"Braver explores the dark side of clinical trials and what can happen when the fortunes of doctors and drug companies become intertwined. He creates a nightmare world, then ratchets up the terror with vividly rendered flashbacks that are not for the faint of stomach. A thoughtful book with an intriguing premise and sprawling plot, pulled together with a twist at the end." —*The Boston Globe*

"Gary Braver has proven in *Flashback* that he is master of the medical thriller. Readers should enjoy the abundance of scientific details, the compelling characterizations, the spellbinding conclusion, and—most significantly—the frightening plausibility of the story itself." —*Mystery News*

"In *Flashback*, Braver delivers once again what we have come to rely on from him: hallmark intelligence, eerie believability, and fear." —*Bookreporter.com*

"As with each of his books, Braver proves himself to be not only a skilled novelist, but an exceptional writer, investing his prose with lovely cadence and rich evocation, and endowing his characters with inner lives full of turmoil, need, hope, regret, and humor. 'Thriller' is almost the wrong word to use for his books; 'drama' might be a better choice. In any event, Braver proves that the novel is not dead even as he demonstrates that realistic speculative fiction is neither kid's stuff nor a trivial time waster, but essential to confronting and controlling the technical marvels of our own modern world." —*EDGE Boston*

"*Flashback* is one of the best medical-science thrillers I have ever read. With an amazing attention to detail, Gary Braver has woven together a story that is as timely as it is

OTHER NOVELS BY GARY BRAVER

Gray Matter
Elixir

WRITTEN AS GARY GOSHGARIAN

The Stone Circle
Rough Beast
Atlantis Fire

gripping and as telling as it is touching. This one's a page-turner with a point."

—Michael Connelly, *New York Times* bestselling author

"A knockout. Braver has written a brilliant cautionary tale. At once chilling and heartening, *Flashback* is thriller fiction at its best."

—Robert B. Parker, *New York Times* bestselling author

"*Flashback* grabs you by the throat, and the heart, from the first page to the last. The superb writing carries you away. . . . Chilling!"

—Ridley Pearson, *New York Times* bestselling author

"Combines an irresistible premise with the medical intrigue of Robin Cook and the scientific plausibility of Michael Crichton—a powerful, gripping, and moving tale with a beating heart."

—Joseph Finder, *New York Times* bestselling author

"Gary Braver does it again. Another taut, suspenseful medical thriller from the new master of the genre. Strong characters, a powerful plot . . . you won't want to put the book down until you're done."

—William Martin, *New York Times* bestselling author

"*Flashback*'s compelling, fact-based medical thriller resonates with the clear pure notes of reality and positively blurs the line between reality and imagination. Braver has created a fictional world you are dying to believe in."

—Lewis Perdue, *New York Times* bestselling author

FLASHBACK

GARY BRAVER

A TOM DOHERTY ASSOCIATES BOOK
NEW YORK

FLASHBACK

A Tor Book
Published by Tom Doherty Associates, LLC
175 Fifth Avenue
New York, NY 10010

www.tor.com

Tor® is a registered trademark of Tom Doherty Associates, LLC.

ISBN-13: 978-0-7653-4853-1
ISBN-10: 0-7653-4853-5

First Edition: October 2005
First Mass Market Edition: November 2007

Printed in the United States of America

0 9 8 7 6 5 4 3 2 1

This book is dedicated
to the memory of my mother,
Rose Goshgarian,
and my aunt,
Nemza "Nancy" Megrichian.

ACKNOWLEDGMENTS

For their contributions on various technical matters, I would like to thank the following people: James Stellar, Roy Freeman, Alice Janjigian, Gail Grodzinsky, Karen Chase, Alice Gervasini, Tweedy Watkins, Deborah Copeland, Jack Reynolds, Karen Hutchinson, Karen Zoeller, Michael Ku, Richard Deth, Marjorie D'alba, Amy Sbordone, Peter Mollo, Michael Carvalho, Kate Flora, Kenneth Cohen, Charles O'Neill, and Malcolm Childers.

A special thanks to Dr. Daniel Press for his generous time and great help with medical matters. Also to Barbara Shapiro for her great advice and encouragement.

A very special thanks to my own special muse, Wanda Hunt, for her extraordinary assistance, her patience at the tape recorder, and her inspiration.

And, of course, my deep gratitude to my agent, Susan Crawford, my editor, Natalia Aponte, and my publisher, Tom Doherty, for their continuing support.

I'm also indebted to the books *Alzheimer Solutions: A Personal Guide for Caregivers* by Jim Knittweis and Judith Harch and *The Story of My Father* by Sue Miller.

So many dreams—it's hard to pick out the right one.

— E. B. WHITE, who died of Alzheimer's disease

When I was young I could remember anything whether it happened or not; but my faculties are decaying now and soon I shall be so I cannot remember anything but the things that never happened.

—MARK TWAIN

PART
1

1

Homer's Island, Massachusetts

From his perch on Skull Rock, they looked like pale eggs sunny-side up moving just beneath the water's surface. Some kind of jellyfish. Half a dozen, pulsating vigorously through the black surf like muscular parachutes.

Odd. Jack Koryan had spent several summers of his childhood out here and could remember only a few occasions seeing jellyfish in the cove, most of them washed ashore by the night tide—dinner-plate-sized slime bombs with frilly aprons and long fat tentacles. But these creatures were small round globs, translucent jelly bells with nothing visible in trail.

Maybe some tropical species that the warm water brought in, he thought.

Jack watched them pump by in formation, driven by primitive urgings and warm eddies. Somewhere he had read that jellyfish were ninety-five percent water—creatures with no brains, bones, or blood. What enabled them to react to the world around them was a network of nerves. What a lousy fate, Jack thought—to relate to the world only through nerve endings: a life devoid of thought, passion, or memory.

The cool, moist air had picked up, ruffling the water's surface. The tide was coming in, and soon the rock would be covered.

Skull Rock.

It looked just as it had forever—a domed granite boulder rearing out of the surf about fifty yards offshore, its crown whitened by generations of barnacles, the base maned with sea grass, a necklace of shiny black mussels hugging the high-tide line like exotic pearls. When they were kids, he and his cousin George would fill a pail with the mollusks for his Aunt Nancy's Armenian dishes or bouillabaisse.

It had been fifteen years since Jack had last swum out to the rock. Back then he'd spend hours there with his cousin and other summer kids. At low tide they'd pack as many as ten wriggling bodies onto the crown, holding their perch by little more than the worn barnacles under their feet. He could almost hear the yowls of laughter as they lost balance or got elbowed off. *First man in is a rotten skate.*

Behind him a sea like liquid iron rolled off to the dark rain-sagged clouds swelling down from the north. Someplace out there Jack's mother had died—August 20, 1975. She had paddled out to her small sailboat, moored just beyond Skull Rock—probably within fifty yards of where he was now standing. It must have been a nor'easter since the tender had washed up a half mile down the beach with lifejackets still in it. Her body was never recovered.

Today was the thirtieth anniversary of her death. Every few years he'd come out in quiet commemoration. He was not even two years old at the time she died. His Aunt Nancy and Uncle Kirk had raised him as their own.

Below, more jellyfish floated by—a skewed phalanx of them. Translucent bodies with intersecting purple rings at the centers just below the surface.

This was a special place, a caretaker's cottage to Vita Nova, the large Sherman estate on the cliff above. His mother, Rose, had rented it decades ago for vacations, attracted to the unusually warm water, the results of complicated weather phenomena involving El Niño. Periodically, eddies from the Gulf Stream would bring into the area creatures from the tropics—

sunfish, hawksbill turtles, bonito, and smaller creatures that fascinated his mother. According to Aunt Nancy, Rose had a half-mystical yearning for the sea and would spend hours walking the beaches collecting odd critters. But Jack had no memory of her—only scraps of information from his aunt, who had died thirteen years ago. His father perished in a plane crash when Jack was only six months old. So he had no memory of him, either.

But Jack did remember getting stung once by a big orange lion's mane jelly in shallow water. It had felt like a hot lash across his calf. As he choked back tears, Aunt Nancy calmly walked him into the house and flooded his skin with vinegar. "Never rub," she had said, "that only makes it worse." Then with the dull edge of a knife she had scraped off a small scrap of tentacle. An old Armenian remedy—something she learned from his mother, she had said. He wondered if that was true.

On shore, in the dimming light, Jack could make out his clothes where he had left them to swim out and, just up the beach, the dark silhouette of the cottage. The sandy beach that rimmed Buck's Cove was completely empty, although lights burned in the Sherman mansion above. It was a private island, but on summer weekends the cove would draw boaters to its pristine beauty. Tonight the place was empty of life.

Lightning lit up the horizon. The storm would break soon.

From the rock the lightless cottage brooded in the shadows of the shore, yet it was a place incandescent with memories. After his mother had died, the Shermans continued to rent the place to his family for a summer week or two. He could still recall how he and his cousin charged down the sand and plunged into the water, inured to the chill that stopped adults dead at the knees.

From out of the gloom a seagull sliced low to catch something in the water then shot up with a squawk at the last second as if spooked. It came to rest on shore near Jack's clothes, still protesting.

Jack felt a jab to his chest. Under the flashing sky, the half-dozen jellyfish had turned into a school. He looked at the water behind him.

"Jesus Christ!"

Not a school. He was standing in the middle of a damn jellyfish bloom. Hundreds of them were bobbing en masse by the rock. The cove was infested with them.

In the dimming light he could make out his clothes on shore, the legholes of his jeans beckoning him to slip back in and pull them up. They looked a mile away.

Where the hell did they come from?

What if these were stingers?

But aren't there a hundred different jellyfish species, and only a handful that sting?

He thought about putting his foot in to test. That would be fine if he got no reaction. But if he got stung, then what? Wait out the storm so lightning could turn him into a charcoal briquette? Besides, in an hour, the rock would be underwater, and jellies would be streaming over his feet. *Jesus!*

He estimated the black expanse separating him from shore. His best high-tide time was one minute twenty seconds. But that was when he was eighteen years old. He was thirty-two, and at best he could reach shore in two minutes. *Two little minutes,* but the thought of swimming through water thick with jellies was repulsive. And if they were stingers, the trip could be nasty.

But they're no bigger than a baseball and probably eat minnows.

True, but doesn't their venom paralyze their prey like that?

But you're not a minnow.

No, but a hundred hits could balance the books.

Sweet Jesus!

The sky lit up in a sickly green, then a high-metal crash exploded the air. With the incoming tide and the onshore wind, he could possibly make it in maybe a hundred adrenaline-driven seconds.

(His mind lit up with Aunt Nancy grinning on shore with a stopwatch. *Three, two, one. Go!* George was two years older, but Jack was the better swimmer.)

One hundred measly seconds.

The water was dark, but the jellies seemed to occupy the upper foot of surf. Jack could dive deep and swim half the distance just above the bottom, then he'd only have to stroke maybe another twenty feet to the shallows and go the rest of the way on foot.

He tried to tell himself that they were just harmless blobs whose mucus coating would slip by his body—that it would be like swimming through a tide of silicone gel bags.

Don't think, just get your ass to shore. Three . . . two . . . one.

The sky exploded again, strobe-lighting the cove. His heart almost stopped: The water was flecked with jellies all the way out. He uttered a silent prayer, filled his lungs, and dove into the water.

But he was wrong. These jellies had three-foot-long invisible tentacles.

And they were stingers.

Jack kicked his way for maybe thirty feet, then shot to the surface.

In those first microseconds of awareness as he sucked for air, Jack could not determine the epicenter of the pain. The tentacles had slashed his arms, back, and legs and made a repulsive mucus mat of his head.

"Don't rub."

He brushed the things out of his hair, their spaghetti strands cutting across his face and ears. He screamed so loud that his throat nearly shattered. He was on fire, as if he had been caught in a hotwire mesh.

"Don't rub. Don't rub."

In the chatter of lightning, he could make out a woman looking like Aunt Nancy waving to him from shore.

But it was too late, his hand was ablaze with poison. And his shoulders and back felt as if he'd been gashed with machetes. Jack had never known that pain could be so exquisite. He gasped in more air, closed his eyes, and kicked to get under the creatures. Pumping blindly, he could feel the blobs ripple by his face, cross-slashing his body.

He shot to the surface sucking for air, his mind screaming against the horror, fighting to focus on making it to shore no matter what, before the toxins began paralyzing his muscles.

On shore the woman had disappeared, and in her place a large white seabird pecked at his clothes.

Somewhere thunder crashed, but Jack did not register it. He did not register anything but the pain flashing across his body. It was like swimming through eddies of molten lava.

With a porpoise kick he shot ahead.

He was halfway there. On the hill above, the Sherman mansion glowed against the black sky. Even if he could find the voice to scream, it wouldn't reach that far. And he could not summon the air. So he concentrated on pumping his legs and arms and keeping his face out of the water.

Your eyes. Close your eyes! his mind screamed.

Don't want to go blind. Can take the skin burns, but, God, you don't want to lose your eyes.

He pressed them shut. A tangle of tentacles made a partial noose under his right ear, searing his skin.

"Never rub."

But in reflex he swiped them off, making it all the worse because that smeared the toxins into his ear and across his jaw and lips. God! The stuff was in his mouth, burning his tongue and throat as if he had swallowed hot water. He scraped his fingers on his bathing suit to remove the slime.

"NEVER RUB!"

Now both hands were on fire, like the rest of his body. And in that slender margin of sanity, he knew that his shoulders, back, and legs would be crosshatched with blistering welts—and that if he got out of this alive, he'd be a mess.

In the flickering light he made out the shore and the bird watching him. Maybe forty feet. He was in five feet of water. But he couldn't wade in. So he pressed shut his eyes and kicked furiously, trailing his hands because they were useless balls of agony. He did all he could to keep his face up. But his eyes were beginning to burn. *God, don't let me go blind. Please.*

As he kicked, he could feel jellies slip over his skin, the hot-poisoned strands streaming across his torso.

At maybe another twenty feet, he snapped open his eyes to see the waves crash on shore just a few body lengths ahead.

Acid tears flooded his vision, but he could still make out the pile of clothes. And he locked his eyes on his shirt and pants which that bird picked at like some carrion vulture.

With every scintilla of muscular will that he had left, Jack Koryan kicked.

Suddenly the burning began to fade.

Thank you, sweet God.

It was miraculous. His arms and legs were rapidly cooling. Maybe the toxins had worked their evil and were being neutralized by his body's natural defenses. Or maybe he had somehow adjusted.

He tried to stand up to wade in, but he could not feel his feet touch ground. Nor could not even right himself up. He tried to continue swimming, but his legs did not obey the command.

God in heaven! His body was going numb, as if his blood were hardening wax.

He was maybe fifteen feet from shore, but he could not move. He was paralyzed in a dead man's float, bobbing in the surf, staring at his running shoes and clothes, just this side of the finish line, some dumb seabird gawking at him, its milky eye flicking in the lightning.

Then coming down the sands from the cottage was that woman beckoning him with open arms. She was Aunt Nancy and she wasn't Aunt Nancy.

My mind. My mind is going. The last delusions of a dying man.

He looked at the bird and felt a fog fill the sacs of his brain like a miasma.

The bird let out a long harsh cry.

This is my death.

In the surf, just a few feet from home. Three . . . two . . . one.

Those were Jack Koryan's last thoughts before his brain went black.

2

Beth Koryan was in a deep sleep when the phone rang. Through the murk, the cable box clock read 12:22. Jack's side of the bed was cold, so she rolled across it to catch the phone, thinking that he had probably stopped off at Vince's to rehash out the menu for next month's opening of Yesterdays, Jack's dream restaurant that had sent them into huge debt.

Even though she and Jack didn't have children, Beth could still hear her mother's words about no good telephone call after midnight: "Pray it's a wrong number." Maybe there were problems with the water taxi; or maybe his car had broken down again and he needed to be picked up someplace. Just what she'd want to do at this hour—jump out of a warm bed and drive off. She'd warned him that the car might not make it to New Bedford and back, but no! He had to go out to that damn island—a little trip down Memory Lane.

Jack was strong-willed and fiercely independent, but he had nostalgic hankerings that could squelch his better judgment—like announcing his resignation from Carleton Prep's English Department to open a place that served eclectic old-world cuisine—thus the name, Yesterdays.

Jack liked teaching and was popular, but he could not see himself committed for life—and after ten years he was growing weary of the budget cutbacks and increased class sizes to the point that education was losing out. So in a carpe diem mind-set, he decided to follow an old passion. From his Aunt Nancy he had developed a talent for cooking. And his old friend Vince Hammond had agreed to be his partner. The risks were high, of course, and in spite of Beth's protests, Jack had broken the bank. But that was Jack: a can-do will, propelled by mulish single-mindedness.

She was still furry with sleep as she caught the phone on the fourth ring. "Mrs. Koryan?"

"Yes?"

"Is Jack Koryan your husband?" and the man named their address.

A spike jabbed her chest. "Yes."

"This is Dr. Omar Rouhana. I'm an ED physician at the Cape Cod Medical Center in Barnstable. Your husband is here. There's been an accident and he's seriously ill."

"What?" Beth was now fully awake. *ED. What's ED? Emergency Department?* "What happened?"

"We think it's very important for you to come down to the hospital. Is someone with you—someone who can bring you in?"

"Is he alive? Is he alive?"

"Yes, he's alive, ma'am, but it's important for you to be here, and we'll explain the details when you arrive. Do you have children?"

"What? No. Will you please tell me what happened? Was it a car accident?" There was a long pause during which Beth could hear her own breath come in sharp gasps.

"Your husband was brought in by a Coast Guard rescue squad. He was found on a beach on Homer's Island. What we'd like you to do is to come in so we can talk about this further. Can you get a ride?"

They were stonewalling her, refusing to give details. She did all she could to control herself. "Is he conscious? Can you please tell me if he's conscious?"

"Well, I think it's best—"

"Goddammit! Is he conscious?"

"No." Then after a dreadful pause, the doctor added, "Would you be coming from Carleton, Massachusetts?"

"Yes."

"Well, that's about ninety miles away. Can somebody drive you, or would you like us to call the local police to bring you in?"

God! Was it that bad? She did not want to spend the next two hours riding in the back of a police car with a perfect stranger. Nor did she want to bother Vince or other friends. "I can drive myself."

The man gave her directions that she scribbled down.

"What happened to him?"

Again the doctor disregarded the question. "And please bring any medications your husband's been taking."

It was a little before three A.M. when Beth pulled into the lot of the CCMC. From the scant details, she guessed that Jack had probably blacked out while swimming, which meant he had suffered a lack of oxygen. As she entered the emergency entrance, she wished she had called Vince.

The ED lobby was a tableau in bleak fluorescence. Two people occupied the reception area—one man asleep across two chairs, and an elderly woman glaring blankly at a television monitor with the sound turned off. The woman at the reception desk had expected her, because when Beth identified herself she stabbed some numbers on the phone. "Mrs. Koryan is here." In seconds a physician and a nurse emerged through the swinging doors. Their faces looked as if they had been chipped from stone. They introduced themselves, but Beth didn't register their names and followed them to a small conference room off the lobby and closed the door.

"He's dead, isn't he?" Beth asked.

"No, he's not dead, Mrs. Koryan," the doctor said. "Please sit down. Please."

Beth slid into a chair across from them. Their faces were grim. Their badges read Omar Rouhana, M.D., and Karen Chapman, R.N. "Mrs. Koryan, before we let you see him, we must first warn you that your husband experienced serious trauma. Besides nearly drowning, he suffered acute toxic burns on his body."

"Burns?"

"He got caught in a school of jellyfish."

It sounded like a bad joke. "Jellyfish?"

"We don't know the details, but a coast guard officer at the scene reported a large school of them. Fortunately, he bagged a couple, and we're in hotline contact with marine biologists at Woods Hole and Northeastern University's marine labs at Nahant to assist with toxicology screening."

"Wha-what are you saying?"

"That your husband got badly stung," Nurse Chapman said. "And he's not a pretty sight, I'm sorry to say."

Beth nodded numbly. Then the nurse got up and took her arm and led her through the Emergency Department door and down a hall toward the curtained bays, an orchestra of electronic beeps and hums rising around them. They stopped by the third bay, and the nurse pulled back the curtain. The doctor and nurse had done their best to dull the shock, but they could never have prepared Beth for what her eyes took in.

The immediate impression was that this was not her husband but some hideous alien parody: Jack was spread-eagled on a stretcher. His eyes were patched with gauze, his genitals were draped with a white cloth, and his feet were balled in bandages. Tubes connected to monitors, machines, and drip bags from all parts of his body—mouth, head, arms, and privates. One had been surgically implanted under his collarbone and connected to drip bags. But what nearly made Beth faint was Jack's body: It was bloated to twice its size, and his neck, chest, arms, thighs, legs, were crosshatched with oozing, angry red welts and glistening from head to foot with analgesic goo. He looked as if he had been brutally horsewhipped then pumped with fluid to the bursting point.

Instantly the air pressed out of Beth's lungs in short staccato gasps, as she stood there stunned in horror while trying to process what had become of Jack—that beautiful man she had married with the thick black hair and starburst green eyes that drove his female students to distraction. Beth's own eyes fell on the small rose tattoo on his right arm in memory of the mother Jack never knew. Then she burst into tears.

The nurse put her arms around Beth. "I know, but the good news is that his heart rate is strong, and that his vital signs are good."

"Wh-why's he so *bloated?*"

"The toxin. It causes water to leak into the tissue and cavities of his body, which is why we're hydrating him."

"The tests won't be back for a few days," the doctor said, "but so far the lab work shows no major abnormalities in his blood."

"What did this to him?"

The doctor took the question. "The marine-lab people think it's some rare kind of creature found in the tropics. Until we get a tox screen, we're treating him with steroids and anti-seizure meds to keep him stable." The doctor checked Jack's chart. "Already his temperature is approaching normal."

Jack's eyes were wadded with dressing, and what little of his face she could see was a puffed mask of red and purple. His lips looked as if he had been beaten with fists—blue, swollen, bloody, painted with disinfectant, and an endotracheal tube jammed down his throat. Except for the tattoo, there was no reminder that this was the same man she had fought with just hours ago. Her heart twisted: Their last words had been contentious—about his going out to the island.

"What's that on his head?" Jack's hair had been roughly chopped to the scalp, and something had been implanted in his skull.

"An ICP gauge. We're watching the intracranial pressure in his brain." It looked like a tire pressure gauge buried in his head and had lines connecting it to an electronic monitor.

"As with some snakebites," the doctor said, "toxins from marine organisms cause a rapid rise in blood pressure and cerebral hemorrhaging."

On the wall was a light display and what looked like X-ray images of Jack's brain. The nurse caught Beth's eyes. "We had an MRI done to check on any edema . . . swelling and bleeding."

"The good news is that we don't think we'll have to operate," the doctor said. "The ICP trend has turned negative—no increase in intercranial pressure over the last two hours."

"You mean there was bleeding in his brain?"

The doctor nodded. "But to what effect we can't determine. We really don't know how long he was unconscious. But we're treating him with steroids to prevent brain inflammation and antiseizure medications hopefully to prevent seizures and keep him stable."

Beth nodded as a hideous thought cut across her mind like the fin of a shark: *Jack could be brain-damaged.*

She scanned the various monitors with blinking blips and graphs and orange and red squiggles, quietly chittering away, the IV stands with drip bags, the ventilator chuffing in his throat, the catheter drainage bag, suction jars, and oxygen tanks along the side of the bed, tubes of urine connecting to some machine on the floor.

I'm going to lose him.

Her eye rested on the heart monitor. It was still pumping, that big stallion engine.

Jellyfish.

In a voice barely audible, Beth asked, "Is he going to make it?"

"We're doing all we can," the doctor said. "If he remains stabilized, we'll move him to Massachusetts General where there are specialty neurologists and some of the best equipment in the world. And he'll be closer to home."

Nurse Chapman handed Beth a wad of tissue to absorb the tears that were now flowing freely down her face.

"His feet . . ." They were wrapped in dressing.

"Well, they were exposed to the water when he was washed up."

And she imagined Jack's feet marinating for hours in jellyfish toxin. Another nurse came in with a tray of medications. "Mrs. Koryan, we have to turn him over to dress his back, so it might be best if you waited in the waiting room. If you're hungry, there's a coffee machine and bunch of canteens down the hall."

They wanted to spare her the sight of Jack's back. Beth nodded. She wasn't hungry, but she could use a coffee since she'd be up the rest of the night. They said to return in half an hour. As Beth started toward the door, her eyes fell on Jack's hands. His fingers looked like purple sausages. His ring finger was bandaged. Then she noticed a small plastic Ziploc bag on the bed table. In it was a twisted piece of yellow metal. Like a Polaroid photo rapidly developing, she realized it was Jack's wedding band. They had snipped it off his finger to prevent it from cutting off the blood flow.

"You may take it," Nurse Chapman said, handing it to her.

But Beth shook her head and left.

3

Eddie Zuchowsky thought it would be a bad day, but not like this.

First, he got stuck in traffic for half an hour on Route 3, no more than two miles from Cobbsville center, causing him to arrive at the store ten minutes before opening. Then two of his girls left messages that they were sick and wouldn't be coming in—which really meant that they had gone to the Dave Matthews concert at UNH and got home at five A.M. And because it was Friday—always a busy day—Eddie would have to man the Hour Photo counter and still perform his other duties as assistant manager.

And now some old woman was at the Cover Girl shelf pocketing tubes of lipstick. He could see her on the security videos.

Good God, I don't need this, Eddie told himself.

As he stared in disbelief at the monitor, he could swear he recognized the woman although he couldn't quite place her. He adjusted the set, and then it came to him: Clara, one of the regular Seenies. That's what some of the store staff had dubbed the residents from the Broadview Nursing Home up the street. Seenies, short for "Senile Citizens."

Of course, that was a tad cruel—and as assistant manager of the Cobbsville CVS, he forbade any of his staff to use such insensitive language about customers. In fact, he once threatened to report a stock boy to the district manager when the kid announced to other staffers, "Here come the Alzies but Goodies." (Eddie had to admit it was a funny line, although he reminded the kid that they could be us some day: "There but for fortune . . .")

Their visit to the store was a common event, as they'd stop by on the way back from a field trip to a local baseball game or restaurant so that the nurse's aides could pick up patient prescriptions. But instead of leaving them to sit restlessly in the vans, the aides would bring them into the store to wander around—in monitored groups, of course. As one aide dealt with the pharmacy, the other two would stay with the residents as they bumped up and down the aisles like sheep.

They'd never make any trouble or bother other customers. At times they could be a bit noisy. Once in a while one would yell something out of the blue—nothing that made sense—or if they got confused or frightened and started crying, the aides would hush them up or take them out to the van. Some of the bolder ones might speak to the customers, say harmless nothings—like retarded kids. A couple weeks ago one man asked Allison at the cash register if his daddy could move back in with them, apparently thinking he was a kid again and she was his mother who had ditched the old man. Allison, who's pretty sharp, said, "Sure he can," and the old guy grinned with joy.

Usually the nurse's aides would let them select a little something—a picture book, a toy, a package of cookies, makeup—whatever caught their eye. If the items were inexpensive and appropriate, the aides would usually pay, then herd the patients out the door and into the van. (The patients each had small accounts back at the home, Eddie learned.) What amazed Eddie was that although Broadview was only three miles away, an excursion to the local CVS was a big deal to these folks—like a trip to Disneyland. The sad thing was some barely knew the difference.

But they seemed to enjoy these outings, and, frankly, it was good for business, because it let the community know that its local CVS was a good neighbor. Over the months, Eddie had gotten to know a few of the individual residents—like Clara, who was actually not a little old lady but a large blocky woman with a big flat face. She didn't say much, just shuffled around sometimes holding the aide's hand and studying the shelves. You'd say something to her and her only comment was "Yeah"—no matter what you said.

"Hi, Clara. Is everything okay?"

"Yeah."

"You feeling good today?"

"Yeah."

"You have a very pretty dress on."

"Yeah."

"Would you like to eat a bowl of maggots?"

"Yeah."

Eddie left the photo counter and headed for aisle 1A. But as soon as he rounded the corner he froze.

Clara was at the Cover Girl shelf. For a moment she appeared to be bleeding from the mouth. But as his eyes adjusted, Eddie realized that Clara had smeared her face with lipstick. She was also making awful moaning sounds, and scattered on the floor were shiny tubes and packages of bright-handled scissors—on special this week for $3.39. One big pink one sticking out of a hip pocket, the other, bulging with lipsticks.

"Clara, wha-what the heck you doing? Don't do that!"

And where the hell were the damn nurses and aides? The woman's nuts.

And she smells. And her feet and legs are all muddy, as if she'd spent the night in the woods. And she's making a damn mess of the place.

But Clara was lost in smearing herself and groaning, her eyes rolling like she couldn't get them to focus anywhere. *God, this is horrible.*

At the far end of the aisle Eddie spotted a young mother and her two young kids.

"Stop that, Clara!" Eddie shouted, thinking he'd have to

page for the aides, get Allison or one of the older sales assistants to deal with her because this was out of hand, and he didn't want to touch the woman. She was having some kind of loony fit.

Suddenly Clara noticed Eddie. Her eyes saucered and Eddie felt something jagged shoot out from them.

"Donny Doh, tsee-tsee go."

"What's that?"

"Donny Doh, tsee-tsee go," she cawed again and again and again until she was screaming and her huge red face was contorted, and her bright raw mouth kept spitting at him: *"Donny Doh, tsee-tsee go."*

Shit! I don't need this. "Clara, *stop*. It's okay. Everything's going to be okay."

The mother at the top of the aisle grabbed her kids and scurried off the other way.

Where the hell are the aides?

Hearing all the commotion, Audrey, one of the older customer assistants, came hustling down the aisle. "Oh, my god."

"Donny Doh, Donny Doh, tsee-tsee go, tsee-tsee go."

Clara paid no attention to Audrey coming up from behind. Her face was a huge red melon, and her eyes bulged so much Eddie was half certain they'd pop out of her skull. She looked positively possessed. "Clara, stop it!"

But Clara did not stop and began to rub herself, smearing lipstick on her dress and filling the aisle with those awful groans.

"Call 911," Eddie barked to Audrey. *"Go!"* Then to Clara: *"Clara, stop it! Stop it!"*

"Tsee-tsee go!"

Eddie reached his hand toward Clara in a desperate attempt to calm her down when he heard more shouting behind him— customers, other workers, maybe the nurse and aides, he thought.

As Eddie turned to check, he saw out of the corner of his eye a flash of pink as Clara lunged at him still screaming that refrain—that hideous screechy baby-talk phrase that he would take to his grave as she buried the pointy blade of the scissors in his neck.

There was yelling and commotion, but for a long gurgling moment Eddie tried to process that he had been spiked in the throat with a $3.39 pair of scissors with pink handles by a seventy-something-year-old Alzheimer's patient with her face smeared with Cover Girl Rose Blush and screaming nonsense syllables at him.

Eddie slipped to his knees while faces swirled in his vision and shouting clogged his head. He pressed his hand to his neck and felt the scissors and sticky warm blood seeping through his fingers—and the last he remembered was being lowered to the floor and the overhead panels of cool fluorescent lights dimming into a soft furry blur as his life pulsed out of his jugular vein.

"Donny Doh, tsee-tsee go."

4

Jack slept through the next two nights and days without change.

Beth did not leave the Cape Cod Medical Center until they told her he had been stabilized and that he was ready to be moved to the intensive care unit of Boston's Massachusetts General Hospital. Because she could not ride in the helicopter, Beth drove, stopping at home in Carleton to change and to update Vince Hammond. Once again he offered to accompany her, but she declined. Jack would not want anyone to see him in such a hideous state.

While they prepped Jack, Beth waited in the lobby of the ICU. Forty hours had passed since that awful call; yet she was still in a state of disbelief. Aimlessly she thumbed through the magazines and newspapers. The headlines of the *Boston Globe* were about the war in Iraq, another suicide bombing in Israel, a shooting in Dorchester. The usual horrors. But at the bottom of the front page her eye caught the headline, "Nursing Home Resident Arrested for Murder." The story went on to say that yesterday a seventy-six-year-old woman had fatally attacked the floor manager of a local CVS with a pair of scissors. Witnesses reported that the woman had acted strangely; and when the store manager went to investigate, the woman plunged a scissors blade into his carotid artery. "It doesn't make sense," reported Captain Steven Menard of the Manchester Police Department. "Clara Devine was a docile old lady."

Nothing makes sense, Beth thought, and put the newspaper down. After nearly an hour, Nurse Laura Maffeo came out to announce that she could go in now. "How is he?" Beth asked.

"He's still asleep but stable." The nurse led Beth to a room down the hall. Jack was suspended in a contraption that looked like a medieval torture device in chrome, his body sandwiched between two platforms that were attached to a large circular frame resembling a giant hamster wheel. One of the two nurses hit a button and the structure—what the nurse later called a Circo-electric bed—rotated Jack a few degrees so he was faceup.

"It's so we can dress him front and back without moving him."

Although Beth had last seen him only eighteen hours ago, his appearance this morning was nonetheless shocking—still bloated, lashed with fat red and purple welts, and basted all over his torso and limbs with a thick white ointment. His eyes were still taped and he was hooked up to half a dozen electronic monitors, drip bags, catheters, IVs, and an ICP plug taped to his skull. He was still on a ventilator, which snapped and hissed in persistent rhythm as his chest rose and fell, as if he were playing some strange wind instrument. But in a reverse illusion it appeared as if the machine were playing him—filling the bag of Jack as if he were some kind of inflatable Michelin Man.

"Most of his vital signs are stable," the nurse said. "His heart is strong. His liver and kidneys are functioning well. We've given him medication to keep his blood pressure at an appropriate level."

A woman in white entered the room and introduced herself as Dr. Vivian Heller, a neurologist. She was tall and lean with thick red hair pulled back and large dark eyes. "Mrs. Koryan, I'm very sorry about your husband's condition, but we are monitoring him and thus far he's fairly stable. The Woods

Hole people have identified the jellyfish as a creature native to the Caribbean, and they're on line with specialists in Jamaica. The tox screening is still ongoing, but they haven't yet fully identified the agents, although they're reporting unusual peaks on gas chromatography, and the lab is trying to isolate the chemical structure."

Beth looked at her helplessly. "I don't know what you're telling me."

"Just that there's an odd neurotropic signature we've not seen before. But it's conceivable that it will be out of his system by the time it's identified. In the meantime, we're monitoring his vital organs and assessing any damage."

"Will he be . . . Does that mean there's damage?" She could barely word her questions.

"He was without oxygen for some time, we think, but there's no way to tell if there are any effects. There was initial cerebral bleeding, but that's stopped, and the ICP is down to normal."

All the technical jargon was fuzzing Beth's mind. She looked down at Jack. "Why doesn't he wake up?"

"Because he experienced major trauma to his neurological system. And we don't know what the effects are. We just have to wait."

"But how long?"

"It may take another few days before he comes out of it. But so far he's not responded to commands or to stimuli. But that's not unusual given the trauma."

"How long will he have to have the ventilator?"

"Until we're certain he can breathe on his own."

The moment was interrupted by a call on the telephone, and Nurse Maffeo took it. "There's a Vince Hammond who wants to visit."

Beth nodded in relief. "He's a friend."

A minute later he walked into the room. Vince Hammond was a big man, about six-one with an athletic frame from years of working out at gyms with Jack. But as he laid eyes on Jack, he seemed to shrink in on himself. "Jesus!" he whispered, his eyes filling up. "What's the prognosis?"

Dr. Heller repeated what she had told Beth. "In a few days the swelling will go down and the sores will begin to fade."

Vince shook his head in disbelief that this was his old pal and partner who in less than a month was supposed to be popping champagne at the grand opening of Yesterdays. "How long do you expect him to remain unconscious?"

"As I explained to Mrs. Koryan, it's hard to tell. With cases of coma caused by a near-drowning or toxic shock, there is a seventy-two-hour window in which we begin to see responses to stimuli. We're keeping a close watch." Heller checked her watch.

"Uh-huh," Vince said, and put his arm around Beth's shoulder.

Beth nodded in autoreflex to the doctor. But the word "coma" cracked through her mind like an electric arc.

The cafeteria at Mass General was located three floors below. It was midafternoon, and the place had only a few people scattered at the tables. Vince and Beth took a small table along the back wall.

"I'm scared," Beth said, putting her hand out to Vince. He took it in both of his. And it occurred to her that the last time they had held hands like this was when Vince came to their house to announce that he and Veronica were separating. Now it was Jack near death.

"Of course you are. Me, too. What the hell was he doing out there?"

"The anniversary of his mother's death. You believe that? Thirty years ago she gets lost in a boat accident, and he goes out there to commemorate it." She shook her head. "He's got this thing about his mother. He doesn't even remember her, for God's sake. It was stupid, going out there alone with a storm coming. Now he's in a coma."

"He could still wake up any time now. The doctor said so herself."

"But what if he doesn't? What am I going to do? And what about you and the restaurant? I don't believe this is happening." She began to cry again.

He squeezed her hand. "Come on, come on, hang in there."

"It's my fault he went. We had a fight, a dumb fight. Ever since I lost the baby, he convinced himself we weren't going to have kids, that he'd never be a father. That got to him, because he wanted a big family. I don't know."

Vince nodded and let her continue.

"He wanted me to go out there with him, but I didn't want to. So he got mad and went off in a huff." She wiped her eyes. "Jellyfish. You believe it?"

"Did you talk about adoption?"

"He wasn't interested. The thing is that we had other problems. Things weren't right between us . . . I was thinking of leaving him."

"Maybe we should change the subject."

"I didn't mean to make you uncomfortable. It's just if he doesn't make it, I never get to say I'm sorry."

"He's going to make it. And when he does, you can say you're sorry all you want."

She looked at Vince and nodded, struggling against dark sensations roiling just beneath the surface—sensations that she wanted so much to get out. But she couldn't. Nor could she find the right words. And she hated herself. Besides, how could Vince understand when she herself didn't—that when the doctors told her that Jack might not make it, her immediate reaction was relief?

5

It was a little after eight on Saturday morning when the drilling ring of the doorbell startled René awake. Silky, her black-and-white cat, curled around her feet as René padded to the window. In her driveway was a Cobbsville, N.H., police car.

She threw on a bathrobe, made a fast gargle of mouthwash, and went down to the front door. A large man of about forty smiled and introduced himself as Officer Steven Menard of the Manchester P.D., Homicide Division. He was dressed in a navy blue sportcoat over a blue work shirt and chinos. "René Ballard?"

"Yes."

He flashed his badge. "Sorry to bother you, but we're investigating the murder of Edward Zuchowsky at the CVS yesterday. Are you familiar with the case?"

"No. What's the name?"

"Edward Zuchowsky."

"I'm sorry, but I've never heard of him."

"Okay, but I'm wondering if I can come in to ask you a few questions."

"Oh, of course." René opened the door and Silky dashed out as the officer entered. She led him into the living room, where Menard settled on the couch.

From a folder he handed her an enlarged photograph of a man smiling and holding a pool stick in what looked like a basement rec room. "Edward Zuchowsky. He was assistant manager of the Cobbsville CVS."

René studied the picture and shook her head. "Sorry, but I don't recognize him."

The officer nodded and returned the photo to the folder. "Okay, then does the name Clara Devine mean anything to you?"

"Clara Devine?" For the last two months René had been working as a consulting pharmacist who monitored the medication of nearly six hundred nursing home patients in facilities throughout southern New Hamsphire and eastern Massachusetts. At the present time most were still names attached to folders. The officer showed her the woman's photograph—a wide-faced elderly woman with flat dark eyes.

He checked his clipboard. "She was living at the Broadview Nursing Home."

"That's one of my homes." Clara Devine. The name did not register in René's memory. "I'll have to check my records. I'm still new at this." She made a nervous smile, embarrassed that she couldn't place a patient's name. "Is there a problem?"

"She's been arrested for Mr. Zuchowsky's murder."

"What?"

"She stabbed him in the neck with a pair of scissors at the CVS on Everett."

"My God, that's terrible. Are you sure it's the same woman? I mean, nearly all of my patients are elderly and suffering from dementia."

"There were several witnesses, plus, she was caught on security cameras."

"That's incredible." René got up and got her laptop from the other room. In it were the medical records, bios, and pharmaceutical charts on her patients. She set the machine up on a table and began a search. "I'm very sorry about the young man, but I find it hard to believe that someone like her could have done this." She scrolled her files.

"You're not alone. So what's your professional connection to Broadview?"

"I'm a consultant pharmacist for CommCare."

"What's that?"

"CommunityCare. It's a pharmacy that provides medications to patients at nursing homes and rehabilitation centers. It's a federal regulation that a pharmacist reviews all patients' charts. And that's what I do—visit nursing homes once or twice a month to review charts and look for possible medication-related problems. If problems are seen, I'll make recommendations for changes to the patient's doctor."

"Interesting. And what if the doctor doesn't agree with your recommendations?"

"She or he has that right, but they're obligated to respond to the recommendation in order to comply with federal regulations."

"Uh-huh. So how well do you get to know the patients personally?"

"Well, I mostly get my information about them from their medical records and talking with the nursing home staff. But I'm getting to know some of them."

"And when was the last time you visited Broadview?"

"I guess about three weeks ago."

"And you're saying you didn't know the perpetrator."

Perpetrator. It was hard to think of that elderly woman in the photo as a perpetrator—a term she associated with thuggy males in T-shirts. "I don't know her."

"But she's one of your patients." It sounded like an accusation.

"She's on my list. Officer, you say this happened in the CVS. Where were the nurse and aides at the time? When patients go on outings, they're heavily chaperoned."

Menard looked up at her. "She was alone."

"Alone? How could she be alone?"

"There were no staffers from the home with her."

"But residents never leave the ward without staffers. How did she get there? How did she leave the home?"

"That's what we'd like to know."

René's mouth made an O of comprehension. "You mean she eloped, she escaped?"

"Our guess."

"But . . . that's impossible."

"Well, that's what happened." Menard flipped a few pages on the clipboard. "I'm wondering if you could check your records. According to the Broadview nursing staff, Mrs. Devine was not taking any antipsychotic medications. Is that your understanding?"

René scrolled through Clara Devine's file. The woman had mild heart problems, high blood pressure, high cholesterol, and had been diagnosed with depression and moderate dementia. She had been admitted to Broadview by her sister a year ago at age seventy-two. The sister, Cassandra Gould from Dudley, N.H., was the listed sole survivor. Clara was also designated a ward of the state, which meant that her sister had not been willing to assume power of attorney. "As you know, without a search warrant I'm bound by patient confidentiality not to reveal details, including the medications she was on."

"Of course, but that can be taken care of if something comes up." And he gave her a look that said, *Don't play Polly Protocol, lady.*

They both knew that he could have the records subpoenaed; but that would take time, and he wanted to know if the woman was on any medications that might have made her nutty. She scrolled down the list: Atorvastatin for high cholesterol, hydrochlorothiazide, Atenolol, Captopril, and a baby aspirin daily for her heart disease and high blood pressure; paroxetine for depression; donepezil for dementia. It was a pretty standard menu of medications for an elderly nursing home patient. And while some of the drugs had the potential to affect mental status, none could account for a volcanic urge to kill. According to her medication profile, Clara Devine had been on these same medications at the same doses for months, also decreasing the likelihood that any had caused her sudden homicidal behavior. "Looks like the standard laundry list for elderly patients."

"No smoking gun?"

"No smoking gun." Then she moved ahead toward the present. Suddenly René hit a blank. She went back and double-checked. "That's odd," she said.

"What's odd?"

Clara Devine did not appear on René's patient census for the last six months. And all of the woman's medication orders were from last February or earlier. René felt Menard's eyes scratch at her for an explanation. If she overreacted, he'd want to know how she could have a half-year hole in her records; then he'd go to Broadview to complain, and in no time her superiors at CommCare would wonder why they hired her. "A little computer glitch. Okay, here we are," she pretended. "From what I can tell, she hadn't been on any kinds of meds that would cause such behavior."

"Any record of psychotic behavior on the ward or before?"

René checked the nurses' notes to the six-month dead-end, feeling her face flush, and trying not to let on that she somehow had screwed up. "No. In fact, she was pretty well behaved." Then some nurse's notes made her smile. "Apparently she came out with some funny lyrics." And she read: "'Roses are red, violets are blue, look at my titties and say I do! Had us laughing out loud,' one nurse wrote. She also once announced that she was having a baby. Doesn't sound like someone who'd attack a perfect stranger."

"No, but she sounds delusional."

"Many dementia patients are, but that doesn't mean violent."

Menard laid his pen hand on the clipboard. "So what do you think happened, Ms. Ballard?"

"I don't have a clue." But she'd go back to the home and double-check the master charts to see what she'd missed—and why there was a six-month blank in her files. She closed her laptop, feeling distracted that something was amiss. She had prided herself on keeping meticulous details, of being able to hold in her head the hundreds of unpronounceable syllables that made up drug indices, the technical details of complex chemical arrangements, their intended effects and side effects. And she had worked to attach names and faces to the reams of data. Yet here she was missing records of a patient who was the epicenter of a murder investigation. "So what happens to her now?"

"Well, she's been sent to McLean's for evaluation."

McLean's Hospital in Belmont, Massachusetts—part of Harvard Medical School—was one of the top psychiatric hospitals in the nation, and where dangerous patients were evaluated.

Menard got up and headed for the door, stopping by a table with an array of photographs. One of them was a shot of René in her cap and gown posing with her parents and Nick Mavros, her favorite professor at the New England School of Pharmacy. Beside it were pictures of her father, before he got sick. Also one of him as a little boy in a porch rocking chair—an image of him that she adored. Menard picked up a close-up portrait of Silky. "Is this the guy I met earlier?"

"Yes. Silky." In the picture, the black longhaired tabby with the white nose patch looked like a mobster with a menacing wide-eyed gaze—the kind of photo you'd imagine hanging in a mouse post office stamped WANTED. At the moment he was out back thinking about chipmunks.

"For the record, are you living alone?"

The question sent a little ripple of unease through her. Until a few months ago, she had been living in Boston with Todd and planning a June marriage—June 26, to be exact. Then after nearly two years of cohabitation—bridal gown purchase, Mr. Tux reservations, seat upgrades on Delta flights to Maui, seaside view at the Kapalua Bay Hotel, honeymoon-special sunset-mai-tai-catamaran cruise, and one hundred and twenty unused "René and Todd" invitations—dear old Todd, in a last-moment panic, decided he couldn't go through with it and moved back to New Jersey, where he took up with his high school girlfriend.

If the jilting hadn't been so painful, it would've been comic. In her twenty-nine years, René had never met or heard of any woman or man actually being jilted. Todd's announcement raised a lot of screaming and accusations, but he still left. And after three months of wound licking, René quit her job at the local pharmacy and with the help of Nick Mavros accepted an offer with CommCare that brought her here to Dover Falls where she now lived in a converted barn, stripped down to bare happiness. Since then, René had resolved that she didn't need Todd—that she would embrace the split as an opportunity to find new traction in life and a chance to become a part of something good—something bigger than herself, the welfare of others. "Yes, I live alone."

He thanked her and handed her his card. "Just in case you think of anything that might explain what set her off or how she escaped."

"I'm sure you've already checked, but maybe the security door malfunctioned?"

"We checked. It's working just fine."

"And no family member signed her out."

"Nothing like that. And she didn't put a chair through the window."

And there's a bloody six-month hole I have to account for.

6

The story was at the bottom of the front page. "Elderly Nursing Home Patient Slays Cobbsville CVS Manager." It didn't make sense.

René bought the paper and headed to Broadview Nursing Home, an attractive complex nestled in a forest of oaks and resembling a tiny New England village. The Alzheimer's disease unit was in the newly redone two-story wing at the rear. She parked her Honda and went inside where she waved hello to the receptionist. But instantly she sensed tension like the hush before a thunderstorm. Nurses and staff bounced off each other in trailing whispers around the lobby.

René made her way to the Alzheimer's disease unit and with a strange apprehension entered the four-digit code on the keypad. To the sound of the electric bolt release, the door opened onto an intersection of two corridors. Along one corridor some patients sat in wheelchairs staring straight ahead. Others shuffled along the walls. Down the other she spotted Carter Lutz, Broadview's medical director, talking to a tall black-haired man in a monogrammed sportcoat. When they spotted her, they peeled off the walls and into a small office and closed the door.

Unit Nurse Alice Gordon was at the desk. "Hey, hon, thought Saturday was your day off."

"It was. The police just left my place."

Alice's smile played itself in reverse. "Then you heard," she whispered. "They were all over here last night."

"What happened?"

Alice just shrugged and looked away. "One of those things."

Bonnie, an assistant nurse, came by rolling the meds cart. She looked at René knowingly and shook her head. A few patients milled about the halls. One man was pushing a woman in a wheelchair, a few others sat in chairs against the wall, some asleep, others chattering to the air. René ducked into the small files room. The large three-ring folder for Clara Devine was missing. "Where's Clara's folder?"

Something rippled across Alice's face. "Well, actually it's with Dr. Lutz."

"So what do we know?"

"About what?"

"About how she got out and killed a guy at the CVS."

Alice glanced at the newspaper René handed her and shook her head. "Unbelievable." Then she turned her face to her paperwork again.

"What's this 'Donny Doh tsee-tsee go' stuff the paper reported?"

"One of her rhymes, I guess. She had a thing for them."

"Was this something you've heard before?"

Alice thought a moment. "I don't know." Then she flashed her a sharp look. "You playing Nancy Drew or something?"

"Just trying to get some answers. It's not the kind of publicity the home needs."

"I'll say." Alice dropped her eyes to her paperwork again.

"Alice, why do I have this feeling that something's going on that I don't know about?"

Alice straightened up. "Sorry, Sweetie. It's that everybody's pretty upset."

"Six months of her records are missing from my files."

"That right?" Alice said, frowning. "How did you do that?"

Christ! She was turning it on her. "Well, I'm not sure I did."

Suddenly Alice checked her watch. "Oops. Mr. Martinetti needs his meds."

"Alice, I double-checked my computer, and there are no entries for Clara Devine since February. And I didn't delete anything because they're not on my backup disks."

"Beats me."

René felt a blister of anger rise as Alice tried to shake her off. "Also, I don't remember seeing her name, which makes me wonder if her name was on the monthly patient census lists I'd been given."

Alice looked at her without expression. "What can I tell you?"

Just then, Bonnie came back down the hall with the drug cart. She looked at Alice, who held her glance long enough for René to sense something pass between them. Then she continued down the hall. Alice was useless, so René caught up to Bonnie. "Wait a second." Bonnie stopped and René opened the file drawer containing each patient's meds and files. René started going through them until she found Clara Devine's name.

"Look, I've gotta go," Bonnie said, and tried to move away.

Alice came over. "Is there a problem?"

René let Bonnie go but not before she caught the name of Clara's physician. "Well, I'm really not sure. But according to my records Clara's primary care doc is Barry Colette, but those med sheets were signed by a Dr. Jordan Carr."

Alice's face clouded over. "Well, he's taken over for Dr. Colette." She started away.

But before she did, René asked, "So who's this Dr. Jordan Carr?"

Alice nodded toward the exit. "He just left."

Carter Lutz's office was on the first floor near the reception desk. Just as René rounded the corner, she spotted him leaving his office. "Dr. Lutz, can I speak with you for a moment?"

He looked at her, trying to place her face.

"René Ballard, with CommCare."

"Oh, yes, of course. The new girl."

"Yes." *The new girl.* And in his tone she heard: *The girl who doesn't know any better.*

Lutz sneered down at her for an explanation for why she was holding him up. He was a partridge-shaped man in his sixties with an ill-fitting toupee, a slick chocolate brown thing that hung on his brow in oily spikes but which barely covered the fuzzy gray growing around his ears. "Not right now."

"Well, I'm very sorry, but it's kind of important."

His nostrils flared at her like a horse's. "I'm in the middle of this police thing, which I'm sure you heard about."

"Well, it's about the police thing that I'd like to talk to you. Please, it'll only take a minute." He glared at her, then headed back into his office and closed the door. He checked his watch, then looked at her with sour impatience. *Don't let him rattle you,* she told herself. *Your job is on the line here, kiddo.* "I believe that the medical records for Clara Devine are with you."

"Is that a problem?"

"Well, as you know, my job is to check the record of each patient in the home, and I don't have entries for Clara Devine."

"Sounds more like your problem than ours."

"Maybe, which is why I'd like to see her records."

"I can assure you that nothing's amiss."

"But I don't know that unless I see her folder." And she forced a pleasant new-girl smile, hoping to soften his resolve.

"Miss Ballard, you're an employee of the pharmacy, not this home or its corporation. I will not stand you interrogating me."

"I'm sorry, Dr. Lutz, but I'm bound by federal regulations." She tried to maintain a tone of politeness, but his dismissal of her was irritating. It was also unprofessional. And she wondered if he'd dismiss one of the older staffers or male doctors like this.

"Maybe you just neglected to copy them properly."

"That's entirely possible, but I won't know that until I see her charts."

He made a move to usher her out the door, but she didn't budge. "Dr. Carvahlo is my supervisor at CommCare. I'm sure he would like to hear your explanation. May I use your telephone?"

"No, you may not. The charts are being photocopied in the event they're subpoenaed by the police. You can see them when they're returned."

"Thank you. Oh, another thing: Somebody other than her primary care physician is signing off on her sheets."

The skin of his face appeared to tighten. "Ms. Ballard, why at a time like this are you bothering me with trivial details?" And he pressed her outside the office and closed the door. "Dr. Carr is her primary care physician. Good day."

She watched him clop out the front door and into the parking lot, thinking that maybe she was being trivial, maybe even petty, the kind of things that drove Todd away.

"You're such a details person, so damn anal. I can't even leave a fucking cup in the sink without you raising a flag."

After recomposing herself, she returned to the reception desk and asked the operator to page Dr. Carr. *Trivial be damned!* she thought. Minutiae were what they paid her for. When the phone rang, the secretary said that Dr. Carr had left for the day. She jotted down his office number. "By the way, this is for you," and she handed René a reminder about the groundbreaking ceremony on Monday at Morningside Manor, a nursing home in Smithfield. She stuffed the flyer into her bag, thinking it would be a good opportunity to network.

René left the building and headed for her car, where she called Dr. Carr's number from her cell phone. With the answering service she left her name and number, identifying herself. Just as she started the car, something shot through her brain like a dark premonition.

She went back inside and into the AD unit again. Bonnie was alone at the desk and paid her no attention.

René began at the far end of the west corridor and moved toward the nurses' station, then down the north corridor. Most of the doors were left open, and those that were closed she tapped first, then entered. She went upstairs and followed the same route. At the nurse's station she bumped into Alice. "You're back." It sounded like a reprimand.

"Yes." She didn't explain her return, but she could feel Alice's eyes bore through the back of her head as she cut into the activities room, where patients sat around tables doing puzzles or pasting pictures to colored paper. She stopped here and there to compliment some of them.

"You're beautiful," one woman said to her. And she stuck the tip of her tongue out between her teeth the way a child does. She was doing a puzzle of a kitten. "What's your name?"

"My name is René. And you're beautiful, too." The woman's face was soft and powdery, like risen bread dough. Her eyes were watery blue and she wore rimless glasses. She looked like an aged nun. Her hands were dappled with liver spots, but they worked the puzzle pieces with methodical care in search of their mates.

"I'm going to pray to the Virgin Mary for you."

"Thank you," René said. "And what's your name so I can say a prayer for you?"

"Ma-ry Cur-ley," she said in a singsong voice. Then she wrinkled her face and stuck her tongue out again like a child.

René felt a small shock. There was no Mary Curley on her census. This woman officially was not on the ward. "I'm sorry, what is your name?"

"Ma-ry Cur-ley, and I have a dog named Jello."

"Jello. What a wonderful name." René felt as if she had entered an alternate universe.

Mary took René's hand and made an odd tongue-sucking sound. Then she said, "I have a dog named Jello. And he's out back asleep in his house."

"Well, I'll be sure not to wake him." And she patted Mary on the shoulder.

On the way out of the dayroom René passed a room with its door open. Inside was a male patient sitting by the window wearing a khaki U.S. army cap with insignia. She stepped inside. The man looked up at her blankly.

"Hi, my name is René."

The man said nothing.

"I like your hat." The man still did not respond, but he kept staring at her. "And what is your name?"

Still no answer. On the bureau behind him were several framed photographs with labels. One colored shot, presumably of his wife and daughter, was labeled "Marie and Christine." Another showed the same woman Christine with a young boy named "Steven," probably the man's grandson. Beside them was a large blowup in black-and-white showing two young men posing in army fatigues and helmets. Each was holding a weapon. The label under the photo read: "Louis Martinetti and Sam Swenson, 187th Airborne Regimental Combat Team, Hill 329, Sukchon, Korea, October 1950." A gold star was pasted under one young man—a black-haired slender kid with the same eyes as the elderly man she was addressing.

"Are you Louis Martinetti?"

He looked at her with shock. "You're Fuzzy Swenson's sister."

"Who?"

"Fuzzy Swenson."

René looked back at the black-and-white blowup. "There's a Sam Swenson in the photograph of you. Is that who you mean?"

He squinted at her to sharpen his focus. "You his sister, um . . . Rita?"

René stepped closer so he could see her better. "No, my name is René Ballard. I'm the consulting pharmacist here." She wasn't sure he understood but she put out her hand.

He did not take her hand but stared at her until he was convinced that she was not who he thought. "Just as well . . . what they did to him." He winced as something sharp passed through his mind.

She would have liked to talk, curious about Fuzzy Swenson and hoping to bring Louis out more. But Alice was standing in the doorway staring at her through hard eyes.

"Nice to meet you, Mr. Martinetti," René said. As she turned to leave, she noticed that on the bed was an army uniform neatly pressed and still on hangers. She stepped out of the room and looked at Alice who just glared at her. René flashed her a smile and said, "Well, see you tomorrow."

Alice did not respond, but René could still feel the press of her gaze as she made her way down the hall to the exit.

She passed down the stairs and out into the parking lot to her car. According to the road atlas, Dudley, New Hampshire, was about an hour north of here. She had the day off and it was a beautiful late August morning and maybe during the ride things might start making sense to her.

Especially why she had counted four more patients on the Alzheimer's disease unit than were listed on her census.

7

"Mrs. Cassandra Gould? My name is René Ballard. I called you from the road."

"Yes, yes, I remember," the woman said through the screen door. "I'm not the one with dementia. At least not yet. Come in, please."

René followed her into a living room, which was furnished in floral Queen Anne wing chairs and sofa.

"And it's Cassie," the woman demanded. "Who in their right mind would want to be named after a woman who prophesied doom while nobody listened." She gestured for René to sit in a chair. "You're here because of what my sister did, no doubt, so you'll probably need a coffee, unless you prefer something stronger."

"No, water would be fine, thank you."

"Well, I'm having coffee. The only way to get my heart going in the morning. Still want the water?"

"I've already had three cups. Any more and I'll need a straitjacket."

Cassie smiled. "A pharmacist with a sense of humor. Now there's a rare duck." And she left for the drinks.

Rare duck. C'est moi, she thought, *the new girl, and now Ms. Popularity at your local nursing home.* René strolled to the back wall, which consisted of built-in shelves full of books. Clearly Mrs. Gould was a well-read woman. Most of the books were hardback novels, including classics—Tolstoi, Steinbeck, Dickens, the Brontë sisters, Iris Murdoch—as well as Greek and Shakespearean plays.

On the small fireplace mantel were framed photos of children, perhaps grandchildren. One was a formal portrait of Cassie and a man, perhaps her husband. Also one of Cassie and, she guessed, Clara, from the resemblance, taken when they were much younger—probably in their twenties. Cassie was dressed in a high-fashion dress and hat and Clara in a skirt and polo shirt; Clara was holding a golf club. They were both strikingly handsome, Clara a bit shorter and less willowy than her sister, but with a round, elfin face that could barely disguise high spirits. She was caught midlaugh, as if somebody had just told a joke.

"She had just won a club tournament," Cassie said, entering the room with a tray. "She was quite the sportswoman in her day." She set the tray down and handed René a tall glass of ice water with a slice of lemon.

"That's Walt, my third husband. Clara never married, but I made up for that. Buried three of them. Walt died six years ago, and that's when the word got out I was a high-risk bride." She smiled and sat opposite René. "Shortly after that my sister moved in. And now she's up for murder." She took a sip of coffee. "On second thought, maybe my parents had foresight when they named me."

René smiled. The woman's directness was refreshing. "So the police were here."

"No, they called with the details. I'm sure they'll be dropping by with a lot of questions. They tell me she's being evaluated at McLean Hospital in Belmont, Massachusetts. But I can't visit her for a while."

Cassie was remarkably sharp of mind and still attractive for a woman of eighty—tall and broad-shouldered, although now rounded and padded by time. She had a regal face with wide cheekbones and arching, slightly supercilious dark brows that were enhanced by round, dark wire-framed glasses. Her brown eyes were large and heavily lidded and the skin around them was papery, but they held a person with a fierce intensity. Her hair was gray and pulled back in a bun. She wore no makeup. She was dressed in a red pullover, jeans, and white tennis shoes. Perhaps she was getting ready for a morning walk.

"On the phone you said you had some questions about what might have led up to her assault on that unfortunate young man."

René handed her a photocopy of the murder story from the *Manchester Union-Leader.* "I take it you've not seen this?"

Cassie read the article, at one point wincing at something. When she finished, she laid the article on the table and looked at René without a word. René was sure the police had spelled out the details of the killing, but something in the woman's manner set off uneasiness in her, as if the written words had confirmed the enormity of her sister's act. "You no doubt know your sister better than anyone else. And I know you visited her at Broadview. I'm just wondering if you saw anything that might explain her behavior."

"My sister was a high-energy woman—a fighter, as you can see," and she nodded to a cabinet full of golfing trophies. "She had a temper and would lash out if she felt wronged. But my sister was not a violent woman or capable of murder."

"And as far as you know Edward Zuchowsky was a perfect stranger to her."

"Yes, besides, how could she know him, being stuck in the nursing home?"

"What's baffling is that she wasn't on any medications that would have led to such psychotic behavior."

Cassie took a sip of her coffee. "But she was demented."

"True, and demented people do have fits of violence, but there are always signs of that, and from her records Clara never harmed another patient or staff member."

Cassie raised her cup to her face again, her eyes locked on René's so intently that for a second René felt their heat. Then the woman looked down and the moment passed.

"Did you notice any changes in Clara while in the home—any alterations in her behavior from visit to visit?"

"Frankly, I'm embarrassed to admit it, but I haven't visited my sister in several months. My eyesight is poor and I don't trust myself on long drives. And to be honest, watching her bump down the staircase is very depressing, as you can imagine."

Bump down the staircase. René nodded silently. *Depressing doesn't come close.*

"As I said, she moved in with me after Walter died. And for a while it was fine. Then she began to have memory problems. We had her diagnosed, and within a year she began to get worse—confused, disoriented. She was forgetting things from one moment to the next. It was like watching her being peeled away like an onion. God, what a cruel disease."

"Yes, it is."

"When it became too much for me to handle, even with visiting nurses and day care, we found Broadview. I must confess that the early visits were stressful. I love my sister, but seeing her disappear like that took its toll. She would flicker in and out, asking me the same questions over and over again until I felt my own mind begin to go. Of course, the driving became an issue. So I stopped visiting her, which didn't make any difference to her by then."

"The last time you saw her, how did she seem in terms of mental abilities?"

"Half there. She'd sit around the activities table and try to fill in the blanks. The aide would read a familiar adage for patients to fill in the rest: 'You can't have your cake and . . .' pause. Or 'Nothing ventured, nothing . . .' pause. 'A stitch in time saves . . .' et cetera.

"Clara would struggle to beat others to the answers. Sadly, she was a book person with a master's in history and a doctorate in education. A former high school principal. Most of these books are hers. The last time I visited her she couldn't read the name on the box of chocolates I'd brought.

"I have a good dozen ailments, not the least of which is degenerative arthritis of the lower back—which sounds much kinder in Latin. But I don't know what happened in the genetic throw of the dice that caused her to start blanking out while I'm still festering with useless memories. There are times I envy her. You reach a certain point in life when even your recollections begin to feel made-up. I think Mark Twain said it best—something like, 'I can't remember anything but the things that never happened.'"

"I understand."

Cassie took a sip of coffee. "No, you don't understand."

René wasn't certain what she meant but felt as if she were engaged in some odd sparring match. "No, I can understand the anxiety of seeing her fade. It's horrible, I know, and there's nothing to feel guilty about." René did all she could not to stumble on her words.

"It's different. It's part of your job."

"My father died of Alzheimer's." The words jumped out before René could catch them.

Nothing to feel guilty about. Not true, René thought. She had felt guilty for getting angry with her father when he got confused or abusive; guilty for not being able to give him comfort against the awareness that he was demented and getting worse and that he would never go home again; guilty for losing her patience with him, for not knowing how to act when she visited the nursing home, for not knowing what to say when he wasn't responding or was unaware of her presence, for hating the fog in his eyes and the slack-jawed mouth as he descended farther into the gloom. Guilty for breaking down in his presence after he'd confused her for his dead wife; when he begged her to remove his restraints and they wouldn't let her; when in a fit of rage he swung at her cursing; when it got so bad she no longer wanted to visit him. She felt guilty for trying to get on with her life. For allowing the nursing home staff to avoid taking extraordinary measures when he would no longer eat. For letting him die.

The woman looked at her for a moment as if reading her thoughts. "Then I'm sorry for you. I suppose the only consolation is that the disease blots out the victim's awareness of one's offenses."

"Yes." *It also has a shared effect on the caregiver: It eventu-*

ally renders you numb and ineffectual. And you at last come to realize that nothing you can do will stop the deterioration. Yet, ironically, you can't help but feel that you could have done more. That you failed. Yes, a cruel disease.

Cassie glanced at the newspaper story. "We had a fine sisterhood that lasted until we were old ladies. Certainly there was the usual sibling rivalry stuff, but there were enough years between us so that I was more the older sister and confidante than competitor. We would talk all night in bed, laughing, sharing stories, little truths, and secrets. And as trite as it sounds, I recall some of it as if it were yesterday.

"In many ways we were blessed with exceptional parents who were smart and loving and who provided us with a childhood full of laughter and beauty that should have lasted longer than it did, at least until the age when the world begins to dull and harden the child. Unfortunately, that happened much too much sooner than it should for my sister."

The woman looked away for a moment. "Clara was raped by a neighbor when she was five years old."

"Oh, how horrible."

"By a drunken pig of a man who would sit on his back porch and drink beer out of large brown bottles and snort because he had some kind of sinus problem. One day he enticed Clara to come inside because he wanted to show her something. His name was Donald Dobretsky, the man my father lent the lawn mower to, the man whose wife was our mother's shopping friend. The man we shared Christmas parties and barbecues with.

"He would encourage Clara to recite jingles, silly rhyming things she picked up from radio and TV like 'You'll wonder where the yellow went when you brush your teeth with Pepsodent'—way before your time—or 'Mary, Mary, quite contrary' or 'Ding, dong, bell, pussy's in the well.'

"Or 'Donny Doh, Donny Doh, tsee-tsee go, tsee-tsee go.' As clear as it was last evening, I remember her small, frightened voice cutting the warm night air of our room. Donny Doh was the name she had given Mr. Dobretsky. Just one of the many sweet names her magical little word box had created for people she knew."

"And what's 'tsee-tsee go'?" René asked.

Cassie looked at her point-blank and said, "What he stuck in her mouth."

"My god."

"It took me a while, but she told me everything. She was still too innocent to know she was being sexually abused but old enough to know that what he made her do was bad. So she never told our parents, and I was too afraid. Besides, back then people didn't talk about child abuse. The term wasn't even part of the public lexicon. And if children were abused, nobody talked. And nobody believed kids even if they made such claims. Such things didn't exist in our nice world of Barton Glen. Today, a little whisper can send a man to jail for life or close down a church."

"Was it just that once?"

"No, no. And the SOB told her that our parents wouldn't believe her if she said anything. He was clever not to rape her because that would leave torn tissue. But he left her so deeply scarred that for days she wouldn't speak or eat and had nightmares. Our parents thought she had meningitis or some brain fever and put her under the care of the family doctor because she was wasting away. Of course, all the tests were negative because it was that monster's filthy pleasure."

She was shaking so much that her composure began to fracture. But she took a breath and found her center again. "I tell you this only to explain what's beneath the layers—a wound that never, ever healed. Whatever it was, something in the encounter with poor Mr. Zuchowsky cut to the quick of that, and she exploded."

Mrs. Gould closed her eyes for a moment. When she opened them, she seemed recomposed. "Besides, Clara's nearly gone, so it doesn't matter that I tell you."

She suddenly looked very tired and old, as if she were staring into the narrowing corridor of her own last days. René got ready to leave. "What happened to this Donald Dobretsky?"

"Died of old age."

"I'm sorry to hear that."

"Me, too. And a perfect stranger paid with his life."

8

Died of old age.

The phrase stuck in her mind like a thorn—all the way to Rose Hill Cemetery.

Well, my father didn't die of old age. I let them pull the plug on him.

Rose Hill was located in Paxton, a small town outside of Peterborough, N.H. The place consisted of narrow tree-lined lanes like an arboretum. Since her father's death, René had been coming here maybe once a month and on special days such as Memorial Day, Father's Day, or Christmas. This day would have been his eighty-second birthday.

Her mother was also robbed of her golden years, dying of cancer three years before her father, two years after he was diagnosed with Alzheimer's. She was buried beside him.

René had always been close to her father, but never so much as when he began to fade and especially after Diane died and his dependency fell full-weight on her, his only child. She had made regular visits each week to her parents' home. She had arranged for visiting nurses, then hospice when her mother's condition had begun to worsen. After her mother's death, René moved her father into a long-term-care home, where he rapidly declined into the disease. She cleaned her mother's headstone and laid down a pot of geraniums, then moved to her father's.

"Hi, Dad."

With paper towels she wiped the headstone, a black marble speckled slab that still glistened like glass in the sunshine. She removed some dead leaves and set down the second geranium pot.

THOMAS S. BALLARD

BELOVED FATHER AND HUSBAND

She wished they had picked a less generic inscription. Three-quarters of the headstones had the same wording, just change the gender terms. She wished she had selected lyrics of one of his favorite songs—maybe a few bars of "As Time Goes By" or "Let Me Call You Sweetheart" or "Bridge Over Troubled Waters" or a hundred others. But the funeral director had talked her out of it, which made sense, since they'd probably have had to get copyright permission. And wouldn't that look cute: a footnote with something like "© 1931 Warner Bros. Music Corporation, ASCAP, Music and Words by Herman Hupfeld." Dad would have appreciated that.

"Well, eight weeks on the job, and I'm caught up in a murder investigation because one of my patients escaped from a locked ward and killed a guy. Half her records are incomplete, there are patients on the ward that shouldn't be, and everybody's stonewalling while my head's on the block. Otherwise, it's been a great week."

She finished buffing the stone.

The end was in sight when he began to stop eating, something common with dementia patients. Most of his cognition was gone, but he had had no medical condition and was strong enough physically to shuffle about the ward on a walker or to sit up in a wheelchair. Hoping to stimulate his appetite, the nursing home staff treated him with antidepressants, which worked for a while. But eventually he refused food no matter how much they encouraged him. Sometimes he'd spit it out or he'd keep it in his mouth, not chewing. Or he'd chew it and not swallow, pocketing the mash in his cheeks. Because René was at pharmacy school fifty miles away, she couldn't visit as often as she wanted—a fact that ate at her heart like acid. But when she did, his mood would perk up and he'd eat a little for her, sometimes recognizing her, sometimes just responding to a smiling face that encouraged him to cooperate. But without her, staff just could not get him to eat.

Eventually the options wore down to two: aggressive invasive measures—tube feeding and IVs—or letting him starve.

Because René was a pharmacy student her father had given her power of attorney. She had discussed the options with her father in the early days of his disease. Emphatically he said he did not want aggressive medical treatment. He did not want to simply hang on with tubes down his throat and wait to become riddled with infections. He did not want to put her through this.

"Promise me this," he had said, taking her shoulders in his hands. "When I get really bad, you'll let them do what has to be done to let me go out with dignity, okay? Promise? I don't want to end up just some gaga thing attached to a diaper."

She could barely get out a yes.

She told the nursing staff that she knew how her father viewed life and that he wanted it this way. So she signed the papers:

Do Not Resuscitate—DNR

Do Not Intubate—DNI

Do Not Hospitalize—DNH

Some days her recollection of her father was so vivid that she could not accept the fact of his death. And she could still recall that first day as if it were last week, when she realized that her father—former mechanical engineer, a man of extraordinary discipline, a book lover, a good-time piano player and crooner, an avid fisherman, a jokester, and a gentle, loving, fabulous parent—was beginning to bump down the staircase.

And in an instant René was in the backseat of his Lincoln Town Car, listening to him.

"You must remember this, a kiss is just a kiss, a case of do or die. The fundamental things in life as time goes by. Dah DAH dah DAH dah DAH . . ."

"Come on, Dad, you're spoiling a great song. For old time's sake." It was his birthday, and she was home from college.

"Only if you lead." He had pulled up to the stop sign at the top of their street.

"Yeah, like you don't know the words. You could have written them, for God's sake." She was hoping he'd kick into an old sing-along as they did on long trips when she was a girl. But for some reason he wasn't interested. And her mother sat in the passenger seat looking tense. *" 'You must remember this, a kiss is just a kiss, a sigh is just a sigh . . .' "*

"Oh, that version," and he gave her a wink in the rearview mirror.

Her dad was still such a kidder. *"You big goof."*

"What time are the reservations?" Diane had asked, her voice devoid of inflection.

Because of traffic, René had arrived late, which probably explained Diane's mood. Her face was out the window and she dug in her handbag for a cigarette.

"Seven-fifteen." René tried to ignore Diane's grimness, especially on her father's birthday. *"Okay, from the top. 'You must remember this, a kiss is just a kiss . . .' Mom, feel free to join in. 'A sigh is just a sigh . . .' "*

Her father sang along haltingly, as if waiting for René's prompting.

" 'No matter what the future brings . . .' Dad, you're punking out."

"He doesn't want to sing."

"Yes, he does. Right, Dad?"

"Actually, I'm a little fuzzy on the lyrics," he said to the mirror.

"How could it be fuzzy? It was your wedding song." It was also part of their "repertoire"—old Sinatra, Bennett, and Johnny Mercer numbers.

He didn't respond.

"Right," Diane said under her breath.

His head jerked and he turned into the northbound lane of 6A. They were heading for the Red Goose, a favorite restaurant near their cottage in East Sandwich. It was a glorious midsum-

*mer's evening with a soft, sultry sea breeze. In spite of a grow-
ing uneasiness, René persisted. "Then how about 'I Remember
You'?" She could hear the note of desperation not to let go of
their old-time ritual.*

"Sorry, Honey. My voice isn't what it used to be."

"You've got a great voice, Dad."

*Diane snapped her head around and hissed, "He doesn't
want to sing."*

*It was as if she had stung René with venom. All she had done
was try to lighten the air. Then she saw something in Diane's
eye just before she turned forward again.* Something was
wrong. *Diane muttered under her breath to her father.*

"What?"

"Next left."

"You don't have to tell me, for chrissake."

"You passed the street."

*For a split second it occurred to René that her father was
joking, that this was one of his elaborate charades to twist Diane's tail—something he'd do when she was in a bad mood. It
was slightly perverse but it always got her laughing. Like when
he'd pretend that his leg had fallen asleep and that he'd have to
limp to the movie or restaurant, stopping every so often to
whack his thigh awake, then suddenly stop limping as if he
were one of those miracles at Lourdes and look up to the sky in
a gaze of beatific gratification. It would send both of them into
laughing jags. Or the time he spent the entire evening speaking
like Peter Sellers's Inspector Clouseau because René was taking French lit. And the more Diane asked him to stop, the more
he pretended he didn't understand English until she cracked
up.* That was it: *One of his routines—playing Daddy Dumb-
Dumb.*

"Christ!" He hissed and he slammed his hand on the wheel.
René felt her insides clutch. No, something else.

*He pulled over to the side to let traffic pass. He had driven
by the turnoff. For several seconds he stared through the windshield as silence filled the car like toxic gas.*

*"What's wrong?" René could hear the fright in her voice.
Ever since her arrival, she had detected a low-grade anxiety—*

her mother's nervous distraction, her father's forced cheer. A horrid thought slashed across her brain: Her mother's cancer was back. During a regular check-up they had found a spot on her lung. And Dad was so distracted by worry that he got confused on a route he could navigate in his sleep.

"Everything's fine," *her mother snapped.*

"I'm just a little tired, Honey." *When the traffic cleared, he made a U-turn, approached the intersection again, then turned.*

"Dad, it's the other way!"

He slammed on the brakes and nearly collided with an oncoming car. Horns blared as they sat in the intersection, her father looking stunned. "Pull over. Pull over!" *her mother shouted. He pulled over, the car facing the opposite way and on the wrong side of 6A. René's chest was so tight she could barely breathe and her mother was crying. Her father sat staring straight ahead.* "I don't know what I'm doing."

"What do you mean?"

"I'm getting senile. I forgot how to get there."

"You're not getting senile. You're not." *But she could sense the ugly snout push its way up.* "You just got a little confused, people blowing their horns like that. We don't have to go, if you don't want to."

"We're going," *her mother snarled.* "You can turn now."

Her father checked the road. "What happens when you get old."

"You're not old. Seventy-two is not old," *René insisted.*

"Straight," *Diane said under her breath.* "Straight."

And her father pulled through the intersection up toward the restaurant.

And in the backseat René uttered a silent prayer. Please, God, no.

Seven years later they buried her father under that stone. By then he had forgotten he had once been a full human being.

René finished cleaning the headstone. "I'm doing better, Dad," she said. "Making an effort to stay active. Even Nick is after me. 'You're too holed-up with your computer.' 'You have to end this self-exile,' he says. 'Meet a nice guy.' Well, I'm going to a party tomorrow. Should be some interesting people there besides Nick."

Birds fluttered overhead and changed direction with a flick. She watched them swirl around and return overhead, then blow away toward the west.

"Remember the time we went fishing off the pier at Scusset Beach? Caught a striper the size of my leg. Missed being a keeper by two inches, but you let me bring it home and scale it. You said they looked like quarters flying off it. Always had a way with words." She touched the stone.

"I miss you, Dad." *I miss us.*

9

René arrived at Broadview around nine the next morning. The receptionist told her the old 3-2-1 security code had been replaced by 63082, which struck her as excessive given that the ward was for dementia patients, most of whom were bèreft of short-term memory. She tapped the code on the keypad and the door to the AD unit clicked open. She passed through and the door closed and locked behind her as it was supposed to. Just as she started down the hall, her attention was arrested by something above her head—the ceiling security camera.

Even though it was Sunday, Alice was in her office. "Her records aren't back, if that's what you're wondering. The police still have them. Sorry." She looked away and began shuffling papers.

"Okay. Then maybe you can call me when they're back," she said, wondering why Alice was acting as if René were a giant botulism spore.

"No problem," Alice said without looking up.

"Oh, one more thing," René said, as Alice started away.

"The patient census you gave me? There are forty-two names and forty-six patients on the ward."

Alice looked at her blankly.

"Mary Curley, Louis Martinetti, Anthony Marsden, and Gloria Breed. According to my records, none of these people are residents."

Alice gathered her things. "Well, they're under Dr. Carr's care."

"Meaning what?"

"Meaning you should speak to him." She began to move away from the desk.

"But you're head nurse on the unit."

"And Dr. Carr is head physician," she snapped.

She tried to get away, but René stopped her, "Alice, are you telling me there are patients here whose medical records I don't have access to?"

Alice took a deep breath, puffing up like a bird in defense. "Really, I have to go."

"Sure, but maybe you can tell me about the security cameras."

"What security cameras?" Alice's voice skipped an octave.

"Outside the unit doors. Has anybody checked them?"

"Checked them?"

"To see who might have let Clara out of the ward?"

"Let her out? Nobody let her out." Again she tried to get away. But René took her arm. "Alice, I don't know what's going on here, but let me just say that if word got out to the state and federal regulatory boards that there are irregularities in the medical records of a patient arrested for murder, that there are more patients on the ward than listed, that critical pharmaceutical documentation is missing or locked away—there are going to be questions about patient neglect and patient abuse, and we could see a SWAT team of regulators come down on us like banshees demanding to know what other irregularities Broadview is up to, raising questions about patient security and wondering all sorts of things about the nursing staff and criminal negligence or, worse—that somebody here let Clara Devine out of the home, intent on murder. And since I'm professionally responsible for reporting irregularities in patients' status, my job is on the line. So maybe somebody should tell me what's going on or I'm calling the state."

Alice stared at René for a long moment, her face rippling with expressions under the glare of René's threat. Finally she sighed, and her body deflated like a balloon. She glanced down the hall to an aide. "Bonnie, I'll be right back." Then she nodded René inside a small back office and locked the door behind them. "They'll probably have my head, but I'm sure you'll find out anyway."

"Find out what?"

"You know nothing about this," she whispered, her eyes full of pleading.

The axes of the room felt as if they had shifted a few degrees. René nodded. "Okay."

Alice unlocked a desk drawer and removed a videocassette. On a table behind them was a television monitor and VCR where they often viewed patient behavior or educational videos. Alice popped in the video, and after some flickering the screen filled with a grainy black-and-white ceiling shot of the unit's security door from maybe ten feet back. For several seconds nothing moved, as if they were looking at a still. Then a figure appeared in the jerky time-lapsed motion of security cameras. Clara Devine.

She was alone and carrying a shopping bag. She looked about her, then, unbelievably, she went to the wall and with a finger she tapped the keypad and pushed her way through the door, which closed behind her. It happened so fast that René just said, "What?"

"Yeah, I know. She let herself out."

René felt a flash of gooseflesh across her back. What she was seeing could not be—like witnessing a dog suddenly speaking English or seeing someone levitate. Dogs don't talk, and Alzheimer's patients don't recover their short-term memory. The disease, like gravity, was a downward, persistent force.

"I don't believe this." René's mind raced for a rational explanation: Clara had been misdiagnosed all along. She had faked her dementia. It was somebody else. None of the above.

"There's more," Alice said, her voice grim. She hit a few buttons and the tape switched to another venue. The main entrance outside. Again a shadowy figure, but with Clara's face and body, and this time she was dressed in a rain poncho pulled over her head.

"We think she changed in the elevator and slipped by the front desk. It was raining out."

On rare occasions, a patient managed to elope from a nursing home, usually because of understaffing. Two winters ago a man wandered outside and froze to death. As a result, Broadview had installed an elaborate security system. But no Alzheimer's patient was capable of figuring out a pass code or remembering it even if she had heard it from one of the staffers. Nor were any of them capable of long-range planning of a disguise on a rainy night.

"My guess is she must have watched one of us use the keypad, and she memorized the combo."

"Alice, she has middle-stage Alzheimer's. She's not capable of memorizing anything longer than a second, and you know that."

Alice didn't respond.

"Do the police know about this?"

"No. They never asked. Their job was to solve a murder. Broadview's security is Broadview's problem and not a police matter."

"If they ask?"

"The system was down, the cameras weren't working. Not my area." Alice popped out the cassette and locked it in the drawer again. Then she got up and put her hand on the doorknob to leave.

Not my area.

"Alice, what the hell's going on up here?"

"I think you'd better ask Dr. Carr. He'll be in tomorrow." And she hustled away.

10

Morningside Manor was a red brick, three-story nursing home nestled among birches and evergreens and adjoining conservation land in Smithfield, just below the New Hampshire border. It was an adult long-term-care facility with a hundred and ten beds and was a cut above most of the homes and rehab centers that René regularly visited. It was Monday afternoon and she could not believe the number of cars in the parking lot including several limousines, all here for the groundbreaking of a new Alzheimer's unit.

A large white tent had been pitched on the lawn, and waiters and waitresses were circulating through the crowd with champagne and fancy hors d'oeuvres. This was not the typical jug-wine-and-cheese-cube affair afforded by nursing home budgets.

René parked and made her way toward the tent, seeing no faces she recognized until she spotted Nick Mavros. He was standing with a small knot of people and waved her over.

"Now here's a young woman for whom the expression 'teacher's pet' was coined. Hello, beautiful," he said, and gave her a hug and double-cheek air kisses, vestiges of a Peloponnesian birth some sixty years ago.

Nick had a strong face, thick bold features, and large eyes that lit up his face. "And now I've embarrassed her."

"I'll survive," she said, and shook hands with another physician introduced as Peter Habib from Plymouth, a man about Nick's age.

Nicholas Konstantinos Mavros had been her professor in pharmacy grad school and her thesis advisor for two years, during which time they had become more than student and professor. During her father's decline, Nick had taken René under his wing, consoling her, bringing her to his home, giving her solace when she needed it the most. Over the three years since her father's death, Nick had helped fill the void with warmth balanced by keen intelligence—traits which accounted for his position of respect in the community of neurophysicians. He was one of the few men whose mind never abandoned his heart, and René was grateful that there were people like Nick Mavros in the world.

Nick no longer had time to teach and was cutting back his private practice. He was senior neurologist at Mass General Hospital and chief collaborator at that institution's MRI Imaging Center, where he and a team of physicists had pioneered new techniques for diagnostic imaging of the brain.

"They've got a tent the size of Fenway Park and half the medical community of the Northeast. What's the big deal about a new nursing home wing?"

Nick made a happy grin and held up his glass. "Free champagne." His eyes had that white-grape glow. He liked his wines and had a collection in his cellar.

"You have no shame," René said.

"He's a Greek. What do you expect?" Dr. Habib joked.

"Then they're all Greeks here," Nick said.

"Good stuff?" she asked, hinting that he's probably had more than he should.

"Excellent, and brain cells be damned." Then his eyes widened. "Uh-oh! There go another ten thousand."

She laughed. "You can spare them."

"Nice to meet you," Habib said, excusing himself. "Something about the powers that do reckoning with the powers that be." And he walked off.

"I love that guy," Nick said through his champagne. "He knows how to live. He just bought himself a brand new Harley-Davidson for his semiretirement. Carpe diem."

Habib had moved to a small group of people clustered around a large bald-headed man near the podium. "So what's the big deal?" René asked. It was a crowd of at least a hundred and fifty and clearly was no shoestring celebration.

"It's not Health Corp. who's picking up the tab," Nick said. Then he put his mouth to her ear. "The fella in the gray suit and bald head talking to Preston Van Dyke and Carter Lutz and now Peter. Gavin Moy."

"Who?"

But just then Carter blew into the microphone. "May I have your attention, everybody?"

When the crowd quieted down, he introduced Preston Van Dyke, CEO of Health Corp., the parent company of the nursing homes that included Morningside and twenty-six other homes and rehab centers. Van Dyke began by thanking Carter Lutz and other dignitaries gathered there. "I'd like to say that this is a great day for Morningside as we break ground for our new long-term-care unit, which, as you may know, is to be constructed with another generous gift from GEM Tech." And he motioned his hand toward Gavin Moy. When the applause died down, Van Dyke continued: "With your wonderful support, we will expand our already fine facilities and increase the quality of health care for years to come."

Van Dyke continued briefly, and when he was finished, somebody handed him and Gavin Moy a chrome shovel with which they posed over a plot of dirt for a flurry of photographs and applause. The groundbreaking still didn't explain the large crowd of suits, including someone she recognized from the FDA.

"Exciting, huh?" Nick said.

"Overwhelming," René said, as they walked to a table of

fancy snacks. Her mind was pulsing to tell him about the video of Clara Devine. "Do you know a neuro doc named Jordan Carr?"

"Yes. In fact, he's here somewhere. Why?"

"I'll catch him another time." This was not the occasion for a confrontation.

"Well, if you change your mind, I'd be happy to—" But Nick was cut off.

"René Ballard?"

She turned to see a tall, good-looking man with shiny black hair.

"Speaking of the devil," Nick said. "René Ballard, Jordan Carr."

He held his hand out to her. "I understand you were looking for me."

"Well, yes. I was."

"Then I saved you the trouble." His smile spread over a perfect set of upper teeth.

Nick grinned and took the invitation to depart. "If you'll excuse me."

"No, you don't have to leave," she said to Nick.

He held up his empty glass and nodded toward a waitress. "The champagne lady's here and all's right with the world," he said with a wink. "Besides, there's someone I have to say hello to." And he headed off, grabbing another champagne from the waitress on the way to Gavin Moy.

"So," Dr. Carr said, smiling down on her.

"We can do this at another time."

"This is as good as any."

He had a thin, boyish face with a high forehead and large, dark almond-shaped eyes that made him look Polynesian. His hair was perfectly black and parted on the side with optical precision. René stood five-five, maybe five-six in heels, and he was nearly a head taller than she was. "Okay. Then perhaps where we can have more privacy," she said, and led him to an opening away from the crowd.

"My, my, this *must* be important," he said, following her.

She couldn't tell if he was being serious or condescending.

It didn't help that he spoke in a crisp English accent, which blurred the distinction. When they were on their own, she said, "I have some questions about Clara Devine."

He kept his face in a neutral state of bemusement. "What about her?"

René was conscious of the professional divide between them—he a nationally recognized neurophysician probably on the board of a dozen important institutions and she a twenty-nine-year-old consulting pharmacist. She also reminded herself that a misstatement could get Alice Gordon and the other nurses in trouble. "I'm wondering how she managed to escape Broadview and get herself to the CVS and kill a complete stranger."

"I'm familiar with the case, Ms. Ballard." He smiled and sipped his wine, studying her with unblinking eyes.

She was not going to let his porcelain smugness derail her. "As you may know, I'm responsible for monitoring patients' meds each month. When I went to check her folder, I discovered that several months' worth of her charts were missing. Also, the order sheets were signed off by you rather than her primary care physician."

"Because I've taken over for Dr. Colette." His words had the honey-glaze patience of a teacher addressing a slow child.

"I see, but that still doesn't explain Clara's missing medical charts and those of four other patients under your care."

If her discovery surprised him he did not let on. "They're in Broadview's computers." His smile shaded into irritation, and he checked his watch.

"Then why was I told to consult you first when I asked to see them?"

"Just another firewall of patient confidentiality. Next question."

Yeah. How did you get to be such an arrogant creep?

"Dr. Carr, I am licensed to have access to patient records—all patients' records—not just some of them."

"Then it's an oversight to be corrected. Is that it?"

The feigned civility of Carr's manner was annoying. *Illegit-*

imi non carborundum. Dad's counsel. "No. The census sheets list forty-two patients, and a head count turned up forty-six."

"Beg pardon?"

"There are four more residents in the AD unit than are registered. Four names I've not seen before, yet who have beds. And, frankly, Dr. Carr, I'd like an explanation because I've got to give one to my boss."

Carr looked a bit nonplussed. "You're very clever, Ms. Ballard. And may I call you René?"

"Dr. Carr, I'm responsible for the accuracy of all patients' medical records on that ward as I am at all the homes I visit—"

Carr flapped his hand as if her words were gnats. "Yes, yes, of course." Then he scanned the crowd, looking like a Serengeti gazelle testing the air for cheetahs. And while he did she noticed his outfit—tan hand-stitched boots that probably cost more than her Honda and a blue blazer with a breast-pocket shield of a black rearing stallion in a field of gold. Some designer's logo she didn't recognize.

"Ms. Ballard, I'm wondering if we might discuss this some other time."

"Dr. Carr, I've been getting stonewalled on this since yesterday and possibly since I've been on the job. And given that this has become a police matter, I think I have a right to know what's going on with residents in my homes."

"Nobody is questioning your right to know. It's just not the proper place." He smiled widely and waved at someone in the crowd. "And now I'm being paged. Do you have a business card?"

She was being dismissed. She dug into her bag and pulled one out.

He produced a gold pen. "No, your home number and address, if you don't mind."

She looked up at him for an explanation.

"Chateau Dominique at eight tomorrow. Are you free?"

Christ, he's making a damn date with me. "I guess," she could hear the thinness of her voice. "But this is not a social matter."

"No, but a much better venue."

Go with it, she told herself, and wrote down her number and address.

"Is seven-thirty good?" But before she could file that away, Carr took her elbow. "Here's someone I'd like you to meet," he said, and took her to Gavin Moy.

Moy smiled and shook her hand. It was soft and warm, like a fine glove left in the sun. He had a weathered, tanned face that looked as if it had spent time on a yacht or a golf course. What was striking about his appearance was his brilliant green eyes, which made her wonder if he wore colored contacts. His head was a perfectly tanned dome with a mixture of white and auburn on the sides. "A pleasure to meet you, Ms. Blanchard."

"Ballard."

He nodded and scanned her up and down. "Nice pin," he said looking at her lapel cat pin fashioned in black and white.

"It's supposed to be my cat," she said, feeling foolish.

Moy nodded and began searching the crowd. She could have announced that she had eaten the cat for breakfast and he could not have cared less. So why Dr. Carr's insistence on their meeting?

"Nice to meet you," he said, and pulled away with Carr.

Apparently Nick had taken in the scene, because he sauntered over with a fresh glass of champagne and took her arm. "Having a good time?"

"A blast." She swallowed half her glass of wine. "Why do I feel like I'm stuck in a conspiracy movie and I'm the only one who doesn't get it?"

"Maybe you are. What time is your date?"

"How do you know I have a date?"

"Because I know Jordan Carr. I also knew his ex-wife."

"If first impressions mean anything, I'm on her side."

Nick smiled broadly. "Well, maybe you should give him a chance. He's a brilliant physician and someone who's going places."

"So, what should I know?"

"That you're in for a lovely meal and some good wine."

"Want to chaperone? Please?"

He laughed. "I'm sure you'll be just fine."

"What about the fifty questions I want answered?"

"I'm sure you'll be satisfied." He looked around for the waiter for a refill.

"And I think it's time for Pellegrino." And she plucked the fluted glass out of Nick's hand and headed over to the bar feeling like Alice at the Mad Hatter's jubilee.

When she returned Nick had removed from his jacket a magazine ad for a camera. "Not exactly a new Harley," he said, and unfolded a photo of a large-format Mamiya camera. In what spare time he had, Nick liked to take nature photos and talked about taking time off to do a photo safari in the Canadian Rockies or the Grand Canyon someday. His office walls were covered with shots from Switzerland and Hawaii. "But it's how I plan to enjoy the overrated golden years. And speaking of pictures, I'd like you to drop in at my office at the hospital. Got some interesting images you might like to see."

"And, of course, you're not going to tell me until then."

"The next time you're in Boston." He checked his watch. "Thalia's expecting me." His wife of thirty-five years was suffering from Parkinson's disease.

"Okay."

"If he touches you I'll kill him," he whispered.

"You won't have to."

They double-cheek kissed and he headed for the parking lot. She watched him go, thinking how happy she was to have him in her life. Thinking that if he were a dog he'd be a graying black Lab—solid, strong, smart, loyal, and affectionate.

Across the crowd she spotted Jordan Carr holding forth to several admirers clustered around him. And you, a Doberman, she thought—sleek, angular, and a little dangerous.

11

"**H**is eyes are moving."

"That's good, he's dreaming. See those spikes? There's activity."

"*Jack!* It's me, Beth. Wake up. Please." Gently, she tapped his hip, one of the few places where he had not been stung.

"I think we're ready to take him now," the nurse said. "We'll be back in an hour."

They were preparing to take him to the Magnetic Resonance Center to record images of his brain for signs of strokes or other structural abnormalities. Also to check blood flow in the occipital and neotemporal lobes to be certain there were no occlusions. That was the nurse's explanation to Beth.

And Jack could hear them.

They were on the other side of the door. Beth and the others . . . The door near the big window.

Don't look out. Don't look out.

Bad stuff . . .

"But he's so agitated, he's having a nightmare," Beth pleaded. "Can't you do something? Jack, wake up."

That awful creature with the pointy head . . .

"They'll give him some anesthesia so the images won't blur. But his brain's still active, and that's what they want to capture."

If this was a dream, he didn't like it. Not dreaming. No way. This was too real. As real as those feet. Those horrible twitching feet. And the big brown mouse.

(That's one smart mouse.)

Nice mouse. Big mouse.

They lifted Jack onto the gurney and wheeled him down the hall to the elevator and up to the MRC.

And the noise. Don't tell me that's a goddam dream . . . explosions rattling the dishes in the hutch . . . and that sound . . .

That sickening terrible sound . . .

And don't telling me to stop screaming . . .

"Jack, I'm right here. It's going to be all right. They're just going to take some pictures."

He could hear her through the door . . . Beth . . .

"You won't feel a thing."

His body was a cross-patch of slashes from scalp to foot and covered with antibiotic ointment. But as if by the snap of a magician's finger all that was gone . . . and his body was clean, whole, pain-free.

He grabbed the mouse and climbed out of the cage. The floor was cold and wet. Beth, it's me.

"Almost there."

I'm coming.

He padded toward the door by the big black window . . .

Don't look out.

He could feel the night watching him, pulling him to climb up and take a peek. To see the bad stuff out there.

Don't do it . . . The door. Go to the door. It's Beth.

He made his way to the door feeling all the eyes scrape him as he passed, feeling the jelly stuff making his feet sticky.

He was scared. So scared that he was panting . . . making queer noises. So scared that he pissed himself.

Bad sounds. Bad sounds.

"Stop that screaming. Stop that screaming."

The door. The brown paneled door with the little windows. He put his hand on the knob. It was cool and slick and he tried to turn it to let Beth inside, but it was frozen. God, please help me.

"Jack, we're just going to give you a little something to keep you still, okay?"

Beth! Open the door. Please let me out of here before it comes back in. Please.

"You won't feel a thing . . . just some noises . . ."

Beth, somebody, let me out, let me out. Please.

Pounding. He pounded for it to open, pounded so hard he thought he heard his hand bones crack.

Please, somebody.

God, make the door open.

His feet. He looked down at his feet and they were covered with sticky stuff that left prints when he walked, and it was seeping under the door . . .

And the room instantly flooded as thick glutinous fluid rose up around him, engulfing his body, blotting the light and pushing him backward, black dark thick water rushing him along . . . and the jellies—hundreds of pulsing blobs streaming by his face out of the gloom. He braced for the sting of the tendrils, yet he felt nothing. Maybe they were friendly. Or maybe he really was dreaming.

"You are my sunshine . . ."

He tried to swim, but nothing worked. His feet and arms were dead—as if his blood had turned to concrete. His brain screamed commands to his body, but nothing moved. Nothing. Couldn't even lift his head.

And the voices beyond the door.

He was paralyzed.

"We're all done, Jack. We're taking you back now."

The goddam fucking jellies had paralyzed him.

"Jack, you did good, real good." *Nurse Maffeo.*

Movement. He felt himself being lifted and rolled away. He wiggled his fingers. Then his toes and feet. God, thank you. He could feel his body come back. He didn't know how, but he was going to keep them purring before more vapor lock.

"He's agitated."

"The anesthetic's wearing off."

"Jack, it's me. Wake up. Please."

He grabbed the knob again and felt it turn a little.

"Push, Jack. Push."

I'm trying, but it won't budge. Whatever they did it locked the goddamn door . . . and everything's turning black. Oh, shit!

"See the lines? Let me turn up the gain. He's stable again. Just a bad dream. Happens with trauma cases."

And the voices faded like muffled music.

12

At seven-thirty sharp on Tuesday evening, Dr. Jordan Carr pulled up in a long, shiny red sports car. René met him at the door. She had on a black sundress and heels—her only dressy outfit, the rest being pants suits, long skirts, and button-down blouses, which were fine for nursing homes and the declared moratorium on her social life. And he stood there in a suede camel-colored sportcoat with the same logo as yesterday's blazer.

He walked her to the car that in the house lights glowed like a piece of jewelry. "Yikes, what is it?"

"Ferrari Testarossa." He said that with the aplomb of announcing that the stars were visible.

The vehicle had been polished to a wet ruby sheen. "Very pretty," she said, taking in the long sinuous lines and sculpted vanes.

"Thank you."

As he let her in, Silky meowed down to them from an upstairs window. "Good night, Silky."

Carr got in, looking up at the cat. "Funny, but you seem more the dog type."

"How's that?"

"I guess I'm thinking of how pets reflect their owners. Maybe it's silly, but how dogs are more aggressive than cats."

"And?" She drew out the syllable to see where he was taking this.

"And, well, you impressed me as being aggressive and tenacious."

"Tenacious, as in a pit bull who gets her jaws on something and won't let go?"

"Something like that."

"Would it make you feel better to know that Silky is actually a panther cub?" He looked at her to see if she was making mock of him. She smiled and changed the subject. "I've never been in a Ferrari."

"Welcome aboard." He turned the key, and the car growled to life.

The interior light lit up a medallion on the gearshift—a rearing black stallion on a field of gold. "That's the logo on the blazer you wore yesterday."

"Yes," he said as he pulled away. "I used to have a few other models until a divorce lawyer entered the picture."

For a moment she imagined that he had a whole wardrobe of Ferrari outfits—blazers, polo shirts, Windbreakers, hats—probably even had rearing stallion undies. "Sorry to hear that," she said, but found it hard to feel sympathy for a guy who was down to his last Ferrari. "I collect Honda Civics."

Carr turned his face toward her. "Is that supposed to be funny?"

"I guess not." The guy seemed devoid of humor. Or maybe he wasn't used to teasing from underlings. Whatever—she decided that this was not going to be a long and tedious night.

They came to a stoplight and Dr. Carr turned full-face toward her. "I think if we're going to have a pleasant evening, it might be a good idea to clear the air."

"Fine," she said, feeling as if a valve had opened up. "Then maybe you can tell me what exactly is going on in Broadview Nursing Home, since that is what this is all about."

Carr stared at her, no doubt offended that an inferior in the medical Great Chain of Being had spoken to him with such bluntness. "You *are* a feisty one, I'll say."

"And I think you're playing coy with me, Dr. Carr."

"Do you always say what's on your mind?"

"I guess I do."

He nodded. "Okay, fair enough, but over the wine. And it's Jordan."

Silence filled the car as they headed toward the restaurant, while René kept wondering what this was all about, why Chateau Dominique and escort service by this high-powered neurologist who collected Ferraris.

To break the tension, Jordan looked over at her. "So, how did you end up in a profession like yours? I mean, really, you're an attractive, bright young woman, yet you chose to work with geriatrics and dementia patients."

The question was as familiar as the answer was boring. "I like the elderly. And I guess it's because I've always had an interest in caring for those who get overlooked or scorned by society. Before pharmacy school, I worked at a homeless shelter and then at a substance-abuse clinic. That put me in touch with what it feels like to be a social outcast."

"And now it's geriatric nursing home residents."

"Yes. There are plenty of people in the medical professions who care for babies and the middle-class Americans with health insurance."

"Thus you've chosen the underserved."

"That or I'm suffering some kind of psychopathology. I'm also comfortable with the elderly. I grew up in a small Maine farm town that was impoverished and that didn't have a lot of young people. All around me were older folks—grandparents, great-aunts and great-uncles, and neighbors who were surrogate grandparents to me. The only doctors I remember were those who cared for older people. In fact, I grew up thinking that all doctors were gerontologists. Besides, somebody has to take care of them, right?"

"That's hardly psychopathology."

She was silent for a moment. "Well, there's a personal motive, I suppose. My father died of Alzheimer's."

" *'You must remember this, a kiss is just a kiss, a case of do or die . . .'* "

"I see. So you're trying to help others cope with the dragon."

"Something like that."

In the lights of the other cars she could sense him turn something over in his head that was making him grin slightly. "Was it bad—your father's demise?"

" *'No matter what the future brings . . .' Dad, you're punking out.*"

"Ever treat a *good* case of Alzheimer's?"

"I meant, in the severity of the disease."

"It was fast toward the end, and worse on us than him."

Punking out.

"How old was he when he was diagnosed?"

"Seventy-two."

"Not very old."

"Only seventy-two, Dad. You're not getting senile. You're not! You're not."

"He died seven years later."

"Listen to me, honey, no matter what happens to me, keep strong for your mother, okay?

"And don't let the laughter go away. You'll be my big hero, okay?"

She could still hear the gentle, consoling voice.

"We all have to go someday, and I had a wonderful life. I still do."

"Well, I hope I didn't upset you, but it's what we're trying to do something about."

"I'm fine," she said. "What about your becoming a doc?"

"Well, my father was a physician in Singapore. So I guess it's in the blood. Also, it's not a bad life."

Ferrari Testarossa. No, not bad. "Singapore? Is that where you're from?"

"Originally, yes. My mother was Chinese, my father Canadian, but originally from London."

That explained his exotic appearance. Maybe even his aristocratic demeanor.

Jordan looked over at her when they approached the restaurant. "You're very attractive. Just wondering why someone like you is unattached."

"Thank you, but who says I am?"

"Well, you caught me. I was talking to Nick Mavros."

Nick was a mentor, perhaps a father figure, and a friend, but there was a strain of village matchmaker in him. "I see. Well, I'm fairly busy. And frankly I'm downsizing."

"Downsizing. Ahh, a recent parting of ways?"

"Something like that."

"Clearly bad judgment on his part."

"Thanks. And what about you?"

"Divorced, two children, and paying dearly because her attorney's a velociraptor."

They turned into the restaurant parking lot.

13

The hostess greeted Dr. Carr by name and led them to a private candlelit table in a far corner.

While Carr read the wine menu, René studied his face. In the soft candlelight he was very handsome, with long-lashed quasi-Asian eyes, smooth fine features, hair that closed over his brow like a leather flap, and an absence of beard shadow. Adding to the effect was the silky voice and manner. And despite his obvious avoidance of the issue at the forefront of René's mind, Jordan Carr was very charming—another lesson for her that people aren't what they seem. He ordered a sixty-dollar merlot.

Awkward silence filled the air after the waiter left. René studied the menu just to fill the gap. Then she looked up. "So . . . ," she said. "Clara Devine."

Carr lit up. "Ahh, the wine." And almost by magic the waiter appeared and filled the glasses. Jordan raised his glass. "To a better future through medicine."

"Sounds more like a slogan than a toast."

"Maybe a little of each." And he took a sip and settled back in his chair. "So, what do you want to know?"

René leaned forward. "Okay. You are not Clara Devine's primary physician."

A bemused smile spread like an oil slick across Carr's face. "Correct."

"Why have her medical charts not come back to me?"

"I believe the police have impounded them."

Maybe.

"Next question."

"There are four more patients on the AD ward than in the census—which is highly irregular."

He nodded. "They're under special care with me."

"Special care?"

"Yes," but he did not elaborate.

"You know, of course, that I'm supposed to have total access to all patients' records in order to determine the effect of their meds. If there's a problem, I need documentation, nurses' observations, et cetera."

"Of course. And that's all been documented. Next question."

Stonewalling again, and with an irritating glint in his eyes that said he was savoring her annoyance. One call from her could get the state to review the practices at Broadview, but she pushed that to the back of her mind. "And where are they documented?"

"In the home computers." He took another sip of wine. "Next."

"Clara Devine is a seventy-six-year-old AD patient who mysteriously eloped from a locked unit and ended up the next morning three miles away in a CVS where she killed a guy. None of that is supposed to happen."

"Do you know how she got out?"

She could not betray Alice. "Pardon me?"

His gaze hardened. "Do you know how she got out, how she eloped?"

Yes. "No."

"Then how do you know she *eloped* and wasn't let out?"

Shit! "I don't. That's probably what the police are wondering."

"I know you saw the security videos."

Her chest tightened. "Security videos?"

"It's okay. In fact, we were eventually going to show them to you." He leaned forward and lowered his voice. "Tell me exactly what you saw on those videos."

René wondered if this was a trick to get the nurses in trouble. "I saw an elderly woman with Alzheimer's tap a security code and let herself out, then emerge in disguise at the front of the building and disappear."

"Yes. And how do you explain that? What are the possibilities?"

"That she'd been misdiagnosed. Or that somebody had instructed her how to do it. Or that it wasn't Clara Devine."

"And what does your gut tell you the most likely explanation is?"

"My gut tells me nothing."

"Exactly." Then he ticked them off on his fingers. "One, you know she was not misdiagnosed since you saw her admission profile: a seventyish woman with moderate AD. Two, she was too far gone to be trained to escape or recall the code. And, three, it was Clara Devine because that was her face on camera, correct?"

René's heart kicked up a beat. Then out of some half-glimpsed premonition she heard him say, "What you witnessed was a medical miracle."

"A medical miracle," she said, as if taking an oath.

"Yes. For the last six months Clara Devine and other dementia patients have been part of a large clinical trial of a new compound for the treatment of Alzheimer's disease. As I am sure you're aware, the brains of patients with Alzheimer's on autopsy and on MRI have been observed to have deposits of beta-amyloid protein, or plaques, which do not form on the brains of people without Alzheimer's. So we know that these plaques are a major cause of dementia, though we're learning there are other factors as well—a loss of key brain neurotransmitters such as acetylcholine, which is important in learning and memory functions.

"This new compound has been shown not only to dissolve the plaques but also to stimulate neuronal growth, all but reversing the degenerative effects of the disease. In short, patients are getting their memory and functionality back. And what you saw in that video is the result of that reversal."

It was as if the speech centers of René's brain had tilted out.

"The woman's elopement was an unfortunate consequence of a recovered ability to function. My guess is that she overheard a staffer tell someone else the code, which she memorized. Then she escaped, put on a disguise, and walked out of the building. What you witnessed was a woman in the process of being cured of Alzheimer's disease." His face was beaming.

For a long moment René tried to process his words, running through her head the crude black-and-white video, trying to find cracks in his explanation against those images of the woman purposefully making good her elopement.

"Like I said, *a miracle.*"

René felt a fist grip her organs and it had nothing to do with protocol. "I'm having difficulty digesting all this. A cure for Alzheimer's disease?"

"Exactly. And keep in mind that until a few years ago nobody thought it was possible for nerve cells to reproduce. Now we've learned that they divide even in adults, that we're not born with all the brain cells we'll ever have. And that's what this stuff does—stimulates new cell growth in the hippocampus and with it memory functions."

"But that's impossible."

"Only because you're thinking of meds currently on the market—Aricept, Exelon, Reminyl—which, at best, only slow the progress of the disease. I am sure you know the pharmacology of those as well as I do, right? Why they only slow the progress of the dementia without curing the disease?"

René tried to concentrate on his question around the fist tightening on her internal organs. He was testing her, she told herself. Suddenly this was classroom. So she decided to humor him. "Aricept and the others are cholinesterase inhibitors. Cholinesterase is an enzyme that destroys the neurotransmitter acetylcholine, which, as you said, is crucial in learning and forming memory. By inhibiting the action of cholinesterase, acetylcholine is not destroyed as quickly. Yet the amount of new acetylcholine produced in the brain continues to decline.

And these drugs keep the acetylcholine that's produced around longer, but they don't stop the continuing decline of acetylcholine production. So the dementia continues, but at a slower rate than without these medications."

Carr's eyes lit up. "Very good!"

Yeah, because I researched the pharmacology of every damn drug on the market to save my father.

"And, of course," Carr continued, "the other reason is that the loss of acetylcholine isn't the only cause of dementia. The big problem is the plaque deposits that spread throughout the brain, causing changes in the levels of other important neurotransmitters. And that may explain the different rates of disease progression seen in different patients—or why some dementia patients slowly become mute, docile, and isolative, while others become very agitated, combative, and aggressive. We don't understand all the reasons for this, but so far we only have the cholinesterase inhibitors to help deal with the disease."

She took a deep breath against the conflicting sensations. "So you're saying you've developed a new approach."

"More than that, *a cure.*"

And at the core of her body the fist tightened.

"And it's a completely new drug entity. A proteolytic compound that actually degrades the beta-amyloid protein plaques that cause the dementia. I'm telling you it's amazing: We've seen the plaques recede on MRI in these trials while patients regain functioning and memory. The stuff actually reverses previous damage, not simply slowing the progression. There's also a mysterious secondary effect—the regeneration of nerve cells. Whatever, the compound's been in the GEM Tech pipeline for years. And its trade name is Memorine."

"Memorine." All those fancy people under the tent yesterday. "GEM Tech."

A cure.

"Yes, GEM Neurobiological Technologies. As in Gavin Edward Moy."

The waiter arrived for their orders. René's appetite had suddenly died, so she ordered an appetizer.

"That's all you're going to eat?"

"I'm not very hungry."

Carr ordered a steak. "You don't seem very impressed," he said when the waiter left.

"I'm still trying to process it all."

"Of course," he smiled. "It *is* mind-boggling. But maybe this will help." From his coat pocket he removed a Palm Pilot. He hit a few buttons, then turned the device for her to see. "You recognize Clara there in the blue sweatshirt."

"Yes." On the small screen was an interior shot of patients at a table.

"That was taken seven months ago." The camera zoomed in on the *Manchester Union Leader* to confirm the date. Clara was at a table doing a picture puzzle of a puppy. She randomly picked up pieces and tried to fit them together, clearly having difficulty.

"Hi, Clara, how you doing today?" The feathery voice of Jordan Carr off camera.

"Fine," Clara said, not looking up at the camera.

"Clara, look what I have here."

Clara lowered her eyes into a shoebox. "See, a button, a hairbrush, and a lollypop." She inspects them. "You can touch them. Go ahead." She picks up each item, awkwardly running the brush through her hair. She inspects the button and puts it back, then picks up the lollypop and sniffs it. Carr puts the items back into the box and asks her about the puzzle she's doing. For maybe a minute she picks up pieces and begins to try to find mates. She's unsuccessful. Then the lidded shoebox appears. "Clara, remember this? This box?"

Clara looks at it blankly.

"Remember what's inside?"

She continues to look at it blankly.

"What's inside?"

"I don't know," she says and turns back to the puzzle.

"Remember the lollypop?"

"No," she says, fingering the puzzle piece.

Carr pokes a few keys with a stylus. "Now this is Clara six months later."

Clara is sitting at the same table. A wall clock behind her. Dr. Carr's disembodied voice: "Good morning, Clara."

"Good morning." She smiles at the man beside the camera.

A shoebox slides into view. "I'm going to show you what's inside, okay?"

"Okay."

A hand opens the box and removes a spoon, a small Mr. Goodbar, and a pencil. Carr identifies each out loud, then puts them in the box and puts the lid back. "Now, do you remember what's in the box, Clara?"

"Yes. A spoon, a Mr. Goodbar, a pencil."

"Very good." And Carr opens the box and removes each and replaces them. With the clock in constant view, he has her put together a child's puzzle over the next fifteen minutes. She moves very slowly but manages to fit several pieces together. When time is up, the shoebox reappears. "Now, do you remember this shoebox?"

"Yes."

"Do you remember what's inside the box?"

Clara blinks at the box for a few seconds. She looks uncertain for a moment, then says, "Yes. Mr. Goodbar, a spoon, and a pencil."

"Very good," Carr says, and behind them the nursing staff cheers.

Carr laid the Palm Pilot on the table, the freeze frame of Clara smiling proudly.

The waiter delivered the food while René stared dumbly at the image of the woman smiling back at her. All she could think was, *That could have been my father.*

"So what do you think?" Carr said, digging into his steak.

"Well, that's incredible." And for a second René wondered almost hopefully whether it had all been staged—that she wasn't actually looking at Clara Devine but some imposter partaking in an elaborate conspiracy for whatever reasons— perhaps some security test gone awry.

"Even more remarkable, her cognitive test scores were double what she got before she was institutionalized and two to three times that of the placebo group—not to mention a five times response rate and enhanced ability to perform her activities of daily living. Six months before she took the drug, she could not dress herself or go to the bathroom alone. Now she's undergone a clinical regeneration in twenty-four weeks at two ten-milligram dosages daily."

"I'd very much like to see those results."

"Of course." Carr's eyes beamed like a child sharing a secret.

She was forgetting things from one moment to the next. It was like watching her being peeled away like an onion. Cassandra Gould's words buzzed in René's brain.

And cutting across those her father's plea: *"Promise me . . . I don't want to end up just some gaga thing attached to a diaper."*

Maybe Clara Devine was just some extraordinary anomaly. "Are there other test subjects?"

"Of course."

"So why all the secrecy if it's such a miracle drug?"

"It's a blinded study to keep people unbiased."

Clinical trials were blinded so that the people responsible for patients wouldn't attribute any and every change to the drug being tested. And while in such studies the caregivers may not know which patients receive the active drug and which patients receive a placebo, they are made aware that patients are enrolled in a clinical study. "But why wasn't I or my pharmacy informed?"

"Because technically the trial compound is not among the active meds supplied by CommCare, your pharmacy. The Memorine tablets came from GEM."

"But these patients were on other meds that CommCare supplies."

"Look, their medical charts were meticulously kept by the nursing staff."

"You mean a separate and hidden set."

"Yes, but the trial data wasn't kept from those who need to know at the FDA."

"That still doesn't explain why there are no nurses' reports of the trials in my records or the alleged improvement of patients' behavior and functionality. Or why I wasn't told." Because her job centered mostly on paperwork, she had only minimal contact with nursing home residents—something she hoped to change as time passed. Therefore, she could not personally have witnessed any actual improvements in the behavior of these trial subjects. Nonetheless, nurses and other staffers at her homes often talked about patients' health, behavior, affect, the funny things they may have said. Yet, remarkably, nobody had uttered a word about the extraordinary changes in Clara Devine or any other patients in these trials.

"Well, I'm telling you now."

"But only because Clara Devine eloped and murdered someone."

His face darkened. "That was unfortunate."

"Doctor Carr, this isn't a blinded study, it's a *concealed* one."

He stared at her for a moment, then shrugged. "If you wish."

He was trying to disarm her with a concession because he knew that she could report him. As an employee of CommCare, she was an outsider to the nursing home and bound by state and FDA regulations. And they both knew that she could lose her job were she not to report a secret clinical trial. "Doctor, you're not answering my question: Why was I kept in the dark?"

"It was nothing personal. Even the nursing staff didn't know what the subjects were on, though they were aware they'd been enrolled in trial of a dementia drug."

"That still doesn't answer my question."

He drained his wineglass. "Because GEM Tech did not want to risk the competition getting wind of what we have. Period."

The *we* floated like a lazy feather in the air. "They're really worried some other drug company's going to whip up a me-too compound?"

"In a word, yes. They don't want somebody else beating them to the market. You know what a rat race the pharmaceutical industry is. Somebody invents a Ford, and a Chevy is right on its bumper." He lowered his voice to a conspiratorial whisper. "René, we're talking about a supreme blockbuster drug here—a fifty-*billion*-dollar pill."

The waiter arrived to clear their dishes. When he left, Carr said, "I know it's premature, but the FDA is very excited about this, *very*. And I won't be surprised if they fast-track its approval."

That still didn't justify burying data. But the more he talked about the miraculous results, the more she became self-conscious about raising niggling issues of policy regulations. Here was a celebrated senior neurologist sharing with her what might be the greatest breakthrough in medicine since penicillin, and two months on the job and little Polly Protocol was souring the air with fumes. "I can imagine."

"In four months we'll be submitting trial reports to the Institutional Review Board—all the data and documentation thus far, everything with all the *T*s crossed and *I*s dotted as required by the FDA, to be followed by the necessary publications, which will no doubt make the press. This is going to be huge."

"You're talking as if you're the principal investigator."

"Actually, I'm one of them. A chief has yet to be named."

The chief principal investigator on any clinical trial occupied a post heavy with responsibility and prestige, especially if the compound tested showed promise. That Jordan Carr was a prime candidate was evident. So was his yearning.

"So, what about Clara killing a man? How is that being explained?"

"That was unexpected, of course. And we'll have to make the best of it. Thankfully, patient confidentiality protects us. Meanwhile, she's at McLean for observation."

She remembered Officer Menard's question: *Was she on any antipsychotic medication or other stuff that might have caused her violence?* "So, what do we tell the police?"

"That there was a security breach and that it won't happen again because new safeguards are in place."

"I mean the murder." He kept avoiding that fact.

"Simply that she was a woman suffering from dementia, that she just went berserk. And that's not so far-fetched. These *are* crazy people, after all."

René could hear her father's voice. *"Honey, I can feel it. I can feel the holes."*

The chilly touch of his words bothered her. "So you're saying that Memoring—"

"Memorine," he said, pronouncing it like a talisman. *"Memorine*—and file that away because it's going to rock the world."

"So you're saying that Memorine did not cause her to attack the man."

"That's exactly what I'm saying."

"But how do you know that if the drug's been in its final phase of study for only six months?"

A smile spread across his face like a rainbow. "René, we've been running trials at Broadview and testing efficacy and safety for months, and there've been no adverse reactions whatsoever. The Clara Devine incident is an unrelated anomaly. Period."

"She was sexually abused as a child."

"Beg pardon?"

René did not want to violate the woman's privacy, nor did she want to betray Cassandra Gould, but this was vital information. "A neighbor next door did things to her." And she explained what she knew.

"How unfortunate, but what does that have to do with anything?" He took a sip of water.

She wasn't sure if he was playing coy again or drawing her out. "Doctor, I'm saying that Clara Devine attacked the man because in her mind she was seeing her abuser. I'm just wondering if it had anything to do with this Memorine."

Carr laid down his water glass with a definitive snap. "Well, it didn't."

"But how can one be certain if the stuff's improving memory?"

"Because half the people in your nursing homes are seeing dead people all the time. Their husbands are their baby brothers, their sisters are their kindergarten teachers. You spend your days on these wards, you should know that. Clara Devine was no different, except she's had some kind of post-traumatic stress experience—which happens to people all the time. VA hospitals are full of them."

"There's also the matter of informed consent. Her sister had passed on power of attorney, which meant that Clara was a ward of the state. Essentially, nobody was watching out for her."

Carr made another audible sigh. "And I suppose you're going to quote the Nuremberg Code on the principles governing ethical experimentation on humans."

"Actually, I was thinking of the Declaration of Helsinki."

"Look, this is not some hideous conspiracy. We're not conducting Josef Mengele experiments on the elderly, shooting them up with voodoo compounds. We're bringing them back from a killer fog. You saw Clara Devine, and you're going to see others in the next year. So, think of this as our apology for keeping you in the dark, as you said."

She nodded, feeling as if she were being bought. "I'd like to know what other patients of mine are in these trials."

"Of course, but you've got hundreds of patients, and I don't know the overlap."

"Dr. Carr, every clinical trial is bound by very detailed, very stringent protocols established well in advance. Were I to approach the Institutional Review Board and raise the question about their approval in advance of GEM Tech clinicians sequestering documentation of trial patients from the consulting pharmacist, what might be their reaction?"

For the first time that evening Jordan Carr's face froze, his cheeks mottled with red as if he had been hit with a flash case of the hives. "Ms. Ballard, you're very sharp and very responsible. I'll make certain that you will have total access to all your patients enrolled, as soon as possible. But I ask that any indiscretion or irregularities you please overlook, okay? And I ask you because this is a turning point in the treatment of dementia, and any regulatory roadblock could be disastrous. Can't you appreciate that?"

He was asking her to look the other way, and that made her very uncomfortable. And it wasn't just being in complicity with regulatory violations. She didn't like the power she suddenly possessed. One word from her and some very important people would end up on the proverbial red carpet and the trials of

GEM Tech's hot drug could be suspended. "Then I expect a full list of patients who are enrolled at Broadview and elsewhere."

"Of course."

"And full documentation of meds including Memorine, schedules, and nurses' observations, et cetera." If he proved as good as his word, she would not contact the IRB.

"Certainly. Absolutely." The relief was clearly visible in his face.

The waiter returned. "Would you like to see the dessert tray?"

René shook her head.

Dr. Carr studied her face for a moment. "Irregularities aside, aren't you impressed? A cure for Alzheimer's?"

"If it's the real thing, of course." She could hear the forced brightness in her voice.

"Well, take my word for it, it's the real thing."

"And how long have these trials been going on?"

"The last phase for eight months. But we've known about the neurological benefits to dementia patients for years."

She nodded, and felt something rip inside her heart.

14

Jack was at that door again.

The same brown stained wood-panel structure with the hanging herbs and tarnished brass knob. He had lost count how many times it had been. How many times he had grabbed the mouse and padded to the door through the sticky wet. Then how he had frozen again, knowing on some level that horrible things were happening out there, but also knowing he had to get out to Beth and the others.

Jack stared numbly at the doorknob as if something profound were about to occur. Then he heard a voice full of gravel: "Goddamn you, die."

Then that horrible sound that pounded through his brain over and over again, every time he got here, every time he put his hand on the knob—a sound that set loose a flock of bats in his chest: The crack of iron against bonecap.

Somebody, please, I beg you. Make this stop.

He folded into the corner on the floor, still clutching the mouse, his eyes pressed shut, his own whimpers humming in his head.

"Jack, you're having a dream. Can you open your eyes for me?"

He opened his eyes and the window at the top of the door flashed down at him with a blue-green light.

"He's saying something."

Safe. The thing with the big head has gone away.

Jack got up from the floor and put his hand on the doorknob. Cold metal. He turned it . . .

"Jack, wake up. Come on, you can do it. Just push."

. . . and he pushed.

Instantly the wind sucked open the door with a bang. His heart nearly exploded. The thing with the pointy head stood before him, its arm raised, the shiny club glinting in the light.

"Close the goddamn door."

He closed the door.

"What did he say? I didn't catch it."

"I think, 'Nice Mookie'?"

"Who's Mookie?"

"I haven't got a clue."

15

"**D**id you know about these Memorine trials?"

Nick looked over his glasses at her. "Yes."

"It seems as if everybody does but me." She could barely disguise the emotion crackling in her words.

"Then someone should have told you, of course."

"Dr. Carr was going on as if it was the medical breakthrough of the millennium."

"From what I understand, the results are quite promising, but it's too early to call a press conference."

She nodded, feeling a swirl of hot emotions.

It was Thursday afternoon and they were sitting in the control room of the new MRI imaging suite at MGH. Glass windows separated the bank of computers from the huge scanner, the ring-shaped apparatus with an attached patient table, in the next room. Behind them were three technicians working at their own monitors. Nick was a regular here because he had helped pioneer new imaging techniques for studying Alzheimer's—techniques that aimed at detecting the disease in the presymptomatic phase and diagnosing its progress.

"So, you had a pleasant evening with him?"

"It was interesting." She knew how evasive that sounded.

"He's a very bright and capable physician."

"And very charming, and I'm not interested." There was an awkward silence. Her relationship with Nick was warm and mutually gratifying. He was the older mentor-cum-father-figure and she the pretty former student who made him feel young and charming. She had always sensed that he regarded her with an admiration that exceeded the professor-and-student relationship. It was evident in the way he lit up when he looked upon her, or touched her arm when he was explaining something. He was also intent on seeing her find a boyfriend.

"Okay," he said. "Did he show you the Palm Pilot images of Clara Devine's tests? It's all right, I've seen them. All these years and all the research, and this is the first time that anything out of a lab is showing promise of a cure. Quite remarkable, wouldn't you say?"

"If it is, I was three years too late." Tears filled her eyes.

Nick looked at her, and in a moment realization clicked in his eyes. "Ahh. You mean your father." He took her hand. "Good God, woman, there was no way for you to know. How could you? Besides, he could not have lasted this long."

"He was still strong."

"Maybe physically, but there was nothing left of him inside, and you know that. I would have done the same thing if it were Thalia. I would have wanted the same thing if it were me." He squeezed her hand with assurance.

"I did it for me."

"No! You did it for him. It's what he wanted."

But if I had only waited . . .

"Listen to me. The first dementia patients were not enrolled in these trials until eight or nine months ago. That's two and a half years after he died. You know as well as I what could have happened in that time. He would have continued to waste away, kept alive by machines and tubes and IV drips. Was that something you'd want? Of course not, and neither did he. And who's to say this stuff would have worked for him? Or if he would have lived so long even full-coded. No, you did the right thing. So put it away for good."

She nodded and gave Nick a hug. He was also the one person for whom she had unguarded respect and not a little affection. If it weren't for him, she would have dropped out of pharmacy school and would probably be wiping counters at Starbucks. It was also Nick who had held her hand during her father's demise.

Nick got up and poured her a cup of coffee from the small machine sitting on a back table. René took a few sips and let his consolation take effect.

"So, back to reality. You're having some problems with administrative procedures, right?"

"I think I'll feel better when I see Clara Devine's records."

"Dreadful story. I read the paper."

"Nick, she was sexually abused as a young girl by some creep neighbor." And she told him what Cassie Gould had said.

Nick's face clouded over. "So, what are you saying?"

"I'm saying that in her head, Clara Devine may have been defending herself against the guy who raped her seventy years ago."

"A flashback seizure."

Flashback. The term lit up in her mind as if it were an established syndrome. "Yeah, exactly. A flashback."

"It's a Peter Habib term," Nick said. "I guess it's possible. We're talking about axon connections rethreading the hippocampus. What does Dr. Carr say?"

"He says it's the dementia, not an adverse drug reaction."

"Because post-traumatic stress hallucinations can plague dementia victims. I suppose that will have to be determined. In the meantime, what are you thinking of doing?"

"Nick, for nearly two months I've been up against some clinical code of *omertà* while secret trials were going on right under my nose."

"So you're thinking of filing a formal complaint against the record-taking procedures of a senior clinician working on a potential cure for Alzheimer's disease."

"Not when you put it that way."

"Then let it go. You'll get the charts. Look through them, check the nurses' reports, and if anything looks irregular, then write your letters. In the meantime, visit some of the trial patients. I think you may be impressed with what's happening."

"And what's that?"

"Maybe medical history."

"Wait a second. Are you part of this?"

"GEM's made some recent inquiries."

"How long have you known about the stuff?"

Nick must have heard her words skid because he narrowed his eyes. "I'm telling you it was not an option for your father. They hadn't even begun phase one trials on animals yet. Nobody had any idea if it would work with AD patients. And had I known, you would have been the first to hear."

She nodded. "I know." She had scoured the journals and the Internet looking for every experimental drug in clinical trials, and nothing had held any promise for her father's condition. Memorine was still deep in GEM's pipeline.

"And in case you're wondering, I haven't committed myself."

"Maybe you should. Given how they've been operating, they could use some ethical standards."

"That's very kind, but what do you think that'd do to my retirement plans?"

"You're still young and energetic."

"Kinder still. But Thalia has got her health problems, and I have a new grandchild, number three."

"Okay. When I asked him why I was kept in the dark, Dr. Carr said that GEM wanted to guard against the competition. That seems rather paranoid to me."

"Might also be good business. First of all, clinical trials are almost never done with geriatrics in nursing homes, as you know. So they wanted to keep things quiet for as long as possible. Secondly, GEM's a small, tight drug company and nervous about some Goliath out there stealing its hot molecule. It's happened before. I suppose if this compound turns out to be the real thing, the benefits will more than make up for minor irregularities."

He, too, was saying to look the other way. "And what about Dr. Carr? I'm sure he's doing well by GEM."

"There's nothing unethical or illegal in a physician's getting a fee for enrolling patients in trials. It's how research progresses."

"That's the one gray area that frankly bothers me. Doctors get paid thousands of dollars for each patient they enroll in a trial, plus research grants, equipment upgrades, staff support, travel perks, plus stock options in the company. With all those incentives, it's hard to write up a negative report to the FDA."

"Except actual scientific results don't lie. And from what I hear, this Memorine is looking remarkable." Nick fixed his glasses and rolled his chair. "Now, come here and look at this." He inserted a CD into the computer and ran his fingers across the keyboard. In a matter of moments multicolored images of a brain filled the screen. He moved the mouse around and clicked a couple of times, and the colors began to change, pulsing in yellows and reds. "Thanks to the genius of imaging physicists and computer technicians, we now have the first quantitative, dynamic visualization of the destruction of cortical brain regions in people with dementia. What you're seeing is a 3-D sequencing movie of a seventy-five-year-old male's brain under the siege of plaque formation and neuron tangles over a thirteen-month period."

As best she could, she tried to dissociate herself from thoughts of her father. "What do the colors represent?"

"The base image of the brain is blue. And in red is the beta-amyloid plaque."

"God, it looks like a blight spreading across the brain."

"And of the worst sort. What makes this technology very special is that we can directly monitor both the progressive damage as well as any therapeutic responses from Aricept and other treatments." Nick ran the serial scan images several times.

"It's moving right across the parietal and temporal lobes."

"Exactly, the areas controlling language and major cognitive functions."

"And obliterating memories, personalities—everything that made them who they were," she said.

"His name is Louis Martinetti. He's at Broadview. Maybe you've met him."

"Yes. The Korean war vet."

"And former POW. Well decorated—a Purple Heart, in fact. And a very sweet man."

René felt a little sick as she watched the fast-forwarded sequence of his brain's deterioration. Her father had been a Korean vet also. "What stage is he in?"

"Moderate, but it seems a particularly aggressive case." The red blotches spread from frame to frame. "At this rate, the stuff will probably cover a good part of the frontal lobe within a year or so, rendering him incapable of speech and most memory."

Although one could only imagine the man's cerebral cortex becoming clotted with plaque, this new technology let them witness the brutal unraveling of the man's mind and memory. But if they could have looked inside Mr. Martinetti's brain they would have seen the same landscape of destruction that a hundred years ago in Munich had startled the German physician who described the disease that bears his name. It was Alois Alzheimer whose investigation of what had been diagnosed as premature senility in a fifty-one-year-old woman led to his discovery of the disease's gruesome signature: the brownish nodules of plaque and the dense tangle of neurofibers that eat away the upper layers of the cerebral cortex and destroy a person cell by cell. What had wasted her father.

Nick reran the sequence. "Now, imagine seeing this played backward—all that red turning blue again." And in his eyes she saw a flicker of promise.

Three years too late.

René tried to deflect the voice and looked away. At a station nearby was another computer monitor showing another brain image. "Is this the same patient?"

"No, that's the image of a patient of Dr. Heller, another neurologist here in the department."

René welcomed the distraction.

"But it does look similar." Nick rolled in his chair to the monitor. "And that's rather interesting because he's not an AD patient but a young fellow in a coma. He nearly drowned last week after being stung by jellyfish—some rare creature found in the Caribbean."

"How did he end up here?"

"Actually, it happened up here. On very rare occasions tropical creatures get caught in the Gulf Stream. And when the waters are as warm as they've been, they get caught in eddies that bring them close to shore."

"Where'd it happen?"

"Homer's Island, a private island northwest of Martha's Vineyard. The only place they've ever been reported in the northeast. The Coast Guard found him."

"Lucky for him. What's his prognosis?"

"Not good, though his unconscious mind is quite active." Nick moved the mouse around and hit a few keys as new brain images filled the screen in quarters. Then with a pen he pointed to an area of the frontal lobe of his brain. "This is what interests me. See how the yellow area appears to be expanding. Unlike the other, this is a structural MRI that measures brain tissue volume. And if you look here, the active area is his hippocampus and frontal lobe."

"Meaning what?"

"I'm not really sure, but if I didn't know better, I'd say the tissue was getting denser."

"Denser? You mean his brain is growing?"

"Unless I'm mistaken, there's active cell growth. Unfortunately he's in no condition to tell us what he's experiencing. But if he wakes up, it might be interesting to interview him."

"Meanwhile, he's turning into a Conehead."

Nick laughed. "Or someone with a pretty rich memory bank."

When Nick looked away, René fingered open the folder with his name tab and that of the unit he was in. "Any way to tell how long he might be unconscious?"

Nick shook his head. "Could be a week, could be five years. Could be forever."

"It must be very hard on his family."

"I think it's only his wife, and I hear she's not doing too well. He has seizures but is settling deeper into his coma. The EEG measurement of his brain-wave activity is around three

Herz, which is very low, nearly a third the activity of adults in normal sleep."

"Which means he'll probably be moved to a rehab center soon. I'm sure the caseworkers are probably already talking about that. Maybe I can suggest some possible facilities."

"I think she'd appreciate that. Also, on the off chance that he wakes up, it might be useful to make contact. He's experienced a unique restructuring in his brain, so he might be a treasure trove of data. And it would be good for his wife to have another arm of support."

Jack Koryan. And she filed away the name.

16

*J*ack Koryan.

It was later that evening, and René was back home and at her computer with a glass of chardonnay and Silky in his basket at her feet. Over the hours she had let Nick's words help her come to terms with the reality that she had done the right thing by her father. That at the time there were no other options. *"Promise me this . . ."*

She typed the name in the Google search box, and instantly a community newspaper site came up with several hits of the same article:

MAN COMATOSE FROM JELLYFISH ATTACK

A man was found washed up and unconscious on a beach on Homer's Island. Jack Koryan of Carleton, Massachusetts, was barely alive after being stung by dozens of rare jellyfish while swimming.

Koryan was taken by emergency helicopter to the Cape Cod Medical Center. . . .

Scientists from Northeastern University and Woods Hole Institute said that Koryan had gotten caught in a large school of Solakandji jellyfish, which is only the size of a tennis ball but which has three-foot-long stinging tentacles. The highly venomous creature is a native of the waters of the Caribbean. Dr. Jason Marchi, a marine biologist from Woods Hole, said that the increased water temperature and the rise in nutrients from fertilizer runoff tend to support a rise in jellyfish populations. . . .

Like other species of toxic jellyfish, the Solakandji tentacles have millions of stinging cells called nematocysts. . . .

According to medical experts, there is currently no antivenom available for the Solakandji sting, which has caused deaths in Jamaica. . . .

She finished reading the story, then stretched out on the couch with her wine and Silky on her lap. She clicked on the television and lowered the volume just to decompress before getting ready for bed. On the news were the usual grim stories about the Iraq war and some local crime. She listened with half interest. Something was bothering her and she could not put her finger on it. Something to do with that Jack Koryan guy— something that sat under the upper layers of her mind and kept sending up little tremors.

After maybe fifteen minutes of distraction, she got up and went back to the computer and did a search for *Solakandji* jellyfish. Amazingly, she got over three hundred hits. And she spent the better part of the next hour clicking on different sites. Most were divided between news stories of attacks, treatment of the stings, general information about jellyfish, and a few scientific papers. Several of the technical sites had photos of a creature that looked like a translucent mushroom with four interior rings and spaghetti tendrils.

The Solakandji jellyfish (related to Irukandji jellyfish of Australia's Great Barrier Reef) is found in warm waters of the Caribbean and southern Atlantic.

Minor envenomations cause pain, swelling, and localized numbness that often subsides within hours of onset. Serious envenomations are associated with a rapid progression of symptoms, including erythema, paralysis, respiratory arrest, cardiac failure, and death. . . .

Other sites offered information about how to treat stings with vinegar, news stories about how victims in the Bahamas and elsewhere suffered a rapid rise in blood pressure and a cerebral hemorrhage that led to their deaths. Her mind returned to poor Jack Koryan in a deep sleep, unfortunate victim to happenstance, his entire universe reduced to a bed and that bank of monitors and destined never to open his eyes again.

She clicked onto more technical sites intended for dedicated marine scientists and scrolled down until she came to a dead stop.

N. A. Sarkisian, Mavros, N. T., et al. Neurotoxic activity on the sensory nerves from toxin of the deadly Solakandji tropical jellyfish *Chiropsalmus quadrigatus* Mason. *Chem Pharm Bull* **17**: 1086–8, 1971.

Mavros, N. T.
Nick. He had published a paper on the toxin thirty-five years ago. She read on.

The abstract described the Solakandji toxin as a novel proteolytic agent whose molecules functioned as an NMDA receptor antagonist. Furthermore, the substance was identified as a glutamate inhibitor affecting aspartate—an excitatory amino acid-transmitter in the brain, similar to glutamate.

"Glutamate inhibitor affecting aspartate."

The words jumped out at her.

That was the same neurochemical function that Jordan Carr had described—the same neurotransmitter was linked to seizure activity and agitated behaviors of people with dementia. By inhibiting glutamate, demented patients were demonstrating better behaviors and enhanced cognitive capabilities.

My God! Jack Koryan was attacked by a jellyfish whose toxin was the chemical basis of Memorine. And Nick had helped pioneer the stuff.

PART
2

17

"Who the hell's this CommCare woman?" Gavin Moy's eyes blazed down on Nick. He pulled a letter out of the folder. "René Ballard, Consulting Pharmacist. CommunityCare Pharmacy." He handed the letter to Nick. "Isn't she your friend?"

The letter was elegantly blunt, like a silver-plated bullet. "Yes, and former student," Nick said.

"Well, your friend and former student says that medical records of some patients are missing—'a violation of regulatory procedures,' and she quotes the state and federal codes—blah, blah, blah—and she expects that all the records 'complete and intact' be returned immediately or she's obligated to file a report with the IRB and request FDA review of our trial protocols. Jesus H. Christ!"

Nick had to repress the smile. "I believe she's just doing her job."

"Doing her job? She may be doing a job on friggin' medical history."

"Then maybe somebody should comply with her requests. Rumor has it that withholding nursing home records from consulting pharmacists is a violation of regulations."

"Who the hell's side you on?"

"Truth and beauty." Nick smiled broadly.

Moy snickered. "Which is why I called you. But I must say, she has balls."

"Because I taught her everything she knows."

"Well, Jordan Carr says everything's being returned, so tell her to wrap up."

"What about the other nursing homes serving as research sites?"

"There, too. We want everything on the up-and-up."

They were alone in Gavin Moy's office at GEM Tech—a handsome, voluminous space with windows on two sides, one with a view of oak woodlands, the other commanding a view of the Boston skyline, shimmering in the distance.

On a table behind him were pictures of Moy's wife, who had died five years ago. Moy had adjusted well to his widowerhood. Following her death he redirected his energy into his company, hiring the best and the brightest. And now he was consulting senior medical execs and leaders in hospitals and academic institutions to put together a Dream Team of clinicians. Likewise, his board members were major venture capitalists who would have eaten their own children to be part of GEM's future. And who wouldn't—since Gavin Moy might be sitting on the pharmaceutical equivalent of the Holy Grail: a cure for Alzheimer's disease in an ever-aging world.

On the wall behind his desk hung framed patents with his name on them—each for a variation of the same parent compound, just to keep competing labs from making look-alike compounds—the first, now faded, was dated January 10, 1976, the latest, from eight years ago, represented the final molecular structure whose trials would eventually be presented to the FDA for market approval. Trademarked Memorine, the compound not only had enormous pharmaceutical and commercial potential, if successful Gavin Moy could find himself in Stockholm, Sweden, when they passed out Nobel Prizes.

"We're going to make an announcement at the meeting of shareholders in a few weeks, so the word will officially be out instead of leaks and speculations."

It was a risky plan, because formal announcements about the success of a drug are almost never made in the middle of trials. But given the early success, Moy's strategy was to create a market for Memorine before the first pill hit the shelves.

"Until then, we're playing mum."

Gavin Moy was paranoid and for good reason. He had sunk millions of his own and hundreds of millions of investors' dollars into Memorine against a history of adventures that had turned out to be duds, including development of a cure for a rare neurological disorder; it proved disastrous in the Phase III clinical trials, costing GEM eighty million dollars and nearly tanking the company. Another agent targeting Parkinson's disease was beaten to market when a competing lab offered a disgruntled GEM science director an offer he couldn't refuse—the results: a look-alike that became a blockbuster while GEM fumbled around in Phase III trials only to scrap the project and end up with huge go-nowhere litigation fees. Those fiascoes were why Gavin Moy had guarded Memorine as if it were the Manhattan Project.

It was also why Nick had played coy with René. Only when she called to ask if the jellyfish connection was true did he confess a minor role in its development, breaking ethical protocol. Since learning about Memorine René had been flagellating herself with guilt for having consented to let her father die instead of holding out for some breakthrough cure. So he reiterated the fact that the compound had not been targeted for clinical trials of dementia patients until two years after her father's death. Even then Gavin Moy had sworn Nick and others to secrecy in face of the Darwinian competition for a cure and the fact that when the patent would run out in a few years generic knockoffs would fly. But before that eventuality, GEM hoped to establish a global franchise on Memorine.

"We've tried to keep a low profile, but we're getting calls from physicians and AD organizations wanting to know if it's true we're working on a cure, can they volunteer patients. Christ, this is going to be the biggest thing since the Salk vaccine, maybe penicillin."

"We can only hope."

As Moy scanned Walden Woods out his window, Nick thought that he was like one of those reptiles with independent turretlike eyes constantly alert to opportunities and dangers. That was how he had been decades ago, and, perhaps, that was the secret of his successes and failures. On his desk was a brass plaque with the inscription: "It's not over until you win." Quintessential Gavin E. Moy.

Although Nick had seen Moy over the years at conferences and colloquia, they went back to a time before GEM Neurobiological Technologies existed. They were residents together at Mass General back in the late 1960s, when Gavin had started the forerunner of GEM Tech in the cramped basement behind MIT and where Nick helped in the research before finishing his residency. For years, some antecedent of Memorine had been in Moy's pipeline, going through molecular reconfigurations and testing until the final form was developed. Today it was the flagship product for GEM Tech—and virtually their only product.

The promise began when it was discovered that the toxin from the Solakandji demonstrated an extraordinary neuronal property: it enhanced long-term memory. Fetal rodents injected with the compound learned to whip through complex mazes as if radar-directed while their untreated siblings stumbled along. Even more remarkable, mature rats demonstrated enhanced long-term recall, mastering maze problems that they hadn't been exposed to since they were juveniles. The immediate thought, of course, was what it could do for people suffering memory loss—a speculation that raised hope against the scourge of Alzheimer's disease.

The first breakthrough came when it was discovered that Memorine treatments had all but eliminated deposits of beta-amyloid peptides in mice genetically engineered to have an Alzheimer's-like disease. Even more remarkable, new brain cell growth explained why treated mice had higher learning curves and functionality than untreated mice. In short, Memorine had converted memory-degenerating rodents into recall wizards. Last year it was tested on human subjects and medical history began to be rewritten.

"Nick, you've read the reports—the results are fabulous and you could share in its success. So don't tell me 'no' again, because I'm asking you to come aboard," Moy's eyes were shooting fire.

"Gavin, I'm very flattered, really."

"On the contrary, *we'd* be flattered. And all bullshit aside, we'd like to have a man with your prestige and reputation." Moy handed Nick a few sheets of paper. "Some of the people you'd be working with. I think you'll recognize a few."

It was a long and impressive list of physicians already taking part in the trials—names of medical researchers and practitioners associated with the best of institutions: the Scripps Institute, Yale, Washington University Medical School, the National Institutes of Health, et cetera.

"Plus some acquaintances of yours—Peter Habib, Jordan Carr, and others. We're expecting the FDA to fast-track the application so we can get it to market in eighteen months." Moy spoke with serene conviction. "Word is the president might support clinical development as a pledge to older voters in his reelection campaign. The long and short is this is a revolution, and we want you to be part of it."

"And you're working out possible ADRs—adverse drug reactions."

Moy's face froze. "What adverse drug reactions?"

"That woman who killed the CVS manager. I've also heard rumors of patients experiencing some deep-past delusional spells."

"Where the hell did you hear that?"

It was actually Pete Habib who had come up with the "flashback" label. "Where I heard it isn't important. The story of the murder was in all the newspapers. But questions have been raised about whether there's a connection to the drug."

The skin of Moy's head flamed. "There *is* no connection, and there are no adverse drug reactions. These people were delusional psychotics suffering dementia. Christ, you see them all the time."

"I'm just raising the possibility."

Moy considered his words for a moment. His face suddenly

lit up. "Then this is just the kind of thing we'd want you to monitor—making sure investigators look for contingencies, side effects, whatever. We need someone like you with uncompromising integrity. But, believe me, there's no connection between the woman who stabbed the store guy and Memorine, and you can take that to the bank."

"Okay, but why do you want me when you have all these top people?"

"Because I'd like you to direct the phase three clinical study, to be chief principal investigator—to coordinate all trial data for our FDA application. I want you at the top."

Nick did not see that coming. "Why not Pete Habib? He's chief neurologist at South Shore and one of the best around. Or Jordan Carr?"

"I said no bullshit: You're senior neurologist at MGH and chief administrator of the imaging lab, and Peter Habib, Jordan Carr, and the rest aren't. Having you in the lead would draw a lot of attention, not to mention investors."

"That's quite an honor, but to do this right will require a large commitment."

"Of course, and you'll be compensated handsomely."

"I'm talking time, not money. I'll have to think about it and talk it over with Thalia."

"Of course." Moy glanced at his watch. "How's tomorrow by noon?" Nothing in Moy's face said he was being humorous.

"Next week."

"All right, next week." Moy leaned into a huddle. "Okay, the ugly stuff: For your own patients, we're offering you twice the standard trial rate—three thousand dollars per patient visit. We expect twelve to fifteen visits. You have a lot of AD patients and you can do the math. In addition, for all your expertise blah blah blah and the privilege of having you as clinical director blah blah blah . . . we're offering you equity in the company in the form of stocks—the numbers to be worked out.

"As you know, about five million people suffer Alzheimer's in the States alone—a figure that's going to double by 2020. The current market is twelve billion dollars for AD meds. We've created a special unit to market Memorine, lined up the third largest pharmaceutical company in the country to distribute, plus a sales force of seven hundred reps on a sales-based bonus system to promote it to practitioners. We've got a projection of three million prescriptions the first year on the shelves, twice that the next year, and multiples once our foreign subsidiaries kick in. Nick, this is a fifty-billion-dollar pill. And for the clinical director and the researchers associated with it, the benefits are incalculable."

Nick smiled. "At least you're not turning up the pressure."

"Hell, I'm just winding up. Your imaging lab is a critical tool toward our end, and our board has authorized a ten-million-dollar grant for its application in the trials, which should cover overhead and salaries, blah blah blah. What do you say?"

Nick was aware of the prestige of being part of the development of a potential miracle drug. But at his age he was not out for glory or the financial rewards—and he *could* do the math. Being a millionaire several times over did not move Nick. He and Thalia did not have extravagant tastes. They lived comfortably in Wellesley and drove a seven-year-old Saab. They vacationed in Fresno because Thalia had family there and Nick liked to hike the Sierras with his cameras. Because of ill health, Thalia no longer worked, nor did they miss her income now that their children were on their own. Money was never a motivating force in Nick's life. And, like René, he harbored old-fashioned academic cynicism toward clinicians participating in studies with drug companies.

But the majority of physicians conducted trials for higher ethical reasons: to benefit humankind. And Nick was one of them. As embarrassing as the financial benefits would be, Nick was hearing that he could be part of a team that might cure Alzheimer's disease—a nemesis that he personally had confronted for most of his professional life—a disease more vicious than cancer since it robbed a victim first of selfhood, then of life.

"You should know that I've been cutting back on my practice and research."

"Christ, you're only sixty-two—too early to be retiring.

Think of the hundreds, maybe thousands of people and patients you've watched waste away with dementia. Two or three
years from now, when the world is singing 'hallelujah' because
the scourge of the aging world has been defeated, where you
going to be, huh?—on top of some mountain taking snaps of
yellow-belly sapsuckers."

Nick laughed. "All work and no play—"

"Bullshit! I want you on this, and so do you."

"All right, all right, give me a chance to catch my breath."
Nick had seen Moy worked up before, but not like this. His
face looked like a giant tomato.

"Catch your friggin' breath and tell me yes, you'll head this
up."

"*If* I agree, all proceedings will be according to protocol."

"Goes without saying."

"Fine."

"Monday."

Moy stood up and shook Nick's hand. As Nick headed for
the door, Gavin said, "Believe me, it's the Holy Grail—what
you've been chasing all your life. You deserve to share in the
victory."

Gavin Moy's words echoed in Nick's mind as he took the elevator down to the lobby—a high-glassed interior and the main
entrance to GEM's state-of-the-art complex. Given the surrounding acreage, there was room for expansion to meet the
anticipated demands of the drug for years to come.

Nick crossed the lobby, which was appointed in marble and
brass, red oriental rugs, and gold leather sofas and chairs. As
was characteristic, Gavin himself had worked with designers.
Basically it was a Gavin Moy decor. So was the large aquarium
in the middle of the floor, its brightly colored sea life looking
like Christmas ornaments floating in the air.

Nick's heels clicked on the marble as he walked to the structure that sat like a fairyland column of coral, anemones, sea
fans, long diaphanous grasses, and a bewildering variety of
polychrome tropical fish. It was GEM's showpiece, which

Gavin Moy had specially designed and which cost a small fortune. According to him, this was one of the few Kreisel non-public aquariums. And what distinguished the setup were its unique water inlets and outlets—essential so that its special residents were suspended in the middle of the tank and didn't get sucked into the filters. To add to the complicated filtration and fluid dynamics, sophisticated monitors maintained the proper temperature as well as delicate chemical and biological levels. In addition to the special filter system and chilling unit, a separate breeder tank provided brine shrimp as a substitute for plankton, the creatures' natural diet. This was not your average pet shop fish tank.

Nor were those pulsing bulbs with the meter-long tentacles your average fish tank denizen. These creatures were the real celebrities of this bottled reef and the secret source of the endless blue skies above, the iconic genus of GEM Neurobiological Technologies—the elusive *Solakandji*.

The fifty-billion-dollar jellyfish.

18

René found Jack Koryan in the intensive care unit of Mass General Hospital.

Sitting with him was his wife, Beth, a slender, attractive woman with thick dark shoulder-length hair that was streaked blond. Her complexion was pale, as if she were getting over the flu. Her brown eyes were bloodshot—probably from a lack of sleep—giving her a muddy glance.

René introduced herself and explained that she was the consulting pharmacist and an associate of Dr. Nicholas Mavros. "I just wanted to come by to see how he was doing." *And to put a face to the brain images.*

The woman didn't seem to care who she was or why she was there. "This is Jack." Her voice was flat.

On the windowsill sat a double frame containing two color photographs of Jack—one of him standing with a male friend, the other a close-up solo that made René aware of how handsome he was—a man with black curly hair, a disarming smile, and lively exotic eyes. He was dressed in a black T-shirt that showed a well-built upper body. It was difficult to believe it was the same man in the bed. What struck her about the close-up photo were Jack Koryan's eyes. They looked like shards of peridots.

"That's his friend Vince Hammond," Beth explained, watching René examining the photos. "They were business partners, or would have been." Then Beth muttered "Shit!" under her breath and looked away.

Nearly two weeks had lapsed since the accident and, according to the nurse, the news was good. Jack Koryan was off the ventilator. But he was still a shocking sight. His body was slightly bloated, and the silver nitrate for his open sores had turned his skin black. The blisters across his torso and legs had eventually dried up and had to be surgically debrided—the dead skin being cut away, leaving red patches against the yellow. He looked as if he had been painted for camouflaging. His scalp and ears were scabbed, and his lips were gray. His feet and fingers had been freshly dressed against lesions. His arms were connected to IVs, and a percutaneous gastrostomy tube had been surgically inserted through the wall of his stomach so he could feed—standard for unconscious patients. Machines monitored his vital functions including his brain waves. It was hard to believe he had survived the attack.

"The nurse says that the brain swelling has subsided and he's responsive to sensory stimulation—which is good news."

Beth nodded glumly. "His EEG is only four Herz; six to eight is for normal sleep. He's still unconscious. How's that good news?"

René let the jab pass. "Well, every brain injury is unique; so is the rate of recovery. He could just pop awake."

"I don't believe that." Then she placed her hand on his arm. "Jack, it's Beth. Please wake up. You've got a visitor. What did you say your name is?"

René told her again and studied Jack while Beth spoke to him in a flat, neutral voice. But there was no sign of response—not a twitch of an eyelid or a finger, not a hitch in his breathing.

"The doctors call it a persistent vegetative state." She made an audible *humpf*. "More like he's dead."

Mercifully, her father had never passed into a coma, at least not technically. Toward the end he was conscious and unconscious at the same time. He could sit up in bed or in a wheelchair, move his eyes and hands. But inside he was nearly blanked out. And that's what René could not take: the loss of recognition that animated the face, the vacant stare, the sudden spike of fright, the reduction of his mind to brain-stem reflexes, his strong voice and articulate words reduced to grunts, his bright eyes to blown fuses. A gaga thing attached to a diaper.

Thank God he had made her promise to let him die. He knew what was coming. It was his final gift to her.

"His vital signs look good," René said, nodding at the steady beat of the monitors.

"I don't know," Beth said. "He's had some kind of seizures and bad dreams that make him agitated and get that thing jumping all over the place."

"But that means there's activity in the frontal and occipital lobes, so his memory and vision sectors are functioning. And there's no indication from the MRIs that he'd suffered a stroke."

As René watched the persistent pulse on the monitors, she wondered what if anything was going on inside Jack's mind. Was he dreaming or aware of his condition, or just suspended in a profound void? His brain had been saturated with the chemistry of Memorine. God knows what he might remember were he to even wake up.

"He never should have been out there. It's got an undertow and all those damn poisonous fish and things. But no! And now he's locked inside himself." Then she looked at René in exasperation. "He could go on forever like this, right? Jesus!" she said in exasperation.

René could hear anger and resentment coiling around Beth Koryan's words as if Jack had done this to her. The more Beth talked, the more it became clear that their marriage had not been a healthy, solid one—a suspicion that explained Beth's chilly manner and the fact that there were no happy photographs of the two together.

"Who found him?"

"The Coast Guard. He was supposed to catch the water taxi

back by seven, and when he didn't show up by nine and didn't answer his cell phone, the rental guy called."

"It's lucky they got to him in time." The woman was not easily consoled, and this was the best René could come up with.

"Is it?"

The question squirmed between them. "Of course."

Beth shrugged. "The thing is, he loved the sea. Look at that, I'm talking in the past tense already, like he's dead. But he did— It's in his blood, like his mother, which is kind of ironic, his getting himself poisoned, kind of like the ocean betrayed him. Those goddamn things show up something like three times in the last fifty years. He was in the wrong place at the wrong time."

René noticed that the woman's fingernails had been bitten to the quick.

"He could go on like this for years. Just lie there with these fucking tubes and wires and just shrivel up."

"And he could still wake up any time."

But it was as if Beth didn't hear her, locked in some long-running narrative. "It's all my fault. I shouldn't have let him go alone. We had a fight, nothing new, and . . . now this is what we've got to live with."

It seemed as if the woman had already consigned Jack to permanent unconsciousness and herself a life of bedside wife. And what René was hearing was blame and resentment.

Suddenly one of the machines made a double chirp. And on the screen the green little sawteeth made a series of ugly spikes.

"Shit! Another seizure," Beth said, and got up. "Jack, calm down."

He let out a high-pitched whine at the same time his eyes snapped open—so open that René half-expected his eyeballs to explode from their sockets.

"Amaaaaa!"

The sound cut through René like shrapnel. His voice must have carried, or somebody at the head desk was checking the monitors, because two nurses dashed into the room. Jack was thrashing and pulling against the lines connected to him. The nurses worked to restrain him since Jack was trying to rise from the bed to follow his cries, his eyes huge and staring at something that was terrifying him.

"Jesus, what's happening to him?" Beth cried.

Jack continued babbling nonsense syllables.

"It doesn't even sound like him. His voice. That isn't his voice. It sounds like . . . a child."

It did. And nobody said anything as the nurses tried to hold him down because Jack was pulling against his dressing and the tubes, his eyes bulging and focused on nothing across the room, but something awful swirling behind them.

"Ahamman maideek amaaa . . . ," Jack continued babbling.

"What's he saying?" Beth asked.

"Maideek."

"It sounds like 'mighty' something."

Jack muttered more syllables. *"Ammama . . ."*

"I think he's saying 'Mama,' " René said.

"That's not unusual," one of the nurse replied. "Patients under stress even in comas call for their mothers."

"That happens a lot," the other nurse added. "We hear it all the time."

"Except Jack didn't have a mother."

René looked at Beth. "What?"

"She died when he was a baby, and he was brought up by his aunt and uncle. He never called anyone mama."

Jack started thrashing again, and to calm him down the smaller nurse produced a syringe of Valium and emptied it into Jack's IV. In a minute or so, Jack gasped and deflated against his pillow, his eyes pulsing against closing lids until he slipped back to sleep with a solitary sigh rising from his lungs.

But before that happened, his eyes shot open again and he looked directly at René. And through his crusted mouth still glistening with analgesic ointment he formed the syllables: "Mama."

"Mama."

Jack Koryan was at the door again. He could hear the wind outside, but that was all. He was safe to go out and the knob wasn't frozen again, so he turned until he heard the latch come free.

Instantly the door sucked open and in the flare he saw the large pointed creature standing over the big mouse, its feet twitching as the club came cracking down on it.

Then the door slammed shut and Jack was back in the cage.

And outside the night raged and flared.

Then all began to fade like distant thunder as black air mercifully closed around him.

19

"**S**ure, I remember how to get there," said William Zett, sitting in the passenger seat of his sister's car.

Greg Lainas drove while his wife MaryAnn sat in the back seat. It was late Sunday morning, a beautiful early September day with a big blue sky filled with sudsy white puffs of clouds. One of those days that reminded you of childhood.

"Yeah, turn up here," William said. Then it came to him. "South Street."

"Son of a gun," Greg said. "You've got the memory of an elephant."

"Told you," William said proudly. "Then you take a . . . let's see . . . a left onto Campfield Ave." The name then opened up in his head like a flower. "Goodwin Park."

"Heck, maybe you can get Dr. Habib to get some of those magic pills for me, too."

"Yeah, ask him for the both of us," MaryAnn said with a chuckle. Then she turned toward Greg in a voice loud enough that William could hear. "Do you know the other day he started reciting one of his physics lectures. Come on, tell him,

William. You know, the Heisenberger something-or-other principle, or whatever."

"Heisenberg uncertainty principle."

"Yeah, that's it. Come on, let Greg hear it."

William hemmed and hawed then after Greg and MaryAnn's
prodding he said, "I don't know, something like . . . the simul-
taneous measurement of two variables like momentum and position . . ." He closed his eyes as it all came back to him the
way it did the other day, as if receiving instructions beamed to
him from afar. "Energy and time for a moving particle entails a
limitation on the precision of each measurement. The more
precise the measurement of position, the more imprecise the
measurement of momentum, and vice versa." Then he closed
his eyes tight and thought. "Delta p times delta q is greater or
equal to Planck's constant over four pi. And delta E times delta
t is greater or equal to Planck's constant over four pi."

And MaryAnn and Greg cheered, "Yeaaaaaa!"

"God, just a few months ago he couldn't put a simple sen-
tences together, now he's doing quantum mechanics again."

And William felt a warm glow of pride in his chest. He had
taught physics at the University of Hartford for thirty-seven
years before being forced to retire. He could have taught well
into his seventies, but he had begun to fade.

"Speaking of pie, you're going to love dessert. And nothing
uncertain about that."

They pulled into the parking lot beside the old watering
hole, the playground off to the right through the trees. The
original lot had been dirt, but it had been asphalted over and
security lights now sat atop some poles. The area had not been
expanded as had other town playgrounds—none of those fancy
new wooden climbing complexes that looked like little
fortresses with castellated towers, bridges, handlebars, and tu-
bular slides, et cetera. The swings were the same, although
they had been repainted a hundred times, and the monkey bars
had been replaced, as had the sandy play area. The two slides,
Big Shot and Little Shot, as the kids had called them, looked
the same. And they sat maybe thirty feet apart.

"God, I don't think I've been back here since the fifties," said MaryAnn, who had packed a picnic lunch for the three of them. While William walked around the playground structures, she and her husband spread a tablecloth across one of the wooden tables and laid out the food and plates.

Meanwhile, William shuffled over to the swing, his feet kicking through the familiar fine yellow sand. He didn't think it was the same old chain that held up the seats, but it was long and rusty as he remembered it. He could still feel the cold metal in his hands as he gripped it and sat in the seat. He could still smell the funny rusty iron odor that the chain left in a moist grip. He lowered himself onto one of the swings.

"Want a push?" MaryAnn hollered from the table. She laughed and waved.

William waved back. "I can handle it."

He gripped the chain and it all came back to him in a rush— his feet pushing himself back against the seat until he was standing, then he raised his feet and felt himself swing forward, pushing his body forward and back until he established momentum and was swinging with the steady period of a clock pendulum.

Amazing, as if it were just a membrane away. He closed his eyes. It must have been sixty-five years since he had last done this. But it seemed like . . .

"Hey, Billy."

Billy opened his eyes, and a hot flame flared in his chest. It was Bobby Tilden on the Big Slide near by. Bobby the Bully. And behind him were three other kids, including Annette, the girl up the street Billy was crazy about.

"Come on, or you gonna chicken out again?"

"Hey, William, you're looking good, kiddo."

"But watch your neck," MaryAnn shouted. Then to her husband she said, "He's got that slick jogging suit on, he could slide right off the seat."

"He's fine," Greg said. "Hold on tight," he shouted to his brother.

William nodded and looked toward the slide.

He was scared. Heart-banging, dry-spit scared, pants-wetting scared.

"Hey, Peepee Boy!" shouted Bobby Tilden, grinning with his broken-tooth smile and sly fox eyes and the baseball cap in a rebel slant. "Come on up. Or you 'fraid of wetting your pants again?"

Other kids on the slide and at the bottom joined in the taunt to give it a try—the Big Slide, what the older kids did—kids ten and up. Billy had tried it before, but it was very high and fast, and he did chicken out and had to climb back down the ladder, which caused everybody to make fun of him, and Bobby called him Peepee Boy and knocked him down and gave him a knuckle haircut that made him cry while everybody hooted with glee.

Billy got off the swing and shuffled toward the Big Shot with the clutch of kids at the bottom—Philly, Michael Riccardi, Larry Ahearn, and Francine with the big yellow buck teeth and Snookie B. in the dirty sailor cap—waving him over and jeering, hoping he'd humiliate himself and chicken out again, wet his pants. At the top, Bobby Tilden snorted deeply and spit a clam that landed near Billy's feet. Then he let out a whooping cry and slid down the slide with his hands and sneakers in the air. He landed on his feet, and the others let out a cheer.

Mikey Riccardi was next. He came flying down lying straight out. At the last minute he lifted his feet and came down on his backside flat. Two more kids came down, all pushing each other from the top of the ladder. Then Bobby raced back up, taunting Billy to join them. This time Bobby came down on his belly, letting out a yowl all the way. He smacked the yellow earth and got up spitting and covered with yellow sand on his front. And the other kids went wild.

"You're next," they said to Billy.

"William, lunch time."

Billy's heart pounded as he made his way to the ladder. The others formed a wall around him so he couldn't run off at the last minute. Philly pushed him in the back to climb up. There *was no backing off now, and he thought that if there was ever a time he wanted to die, this was it. One by one he climbed the rungs toward Bobby, who grinned down at him from the top, green-jelly snot bubbling in his nostrils, his chipped tooth flashing at him, his dirty face in a demon grin as he watched Billy climb.*

"William, what are you doing up there? You're going to break your neck."

"Come on, Peepee Boy." And Bobby slid down to give him room.

At the top, Billy looked down the long shiny metal slide that seemed to go on forever, the knot of kids below arms waving and shouting for him to do it, don't be a chicken.

"Will-iam?"

"BIL-LY BIL-LY BIL-LY . . ."

Billy's heart thudded painfully as he held his breath and said a silent prayer. Then eyes closed, he shot down the slide. At the last moment he caught himself and landed on his feet. And the kids cheered. For a protracted moment he could not believe how easy it was, and how great it felt.

"Way to go, bro," somebody shouted. "Now, come on and have your lunch."

To the hooting of the other kids he climbed back up and came down again. Easy as pie, as his mom always said.

"How about on your back if you're so cool?" Bobby sneered at him.

Billy wanted to go home, but he had to take the challenge. So he climbed back up the slide. At the top, while the other kids watched, he took a deep breath and stretched himself out, and when Bobby cried "Go" he shot down and at the last minute he caught himself and landed on his feet, nearly losing his balance.

"William, that's enough of that," the woman said.

"Now headfirst," Bobby said, his face in a slick grin like J. Worthington Foulfellow.

"William." A man was approaching Billy from the picnic table under the trees. He looked distantly familiar.

"*Come on, Peepee Boy, or you gonna go running home to your mommy?*"

"*Yeah, scaredy-pants,*" Philly C. shouted. *He was Bobby's best friend and did everything Bobby said.*

"*I'm not scared,*" Billy heard himself say. *But he was. So scared he felt himself begin to wet his underpants. But he couldn't cop out now or they'd jeer him to tears then give him noogies and a pink belly in front of everybody, including Annette. He was as certain of that as he was of his own name— because that's what had happened way back and every time he kept going back there in his head. But this time he had to show them. He had to. He had to.*

"*So, do it, Peepee Boy. Eyes closed, headfirst on your back, if you're so cool. Or your ass is grass.*"

Your ass is grass. It was Bobby's favorite threat, although Billy didn't know exactly what it meant.

Billy saw the man approach, so he climbed back up the ladder.

"What the hell are you doing, brother?"

But Billy paid him no attention—as if he were invisible or a ghost of another time.

At the top Billy sat down, his sneakers on the top rung. Below, the kids made a noisy clutch of arms and hats and dungarees and T-shirts that said Naylor Elementary. In the distance, at the picnic tables, were his parents and other parents drinking coffee out of big red Thermos jugs and watching all the kids playing. Billy's mother cried out, "Careful, Billy."

And Billy inched himself backward onto the slanting metal slide, his hands gripping the sides, then he lowered his back onto the warm polished metal, his head straight down. He could feel the heat rising, the sun in his face, his short little legs curled over the top, holding him in place, as he watched a white seabird slice across the blue.

"*William, no!*" *cried his mother.*

"*Billy, go!*" *cried the kids.*

And William Zett raised his legs and slid down the sun-slick trough, his face fist-tight, the hard blue sky running him along, the white bird freezing in flight.

His head jammed into the earth and he heard something in his neck snap like a Popsicle stick. And everything—the sky, the trees, the white bird, the man looking down on him—

"Oh, God, no!"

went black.

20

Even an hour after she'd left the hospital and was on I-93 north to one of her rest homes in Concord, N.H., René could still hear Jack's voice—and the image of his eyes cue-balled in his face as he stared at her transfixed with terror. *Terror.*

That was the only word for it. She didn't have a clue what he was seeing as he gaped at her. But what kept playing in her head was that voice—that weird baby-talk voice.

"Mama."

"Except Jack didn't have a mother."

The jangle of her cell phone snapped her back to the moment. It was the secretary at Broadview saying that it was urgent: Carter Lutz wanted to meet with her as soon as possible. René had no idea what the problem was, but she had a prowling sense it wasn't good.

Half an hour later she reached the home, and as soon as she entered she felt the tension. "He's waiting for you in his office," the receptionist said.

René walked down the hall and tapped his door.

Carter Lutz opened it. He did not smile. "I appreciate your coming by." He closed the door and indicated a seat opposite his desk. He settled in his chair. "I'll get right to the point. The family of Edward Zuchowsky is taking legal action against this home, and you've been named in the lawsuit along with Comm-Care."

"What? On what grounds?"

"Gross negligence in his death at the hands of Clara Devine."

She could barely catch her breath. "That's ridiculous. I never laid eyes on Edward Zuchowsky or Clara Devine."

"That's irrelevant. Within the next few days, Zuchowsky family lawyers will call on you for a deposition. How you respond is critical to the outcome and determination of damages."

René looked at him in blank disbelief.

"But there's something that can be done to avoid a horror show for all of us." Lutz's face appeared to sharpen. "First, let me ask you a question. Your work in this home is dedicated to raising the quality of life for elderly people, am I correct?"

She nodded numbly. "Yes, of course."

"Then you wouldn't do anything to jeopardize the well-being of our patients, correct?"

Another obvious question. René nodded.

"Or of the home?"

Nod.

"Good, because the welfare of Broadview is commensurate with that of our residents. Our moral mission is to our residents. Is that not so?"

Nod. And a worm slithered across René's chest.

"What happened with Clara Devine was a terrible thing, and nobody knows what caused her to do what she did. But everybody associated with this home is responsible for keeping track of our patients and not letting them wander away.

"You're new, but you can imagine that liability is something we worry about here. I don't need to paint a picture, but lawsuits are horrible and the results can be destructive. But if you're a team player, we can all help each other. If not, you'll be alone in the dark."

Team player.

"For your deposition, it is of the utmost importance that you keep in mind our highest priorities and exercise prudence and consistency."

Silence filled the room as if the place were holding its breath. Finally René spoke. "What exactly are you asking me to do, Dr. Lutz?"

"I'm asking that you restrict all you know about the incident to the fact that there was an unfortunate failure in the security system, namely, that the locking mechanism had somehow failed and the security camera malfunctioned."

"You mean you're telling me to pretend that I never saw the video of Clara Devine letting herself out."

"In so many words." Lutz's eyes were intense with conviction.

"And that I make no mention of Clara's being enrolled in the Memorine trials?"

"Only because that's totally irrelevant."

"Dr. Lutz, you're asking me to lie and, frankly, I'm not comfortable with that."

Lutz's eyes shrank to ball bearings. "You'd be a lot less comfortable with a ten-million-dollar lawsuit with your name on it."

"But I never even laid eyes on Clara Devine or Edward Zuchowsky."

"That may be so, but you're employed to oversee residents' medications. And lawyers can make ugly mountains out of molehills. It's for your protection that we're having this conversation." He narrowed his eyes to say that she should be grateful.

"Forgive me, but violating the law and ethical standards is hardly protection."

"Ms. Ballard, we are not talking about ethical standards, but a higher morality—which you agreed was for the welfare of our patients."

"Clara Devine let herself out by tapping the security code. We all saw the video and I'm told she did that because of Memorine. So, why are we denying that?"

"Because if it becomes known that she was a subject in the clinical trials of a drug which may have made possible her escape, massive lawsuits would fly, and everybody associated with this home and GEM Tech would find themselves tied up in a legal free-for-all for years to come—the results of which could be suspension, heavy fines, exorbitant legal fees, and acrimony. It would almost certainly mean the termination of the development of a cure for Alzheimer's disease. And that simply cannot happen."

"But what you're asking me to do is wrong."

"Some abstract notion of right or wrong is not the point. It's to do what's right by our residents."

"What about the others—nurses, doctors, administrators?"

"They're in concurrence with our higher mission here."

So, this was getting the new girl in line. "What about Clara Devine's medical records? Surely the Zuchowsky lawyers will want to see if anything there can explain her attack."

"Her records won't be a problem."

She looked at him in disbelief. "Altering medical records could cost us our licenses to practice."

Lutz took a deep breath. "Ms. Ballard, what is proper and improper are relative matters since the circumstances are unique. Greater issues are at stake, namely, the beneficial outcome of this drug research. Secondly, there is absolutely no evidence connecting the compound with Mr. Zuchowsky's death. Something in her just snapped."

"But once the drug's approved, won't the Zuchowsky family wonder if Clara had been enrolled and attempt to raise a connection?"

"Not unless you say something about it, because I can assure you that the rest of the staff here will not."

Jesus! He was putting the whole thing on her. "Do your lawyers know about the clinical trials?"

His face filled with blood. "No. And let me remind you that Clara Devine was suffering dementia and was known to have delusions even before the trials. Any speculation to the contrary could compromise the trials and the marketing of the compound."

He was telling her to lie and everybody else would swear to it. Because we're team players.

"You are, of course, free to hire your own attorney," Lutz continued. "But I'm sure CommCare will provide you with one."

She nodded, feeling confused and resenting how she was being manipulated. She wished she had never seen the videos, had never noticed the irregularities.

"As you may know, the locking system has been replaced, as has the camera."

"What about the security video of Clara Devine?"

"I really don't think that's something that concerns you."

"But I thought we were all team players."

Carter Lutz's eye twitched reflexively. "Let's just say it's no longer a liability."

Translated: Destroyed.

Lutz closed his hands over the papers and stared at her. "So, are you with us?"

"I need some time to think this over. You're asking me to compromise some basic professional ethics. You're also asking me to withhold information from my employer—that because of Memorine, Clare Devine was able to elope from this home and kill someone."

"There is absolutely no evidence that she did what she did because of the drug. And if you even breathe a hint that there's a connection, the promise of a cure may be destroyed."

Then his manner softened. "Look, Ms. Ballard, I'm asking you to put aside your self-concern and think of the residents in this home and the Alzheimer's patients throughout this country—and throughout the world. Think of your residents. Think of anyone you've been close to who may have suffered or died from Alzheimer's disease."

She nodded.

"And while you're thinking about it, I suggest you visit some of the residents who have experienced a miraculous turnaround. And I suggest you do so soon because lawyers will be calling on you any day." He got up and walked to the door.

René followed him. But before he opened the door for her, he said, "And, it goes without saying, what we discussed in here is to be held in the utmost confidence."

"Of course." She left, feeling as if there were a nugget of ice at the core of her body.

21

They moved Jack to a step-down unit in another wing of the hospital.

He was still being monitored by machines but not at the same intensity level as in the ICU. It was still impossible to predict the speed of recovery. Or that it would ever happen.

"Mrs. Koryan, I know how difficult it is," Dr. Heller said, "but I think we have to prepare for all eventualities and discuss long-term care for Jack. He may wake up in the next hour or day, but given the lack of progress in his condition it's also possible he may go on indefinitely. I've arranged a meeting with his other physicians, hospital caseworkers, and an administrator from the insurance company."

Beth knew what was coming.

"There are some very fine institutions in the area."

"You mean nursing homes?"

"Well, that's an option, but it doesn't make sense for a man thirty-two years old to be put in a facility for elderly patients. There are fine rehabilitation centers in the area. I'm sure we'll find the appropriate place. Do you have any in mind?"

"Greendale Rehab Center in Cabot," she said. It was what that pharmacist René Ballard had recommended the other day.

"Yes, Greendale has an excellent reputation. In the meantime, we're going to move him to Spaulding Rehab right next door."

They wanted him out of the hospital as soon as possible, Beth thought. They had stabilized him, and their job was done. The rest was rehabbing his muscles, monitoring his vital functions, and just waiting for him to surface. She glanced at Jack, stuck wherever he was, his breathing the only sign beyond the electronics that he was alive.

"I'll look into Greendale," Beth said, and Dr. Heller left the room.

A few minutes later one of the machines made a double chirp. And on the screen the green sawteeth made a series of ugly spikes.

Jack began to wince and thrash. This lasted for almost a minute, then subsided. Ordinarily Beth would have called the nurse, but the spells usually passed.

As she looked down at Jack, so wan and withered, it crossed her mind that this was no life for either of them. And even if he were to wake up, it could be months or years from now. And what would they have? What would they do while she hung around nursing him back to health? And even if he got better, regained his memory and physical health, they'd be back to where they had left off—estranged at best. Wishing they were living somebody else's lives.

She hated herself, but she had to admit to a thought which had several times wormed its way up from the recesses of her mind: That it would have been better if Jack had drowned.

22

"They're coming back. I mean, if you saw them a year ago you wouldn't believe it."

René followed Alice Gordon down the corridor toward the dayroom, knowing that she was hoping to sway René into agreeing to the cover-up.

"At first, I thought it was my imagination—subtle little changes we chalked up to ward acclimation and fine-tuning their meds. But then we ran some cognitive tests. Something's happening, and it's for real."

It was Monday morning, and René had returned to Broadview for the records that Dr. Carr had promised her. Also, to follow up on Carter Lutz's suggestion that she meet the trial patients.

Because CommCare was named in the Zuchowsky suit, her boss, Mike Carvalho, had given her the name of the pharmacy's lawyer who would contact her soon. He said he was also confident that the Zuchowskys had no case against her or CommCare—that neither she nor the pharmacy was negligent in their duties to Broadview, the residents, or the Zuchowskys. Of course, he had no idea about Memorine or what she had seen in that video. Meanwhile, because the records contained six months' worth of data on Clara Devine, plus the four other phantom test subjects, it would take René days to transfer everything to her laptop. But a cursory check showed that for these patients on the trial drug a simple "T-drug 10 mgs" was recorded each morning, the nurses not even knowing GEM's big little secret. When asked for an explanation, Alice replied, "What can I say? They told us that it was Dr. Carr's project and he was taking full responsibility. They gave us two cards of pills, one labeled Trial, the other Placebo. It's irregular, but I think they just wanted to keep everything mum until the data started accumulating."

"Were residents' families informed they were in the trial?"

"At first the patients were wards of the state, so there was no need for family consent. The lawyers took care of that, and nobody came by to visit. But you can get just so many wards."

"So nobody outside the home knew about the trials."

"Uh-uh. Now we're enrolling patients with family consent, of course."

"And how did the families react to the changes?"

"You can ask for yourself. But first I'd like you to meet Ernestine. She's eighty-two years old, and two years ago she was admitted here with moderate Alzheimer's." They entered the activities room. At a table sat a little white-haired woman pasting cutout pictures of flowers onto colored paper. As they approached, René could hear her singing to herself.

" 'Mammy's little baby loves short'nin, short'nin', Mammy's little baby loves short'nin' bread.' "

"Hi, Ernestine," Alice said. "How you doing today?"

" 'Put on the skillet, put on the lead, Mammy's gonna to make a little short'nin' bread.' " The woman slowly glanced up at the nurse and René, then looked back down to the puzzle. "Fine, thank you."

"That's good."

" 'Mammy's little baby loves short'nin', short'nin', Mammy's little baby loves . . .' "

"Ernestine, this is René. She's come to say hello."

"Hi, Ernestine. Nice to meet you. Those are pretty flowers."

"It's for my book."

"Isn't that nice. It looks like it's coming along very well." A small pile of pasted pages sat neatly beside her.

"I'm going to call it *My Flower Book*."

"What a great title," René said, a little distracted by the woman's manner. She had pronounced the book's title with the deliberate carefulness of a child.

" 'Mammy's little baby loves short'nin' bread.' "

"Ernestine, do you remember me?" Alice asked.

Ernestine stopped singing and looked up at her again. "Oh, sure." For a moment there was no light of recognition in the woman's face. Then she looked at the woman's nametag and said. "Can't you read? You're Alice." And very slowly and deliberately she recited, "A-L-I-C-E. Alice!" And she went back to her puzzle. " 'Mammy's little baby loves short'nin' bread.' "

"That's great, Ernestine. I'm so proud of you.' "

The woman smiled. And they moved away. "Two months ago I could walk in the room, tell her my name," Alice said, "and twenty seconds later she'd ask me who I was. I'd tell her again, and another twenty seconds later she'd ask me who I was again. She could recognize the face, but forget about putting a name on it." She shook her head in dismay. "If I hadn't seen it with my own eyes, I wouldn't believe it."

"That's incredible."

"Yes, and *that's* what it's all about." And she gave René a knowing look—a wordless plea not to raise a flag—not to report the irregularities to the authorities.

"I hear you," René said, still a little dazed by how complicated life had become. One word from her and all this could explode. "You think it's the drug that brought back her reading?" She hadn't seen Ernestine's cognitive evaluations, but some early dementia residents still retained rudimentary reading powers.

"When she was admitted to Broadview two years ago she couldn't read her own name. But I suppose the proof of the pudding is how she's doing six months or a year from now."

"You mean if she's sitting there reading *War and Peace*."

Alice laughed in relief. "Given the way things are heading, that may not be a joke."

As they walked down the corridor, René remembered how common nouns for her father had faded into "whatchamacallits" and that to avoid the humiliating frustration, she had put big labels on objects around the house—"telephone," "dish," "lamp," "fridge." As his ability to read faded, he began making excuses about needing a new prescription for his glasses. Eventually the synaptic wiring got so clotted that written words were meaningless blotches and books were things that filled shelves.

Alice led René into a room where a woman bedridden with a fractured hip was sitting with her visiting son and daughter-in-law. Alice explained that Lorraine Budd, age eighty-one, had been diagnosed with moderate dementia when she was admitted over a year ago.

Alice made the introductions. "Hi, Lorraine, this is René."

The woman had a pink face flecked with brown spots, but despite the discoloration and the soft folds of loose skin, René could see that she had been a beauty in her youth: the bright sapphire eyes and fleshy mouth and high intelligent forehead. Thick white hair was brushed back neatly and held by combs.

"I knew a René from school."

"You did?"

"René St. Onge."

"And you still remember her?"

"Oh, yes, we were best friends."

"I'm impressed," René said. "And where did you go to school?"

Without a moment's hesitation she said, "North Central High in Kalamazoo, Michigan."

"That's amazing."

Lorraine smiled proudly.

"And do you remember what year you graduated?" her son asked.

Lorraine frowned a bit as she thought about the question. "It was 1946. And I had poison ivy all over me. My face was all blown up and pink with the medicine. And it was very hot and

I had to wear gloves to shake hands so people wouldn't catch it." She chuckled to herself.

"And do you remember your guest's name here?" Alice nodded toward René.

"Yes, René like my friend René St. Onge."

Long-term memory *and* short, René thought with amazement.

Before she and Alice left, Lorraine's son said, "I'm not particularly religious, but this is like a miracle."

"It *is* a miracle, and you better believe God was listening," his wife declared.

"Whatever, the people who developed this should get the Nobel Prize," the son added. "I can't tell you how much better she is. Right, Mom? You're getting your memory back."

The woman smiled. "That's what they say."

"Here you go, Mom. Remember what day it is today?"

The woman stared at the wall as if trying to read a teleprompter. "Sunday."

"Close enough. It's Monday."

"But you usually come on Sundays."

"Jeez. That's right, and today's a holiday. It's Labor Day. I forgot." Then he looked at René. "See what I mean? It's unbelievable." Then he squeezed his mother's hand. "Mom, you're a miracle." And he kissed her hand.

Alice led René back out and into the dayroom, René's head spinning. All her previous suspicions of exaggerated claims were diminishing. And according to Alice the cognitive test scores would bear out the evidence.

Just three years. The niggling voice was back as they made their way into the dayroom. *He could have held on.*

Christ, you're going to let this eat you to death, she told herself.

Promise me . . . to die with dignity.

He would have continued to waste away, full-coded to be kept alive by machines and tubes and IV drips, antibiotics, CPR, emergency trips to the hospital.

You didn't know. You didn't know. And she latched onto Nick's words like a life raft.

"And this is Louis Martinetti," Linda said.

Louis was standing in front of them wearing jeans and a khaki shirt with pockets and epaulets. Hanging conspicuously around his neck was a chain with some kind of dull gray metal pendant.

"Louis and I met the other day. Good to see you again, Louis. How you doing?"

"How am I doing? I've got Alzheimer's." And he gave René a glacial stare to gauge her reaction. "I'm the sum of all I've forgotten."

"Well, I hear you're doing very well," René said.

He looked at René and squinted. Then something shifted in his face. "Your name Rita Swenson?"

"No, I'm René Ballard. We met the other day."

Unconsciously Louis's fingers gripped the pendant around his neck. They were military dog tags.

"Maybe your glasses will help," Alice said, and she pulled the case out of his shirt pocket, extracted his glasses, and handed them to him.

Cautiously, Louis slipped them on and began to study René's face. After a moment, his expression shaded to embarrassment. "Sorry, I sometimes get a little confused. You're the pharmacist."

René was delighted at his recall. "That's right. Very good, Louis. René Ballard." And he squeezed her hand.

Louis shook his head as if dispelling a thought. "But you don't know who she is, do you? Nah, you wouldn't know."

"Well, maybe you can tell me about her and who Fuzzy Swenson was."

Louis thought that over. Suddenly, something passed through him and he became agitated, his eyes flitting and his expression darkening. He moved toward the nearby window and became fixed on something outside. "From the southeast corridor," he mumbled. "Maybe hundred fifty, two hundred men tops . . ." He continued to mutter to himself as if having an interior conversation.

"What's that, Louis?" Alice asked.

Louis did not turn but continued muttering to the window.

"Light armaments the northwest . . . half dozen . . . reconnaissance . . . Seventeenth Infantry Regiment . . ." Then his face
screwed up as if he had just seen something awful. "I'm *telling*
the truth. That's all I know." Then his head cocked and his face
smoothed out again. "Tell them he's only a kid, only a boy. He
knows nothing. I know nothing. Nobody knows nothing."

"Louis, are you all right?"

Louis rotated his head toward René and Alice, and for a long
moment he stared at René. "He was a good guy, a good stand-
up guy is all. Told some good jokes." His eyes appeared to fill
with tears. "I loved him like a brother, you know?" His head
cocked and he nodded as if he were taking in responses from
some invisible companion. "I know, I know. But I swear we'll
get them back is all."

Alice leaned toward her. "Sometimes he talks to himself.
But it's never a problem." And she nodded a reassuring expression at René.

"I promised him that night and I promise you now," he said
to René. "We'll be there—me, Captain Mike, and Jojo. I
swear."

René had no idea whom he was addressing in his head or
what he was swearing, but the look in his eyes sent a small
electric shock through her.

Louis then turned and headed back to his room, still muttering. But he wasn't simply talking to himself. He was engaged
in a full-fledged conversation with people in his head. "His
charts say you've been treating him with antipsychotics."

"Yes, well, only when . . . you know, the delusions become a
problem."

"Like what?"

Alice appeared to squirm. "Well, like when he gets paranoid
or frightened."

"He's on a high dosage of Haldol."

"Well, sometimes he gets pretty upset and doesn't snap out
of it." Then her face brightened. "But the thing is, his short-
term memory is coming back like gangbusters. I'll show you
his scores."

They walked down the hallway. But what bothered René was

how Alice wanted to put the best face on Louis's delusions—and the weird sensation that Louis's mind was toggling between the ward and some dark and faraway time. Yes, that happened with dementia patients. Her own father had had occasional delusions, sometimes thinking René was his wife as a younger woman or someone from television. But what struck her was how Louis had looked at her as he stood there fingering his dog tags. He looked lethal with conviction.

Alice continued her sunny monologue. "When his wife and daughter admitted him last year he had nearly forgotten the first half of his life. He could barely remember anything. Now he's coming back like pieces of a puzzle. It's unbelievable." Alice stopped and took René's arms. "This is what it's all about—not all that team-player stuff," she whispered. "Honey, we're seeing miracles like he said. Real miracles."

"I'm starting to believe it."

From down the hall Carter Lutz stepped out of a conference room with Jordan Carr and two other people she did not recognize—men in suits. Lutz separated from the others and came over to René, his face preceded him like a huge happy-face mask. He extended his hand to her. "Nothing like seeing for yourself. Pretty remarkable, huh?"

The man was the personification of smarminess. "Yes, it is."

"So you can appreciate what we're all excited about."

They both know what he referred to.

"Alice tells us that her meeting with the lawyers went swimmingly."

Alice went into exaggerated nodding. "Uh-huh. Oh, yeah, a piece of cake."

"They should be calling you any day now to prep you for the deposition. I'm sure you'll be fine."

"Dr. Lutz, I appreciate your concern," René said. "But my understanding is that in depositions one is asked to swear to tell the truth. I'm having trouble with having to lie under oath."

Lutz's face looked as if it had just freeze-dried. "Ms. Ballard, we've been through all this." Then he pressed his face very close to hers so that she could smell the sourness of his coffee breath. "If you tell them what you saw, you will bring this all down—everything! And you will hurt many people . . . including yourself. Do you understand? Do *you?*" His voice sounded like an electric saw hitting a nail. Down the corridor Jordan Carr and the other men were silently taking in the scene.

"Yes, I understand, but—"

"Don't!" The syllable shot out of Lutz's mouth like a bullet. Then he turned on his heel and stormed away.

"Well, that was pleasant."

Alice put her hand on René's arm. "Look, hon, I don't mean to turn up the heat, but my brother-in-law was caught up in a lawsuit involving a traffic accident that left somebody crippled. It went on for years and he lost nearly everything. Carter's right: It's not worth it. Believe me. Tell them you know nothing and let the lawyers fight it out. Please. Otherwise, it'll never go away."

God! It wasn't all that long ago she'd been thrilled at landing a job in a community dedicated to doing good by doing right—a profession that was noble and dedicated to the well-being of needy people. The wonderful world of health care, the Hippocratic oath, of good science, healing and all that. Now she was knee-deep in murder, conspiracy, and corporate cover-up. And in her dissent she had ended up on the wrong side of the battle line. She looked at Alice's supplicating eyes and suddenly she felt trapped between trying to sort out the merits of moral rightness versus professional ethics—of good versus the strangulating red tape of law.

"Thank you," she said, thinking that her decision could render a brutal new shape to the universe.

23

The director of the Greendale Rehabilitation Center called Beth to say that there was a bed available for Jack. He could be moved from Spaulding within two weeks.

Meanwhile Jack slept.

And after their visit, Vince drove Beth to Carleton. She didn't want to go right back to an empty house, so she suggested they get something to eat. And Vince took her to a restaurant near the hospital. "He's never going to come out of it," she said in a low voice.

"Don't say that," Vince said. "He'll be back. I'd bet my life on it."

"But I'm okay with it, really. I just wish I could have said I'm sorry." She took Vince's hand. "You were such good friends. I envy that. Really. Jack and I were talking of separating."

Vince's eyes dilated in shock. "Well, he never said anything."

She shrugged. "Pride. But things weren't what they seemed. We had problems. It's just too bad we never worked them out." She could see Vince becoming uncomfortable with the conversation.

"The MRIs are showing activity, which means his brain is still active. He could snap out of it anytime."

"Maybe."

Vince checked his watch. "I think we should go."

By the time they reached Beth's place it was dark. Vince parked around back and walked her to the door. She put her arms around him. "Thanks, Sweetie."

"Nothing to thank me about. We're practically family."

They were standing at the back door. The night was cool and overcast with a hint of autumn in the wind. The house was dark and forbidding. "I hate the thought of going in there. It's so damn empty." She hugged him to her.

Vince didn't say anything, but she could feel him brace.

"You could sleep on the couch," she whispered, and she pressed herself against him ever so slightly.

She felt Vince pull away. "I don't think it's a good idea."

She nodded because they both knew that it was not the couch where she wanted him to spend the night but in her bed—to be made love to without thought, to nestle against the curve of his hard body like spoons, the way she would with Jack. Just this once—a momentary lapse into creature needs absent of reflection or consequence. "Sorry," she said. "It's just that it gets so hard at times."

"I understand."

But she knew that he didn't understand. She kissed him on the cheek and let herself in the house as Vince returned to his car and drove home.

For over an hour Beth rolled around in her bed unable to compose her mind to sleep, thinking that she had in a moment of weakness led Vince on. Thinking that maybe he really did understand and would not see her proposal as an overture of betrayal. Thinking of the emptiness in the bed next to her.

I cannot live this way, she told herself. *I cannot go on. Yes, I'm weak, self-absorbed, starving. But that's me, and I can't spend the next months or years waiting to resume a dying marriage to a man who even if he does emerge will probably be mentally and physically impaired. What's in it for me?*

I can't.

I won't.

24

Saturday could not come soon enough. All René wanted to do was sleep in and not think about lawyers, depositions, and clinical trials.

But that was impossible, since over the intervening five days she got e-mails from Alice, Bonnie, and even the director of nursing at Broadview saying how well the meetings went with the attorneys representing the home. Bonnie actually claimed it was "kind of fun." She also said that she understood René's position, but it was a bit of an overreaction, if you asked her.

Of course, the wording was purposefully vague so as not to leave record of anything incriminating. In spite of the sweet-smelling wording, all the messages read the same: Don't rock the boat. Deny, deny.

According to René's boss, CommCare had provided her a lawyer named Brenda Flowers who would accompany her next week at the deposition with a Zuchowsky lawyer. Over the telephone Ms. Flowers assured René that it would be "a piece of cake."

A little after eight o'clock, Silky began nuzzling her face to be fed and let out. She thought about taking care of the cat then going back up to bed to sleep until noon, the way she did when she was younger. But that was impossible. Her mind was racing with thoughts of the deposition she was required to give in a few days and the words of Carter Lutz, Jordan Carr, Alice, and the others whipping through her mind like hysterical sound stripes.

The stress of the last several days had left her mentally and physically fatigued. It crossed her mind to put Silky in the car and drive until she reached the Pacific Ocean, maybe someplace in northern California or Oregon where in some nice little town she'd get a job as the local pill counter in some little mom-and-pop apothecary where nobody had ever heard of GEM Tech and the McCormick, Hadlock, and Woodbury law firm.

But she couldn't do that, of course. So she slipped on her robe and followed the cat downstairs, his huge fat black tail trailing him like a skunk's.

She dumped a can of Figaro into his bowl, changed his water, and looked out into the front yard. It was a sunny day, and a brilliant blue sky made a dome over the house. At the bottom of the driveway near the mailbox sat rolled-up copies of the *Manchester Union-Leader* and *Boston Globe* that the paperboy had left.

That was when she noticed the red metal flag of the mailbox sticking up. That was odd, since Joe the mailman didn't come around to deliver until after eleven, especially on Saturdays. Maybe somebody else had taken his weekend route.

She opened the back door, and Silky shot between her legs into the middle of the backyard, where immediately he squatted down to assess the bird situation.

The sun was warm, and the air moist, although a touch of autumn laced the air. It was one of those mornings that made her grateful for living in New England. But in a month, the sky would be bleak, the ground crusted with frost, and the air snapping with the scourge of a Puritan God.

She headed down the driveway and picked up the paper rolled in the plastic bag. The headlines were about the war. More dismal news. More dead soldiers and civilians. *"Will the world ever saner be?"* The Thomas Hardy line shot up from college English class. "Seems not," she said aloud as she approached the mailbox. She waved to a neighbor across the street who was packing her young daughter into her car seat. René watched them pull away as she reached the box.

It was the odor that hit her first. She opened the door of the mailbox and let out a scream.

For one hideous moment that telescoped her horror, all she could think was Silky. But a voice inside reminded her that she had just let him out the back door—that he was in the backyard still stalking starlings.

God, please no.

In a microsecond reprieve her mind scrambled—no white patch, no white patch . . . wider nose . . .

Staring out at her from inside the mailbox was the severed head of a black cat.

25

"It was goddamn sick," René said.

"Of course it was," Nick said with a dismissive shrug. "But maybe it was just some random prank."

"Nick, it was no random prank, and you know it. Someone's trying to intimidate me into lying. And I'm ready to go to the police."

"I can understand. But you have no proof who did it."

"Well, it wasn't my mailman."

It was later that day. And Nick, who was at Mass General catching up on work as he often did on weekends, had convinced her to drive to town and jog with him down the Esplanade along the Charles. It was what they did whenever René visited one of her Boston-area nursing homes. This time it was to get out of her place.

But she couldn't leave the cat head in the mailbox for the postman. So, fighting the rise of her gorge, she used a stick to pull it into a paper bag. She hosed out the mailbox, buried the bag in her backyard, and then threw up the contents of her stomach.

"If you go storming into Carter Lutz's office, he's only going to deny it and make it difficult with your boss."

"He already did. I called him at home and told him what happened. He said that he had no idea what I was talking about. Half an hour later I got a voice message from my district manager at CommCare saying that he had gotten a call from the VP of Health Net regarding my overreacting to policy issues. Overreacting! They put a fucking cat's head in my mailbox and I'm supposed to look the other way."

"Did you mention the video to anyone?"

"Not yet."

"Or the cat's head?"

"Just Carter Lutz."

"Good."

"Good *what?*"

"Good you didn't take this any further."

René wasn't sure why, and Nick was turning something over in his head. So they jogged in silence for a few moments. Because Nick was more than twice René's age and thirty pounds overweight, their pace was leisurely. It was also a warm September afternoon and many sailboats were on the river. In the late afternoon sun the trophy buildings of MIT squatted like ancient gilded temples rising above the trees of Memorial Drive.

"You want my advice?"

"Of course."

"Drop it. You don't know who did this. It could be anybody at Broadview as well as friends and associates of them. And it's simply not worth running around accusing people. Yes, it was sick and crude, but the gesture reads more of desperation than menace."

He was right that it could be anybody. Most of the people she worked with knew that René owned a black cat. A photo of Silky hung from a tag on her laptop case and she occasionally wore her cat pin. "But this was well planned. Somebody went to the trouble of finding another black cat at some animal shelter or they stole some kid's pet and decapitated it, then sneaked out to my place in the middle of the night and put the thing in my mailbox. We're talking health care professionals, and that scares the hell out of me. What else are they capable of?"

"I understand."

"It was a warning to shut me up or scare me into quitting my job."

"Well, it won't happen again."

While she wanted to take refuge in his assurance, she couldn't. "Look, I have to continue working with these people, smiling and acting normal, all the while wondering which of them did it and when they're going to strike again—and how."

"I don't think it was any of them."

"But I don't know that."

He gave his head a shake to dismiss her concerns. "Back to the issue. Going to the police would guarantee blowing up everything, the upshot being the termination of the trials. And that's what this is all about. You know how anal the FDA is about protocol. One hint of impropriety, and Memorine would be back-burnered for years. Meanwhile, somebody else would try to get their look-alike on the market, and GEM would be down the tube."

"So it's all about saving GEM's ass."

"We're going around in circles again."

"In other words, look the other way."

"Only because there are more important issues at stake, like our patients."

"Someone threatened me, Nick."

He looked at her directly. "I know, and that will not happen again."

The intensity of his look was almost startling. She didn't have his certitude but let that pass. "What about setting myself up for a perjury charge?"

"First of all, nobody can prove you saw the tape. Second, my guess is that it will be settled before it ever gets to court." Then, as if reading her mind, he added, "I know you don't like lying, but sometimes we have to overlook minor violations for a higher good. You've seen the results, right?"

"Yes, they're remarkable. I also feel guilty about the Zuchowsky family."

"Unfortunately, they can't get their son back. But I'm sure they'll want to avoid trench warfare and would probably agree to a settlement. Besides, what good would it do if the Zuchowskys knew that Clara let herself out instead of slipping through a faulty security system? Tort lawyers would turn this into a juicy malpractice case that would bring a sympathetic jury to its knees and send everybody straight to litigation hell, including you. And three years later you'd probably be jobless and in debt for life."

"But denying that Clara Devine was a subject in a clinical trial violates a whole slew of regulations designed to protect patients and prevent litigation. And now we're agreeing to perjuring ourselves."

"Maybe the lesser of two evils. So, go to the lawyers and tell them what everybody else is telling them, that you know nothing—just to get it behind you."

"But the legal back-and-forthing could drag on for years."

"Not if I have anything to say about it."

She looked at him. "Nick, what are you telling me?"

His expression softened. "That I really didn't want to retire."

She stopped in her tracks. "You're taking the offer?"

"What the hell, I'd get bored otherwise. Besides, look at the mess they got themselves into. Maybe I can put some pressure on them."

She had been after him to accept Moy's offer as chief principal investigator from the start. "That's great. And maybe you can keep their act clean."

"Whatever. I'm not signing any papers until this Clara Devine thing is behind us."

They started jogging again. "Any idea who's behind the cat head?"

"My guess is no one you know. But nothing like that will happen again."

She glanced at him, thinking that dear old Professor Nick Mavros carried more guns than she had imagined.

26

Jack continued in a profound sleep.

And after two weeks they moved him from Spaulding to Greendale Rehabilitation Home in Cabot—a private long-term-care facility just twenty miles north of Carleton. There was a special rehab unit devoted to coma patients. He occasionally muttered meaningless things, but his brain activity held steady and with diminished agitation.

A white two-story stone building that looked more like a restored elementary school, Greendale boasted "high-quality and compassionate" medical care and rehabilitation. It also offered a "coma stimulation program" for patients at low levels of cognitive functioning. Beth was impressed with the staff's professionalism and good nature.

Jack's primary care nurse, Marcy Falco, explained that she had brought several patients out of comas in her twenty-three years. In fact, she was so successful, she said, that others on the staff wondered if she was a witch. She said that she believed in talking to her patients, telling them about herself, narrating her regular tasks, summarizing the daily news and sports scores, playing their favorite music, making simple requests—blink, wiggle your toes, squeeze my finger. "His spirit is trapped inside of him," she told Beth one day. "But it's listening. He can hear you. Tell him stuff, tell him you love him. And above all, tell him the truth, because it may set him free. Honesty is the best therapy."

Beth visited Jack every other day at first, helping out with the physical activities as did Vince when he visited—turning him over, exercising his limbs, changing his bedding. They also helped out in the stimulation program—rubbing his face, his arms and legs, brushing his hair, moving his limbs, using smell stimulation. Beth brought in a CD player to play his favorite music—John Lee Hooker, Stevie Ray Vaughn, Bessie Smith. Vintage blues. She also ordered a television set to be left on as sound stimulation when she wasn't present.

Meanwhile, the jellyfish welts faded and the flesh around his eyes had lost its puffiness. His hair had begun to grow back, although his brow was still slick with antibiotic ointment.

Beth also saw René Ballard on occasion, as Greendale Rehab Center was one of the facilities where René worked as consultant pharmacist. She was very friendly and offered good moral support. She was also interested in Jack's dreams since she said his MRI patterns coincidentally resembled those of some Alzheimer's patients. That meant nothing to Beth.

As time passed, she visited Jack less frequently. She also began to go to bars with women friends. She met single men and talked, and she felt no guilt. She did not wear her wedding ring. When asked, she said she was a widow.

Beth cut her visits to once a week at best, and she sat with Jack for shorter periods. She continued to talk to him when she came by—mostly monologue spurts full of chitchat nothings. But she never told Jack that she loved him.

And Jack slept into his second month.

27

Nick looked at Gavin Moy point-blank. "Here's the deal. If you want me to head up these Memorine trials, there are a few conditions. First, be prepared to spend some money."

Moy smiled. "Why should you be any different?"

"Not me, the Zuchowskys." He held up his fingers. "Two, no more rough stuff."

They met at Gavin Moy's sixth-floor condo at Marina Bay in Quincy, a sprawling oceanside haven for local celebrities, athletes, and other upscale folks who wanted the accoutrements of privacy and proximity to Boston. Because the waterfront was lined with shops and restaurants, the place had the feel of Nantucket crossed with Florida's South Beach, especially from May through September. This was Moy's pied-à-terre, his primary residence being a waterfront mansion on a cliff in Manchester-by-the Sea on Boston's north shore.

The interior six rooms were done in off-white—walls, carpet, draperies, even the large curved leather sectionals, perfectly matched with accompanying chairs. Except for the vases of flowers, porcelain lamps, and watercolors, the place was bled of color. Gavin's designer had opted for understated monochrome elegance. But Gavin's touch was evident. On the fireplace mantel and scattered about the rooms were photographs of Gavin with various VIPs including other captains of industry, state senators, and, sitting dead center above the fireplace, a shot of him shaking hands with the president of the United States. Nick also spotted photos of Moy's son, Teddy, and Moy's late wife.

At the moment, Nick and Moy were sitting on the deck overhanging a spectacular view of Boston Harbor. In anticipation of Nick's acceptance, Moy had opened a bottle of Taittinger. Nick had played coy on the phone, but he said he wanted to discuss the terms of agreement in person. And Moy was ready to meet them, champagne in bucket.

"Why you hitting me with this Zuchowsky stuff?"

"Because this is a cover-up for your welfare. And because a lot of good people are getting poked by lawyers, going about their business in a fog of lies and anxiety over possible perjury suits. It's wrong, and I don't like it. And if we let them, the frigging lawyers will drag it out for years, wrecking lives and pulling the curtains on your miracle drug."

Moy made no response except to sip his champagne and to study Nick's face. It was his ploy to let a person lay out all his cards before he made his move.

So Nick pressed on. "Carter Lutz was given thirty days to fulfill a document production request from the Zuchowsky attorneys, which means he has to provide his own lawyers with paperwork on the security system, insurance records, Clara Devine's medical charts, which have conveniently been doctored to protect the trials."

Finally Gavin asked, "So, what do you propose?"

"That for everybody's best interest, including your own, you muster your resources to getting this settled out of court ASAP."

"Otherwise?"

"Otherwise get yourself another director."

Moy's eyebrows shot up. "Nick, you threatening to go to the FDA?"

"No, and I won't have to do that because someone's going to smell a rat if this drags on."

"So we throw a lot of money at the Zuchowskys and make it go away."

"Yeah. I'm sure the Zuchowskys aren't looking to get rich, just some moral sense of justice. Maybe you can even set up a memorial fund in the name of their son."

Gavin nodded. "Anything else?"

"Yes. Have the lawyers build into the settlement an agreement that no further legal action would be taken against the nursing homes, CommCare, its employees, or any parties associated with it."

"Anything else, *mein Führer?*"

"Yes. I also expect the clinical reports to be legitimate and complete."

Gavin Moy was not used to people dictating behavior. But Nick had the tactical advantage here. "Nor should it be any other way. I'll make some calls."

"I also want to bring aboard my own people."

"I don't care if you hire Daffy Duck." Then Moy's eyebrows shot up. "You mean the Ballard girl."

"Yes. She's smart and capable and has a heart. She's also a fine person, and I respect her intelligence and her integrity." Then he added, "She's also good with these patients. Her own father died of Alzheimer's a few years ago, so she's motivated."

"Fine." Moy raised his glass to Nick.

But Nick did not clink him. He leaned forward so that his face filled Moy's vision. "Somebody put a cat's head in her mailbox."

Moy winced as if trying to read fine print. "Beg pardon?"

"I said somebody put a severed cat's head in her mailbox."

There was a gaping moment. "And you think that was our people?"

"Let's just say I know where you come from."

"What the hell does that mean?"

Gavin Moy was brilliant, handsome, and surrounded with all the accoutrements of wealth and class. Yet under all the

high gloss swaggered a kid from the streets of Everett, where
scores were settled with baseball bats and fists. One night back
in college, some soused frat rat had insulted Gavin to his face
at a party. Because the kid was surrounded by pals, Gavin
sucked in his pride and walked away. But later, when he and
Nick crossed the parking lot, Gavin found the kid's car—a
new model that actually belonged to his parents—and with a
pocketknife he laid into the paint job. Had Nick not stopped
him, Gavin would have turned the hood into a Jackson Pol-
lock. As small a scene as that appeared through a lens of four
decades, it always came back to Nick when he picked up rumors of Moy's dealings with adversaries. "It means that I
know you can play hardball. So let me just say now that if anyone makes the slightest threat against her again, there's going
to be hell to pay."

Moy held Nick's eyes for a few seconds. "You really have a
thing for this woman."

Nick resented the implication. "She's a colleague and a former student."

"Oh, hell, man, I didn't mean anything by it. Just that she's
a real looker."

"Yes, she is. She's also a good person."

"I'm sure."

In the water below, a large, sleek outboard chuffed into the
marina for its slip with two men aboard. One looked up and
waved when he spotted Gavin and Nick. Moy's adopted son
and only heir.

"So we on?"

"Under the conditions specified."

"Fine."

And Nick clinked glasses. "Great view."

They sat in silence for several minutes. Then Moy broke the
spell, the champagne warming his words. "Do you friggin' believe where we've come from? You, a poor Greek kid from
Lowell, and me a son of a shoemaker out of a three-decker in
Everett. Like the old cigarette ad: 'A long way, baby.' " He
raised his glass. "To whatever leads to glory and makes a
buck."

Another of Moy's favorites—one that had been with him since he was half his age.

A few minutes later, his son entered the apartment. "You remember Teddy," Moy said, as the man emerged onto the deck. "Dr. Nick Mavros."

It had been years since Nick last met Teddy. He was a quiet man in his thirties. Except for the implacable expression, he was good-looking. Months of exposure to the sun had bronzed his skin and lightened his hair, which was pushed back to expose the slick V of a high widow's peak. He was not very tall, but he had clearly spent a good deal of time in a gym, because he was wadded with muscles—the tight brown T-shirt making his chest look like gladiatorial armor. He also had large thick hands—the kind that could twist the head off a cat, just like that.

Teddy made a tortured smile and shook Nick's hand. "Good to see you again, Doctor."

From what Nick knew, Teddy had failed to live up to his father's dreams of heading the GEM enterprises after Gavin. He was not the scientist type. In fact, he had dropped out of college and had gotten involved with some real estate schemes that set him afoul of the law and that ended up costing Gavin Moy considerable money. Apparently Teddy did not have any steady employment—just some handyman jobs with different contractors. He lived in the condo and spent his days on his father's boat. He also waited on his father like a valet, removing the empty champagne bottle and asking Moy if he'd like another, refilling the bowl of smoked almonds. As the two interacted, Nick could detect a curious pattern he had noticed years ago when Ted was a boy—behavior that balanced Teddy's need for approval and Gavin's scant servings of it.

While they sipped their champagne, Nick studied Moy's face. The tan made his green eyes blaze all the more, reminding Nick of the handsome young scientist with the shocking red Afro who had charmed female grad students and instructors alike back at MIT, where he was known as Big Red. A ladies' man, Gavin was never without a date, never wanting in his love life. And Nick had envied him because whenever they entered a bar or campus party, women's heads turned as if a film star had walked into the room. And Gavin exploited that advantage, sometimes leaving Nick to whoop it up with other guys while he headed off with some queen. And although he had filled out and had lost his hair, Moy was still attractive, and all the more so because he was about to turn a multibillion-dollar profit.

Nick nodded toward the water. "There were reports of tropical fish around the Elizabeth Islands a few weeks ago."

"Is that right?" Moy shoved a handful of almonds into his mouth.

"Your jellyfish sent a guy into our ICU. He's in a coma."

Moy's eyebrows rose up. "Is that so?" And he crunched almonds in his molars. "What the hell was he doing out there?"

"Who knows? I thought you'd seen the story. I think he was a former summer resident."

"What his name?"

"Jack Koryan."

"Jack what?"

"Koryan."

Moy washed down the nuts with champagne. "Means nothing to me."

"Me, neither."

And they sipped their drink as shadows stretched across the harbor.

28

Jack Koryan looked through the bars to see the door click open and the large dark pointy thing entered with a hiss.

The light was dim. Flashes dashed off the bright equipment in the room—the chrome IV stand, the tubes running from his arms and side. The stacked monitors with their green squiggles. The vase of flowers from that woman.

But the fading afternoon light slashed through the blinds to catch the creature approaching the bed.

Jack's eyes were gummy with stuff they kept putting in them. So he couldn't make out the figure. But it wasn't any of the nurses or aides—God, no—because this thing was big and dark and not asking how he was doing or running on about how the weather was or that movie she saw last night or how the Sox were doing in the AL standings . . .

And Jack was scared. Pissing scared, whimpering scared . . .

And something in the creature's hand caught the light.

Some kind of pipe.

Or club.

It made no difference because he could hear the hard cracks shoot through his soul.

Gonna smash down on you, Jacky Boy. Gonna put a trough in your brow so your brain will mush up out of your ears.

Time to call the cops. The cops.

Through jellied corneas he watched the thing stop at the foot of his bed. Something hard knocked against the bars.

Gonna get cracking.

Call the cops.

Call Mighty Mouse . . . to save the day.

The thing scraped along the side of the bed toward Jack's head. It hunched over him, and he could smell fishiness . . . and a swimming pool.

Better call . . . before . . .

(Whack! Whack!)

Your head implodes.

The creature raised its arm as Jack braced for the blow, and for a telescoped moment Jack reached down to the bottom of his being through all the layers conspiring to hold back the one vital urge not to yield:

"*Meds Gama.*"

And the creature was gone.

"Jack, you call? It's Marcy, your nurse. Jack, wake up."

"Hi, Jack." Another female voice. "Was that you?"

"*Meds Gama.*"

"Nothing."

"False alarm."

No, he screamed. *It was here. The monster thing was here. Right by the bed. Look down at the tracks . . . the wet. He was here, I swear. I swear . . .*

"G'night, Jack."

And a hole opened up and sucked Jack in.

29

"It's a piece of cake, I'm telling you."

Nearly a week had passed since the cat head discovery, and there were no more intimidating incidents. Whatever Nick had done was working. Also, Brenda Flowers, attorney for CommCare, had called René to prep her on her deposition scheduled for the following Monday.

"Unlike a courtroom trial, a deposition isn't cross-examination; it's just a vacuum cleaner for information—lots of broad, open-ended questions and follow-ups. All they want are the facts, and the strategy is to answer the questions as straightforwardly and narrowly as possible."

That's when René felt her stomach leak acid. And she could hear her father's voice: *The softest pillow is a clear conscience.*

Flowers also said that the Zuchowsky lawyer's name was Cameron Beck, and don't be fooled by his baby face. He could be a little pushy.

But Ms. Flowers had grossly understated Cameron Beck. He was a pit bull disguised as a cherub.

Flowers met René the following Monday at Beck's office on the twenty-eighth floor above State Street. She was in her forties and a pleasant woman with a sincere blue business suit and reassuring manner. "Don't be nervous," she said. And instantly René's heart rate kicked up. "You're going to be fine."

After a few moments, Cameron Beck came out to lead them to a conference room with a large shiny table, artwork on the walls, elegant designer furniture, and a million-dollar view of Boston Harbor—all of which conspired to remind René that there was a much larger world outside of wheelchairs, bedpans, and pills.

Also in the room was a stenographer with a dictation machine. She asked René to take an oath that everything she said was the truth. René nodded, thinking that she would throw up. But she didn't and took the oath.

In his early thirties, but looking about fourteen, Beck was a soft and cheeky man with a thick head full of auburn ringlets. He had a sharp, thin nose and intense blue eyes that projected a predatory cunning. As Flowers had said, Beck began with some neutral questions about herself—René's education, job history, her role as consultant to Broadview. René explained in minimal terms, as instructed.

Then Beck asked about the people she worked with at Broadview—their responsibilities to residents, what their jobs were, who their superiors were—boring stuff that helped Beck understand how the CommCare pharmacy operated and what its relationship was with the nursing home. This lasted for nearly an hour. All went well until Beck started to ask about Clara Devine. "Did you know her?"

"Not personally."

"As I understand it, this was the first time that Broadview has ever had a patient escape. Is that your knowledge?"

"That's what I've been told."

"I see. Then maybe you can tell me how you think she got out of a locked Alzheimer's ward."

"I don't know how she got out."

There! It was out, and on record, and under oath. Officially she had crossed the line. *Sorry, Dad. Just made myself a cement bag.*

Apparently Beck sensed the psychic shift because his eyes

locked onto René's. He glared at her for several moments without blinking, probably hoping she'd crack under the strain and fill the dead air with confession. But René held firm and held his gaze.

"Well, Ms. Ballard, maybe you can speculate. Did she go out the door? Or perhaps the window? Or maybe she went up the chimney?"

Brenda Flowers cut in. "Counsel, I don't think this line of questioning is fruitful. It's clear that Ms. Ballard doesn't know how Clara Devine escaped."

"We're trying to establish how a lockdown security system failed, apparently for the first time. So I'm sure that Ms. Ballard, an educated professional familiar with long-term-care facilities, has a theory she could share with me, don't you, Ms. Ballard." And his eyes snapped back to René and dilated in anticipation.

Didn't I see you in The Silence of the Lambs? she thought. "I don't have a theory."

"Then guess."

"Mr. Beck, please. This is a fact-finding exercise, not a courtroom." Flowers tried to sound pleasant, but the lilt of her voice had a serrated edge.

René responded. "My guess is that the door lock system failed, and she just pushed her way out."

"She just pushed her way out. I see, as opposed to somebody letting her out."

"Nobody would let her out."

"How do you know that?"

"I don't."

"How familiar are you with Broadview's security system? To your knowledge, how does it work to keep patients in?"

"A security code pad."

"I see. So you press a certain code and the door opens."

"Yes."

"And it closes behind you and locks automatically."

"Yes."

"And the only way out is to press the code on the keypad."

"Yes."

"So you're saying that something in that system failed."

"If I had to guess."

"If you had to guess. Is it possible that Clara Devine knew the code and let herself out when nobody was looking?"

A prickly rash flashed across René's scalp. And in her head she saw the video of her escape. "Clara Devine was suffering dementia, and such patients don't have the cognitive powers to remember codes or operate a code pad."

And now you're falling behind slippery wording.

"But she did get out and go down the stairs or elevator and slip out the front door past the main desk where staffer members were supposedly on duty, is that not correct, Ms. Ballard?"

"Yes."

"How do you explain that?"

"That the security door malfunctioned."

"Have you heard of it failing any other times?"

"No."

"Have you ever known the security system on the Alzheimer's ward to ever fail?"

"No."

"Then how do you explain it failing this one time?"

"I can't."

"What about the front desk? Did she suddenly turn invisible, or did she turn into a bird and fly out?"

"Mr. Beck, you're bullying my client and I won't stand for it."

But he disregarded Flowers. "Well?" Again he bore down on René as if trying to stun her in his glare. But the more hostile Beck turned, the more resistant René became. It occurred to her how easy it was to lie, to maintain a kind of Orwellian doublethink—holding two contrary thoughts in your head at the same time. And with every question, she felt a separation from her more real essence—like a retreating doppelgänger. To justify the growing split, she kept reminding herself of the "higher good"—of Lorraine Budd recalling her high school friend from 1940-something and Ernestine spelling her nurse's name and Louis Martinetti remembering his army days. "I don't know."

"You don't know. Is it possible the front desk attendant

maybe left for a few moments to go to the restroom or get a coffee, and while she did Clara slipped by?"

"It's possible. But I really don't know."

"And where exactly were you when she got out the door?"

"At home."

"You say your job is to monitor patients' medications, correct?"

"Yes."

"And you have a pharmacy degree?"

"Yes."

"So you understand the medications that are prescribed to patients?"

"Yes."

"Good. So if a patient is taking anything that might be harmful to themselves or others, you would know?"

"Yes."

He opened up a folder and pulled out a sheet.

"Was Clara Devine on any medications that would cause her to become violent?"

Maybe. "No." She heard the syllable rise easily out of her throat but imagined that her eyes were blinking red polygraph alerts.

"Are there any she was taking that could have such violent side effects?"

"No."

He opened a file folder and removed a sheet. "The medication sheets on file at the nursing home lists Atenolol. What's that?"

"A beta-blocker. It reduces heart rate, blood pressure."

"What about Aricept?"

"That's for her dementia."

"No possible side effects?"

"No."

"What about Paxil?"

"That's for her depression and general anxiety."

"How does it work?"

Brenda Flowers tried to protest the line and manner of questioning, but he persisted as if he were on some slightly manic autopilot.

René could see that Beck was enjoying his schoolroom inquisition, but she would not crack as she shot back the answers as if she were taking her orals back in pharmacy school. "Paxil is the brand name of paroxetine, a class of drugs known as selective serotonin reuptake inhibitors. It affects the activity of neurotransmitters in the brain, in particular serotonin and norepinephrine, which help regulate one's mood."

"You've done your homework, I see. So have I," and he whipped out a file card from his folder. "Did you know that Paxil can cause delirium, irrational talk, and hallucinations, irritability and hostility, even manic reactions including 'great excitement and psychotic rage, followed by depression'—all of which this drug is supposed to prevent? Is that not so, Ms. Ballard?"

"All drugs have side effects, and a small percentage may be adverse."

"But are these not side effects that could have led to Mrs. Devine's attack on Edward Zuchowsky?"

"That's remotely possible."

"Remotely possible? Well, did you know that England has recently banned the use of Paxil for children and teenagers under the age of eighteen because the drug has been linked to suicide, suicidal behavior, and violent outbursts? Did you know that?"

"I had heard that, yes."

"And yet your home still prescribed the drug to her."

"Clara Devine was seventy-six years old."

He made wide-eyes. "Oh, so it only adversely affects people under eighteen? How is that possible? Brains are brains, no?"

"No. Childhood depression is different from adult depression, probably because children's brains are still developing. So antidepressants may not have the same effects—beneficial or adverse—in children as in adults or geriatric patients. While it's difficult to weigh the risk-versus-benefits of any medication, Clara Devine had been on the same doses of Paxil and her other medications for many months. So I'd say that it's very unlikely that any of those meds caused such a dangerous impulse."

"So you're saying that nothing she was on could have accounted for her violent behavior."

"Not to my knowledge."

"But how would you know if you've been on the job for only eight weeks?"

"Because I saw her medical charts, and because there's no report of psychotic rage, hostility, or combative behavior that would point to her killing of Mr. Zuchowsky."

Beck rocked back in his seat and looked down at this list. "Once again, are you certain there were no drugs she was on that could have led Clara Devine to kill Mr. Zuchowsky— some kind of stimulant or antipsychotic drug that produced the opposite effect?"

In a flash she saw the nurses' notes: "More alert." "More verbal." "Remembered his granddaughter's name." And Louis Martinetti's swearing, "We'll get them back is all." And she heard her father's exasperation: *I can feel the holes.*

Besides, she really didn't know if Memorine had anything to do with the killing. That was the truth. And that's what the purpose of this deposition was. Furthermore, this Cameron Beck was a royal prick. "Not to my knowledge."

Beck snapped closed his file folder. "Thank you, Ms. Ballard. That will be all." He stood up and shook her hand. "Good day."

When they left the office, Ms. Flowers said, "Sorry about that. But he can get a little intense at times. You should see him in the courtroom. How do you feel?"

"Fine," she said. *Piece of cake?* René felt as if she had just eaten a slab of suet.

30

For the better part of a week, René pored through the various nurses' reports of residents enrolled in the Memorine trials, hearing the nasal persistence of Cameron Beck's voice—"any adverse side effects?" What she discovered was a marked increase in cognitive tests scores of nearly fifty percent of the subjects as well as improvement in their basic daily functions. In fact, Louis Martinetti had progressed twenty percent on his Mini-Mental State tests. That statistic particularly delighted René, as if the demon was being vanquished for both Louis and her father.

But in about a quarter of the reports, nurses had noted spells of "regressive behavior" and of "odd spells" when patients would become dissociated from the moment and lapse into past-time hallucinations—like Louis Martinetti thinking he was back in the army—or "childhood delusions."

Flashbacks.

According to her time line, those residents were part of the first trial group.

"Her mood would suddenly change, like that," Alice said when René asked about Clara Devine. "Suddenly she'd start talking in rhymes. Or she'd have conversations with people who weren't there. That's not unusual for dementia residents." Then she added, "But the thing is these spells could last a long time, and they were pretty coherent. It was kind of weird."

The notes also indicated that flashback spells had been observed in Mary Curley, who, like Clara Devine, was being treated with antipsychotic drugs and tranquilizers. So was Louis Martinetti.

"It's what we did if they became too disruptive or when the families visited."

The medication orders had been signed by Jordan Carr.

Of course, Clara Devine was at McLean's Hospital for psychiatric evaluation and would not be back for weeks or months—if ever.

During his rounds one afternoon, René approached Jordan Carr about his medication orders when he became defensive. "That's what's used for treating psychotic delusions. Do you have a problem with that?" His face had taken on the rashlike mottling again.

He clearly did not like the implication of her question: that they were burying a potential adverse side effect of Memorine. His manner also reminded her of the professional divide that separated them. "No," she said.

"Good." Then to clear the air, his manner changed. "I hear your deposition went well."

"It's not something I'd like to go through again."

"Well, you won't, I'm sure." Then out of his shirt pocket he removed two concert tickets. "By the way, I've got two tickets to the symphony next Friday night. *Mnemosyne* by the Hilliard Ensemble."

She thanked him but said she was busy, which was a lie. It was also the second time she had turned down a date with him. Jordan Carr was handsome, charming, brilliant, rich, and accomplished—a real catch in most women's books. His interest in her had not gone unnoticed by some nursing home staffers who wondered if her relationship with Jordan had transcended the professional. It hadn't, and René did not want to encourage that. She was not comfortable dating a professional colleague. Nor was she ready for another boyfriend. All she wanted was to continue carving out her career without complications.

From the upstairs window she watched Jordan leave the building. A couple of weeks ago he had purchased a second Ferrari, a silver 1999 Maranello. Out of curiosity, the other night she went online and looked up the model. She came up with one hit from Atlanta with the same red with tan interior. The asking price was $240,000.

As he pulled out of the parking lot, her eye fell on her little blue Honda Civic with the dented front fender. She felt like the member of a different species.

"Did Dr. Carr leave?" Alice asked, as René returned to the nurse's station.

"Yes."

"Oh, well. A fax just came in for him."

Just then one of the aides called her to help with a patient. "Here, hon, slip this in Dr. Carr's mailbox for me like a good kid, okay?" And she handed René the sheets and scurried away to the aide. Even Alice was beginning to perceive René as Jordan's girl.

René walked over to the mailboxes and happened to glance at the sheet. It was from Massachusetts General Hospital Emergency Department, Archives. It was a blood assay made back in August.

She glanced at all the chemical analyses, but what caught her eye was the name of the patient. It struck her as odd since he was not one of Jordan Carr's patients. In fact, when she had mentioned her visit a few weeks earlier, Jordan had said that he was unfamiliar with the case of Jack Koryan. Never heard of him.

31

René found Mary Curley in one of the activity rooms. Three other women were at the main table doing cut-and-pastes with an aide. But Mary sat alone in a corner with puzzle pieces piled in front of her.

As she approached her, René became aware of Mary's outfit—a ruffled white blouse under a pink and white jumper. Some residents needed help getting dressed. Others could dress themselves. According to the charts, Mary was in the latter category because of her improved functionality. But what startled René was that Mary looked like a geriatric Little Bo Peep. "Hi, Mary. Remember me? My name is René."

Mary looked at her. "I remember you."

René didn't really believe her since several weeks had passed. "The last time we met, you were doing a puzzle of a kitten."

"That was Daisy. She's over there." And she pointed to a shelf of puzzle boxes.

René was shocked at her recall. But Alice's words shot through her head: *This is what it's all about.*

"That's right!" But as soon as the words were out, René's

eyes fell to the picture puzzle—a little girl with a dog. And the little girl was dressed in a pink and white jumper. "Mary, that's a very pretty dress. Where did you get it?"

Without missing a beat, Mary said, "My daddy." She clicked another piece into the puzzle. "He's going to take me to the museum today." And she checked her naked wrist as if reading a watch.

"He is? Isn't that nice? Which museum?"

"The Museum of Fine Arts in Boston," and she enunciated the words with slow deliberation.

But what sent a jag through René was the woman's voice. As if somebody had flicked a switch, Mary sounded like a little girl. Even her deportment seemed to shift as she rocked her head with each syllable, the pink tip of her tongue wetting her lips.

"He's going to take me to see the mummies. You like mummies?"

"Yes. I like mummies," René said, feeling as if the room temperature had dropped ten degrees.

"No, you don't. That's not what you said yesterday. You said you didn't like mummies. You said they were all dry and scary-looking, and you didn't want to go the museum."

"But I didn't see you yesterday."

"You did so."

"Mary, what's my name? Do you remember?"

Mary looked up at her with a slightly quizzical expression. "Barbara Chin, silly."

"My name isn't Barbara Chin. It's René."

Mary snapped another piece into the puzzle. "I'm not afraid of mummies. And you shouldn't be either. They're dead."

As Mary continued her weird monologue, René noticed how she kept licking her upper lip like a child and how she fidgeted with the folds of her dress and twisted strands of her hair as she studied the scattered puzzle pieces, or put a twist of them in her mouth, sucking the ends as she searched for connections.

But what unnerved René was not just the full-faced innocent hazel eyes entreating her to explain her fear of mummies. It was that voice: It had none of the resonance and timbre of an elderly woman but the thin violin sharpness of a little girl's.

"I remember you have a dog also," René said, as Mary completed the spaniel's head in the picture.

Mary licked her lips and her face lit up. "His name is Jello."

"Yes, Jello. I like the name. What kind of dog is he?"

"He's a golden retrieber."

"Retriever."

"That's what I said, *retrieber*."

René kept feeding her questions not just in fascination at Mary's recall, but the weird sense of double exposure. Half the visual cues told her that René was having a conversation with a seventy-eight-year-old woman. But the dress and gestures and voice were those of a child. Every so often Mary would look up full-faced at René, her watery eyes staring at her full of little-girl innocence but through a face of crinkled, doughy flesh and liver spots. These were not the eyes of a dementia patient who looked out in fear and confusion at a meaningless kaleidoscope of colors and shapes. Nor were these the eyes of a woman who was being stripped away inside. These were the eyes of a child pressed into the face of an old woman.

"Mary, can I ask you a question?"

Mary looked up at her blankly, her eyes perfectly round orbs of milky blue innocence.

"Where are you?"

For a hushed moment, Mary just looked at her with that broad soft open face. "Henry C. Dwight Elementary."

"And how old are you?"

"Seven."

"No," René began. But she was cut off as Mary grabbed her hand, and for a second René thought she wanted to be helped up. But she pulled it to her mouth and in the instant before she took a bite out of it, René snapped it away.

Mary hissed at her. "I don't like you." Then she pushed her chair back and stood up. She inspected her wrist again and started moving away.

"Mary, where you going?"

Then in that little-girl voice again, she said, "Jello needs to go out." And she got up and shuffled out of the room.

32

"It was creepy. She was in a time zone of seventy years ago."

"That's not unusual with these patients," Nick said.

"But this was different. She was coherent, not scattered or fragmented. Neither was her delusion. She was back in her childhood and apparently enjoying it, except when she tried to take a bite out of me."

They were jogging along the river again. The day was cool and overcast, and because it was October only a few sailboats were on the water.

"Then that's something we'll be looking into," Nick said. "Which brings me to why I called. Feel like moonlighting? I'm going to need help tabulating data for the trials. We're getting lots of positive results, but I'm concerned over these flashback events."

She was relieved to hear him say that. She was beginning to wonder if she was the only one who saw this as a potential problem.

"That's something we have to deal with. And that's going to mean cross-referencing these events with population demographics, genetic profiles, et cetera."

"What exactly would my job be?"

"Your title would be behavioral data analyst."

"Why do I have the feeling that you just made that up?"

"Because I did, but who'd be better than a consulting pharmacist?"

"I'm flattered, but won't that be a conflict of interest?"

"*Au contraire,* and didn't I see that coming? You're an employee of CommnityCare pharmacy, which makes you an outsider to both the homes and GEM Tech. And since you'll be in my employ, that puts you out of range of GEM."

She thought that over for a moment, feeling a slight uneasiness.

"Unless, of course, you have problems with receiving compensation from me."

"No, but my guess is that it will be coming from GEM Tech, right?"

"Yes, but you're participating in clinical research for me, and God knows I can use the help. And you can use the money."

Was this ever true. Nearly forty thousand dollars remained to be paid off in student loans. And on a salary of seventy thousand dollars, she'd be paying it back for years. Plus her car was beginning to break down, and her wardrobe was full of gaps, and her credit card debts were mounting up.

"Also, you're the last person who's going to look the other way if there's a problem."

"What exactly would I be doing?"

"Compiling data on meds and behavior from the clinical nurses, maybe even taking note yourself of any changes in the behavior of patients."

"How long do I have to think it over?"

He nodded down the path. "Until we reach that tree. And the rate is fifty dollars an hour."

"That's ridiculous."

"So is GEM's potential profit."

"How many times can I sell my soul to them?"

Nick laughed. "Do I hear a yes?"

Screw it. "Yes."

"Good."

They jogged silently for a few yards. "By the way," she said, "is Jordan Carr working with you on the Jack Koryan case?"

"No."

"Oh."

"Why do you ask?"

"He requisitioned a blood assay of Mr. Koryan."

"He did?" Nick looked genuinely surprised.

"Then later he asked Alice to fax it to another number. I checked," she said. "It's the office of Gavin Moy."

"Gavin Moy?" Nick nearly stopped, but he caught himself and continued his pace again.

For several moments they jogged along without further comment. But René sensed a festering behind Nick's silence and the way he stared at the water as if half-expecting something to surface.

33

By mid-October, Beth had cut her visits with Jack at the rehab center to once a week. In spite of the aggressive efforts at sensory and motor stimulation, the staff at Greendale had failed to elicit any on-command response from Jack. He could breathe on his own, cough on his own, make occasional meaningless sounds. But for all practical purposes, Jack was dead.

Meanwhile, Yesterdays opened to rave reviews in both the *Boston Phoenix* and the *Boston Globe*. Because Beth had no interest in the restaurant she had sold Jack's share to a cousin of Vince's.

And Jack slept.

And one night at the Bristol Lounge in Boston's Four Seasons Hotel Beth met George King, an investor from McAllen, Texas. He was in town for a week of meetings. He was a kind, handsome man, and they spent the evening together walking through the Boston Garden. His wife had died the year before of breast cancer. To Beth's mind they shared a common loss. On the eve of his departure, they shared his hotel bed.

And Jack slept.

When she visited Jack again, Beth felt less conflicted with

devotion and honor than she had been. She knew she was slightly neurotic, more concerned with herself, thinking that she could end up like one of those family members waiting seventeen years for their loved one to wake up. But she had to be honest with herself. That just wasn't her. She was no bed-side wife. Besides, she had considered leaving him before all this happened. If he were awake, he'd understand.

When the nurses left, Beth laid her hand on Jack's and, her eyes pooling with tears, she kissed him softly on the forehead. "I'm sorry, Jack," she whispered.

The next day she filed for divorce.

34

"Who's Fuzzy Swenson?" René asked Christine Martinetti.
Christine looked startled. "How do you know about Fuzzy Swenson?"

"Your father. He was a little confused the last couple times I was in and asked if I was Fuzzy Swenson's sister."

"I don't know about her, Fuzzy Swenson was a buddy of Dad's in Korea. He's got a picture of him in his room."

"I saw it."

"What did he say about him?"

"Nothing. Just that he thought I was his sister. Also became a little agitated."

Christine nodded and sighed. "I think his real name was Samuel. He was in a POW camp with Dad in North Korea. He died over there and I guess it was pretty bad what happened to him because Dad never talks about it. Funny thing is that he's beginning to talk more about his Korea days—the good stuff. Maybe it's the Memorine."

"Maybe. His cognitive test scores are beginning to improve."

They were sitting in the conference room on the locked unit

having coffee and waiting for Louis to finish his shower. Christine, who was about René's age, lived in Connecticut and visited her father maybe once a week.

"He's otherwise so healthy. He could live another fifteen years."

"Absolutely."

Christine was silent for a few moments. "From what I've read, nobody ever dies of Alzheimer's. They die of heart attack or cancer, but not the disease itself, right?"

"Yeah, it's usually some prior condition. But if they're in advanced stages and are confined to wheelchairs or a bed, they're susceptible to internal infections and pneumonia."

"Because they forget how to walk and eat. So they starve to death."

René nodded at the primal reality. "By then they've lapsed into a coma, and the family usually decides to discontinue feeding and not to take any extraordinary measures to resuscitate."

"I don't want him to go like that."

"Of course not."

"I don't think I could take it."

DNR. One of the countless antiseptic shorthands.

It's what René had finally yielded to. *Do not resuscitate*. To spare her own father from pain and more humiliation. Because she did not want him to linger on until the basic circuitry of his brain had become so gummed up that he had lost memory of how to breathe. It was that raw eventuality that caught up to her—when she had come to accept the fact that he would never recover, that no matter what she did or what the doctors came up with he would never come back but continue to descend into the disease. So she signed the DNR order. And the day he died was a release for the both of them. Her only compulsion was to be with him at the moment of his death. And when that came, she held him in her arms and told him over and over again that she loved him, that he and Mom had given her a beautiful life, and that he was going to be with her soon. Of course, he heard none of René's words. And even if he did, they meant nothing to him. They were for her.

His breathing came irregularly, in short gasps and long intervals. Then in a long thin sigh that seemed to rise out of a fundamentally held resignation of all living creatures, he died. In a blink his life and all that had gone into making him who he was ended. She held her face to his and sobbed until she thought her heart would break. When the nurses came, they sat with her. Then they left to give her one final moment with him.

For the last time she kissed him on the forehead and whispered, *"Tell them I remember you."*

Against that memory flash René forced a bright face and matching voice. "Well, if he continues to improve the way he has, that may not happen."

"You really think it's working, that he may actually recover?"

"It's really too early to say for certain, but from what I've seen around here the signs are very promising."

"God, I pray it's true."

René felt the tug in her chest again. "Me, too."

An aide stuck her head into the room. "He's all ready."

René followed the aide and Christine down the hall and into the dayroom, where Mrs. Martinetti was sitting with Louis at a table. Louis was looking at black-and-white photographs. Old photos of the Martinettis in younger days.

"Good morning, Dad," Christine said with a big smile, and she gave Louis a kiss on the forehead. "You look so handsome in that shirt."

His white hair was still damp from the shower and his face had a bright sheen. And although the bright red polo shirt gave a youthful glow to his face, it could not mask the confusion in his expression as he looked at Christine, then back at René.

Christine pulled up a chair beside him. "So, what's new? What's been going on?"

Louis continued to glare at her in bewilderment. Finally he said, "Where's . . . my other daughter?"

"What other daughter? You only have one daughter—me. Christine."

Louis looked at René for help. "I have another daughter. Not her."

Christine's body slumped. "No, Dad, you only have me. You just forgot."

"She's not my daughter," he insisted, looking at René. Then he lowered his voice. "She's somebody else."

"Dad, how can you forget? It's me, Christine. You remember."

The photos were of Louis and Marie posing with Christine when she was a girl. Louis's face turned angry and red. "You're somebody else. You're an . . . imposter." He again turned his face away, clapping his eyes on René for safety.

"I'm not an imposter. You're just a little confused."

René could hear the fracturing in her voice. It had only been a few days since Christine was last here. Remarkably, his scores had increased twenty percent since he had first entered the home eleven months ago.

René knelt down and took his hand. "Louis, you remember me, right?"

He looked at her at first with a disconcerting scowl. But then his face smoothed over. "Yeah, you're the pharmacist woman."

"That's right. We're friends—you can believe me. And this is Christine. Look at her, Louis. She's your daughter, Christine."

Louis did not look at Christine. But he shook his head. She asked him again to look at Christine, but he refused.

René got up and nodded to Christine to follow her. "We'll be right back," she said, and led Christine out of the dayroom and into the hall where Louis couldn't see them.

"How can he not recognize me? I was here three days ago, and he was fine. He's supposed to be getting better." Tears puddled in her eyes.

"It might be that he's remembering you from years ago—the old photos. That happens often. In fact, it's called Capgras syndrome—when they think that loved ones are doubles or fakes."

"Can't you give him something? I means with all those meds you got?"

"He's been treated with antipsychotics."

"Maybe you can recommend they up the dosage or something."

The nursing staff would give him Ativan or Haldol when he got seriously agitated or threatened to disrupt the ward. But they could not medicate back the recall every time he forgot his daughter. Ironically, Memorine was supposed to do that.

Christine looked distraught. René took her hand. "Let's try this," she said, and led her back into the dayroom. "Hey, Louis. Look who's here. It's Christine."

Louis looked at her for a prolonged moment. Then his face brightened into a smile. "Where you been?"

"The traffic was bad." Christine walked over and gave her father a big hug. "So what's going on? How you been?"

They talked for a while. Then Louis glanced at René as she was about to leave them. "I couldn't stop them," he whispered. "I tried, but I couldn't. I'm sorry."

"You couldn't stop who, Louis?"

"Sorry." His eyes filled with tears.

"Dad, what are you talking about?"

But he disregarded Christine. "Louis, you're getting confused," René said. "What's upsetting you? Tell us, please."

He looked at Christine, then back to René. "Sorry about your brother."

"Louis, I don't have a brother."

He nodded. Then his face tightened. "But I'm going to get them back some day, the fuckers."

"Get who back?"

He nodded to himself as if he had just settled something. "They'll know."

35

"**W**ell, you got your out-of-court settlement, and it cost me a friggin' bundle," said Gavin Moy.

"Two years from now, it'll look like petty cash." GEM Tech stocks that morning were up by twenty percent since last week over the rumors about the new Alzheimer's drug. In a year Nick's holdings would double several times over. And Jordan Carr would probably own an entire fleet of Ferraris.

It was a warm late October day, and Nick and Gavin were riding at thirty knots southward on Gavin's boat in celebration of the settlement and Nick's agreement to head up the clinical trials. When Gavin asked where he wanted to go, Nick said he had never been through the Cape Cod Canal. It would be the last run before Moy put the boat in dry dock.

A thirty-eight-foot Sea Ray sport cruiser with twin 350 horsepower MerCruiser engines, the boat was long, sharp, and very fast; and it was named the *Pillman Express,* Moy's punning homage to George Pullman, whose railroad car industry grew into a dynasty. Teddy drove while Nick and Gavin settled back at the stern.

According to Moy, Broadview Nursing Home had assumed

full responsibility for negligence in the death of Edward Zuchowsky, while, behind the scenes, GEM Tech paid the lawyer fees and damages. The Zuchowsky family agreed to accept a settlement of $1.5 million as well as an apology from Broadview and a promise to upgrade the security system of Broadview and other homes in the network.

"So, to use your phrase, 'God's in His heaven, all's right with the world, right?'"

"It's actually Robert Browning."

"Whatever. So how's your colleague and former student doing?"

Nick let pass the sarcasm in Moy's voice. "She'll be relieved it's all behind her."

"Some things are better left forgotten," Moy said.

"I guess."

"By the way, we're going to make an official announcement in a couple weeks—press release, video, you name it—the whole nine yards."

Moy beamed at Nick as if he were Moses glimpsing the Promised Land. Nick nodded, thinking he would not spoil the moment by reminding him of the flashback issues that lay before them—the delusional seizures that had probably led to the killing of Eddie Zuchowsky and the death of one of Peter Habib's patients, William Zett, on a playground slide.

No free lunch in pharmaceuticals. No magic bullet—or very few that don't leave scars.

They had left Marina Bay at nine that Saturday morning, when the sea was like polished marble, and headed down the coast. A little before noon they passed through the canal and out into Buzzards Bay. They lunched at Woods Hole, then by two they headed deeper into the bay at Nick's request.

On the right they passed Naushon and Pasque Islands and some of the others in the Elizabeth chain. Short of Cuttyhunk, Moy asked Teddy to turn the boat around because he wanted to catch the tide and the headwinds.

As they swung around, Nick nodded toward a low blue hump on the western horizon. "Isn't that Homer's Island?"

"Yup," Moy said without even looking.

"You been out there recently?"

"Nope." Then Moy waved at Teddy to head back.

Teddy leaned on the throttle, and the boat roared back up the ferryboat lane toward the canal which would take them back home.

"You remember that guy I was telling you about—the one who got caught out there in the jellies?"

"Yes, Jordan Carr told me something about it. In fact, I saw the blood workup."

"Quite a coincidence."

"I guess. What's the name again?"

"Koryan. Jack Koryan."

Moy shrugged. "Sounds like a countertop. How's he doing?"

"Still comatose. It doesn't look good."

Moy nodded and raised his face to the sun and took a huge breath as if he were trying to drain the atmosphere. "Man oh man, it doesn't get much better than this."

"No, it doesn't," Nick said, thinking that maybe that was that about that.

But it wasn't.

36

Three weeks later it was the lead story. And René clicked up the volume as the Channel 8 anchor made the announcement:

"More good news in the fight against Alzheimer's disease. At its annual meeting of shareholders, GEM Neurobiological Technologies announced some early successes in its trial use of Memorine, the lab's revolutionary experimental drug for the treatment of various forms of dementia, including Alzheimer's disease."

The screen then showed a female reporter outside of Mass General Hospital. "Patients enrolled in GEM's phase three clinical trials of the Memorine compound were diagnosed with early or mild forms of Alzheimer's. And early reports have shown very promising results.

"Heading up the team of clinical physicians and researchers is Dr. Nicholas Mavros, neurologist at MGH."

They shifted to Nick at his desk. "It's very exciting to participate in this historic effort to develop a cure for Alzheimer's. Until now there's been no way to stop the decline in mental functions. And certainly nothing to reverse the disease's progress. It's still relatively early in the trials, but we're seeing cognitive improvement in nearly forty percent of our trial patients."

René could feel Nick's restraint. Successful trial results were not officially made until the study was complete and findings were published in a reputable journal. But, of course, this was Gavin Moy's ploy to start a Memorine fever.

Their faces strategically blocked, trial patients were shown doing puzzles, writing on pads, talking to nurses and aides. Many smiled and looked focused. There was tearful testimony from Christine Martinetti who told how her father was regaining his memory and coming back to his old self. "When we put him in the nursing home, he was confused and frightened. He got people mixed up. He couldn't recognize family members. He struggled to do simple tasks like tie his shoes. Now it's all beginning to come back."

The camera shifted to Louis sitting in a chair with one foot on a stool as he tied his shoes while chatting with an aide. He looked at the camera and waved with a big smile. And René felt a warm surge in her chest.

"He still has a way to go, but it's a miracle what's happening in him. A miracle."

"And a miracle it seems to be," the reporter continued. "We spoke to Mr. Martinetti briefly about the return of his memory."

The camera closed in on Louis. He looked wonderful wearing a blue polo shirt and sitting at a table with his hands folded, his face squared in confidence. "Yes, I do feel things coming back to me, especially from way back."

René's eyes filled as she watched. She could not help but see her father.

"So, you're remembering things that you had forgotten."

"Yes, and I'm feeling more . . ."

There was a painful pause as he tried to come up with the word. Hating dead air, the interviewer began to talk, "Well, that's wonderful—"

"Clearheaded. But sometimes the words take a while to come to me, but they do. Better than before." Louis smiled at the camera and gave a two-finger salute just as they cut him off.

The scene shifted back to the reporter. "Located in Walden, Massachusetts, GEM Tech plans to develop Memorine as an orally available pill."

On the screen were shots of the GEM complex, the camera panning the main building and surrounding complexes. "The president and CEO of GEM Tech is Dr. Gavin Moy." Moy's large, fleshy face filled the screen. "Dr. Moy, what do you see as your goals in these clinical trials?"

Moy adjusted his glasses. "Alzheimer's disease is the most common and deadly form of dementia affecting people over age sixty-five. Some five million Americans are afflicted, and it's the major reason why people are institutionalized in the United States. Left unchecked, there will be fifteen million cases in this country by 2025. And that's what we're trying to prevent here at GEM Tech. And every indication tells us that we're heading that way."

"So, when can we expect Memorine to become available?"

"Based on our great successes so far, we're expecting to complete trials in nine months, maybe sooner if the FDA fast-tracks our application. We're very hopeful."

The camera switched to Nick's video sequence of a blue brain heavily spotted with red blotches of plaque. As the video ran, the red began to recede and disappear. "What you're seeing are time-lapsed MRI images showing the actual reversal of the damage in an Alzheimer's patient's brain . . ."

René watched, thinking that Gavin Moy was brilliant and slick as oil. What he had done was turn a news announcement into a priceless promo for Memorine. And corporate protocol be damned because, no matter how premature the announcement, every prestigious journal in the world would want to publish the results, just as every neurologist would kill to get his or her name attached to the trials. And to potential investors the publicity was catnip. By tomorrow night GEM stocks would probably double again.

The camera closed in on the original patent framed and hanging on the wall of his office. "By the way," the reporter said, "how did you discover that Memorine was so beneficial to the treatment of Alzheimer's disease?"

Moy smiled. "Trade secret."

Nick appeared on-screen again. "What makes Memorine so revolutionary?" the reporter asked him.

"We think that Memorine prompts an immune-system response that destroys amyloid plaques, one of the hallmarks of Alzheimer's that contribute to brain cell degeneration. It also stimulates the regeneration of new cells in damaged areas."

Back to the reporter. "According to GEM researchers, patients tested with Memorine experienced significantly better results than participants in the placebo group in measures of thinking and reasoning, day-to-day functioning, and behavior.

"But the drug did not help every individual who took it. At least not as yet."

Back to Nick: "Some patients may take longer, depending on the stage of their diseases. It may be a genetic factor or a demographic one. That's part of what we'll try to determine in the trials. Also for whom it works best, et cetera."

"Any side effects?"

"That's part of what the trials will determine. Every drug including aspirin has side effects, some more measurable and adverse than others. But at the present time, there are no conclusive side effects to speak of."

The report concluded with a shot in front of GEM Tech's offices. "If approved by the FDA, all indications point to Memorine becoming one of the all-time blockbuster drugs with first-year U.S. sales of five billion dollars. Back to you, Liz."

The final shot was of Louis Martinetti snapping a salute at the camera.

This is what it's all about. Yes, René thought. *Yes.*

And for another one hundred and twenty-seven days Jack Koryan remained in a profound sleep.

PART
3

37

Four Months Later

"*Meds Gama.*"

Nurse Marcy Falco looked up from her chart to Constance Stone, who was tucking in the sheet at the bottom of the bed. "You say something?"

"N-no," Nurse Stone gasped, here eyes bulging like hen's eggs. "*He* did."

"Omigod!"

Jack Koryan was staring at Marcy—eyes locked in purposeful focus, not floating around in their sockets or staring off in different directions. And his mouth was moving.

He repeated those syllables.

Over the six months, Jack Koryan had muttered a lot of nonsense, but this was the first time Marcy saw signs of a breakthrough. "Hi, Jack. My name is Marcy." Then over her shoulder to Constance: "Get the others. They've gotta see this."

But Constance was frozen in place, her eyes transfixed on a man who for the better half of a year had been a body connected to drips and Texas Catheters.

"Constance! Snap out of it. He's trying to talk. Get the doctor."

"Uh." Constance said, but she was still unable to move.

"Meds Gama."

"Jack! Jack. What did you say?"

"He's waking up," Constance gasped, as if just realizing it.

"Jack, say it again," Marcy insisted.

And the same syllables scraped out.

"Something about his meds. 'Meds karma'?" Constance asked.

"Would you *please* get me some help? *Now.*" And Constance bolted out the door. Marcy took Jack's hand. "Jack? Jack, can you hear me?"

He looked at her, his eyes widening in fear.

"Good. Jack, my name is Marcy. I'm your nurse. I'm going to stay with you," she continued. In a strange environment with no frame of reverence, he could panic, maybe even relapse into the coma or, worse, go into cardiac arrest. "I'm not going to leave you. I know this is confusing to you, but you're going to be okay. But I want you to talk to me, Jack. Do you understand? I want you to talk to me."

His eyes closed again. Nothing.

Damn! She squeezed his hand: "Jack, open your eyes again. Tell me what you said. Jack, answer me."

Jack rolled his head and took a deep breath. But he did not open his eyes.

"Jack, squeeze my hand." She raised her voice. "Jack, squeeze my hand." And she felt his hand squeeze ever so slightly. "Good, Jack. Now open your eyes. I know you're in there."

Jack's eyes slitted open.

"Hi. Can you see me?" she asked, hoping even after six months that he would be another of her "witchcraft" wake-up cases. Instantly she shifted into her clinical mode, carefully scrutinizing him for neurological responses. "Look at me, Jack."

At that moment, several people burst into the room—two other nurses, another assistant, the nursing supervisor, and Dr. Clive Preston, director of the facility.

"His feet are moving," one nurse said, and she pulled up the bedding to reveal the tennis shoes.

Greendale was aggressive with its physical therapy of coma patients—regularly exercising their limbs and digits, fixing their hands and feet in splints to prevent drop foot and hands freezing into claws. The shoes were intended to keep his toes pointing upward. Despite all that, two weeks in bed was like losing a year of muscular life. And six months of disuse had reduced Jack to scarecrow proportions.

Marcy removed his shoes. "Jack, can you wiggle your toes for me?"

Nothing. His eyes closed again.

"Then just move your feet a little."

Still nothing.

"Jack. *Jack!* Listen: I want you to open your eyes for me. Please. Open your eyes."

Jack's eyelids fluttered slightly then opened partway. He rolled his head toward Marcy.

"Good. Can you hear me?" She lowered her face to his. His eyes were at half-mast, peering at her. But his tongue moved behind his teeth.

"Mmm."

"What's that?" She had to get him to track her with his eyes, to confirm that this wasn't a false alarm.

Jack's eyes widened and locked on to Marcy's. And in a barely audible voice scraping through a larynx unused for months, Jack said, "You have big teeth."

"I sure do." Marcy's white front teeth protruded slightly.

The paper skin around Jack's eyes crinkled ever so slightly, and the muscles of his mouth expanded into a faint smile. Remarkably he was processing memory, even judging with humor. This was incredible. Also the fact that he had articulated his words so well. "Great. Now, Jack, please look at me."

Jack's eyes opened with gluey effort, his pupils large, parallel, and fixed on her face.

"Good. My name is Marcy. I want you to tell me your name. Understand?"

He looked down at his arm with the IV attached to the drip bags and catheter running to a bag hanging on the bed's side and the wires connecting him to the monitors. In a breathy rasp, he said, "Where am I?"

"You're at Greendale Rehabilitation Home in Cabot, Massachusetts."

Jack rolled his head toward her, blinking against the lights at the circle of faces looking down at him. "Blurry."

Marcy's heart leapt up. Remarkably he was processing thought. "Yes, blurry. That's from the ointment we put in your eyes. But can you see me okay?"

"Mmmm."

"Can you tell me your name?"

"Jack Koryan."

"Great. That's great." Because Jack was her patient, the others let Marcy maintain a running monologue to keep Jack awake and to assess any neurological dysfunction. Nearly glowing with pride, she had him wiggle his toes, his fingers, blink one eye, then the next, tell her his full name, to repeat words after her. But what she dreaded telling him was that he had missed the last half year of his life.

"Hi, Jack, my name is Clive Preston. I'm the director here at Greendale."

Marcy nodded for Dr. Preston to continue. "You had a swimming accident and were unconscious for a while. You're getting better, but you have to stay awake and keep talking to us. Okay?"

"How long?"

Marcy felt her insides clutch. The shock could be traumatic, maybe even bring on a relapse.

"How long?" Preston asked.

Before he could answer, Marcy cut in. "Jack, the important thing is for you to talk to us." She took his hand. It wasn't supposed to happen this way. Patients never just snapped out of deep comas; they emerged gradually, over days—enough time to call in relatives and friends to be there when they woke up. Jack had emerged from a profound coma lasting over six months and was suddenly demanding answers.

His eyes scanned the faces. "How long?"

Marcy wished Beth or Vince were there. The shock could

send him into a panic. "Jack, I want to run a few tests on you. I want you to count to ten, okay?"

He closed his eyes for a long moment. But instead of mouthing numbers, he said, "Honesty is the best therapy."

The words sent a cold ripple through Marcy. Her slogan. What she had said to Beth—but *Jesus!* That was months ago! "Well, now, you've been listening."

"What's . . . date?"

Dr. Preston pushed forward. "Jack, I know how confusing this all is, but we'd like you to just answer a few simple questions, okay?"

Jack closed his eyes again and rocked his head slowly from side to side.

"Jack, don't go back to sleep," Marcy said. "Please open your eyes."

"Dreaming," he whispered.

"What's that?"

"Dream."

"No, you're not dreaming, Jack."

"Jack, tell me your name again."

"Jack Koryan." Then his eyes widened as something passed through him. "What's date?"

Marcy glanced at the others who looked like wax images of themselves hanging over the bed.

A groan rose from Jack's throat. "Whatsa date?" he repeated.

Dr. Preston shot a hard look to Marcy, then nodded. He was deferring to her and her baseline policy. To stall him until Beth and Vince arrived would not work. It could even cause him trauma. "Jack," Marcy finally said, "you had an accident swimming and you've been in a coma. You've been asleep. Do you understand me?"

And in slow deliberate breath he asked, "How . . . long?"

"Jack, can you tell me where you live? What town you live in."

"How long?"

To deflect the question would only make him more agitated. But to tell him the truth could be worse. *God, let me do the right thing,* Marcy prayed. "Six months."

Jack looked at her blankly as he processed her words.

"You had a swimming accident off a beach on Homer's Island—know where that is?"

Jack nodded.

"Good. Well, you blacked out in the water." And she told him how he was brought from a hospital on Cape Cod to MGH to here. She narrated the details slowly and deliberately for him to absorb, repeating herself, asking him if he was following her, trying not to get him too upset or excited. She left out the jellyfish. There was no point adding to the shock. When she finished, he looked down at his left hand. For a moment Marcy thought he was trying to make sense of the IV connection. But he was inspecting his fingers.

"Beth?"

"Beth is on her way in. We just called her. Now, I want you to do me a favor. I want you to wiggle your toes."

"Beth." He repeated her name again as if testing his memory.

"Yes, we just talked to her, and she's coming in to see you."

"Still my wife?"

"Now, Jack, I want you to wiggle your toes for me, okay?"

"Still my wife?"

Marcy knew what he was asking. "I'm sorry, Jack," she said, and shook her head. Gently she gently stroked his hand. Two months ago Beth moved to McAllen, Texas, to remarry.

Jack closed his eyes, and in a matter of moments his eyeballs began to flutter.

"Jack!" She had to keep him talking. "Jack." Suddenly his face appeared to reshape itself. The skin across his forehead smoothed out, blanking the frown and scowl lines at the corners of his eyes; his lips began to move as if he were having a private conversation within. Then he made a sweet smile. And before they knew it his mouth opened.

"He's saying something."

Marcy lowered her ear to his mouth. "I think he's singing."

And in fluttery breaths she heard: "You are my sunshine, my only sunshine."

But what sent a bolt of recognition through her was Jack's

voice: He was singing in the high, thin, honeyed pitch of a woman.

The next moment Jack let out a raspy sigh and sank into sleep, leaving the others wondering what the hell had just passed through their patient.

38

The president of the United States took René's hand. "Great job. We're very proud of you, all of you," he said. "You're making medical history."

"Thank you," said René, still trying to process whose grip she had just been in.

The president made his way down the line of nurses and other staffers of Broadview Nursing Home, being led by Carter Lutz and an entourage of VIPs, including Gavin Moy and other GEM Tech execs, officers from the Alzheimer's Association and other health care organizations. Also with them were Nick Mavros, Jordan Carr, and several other clinical physicians as well as security guards.

The president entered the dayroom and chatted with residents who sat in their chairs and had their photos taken. Some recognized him from television and were delighted. Other patients—those not receiving Memorine—were not sure who he was. One of the women announced that she saw Dwight Eisenhower once. The president complimented her on her memory.

As the president approached him, Louis Martinetti rose to

attention with a crisp salute. He was dressed in his uniform, now two sizes too small for him. Several people chuckled, although René felt a pang of embarrassment for Louis. He did not seem to be playacting but stood there in stern pride with his Purple Heart, Combat Infantryman Badge, parachutist badge, and other medals and looked straight ahead as the president stopped before him, saluted back, then walked on by, smiling and nodding.

Carter Lutz called attention to the gathering and thanked the president for visiting them. He praised the president for his track record of advocating for the elderly and supporting legislation aimed at early detection of Alzheimer's disease. Lutz also thanked him for keeping his campaign pledge and embracing "the Memorine Solution."

The president thanked Dr. Lutz and everybody associated with the Memorine study. "One doesn't have to look beyond this room to see miracles in action. I congratulate all of you and the good people at the other clinical sites and the researchers and scientists who have made this possible. Memorine represents a sea change in the treatment of Alzheimer's disease. I wish you continued success in bringing hope to AD victims and their caregivers everywhere."

A joyous applause filled the room.

The president was right, of course. The AD unit at Broadview was a changed place. In the months since René first entered the ward, the decibel level of the chatter had multiplied. And not just the white noise mumbling and gibberish "word salads," but talk—purposeful, coherent talk. Patients communicating with staffers, other patients, visitors, themselves. Likewise, the collective kinetic energy level had risen. A year ago, a time-lapse video of the ward would pass for a still life, with an occasional nurse or aide scurrying across the camera or a few patients shuffling by on foot or walker across the dayroom set. Today the ward could easily be mistaken for an active senior citizens center. Patients who months ago would sit and gape at nothing for hours on end were now mingling with others or following aides around asking if they could help.

The president concluded, "I need not remind you that a cure

for Alzheimer's disease would save over fifty billion dollars of American taxpayer money in health care."

More applause.

Of course, the president's endorsement was also a public relations bonanza for GEM Tech, whose stock value was soaring as the public anticipated the drug being brought to market soon. And everybody knew that, including Jordan Carr, who was beaming brightly at René from the other side of the room.

When the place settled down, Nick addressed the group, thanking the president for his support. "We are seeing extraordinary progress. And the evidence is in this room, as you have seen, Mr. President. But more work needs to be done, and that's what we're doing in collaboration with researchers at GEM Tech."

Some of the nurses and aides nodded in agreement. Jordan Carr, who was standing with the GEM Tech VIPs, shot a glance to Gavin Moy and the other suits, then turned toward Nick, where all lines of attention converged.

In guarded language, Nick praised the progress of the trials, then added a subtle warning: "But I must caution that the road to success is long and winding and fraught with unexpected turns, although I am very confident that as we continue to make our way, one measure at a time, we will succeed."

More applause.

The president and entourage left the room, and Louis snapped to attention with a salute.

Behind Nick's cautious wording were things that the president did not see: the growing number of recovering patients lapsing into regressive flashbacks. The weird infantilizing of their personalities. The sudden morphing into some past self that talked to people who weren't there while not recognizing those who were. The sometimes frightening lapses into traumatic flashbacks when the only recourse was to dope patients down until they had no more affect than when lost in the fog of dementia.

That's what the president did not see. Or the cameras.

39

They also did not see the Louis Martinetti beneath the chest of medals.

Every health care worker has patients she likes and patients she dislikes. Some are simply unpleasant to deal with—people ill-tempered, mean, or belligerent. At the other end are individuals in whose comfort and well-being one feels an extra emotional investment. For René, Louis Martinetti fell into that special category of favorites.

Yes, Louis reminded her of her own father. Each was a Korean War vet, each had lived an active mental life, and each had been a devoted family man and a great guy. It was those ordinary "great guy" characteristics that over the months were beginning to reemerge and endear Louis to René.

An hour after the president had left, René sat with Louis in the small parlor with a view of the woods. "So, what did you think of the president's visit?"

"Pretty good."

"I think he liked your saluting him like that."

Louis smiled proudly. He was still wearing his army shirt

with the decoration and his old dog tags around his neck. Even in his facial expression he resembled René's father. And in these quiet moments she was brought back to tender intimacies as a girl. Perhaps that was why Louis's progress was of special concern for her—as if, in Jordan Carr's metaphor, she were witnessing the defeat of the demon that had left her father a ragged husk of himself.

Louis's progress was remarkable on all fronts. Nick's imaging sequence over the last several months showed a reduction of protein deposits and neurofibrillary tangles in the frontal temporal lobe—the seat of language and logic functions—as well as the hippocampus, a region of the brain essential to maintaining memory. Likewise, the gray-matter tissue had increased in density. As his functional abilities for his basic activities of daily living (dressing, personal hygiene, feeding himself) approached baseline normal, Louis had become more self-directed and more socially deft than he had been, now mingling with other residents. He had also become more concerned with his appearance, no longer emerging from his room in mismatched tops and pants. And, of course, René always complimented him on how nice he looked, and Louis loved that.

With some effort he could read news headlines. He knew the days of the week and the schedule for his favorite TV shows. He recognized the people and faces in the photos in his room without labels. He'd sometimes talk to the guys in the Korea snapshots by name, often snapping them a salute.

Louis's Korean memories were important to him. As his daughter once said, in spite of the time spent in a POW camp—something he never talked about—the army had been the best time of Louis's life. He was young, feeling immortal, bonding with other guys, and engaged in an effort he deeply believed in. Ironically, Korea was part of why he had been committed to Broadview two years earlier. Louis had thrown a violent fit when he thought that his wife had hidden his Purple Heart. When he calmed down, she showed him that the medal was stored in the special war memorabilia chest in the bedroom where it had always been. An hour later he accused her of taking it once more. When she again showed him the medal, he claimed she was trying to trick him. She denied it, and he pushed over the chest and smashed a mirror. A few days later he pushed Mrs. Martinetti to the floor. It was then he had been admitted to Broadview. Luckily, he remembered nothing of the incident.

The definitive evidence of Louis's progress were the Mini-Mental State Exams, which consisted of different memory tests—lists of grocery or household items that the subject was asked to repeat in any order, word associations, et cetera. For healthy individuals from eighteen to twenty-four years of age with at least nine years of schooling, the median score is twenty-nine out of thirty. For healthy individuals seventy to seventy-nine years of age and older—Louis's range—the median is twenty-eight. When first tested last year, Louis scored sixteen, indicating moderate cognitive impairment. That morning of the president's visit he scored twenty-four. Also impressive was that Louis had developed learning strategies, clustering items according to semantic categories—food, tools, clothes, et cetera—a practice more sophisticated than simply remembering serial order. He also enjoyed taking the tests because he could measure how daily dosages of Memorine were bringing him back.

"You're doing a great job, Louis, and we're all proud of you."

He smiled with pleasure. "Coming along."

"I never told you this, but my father was in Korea."

Louis's eyes widened with interest. "What branch? I was in the 187th Airborne."

"Yes. I saw the photograph from Korea in your room. My father was in the navy, and spent most of his time on a ship called the USS *Maddox*."

"USS *Maddox*. That was the Seventh Fleet."

René was astounded. It was one of the few things she knew about the *Maddox*. "Yes, it was. How did you remember?"

"I remember lots of stuff about the war." He looked away for a moment as he began to gather some recollections. "The guy in that picture. He was my best friend, Fuzzy Swenson. You look like his sister."

René began to feel uncomfortable and thought it best to

change the subject. "Maybe you can tell me about where you grew up."

But he disregarded her. "He was our platoon sergeant. His real name was Sam but all the guys called him Fuzzy. Blond hair, cut real short," and he held up his forefinger and thumb, making a small gap. "Like peach fuzz. Why we called him Fuzzy. He was our gunner, real good kid from . . . Racine, Wisconsin. We used to josh him about being from the land of milk and beer."

"It's great that you can still remember him."

"Yeah, I remember him." Louis nodded then looked out the window.

He looked back at her for a puzzled moment and René felt herself brace against whatever was coming next. His eyes rounded as his glare intensified—and she could swear something passed through them. "Louis?"

His head snapped at the window again. "They said it would be a surgical drop."

"What's that?"

He looked back at her, and his eyes seemed slightly askew.

"Louis, are you okay?"

"Captain Vigna. He said we were going to fly a special mission one night when conditions were just right."

"Louis, I don't know what you're talking about."

He smiled furtively and cocked his head. "I don't know when it's gonna be, but it's going to be a drop behind enemy lines. Gonna take out those bastards for what they did."

"Louis, maybe we should change the subject."

But he did not respond—just stared off someplace and began to get jiggly.

She took his hand. "Come on, let's go to the dayroom." She started to pull, but he snapped his hand away.

Suddenly Louis's face began to spasm with emotions. He grimaced out the open window at the trees, looking as if he had spotted something terrible. He ducked down then shot up, and for a second he looked as if he were going to attack René. Instinctively she pushed back her chair and looked around for help. But in the next instant Louis gasped and pressed the heels of his hands against his brow, as if trying to force back some awful visions.

"They killed him, the bastards. They killed him in pieces."

"Louis, let's talk about something else. You're getting upset." She thought about calling an aide.

He glared at her through wild eyes. "They took care of him good. Oh, yeah. In the Red Tent, the dirty bastards. The Red Tent is where they did it all. Colonel Chop Chop and Blackhawk, the Russkie." Louis began to lick his lips and swallow hard against whatever was afflicting his recall. Suddenly his face contorted. "He was sitting right across from me." Then his voice changed. "Between my goddamn knees," he cried in dismay. "They put it between my knees. In my goddamn helmet. God!" His voice thinned out into a plea. *"Please don't. Please don't. I'll tell you whatever you want."* The next moment his face spasmed into something else, and he sat up straight in his chair, his voice hard. He was wavering in and out of some awful recollection. "Yeah, I was there. Not six feet away, and they kept cutting him—the bastard with the baby face and knife."

Louis's eyes dilated as he seemed to stare beyond René as he addressed her. "I couldn't make them stop, you got me? No matter what, I couldn't make them. And those two bastards stood in the corner telling him to keep going, keep cutting, no matter what I told him. I begged them." Louis's face crumbled, and he looked down at his lap and the sleeve of his shirt. "I got his blood on me."

René took his arm. "Louis, snap out of it. Everything's okay."

From the corridor a nurse and two male aides walking by saw the commotion and shot over to their table. René was on her feet trying to calm Louis, who was trying to get away, his face contorted with anguish. When Louis laid eyes on Malcolm, he started yelling and swinging his arms.

"Hey, Louis, what's the problem?" He tried to catch Louis's arms and keep him from breaking away.

"Louis, calm down. Everything's okay," the nurse said.

But it was clear Louis was beyond reasoning with, lost someplace far away. Malcolm managed to pin Louis's arms from behind and settle him in a chair.

Louis kept looking behind him. "Over there," he said to the aide.

"What's over there?" the aide said, looking at the trees outside.

Louis shook his head. His face was taut, his eyes squinting as if trying to get a clear focus.

"Come on, Louis," the nurse said. "You're upsetting all these people."

But Louis kept looking across the area, his eyes fixed on something else. "Louis, open up." René could see the nurse hold a pill to his mouth.

"They cut one side, then the other," he said to the aide. Then he looked down at his lap, seeing imaginary horror.

"Come on, open up."

Louis looked at the pill and water bottle in the nurse's hand and pushed her hand away. But she persisted. "You have to take this, Louis. It'll make you feel better."

He shot a look at René. "They're trying to brainwash me," he whispered. "It's what they do, they brainwash you."

"Don't be silly, Louis," the aide said. "Nobody's brainwashing you. Open up."

René could see the small yellow pill. Haldol. One of the antipsychotics the staff had been giving patients suffering flashbacks. But to Louis the pill represented something else. "Who, Louis?" René asked, disregarding the others. "Who's trying to brainwash you?"

"The NKPA," he whispered to her. "The fucking Commies. Take it and you're gone, kaput."

He struggled to get up again, still focused on his buddy dying and the blood on his hands and enemy gunners on the ridge. René took Louis's hand. "Louis, it's René. Look at me. Please look at me." Louis turned his face toward her. Tears were in his eyes. "Nobody's brainwashing you. Please believe me. Please take the pill."

He glared at her for a moment, then he opened his mouth to say something, and the nurse pressed a pill inside and put the bottle to his lips and squirted some water. Reflexively Louis swallowed as if drinking from a buddy's canteen. "He's got a kid sister. What're we going to tell her, huh? That they cut him up?"

Then something clicked inside of him, and his expression changed. "Gotta get them back," he said to René in a conspiratorial whisper. "I promised." The aides raised Louis to his feet and began to walk him to his room. "I gave him my word." And he tugged against the grip of the aide.

René's insides squeezed as she took one of Louis's hands, feeling as if she had betrayed him. Because in a few minutes he'd be back in the ward—in the moment, and that was not where he wanted to be.

"It's what they do. They brainwash you."

He wanted to be back with his buddies of the 187th Airborne, going on his "special" drop, avenging whatever they did to Fuzzy Swenson in the Red Tent.

As they approached the door, Louis looked at René, then over his shoulder. "I saw him and his buddy. I saw the bastards." His eyes were huge and blazing.

"Who, Louis? Who did you see?"

"The colonel."

"What colonel?"

"Chop Chop."

"Who's Chop Chop, Louis? Tell me."

"They were here."

"Who, Louis?"

But Louis didn't answer. He just nodded to himself as they hauled him to his room.

40

For a long time René sat in the parlor looking out the window at the rustling leaves of the trees. All was calm again, and outside the slanting sun sent shafts of dancing light into the woods. She could not stop hearing Louis in distress and seeing his face contort and his eyes blaze like coals in the wind.

And suddenly she was at the sink in her parents' kitchen doing the dinner dishes.

Her mother had passed away the year before, and he managed to function well without her. The visiting nurse was gone for the day, and her father was in the basement at his workshop, from which René had removed all the dangerous tools. In a matter of months, she would move him into a nursing home. Over the years, he had built model cars from kits and had become an expert. Nearly every night after dinner he'd go down, turn on his tape player, and while oldies filled the cellar, he'd sit on his stool and work away like some crazed Gepetto. As a girl she had helped him put together several models.

He would sometimes wear a jeweler's loupe for the fine detailing—fitting chrome trim and micro decals in place. He had even built a spray-paint station with sheets of plastic and glove holes. His handiwork was wonderful, and he was at his happiest when engaged in it. After twenty-five years, he had amassed an impressive collection of classic models, from Matchbox-size to over a foot long. And they sat on shelves arranged by size and years—all enameled in brilliant gloss colors and looking like jeweled artifacts from some pharaoh's tomb. René's favorite was a 1938 Packard, which looked like something Clark Gable would have driven. Her father's favorite was the 1952 Studebaker Commander, the car her parents drove after his return from Korea.

"Someday all these will be yours," he once said. "Imagine the yard sale."

It was a little after seven and the slanting rays of the sun lit up the western wall of the house. Suddenly René heard banging below. She shot to the cellar door. "Dad, you all right?" she yelled down.

No response.

"Dad, is everything okay?" She could see that the orange pools of sunlight coming from the window wells mixing with the fluorescent lamp of his bench. "Dad?"

Silence. Then a sharp metallic crashing sound.

René dashed down the cellar stairs, half-expecting to find him sprawled out under one of the tables or machines. Instead he was standing in the middle of the floor and hurling model cars at the wall, pieces ricocheting around the room. "Dad, what are you doing?"

But he paid her no attention. His eyes were wild and he muttered oaths as he pulled car after car off the shelves and flung them at the far wall.

"Dad, stop it. Stop it!"

But he didn't stop. He glanced wildly at René, then took a model fire engine and smashed it to the floor. And when it didn't break, he dropped to his knees and pummeled it with a hammer.

"Dad. Please. Don't," she pleaded.

But he disregarded her and tore another off the shelf and smashed it.

"Dad, I made those with you. We did those together. Please, stop. Please," she wailed.

He froze, the hammer still raised. He glowered at René, and for a hideous moment she thought he would come at her.

"Dad, it's me. René, your daughter."

"You're not my daughter. Where's my daughter? You're a . . . fake."

She moved closer to him and the overhead light. "Dad, it's me. René. I'm right here."

Then for an agonizing moment she watched his eyes soften as recollection registered in his poor beleaguered brain. He then let out a low groan as he surveyed the bright wreckage. The hammer slipped from his hand, and he began to cry. "I hate this," he said as she embraced him.

"I know, I know," she whispered. "I love you . . ."

"I hate this. I can feel the damn holes. I can feel them filling my head." His voice dissolved.

"Don't," she begged, as she felt her heart tear. "I love you, Dad. I love you."

And for a long moment they stood there silently embracing amongst the scatter of dimming light.

René could not bring back her father, nor could she have saved him from the slow and inevitable disintegration—this conclusion she had at last come to accept. But she would do anything to see Louis go home and resume his life with his mind again intact and his memories whole and good and not fraught with throwback traumas of the Red Tent.

41

Six months.

In the muddy light of his room Jack woke up again. The nurses had checked him at regular intervals, wiring his head to monitors to be certain he hadn't slipped back into a coma. He hadn't. He had made it to the other side with his mind and senses open to his surroundings. Green and orange beeps and blips and drips and broken blinds and gray predawn light seeping through like fog.

Six months.

Everybody was amazed and delighted that he was thinking so clearly, so logically, and communicating so well. Some kind of miracle, they had proclaimed.

But what difference did that make to him? Yesterday he was married and planning to retire from teaching to open a first-class restaurant with Vince Hammond—to give Carleton Center some gastronomic panache. And today it's next year, and he's divorced, bedridden, stripped of plans beyond his med schedule, and feeling like roadkill.

God! A coma had punched a hole in the fourth decade of his life.

Beth.

He missed Beth. He missed the way it was years ago. He missed their old life together. He wished they could heal the wounds and go back. While the monitors beeped like birds, he stared at the perforated ceiling.

Holes. So many holes.

And so many vague sensations—wicked ghostly images. Shadowy things doing bad, bad things. And holes . . .

Then he closed his eyes and pressed back into sleep.

42

Nick and René were in the small snack bar off the main lobby of Morningside when René heard the familiar high-compression growl out the window. It was Jordan Carr arriving for the eleven o'clock meeting that Nick had called. He had pulled in with a black Ferrari Maranello he had just purchased.

When he came in, Nick smiled and said, "Did the other one get dirty?"

"Very funny," Jordan said, and forced a smile.

But from the red blotching of his cheeks, he did not like the ribbing. Nor did he want to be reminded that his Italian sports car collection was growing, not from his practice, on which he had cut back, but from the trials. Gavin Moy had named him number-two point man.

Nick led them inside to the conference room. Although it was a regularly scheduled meeting for trial clinicians, Morningside administrators, and staffers, Nick had invited Peter Habib from Plymouth as well as two researchers from GEM Tech to review recent data—Kevin Maloney and a Hassan Vadali.

After some pleasantries, Nick got down to business. "The

good news is that test results are improving markedly in test residents." And he named several patients, including Louis Martinetti, who had shown higher scores on the Mini-Mentals as compared to scores of those patients receiving placebos. "Similar results have been recorded at other sites. Of course, we are very pleased, as the progress demonstrates the efficacy of Memorine."

A summary of the report that René had helped put together had been sent to everybody in the room.

"But what concerns me are the mounting reports of flashbacks," Nick continued. "We're seeing regressive behavior in a number of patients here and at other sites." Nick named several.

"I've had a few also," Peter Habib added. "One particularly troublesome case you may recall was that of William Zett several weeks back. According to his brother and sister-in-law, he got completely lost in a deep-past flashback, talking to kids from his childhood. He went down a slide backward and broke his neck. Nobody knows what was going on in his head, but, according to his brother and sister-in-law, before the accident he appeared frightened, traumatized, as if reliving some disturbing experience. And these are the kinds of things that concern me."

Nick nodded. "The problem is that almost none of these patients experienced flashback seizures before they were enrolled in the trials."

"How many patients have you seen with these so-called flashbacks?" Vadali asked.

The question was disingenuous because René knew that the number was headlined in the report. "About thirty percent. And that could be a problem for a fast-track FDA approval."

It was the first time Nick had raised this warning. Perhaps they had seen it coming, because the GEM Tech representatives looked unfazed.

"And how are these so-called flashbacks characterized?" Maloney asked. "You seem to view these as discrete neuropsychological phenomena."

Nick deferred the question to René, who could feel the pressure from Maloney's expression. "Well, in their reports nurses describe them as elaborate delusional episodes in which residents manifest regressive behavior."

"Such as?"

"Such as talking like children, singing nursery rhymes and Christmas carols, spending hours playing with toys or flipping through children's books. They appear to be locked in some past recollections."

Maloney nodded. "And you think these delusions are the result of Memorine."

Either he was playing dumb or he had not read the regular reports René had forwarded to GEM's R&D people. Or they never took them seriously. "I'm saying that there are indications of a patterned correlation," she said.

"I'm also seeing a frequency correlation between the flashbacks and increased neurological repair in MRIs," Habib added. "It's rudimentary, but there might be something to it, which means an added diagnostic tool for screening."

"That sounds like yes," Vadali said.

"Then yes—they're the result of Memorine," Habib said.

"And what do you think, Dr. Mavros?" Vidali asked.

"I'm being more open-minded, although the correlation is troublesome."

"It's more than troublesome," Habib said. "I frankly think the drug is flawed, and we have to address that."

Flawed. The word fluttered in the air like a bat.

"I don't believe that for a moment," Maloney said. "But even if that were true, these anomalies are more than compensated for by the patients' extraordinary progress in cognition and daily functionality."

Vadali and others in the room nodded in agreement.

René felt a battle line cut across the table like a seismic fault: GEM Tech reps and home administrators on one side; she, Peter Habib, one nurse, and Nick on the other. Jordan Carr had thus far not responded.

"The problem is that when patients get stuck in past experiences and become disruptive, they have to be medicated with antiseizures, antipsychotics, and sedatives that impede their mental recovery." René looked toward the unit nurse, who concurred.

"How so?" Maloney asked.

"They're doped down."

"Our strategy here and at other sites," Nick said, "is to try to come up with just the right dosages and combination of agents."

Maloney kept his eyes on René, but she disregarded their heat. "My suggestion is that instead of simply addressing the events with antipsychotics and other meds, it might make sense to determine the nature of the connection, because I believe these flashback seizures are adverse reactions to the use of Memorine."

Jordan cleared his voice. "If I may, and with all due respect, Peter, in patients with moderate-to-severe dementia, delusions that are related to post-traumatic stress disorders are not uncommon. And that's what I believe we're seeing here, since all these so-called flashback victims are patients within that population. Furthermore, according to nurses' reports, since Mr. Martinetti was first treated with antipsychotic drugs he hasn't had any sustained flashbacks."

"That's not exactly true," René said. "He was lost in a closed loop, reexperiencing some horrible episode when he was a POW."

An uneasy silence filled the room as she described the earlier episode.

René continued: "What bothers me is that according to his wife and daughter, Louis never suffered PTSD flashbacks before, and now he's getting trapped in them." She didn't need to remind them that this flew in the face of the public perception of Memorine as a miracle cure and Louis as poster boy for GEM's half-billion-dollar marketing campaign.

"I'm seeing the same thing," Peter Habib said. "Patients getting caught in some dark past-time traumas. And nothing in their medical history shows they had suffered PTSD disorders."

"But nothing in the reports in the earlier phases point to any such efficacy problem," Maloney said. "So I think Dr. Carr is correct. But that's not to say we shouldn't continue monitoring patients' behavior problems, et cetera." And he offered a conciliatory smile.

"Well, that's our intention." And Nick outlined a plan to measure cognitive progress while trying to determine a medical, demographic, or even genetic cause to any flashback seizures.

As he and the others continued, René receded and took notes. She had already created for herself a reputation as some self-appointed Ralph Nader watchdog. Besides, Nick was in charge and laying out a sensible strategy.

As she sat there, she tried to remind herself that everybody in this room—GEM Tech reps, nurses, physicians—were decent, well-intentioned professionals dedicated to the relief of patients suffering from dementia. Yet she could not help thinking that corporate agendas were at least as important as medicine—that decisions made in this room had as much to do the stock portfolios of GEM Tech investors as with science.

When the meeting was over, Jordan Carr pulled her aside. "I think we've mapped out a good strategy. And maybe to an extent you're right."

"I think it makes sense."

"And if there's something to these episodes, we'll deal with them." And he patted her on the shoulder.

She nodded.

He lowered his glasses. "So how come you don't seem pleased?"

"Because what I felt in there was just more pressure to downplay problems."

"What pressure? What are you talking about?"

She opened her briefcase and pulled out a set of pearl earrings, two complimentary tickets to a Celtics game, more tickets to Boston Symphony Orchestra and Boston Pops concerts, and a year's membership to Kingsbury Club, an upscale fitness center on the South shore. "And I'm not alone. Nurses, aides, and other home staffers are being flooded with GEM gifts including trips to Bermuda and Jamaica."

"Complimentary gestures for working on the trials."

"You mean standard practice in the industry."

"In any industry, and nothing's wrong with that." Then he picked up the BSO tickets. "Not exactly payola."

"No, but this is," and she held up a letter. "From a Tanner Walker, chief financial officer at GEM—an offer of stock options." She did not cite the specifics, but the letter, which had just arrived, said that in recognition of her services to the company and to victims of Alzheimer's disease she was being granted options to purchase five thousand shares in GEM Tech for five dollars each. And that she had three years to exercise her option.

"Well, congratulations."

"Congratulations?"

"Yes, you could be a wealthy woman in a few years."

He was right. If Memorine was approved by the FDA, her own Memorine-driven stocks would in a year wipe out all her loans and still leave her with more money than she had ever dreamed of having. But that bothered her. For as long as she could remember, René had viewed health care workers, especially physicians, as good and trustworthy by nature. But while working on these trials she was witnessing bold-faced avarice—like that growing collection of Ferraris out the window.

As if picking up her thoughts, Carr said, "Look, don't get me wrong. I'm not like that Michael Douglas character from *Wall Street*—you know, 'Greed is good.' But anyone who says they're not interested in money is a liar." Then he added, "And nothing wrong with doing well by doing good."

"Jordan, this isn't an incentive, it's bribery."

"Bribery? That's ridiculous."

"Then tell me what I'm missing. First they intimidate us to silence about the Zuchowsky murder. Now they're buying us off to underplay the flashbacks."

"Nobody is buying anybody off. All that's simply encouragement to do your best work—what you call employee incentives."

"But I'm not an employee of GEM." And she wanted to add that neither was he, or the fact that, under the guise of "incentives," drug companies lined the pockets of doctors, showering them with fancy gifts to spouses and free trips to flossy ski slopes and tropical resorts in order to get them to write prescriptions for their products. And how nobody protested. Nobody raised the conflict-of-interest flag. And the reason was that drug companies had bottomless coffers to buy the best legal defense teams.

"This is about making sure we're all insiders so we put the best possible light on the trials without appearing to cross the ethics line."

"Nobody is asking anybody to cross the ethics line. And just keep in mind that if it weren't for pharmaceutical companies, you wouldn't have a job." Then, as if an afterthought: "Or me, for that matter."

"True, but it just doesn't feel right."

"Well, René, if you're not comfortable with the stock options, then don't exercise them." And before he walked away, he added, "This is a fast-moving train coming down the tracks, and jumping in front won't stop it."

She watched him walk away, thinking that he seemed more interested in his silver bullet outside than Louis Martinetti's private war with Colonel Chop Chop.

43

Three days after he woke up, Jack was moved to a rehab floor referred to as the SNIF unit—shorthand for "skilled nursing facility."

Here Marcy and a therapist wrapped his legs in Ace bandages to prevent his blood from pooling and laid him on a tilt table in preparation for sitting him up. Something about "orthostatic hypotension" and his "autonomic nervous system" adjusting to being upright again. He heard the words but didn't bother to process the explanations.

They also monitored his blood pressure and heart rate, raising him to a slant of sixty-five degrees, moving him ten degrees at a time for five-minute increments. It took an hour to do this and he felt lightheaded. "If you don't use it, you forget how to use it," the therapist explained. "Being upright increases the vascular resistance on your autonomic nervous system. We don't want your blood pressure to drop suddenly."

Jack nodded. Whatever, he just knew that it felt good to be up, since some part of his mind sensed how long he had been on his back.

So much time had passed, yet he felt the heft of elusive

memory just beneath the membrane of awareness—memory that manifested itself in incoherent flashes.

As they had since he woke up, the nurses and staff kept him chatting so that his voice grew stronger and the words came more easily. But it was like starting over, having to relearn how to do things that previously were all but involuntary activities.

In spite of the constant and aggressive physical therapy he had undergone while comatose, he had lost seventy-five percent of his muscle strength. But with the aggressive physical rehab program laid out for him, the therapist said that chances were good that he would be able to walk again in a month, probably with the assistance of a cane.

Since Jack had been fed through a gastric tube for so long, they were afraid that if he ate solids right away he might inhale some and end up in the hospital again. So he had been put on thickened liquids for two days, after which he graduated to mashed foods. It was like being a baby again, he said to Marcy.

In the afternoon of his third day awake, Marcy and the therapist sat Jack in a wheelchair and brought him to an office to meet the neurologist, a tall thin woman with a sharp bird face and reddish brown hair pulled back in a bun. She introduced herself as Dr. Vivian Heller. "Welcome back. How are you feeling?"

Jack's left foot ached, his vision was still slightly blurry, and a beetle was crawling through his brain. "Fine."

"I know how difficult this is, so confusing and all, but you're going to go on the record books for coma recoveries."

"Lucky me."

"Well, you are lucky, since only a small percentage of long-term coma patients ever wake up, and so alert. It's wonderful."

He nodded.

Then she opened her folder. "If you don't mind, I'd like to check your neurological recovery—memory and such. Okay?"

"Okay."

"Good. I'm going to ask you some questions and you answer them as best you can. Do you know what state we're in?"

"Massachusetts."

"What country?"

"United States."

"Good. And who is the president of the United States?"

"George W. Bush."

"Who was the previous president?"

"Bill Clinton."

"Very good. And where were you born?"

"Worcester, Massachusetts."

"What's the capital of England?"

"Fish."

"Fish?"

He closed his eyes. "I smell fish. . . . Fishy air."

"You mean the sea." The doctor tested the air. The window was open and a breeze could be felt. "I don't smell it, although we're only a few miles inland. So you think you smell the ocean."

"More like in my head." He closed his eyes again. "And something else . . . like a swimming pool . . . chlorine."

The doctor made some notes. "The police report says you were on Homer's Island. Do you recall what you were doing when you got caught in the jellyfish? Why you were out there?"

"Summer cottage my family used to rent."

"When you were young."

"Mmmm." The beetle in his brain split in two and began to nibble twin paths into the gray matter.

"I see. But you were out there alone, I understand."

"Anniversary of . . ."

The doctor waited. "Of?"

"My mother's death. She got lost in the storm a long time ago."

"I see. If you don't mind me asking, how long ago? How old were you when she got lost?"

"Two."

"Two? But didn't you say your parents used to rent the place every summer when you were a kid?"

"My father died in a plane crash shortly after I was born. After my mother died, I was brought up by my aunt and uncle." He wasn't sure if the doctor was asking for real information or just trying to jump-start his memory.

"And what were their names?"

"Nancy and Kirk."

"And what were your parents' names?"

"Rose and Leo."

"What kind of work did your father do?"

"He worked in a foundry."

"Did your mother work?"

"Yes, she was a biochemist."

Heller's eyebrow shot up. "Really. How interesting, and for a woman back then."

What she was really wondering, he thought, was how a scientist could end up with a foundry worker. "It was an arranged marriage—what immigrants did back then."

"I must say that your long-term memory retrieval seems excellent. What I'd like to do next is test your visual memory. If you get tired or confused or want to stop, please say so."

"Okay." The beetles had doubled and redoubled again and were humming behind his eyes in packs.

She pulled out a small stack of eight-by-ten cards and laid them facedown on the tray table. "What we'll do first is I'll show you a series of cartoons one at a time. You'll look at each one for five seconds, then I'll cover it and ask you questions about what you saw. Got that?"

"Got it."

"Good." She turned over the first and held it up—a colorful drawing of a house with children out front, toys on the lawn, a cat under a bush, birds on the roof. After five seconds, she turned the card facedown. "How many children are playing in the yard?"

"Two."

"How many birds are sitting on the house?"

"Five."

"On which side of the house, left or right, is the chimney?"

"Right."

"What color is the house?"

"Blue."

"How many windows are on the front of the house?"

"Five."

"What number is the house?"

"Three seventy-nine."

"How many bushes are in front of the house?"

"Two."

"True or false: There is a hydrant in front of the house."

"False."

The doctor continued reading all ten questions, and when she finished recording Jack's answers she peered over her glasses at Jack. "Very good. You got them all right. Now let's try the next one."

The next drawing was more intricate with details—a pasture scene with cows, horses, and sheep in a field, with a farmhouse and barn in the background. The doctor held up the card and then laid it down and asked ten more questions. And Jack responded. When he was finished, Dr. Heller said, "You're doing a great job, Jack." She opened another folder. "Okay, this time I'm going to show you a series of letters for five seconds, then I want you to repeat them from memory."

Jack nodded. The beetle-humming in his head intensified, as if someone had cranked up the volume. She held up the first card for five seconds then dropped it.

"GU."

And in the time allotted, he did the same with each sequence that followed.

"RXW."

"XIURZ."

"APXOZNT."

"QMENRBTJH."

"EIDYTAWXIZBJM."

When he finished the last sequence, something flitted across the Easter Island blankness of Dr. Heller's face.

"How did we do?" Jack asked.

The doctor looked up at Jack with a queer expression and shook her head to say she would hold off on commentary. "Okay, this time I'm going to hold up cards with a series of

words for five seconds and I'd like you to try to recall as many
of the words from the list, and the order is not important. Only
as many words as you can recall."

The first card was short: CANDY, CHOCOLATE, CAKE, TASTE,
SWEET.

After five seconds, Jack repeated the words.

The next sequence followed: NAP, SLUMBER, PILLOW,
DROWSY, REST, WAKE, DOZE, BED.

And the next: DOG, FUR, BARK, FLUFFY, TAIL, LICK, JUMP,
PAWS, LEASH.

And the next: BEACH, SAND, OCEAN, CRAB, WAVES, SHELLS,
SUN, SALT, BOAT, FISH.

Jack answered, but the humming in his head was making his
teeth ache.

KNIFE, CUT, POINT, HAMMER, STEEL.

The doctor stopped. "Jack, are you all right?"

He shook his head.

"Maybe we can finish later."

Dissociated images were swimming in his head like litter in
a muddy whirlpool. And the buzz had produced a material
pressure. "Sorry," he whispered.

"Nothing to be sorry about. Are you feeling faint or dizzy?
Or disoriented?"

He rocked his head slightly. "Tired."

"Fine. We can continue tomorrow, but you should know that
you did amazingly well, Jack. The average adult letter span is
seven, with a deviation of plus or minus two. You did a span recall of eleven. I don't know what to say, but your short-term recall is off the charts."

The beetles had bored their way out of the sac inside his forehead and were making their way toward the rear of his brainpan. He wanted the doctor to leave. He wanted to be left alone.
He wanted to close his eyes and fall into a long, deep sleep.

"I'll let you rest," Dr. Heller said. She got up and began to
pack her papers into her briefcase. "If you don't mind, I have
one more thing I'd like to ask you. No, it's not a test."

Jack looked up at her through pulsing slits. "Sure, but how
about some Tylenol when I'm done?"

"We can do that right now," she said, and produced a two-pack from her smock pocket and placed them in his mouth and held up a cup of water. "If you don't mind me asking, what's the ethnicity of Koryan?"

"Armenian."

Another test question. He was certain that during the course of his convalescence the staff would be tossing him offhand little bio queries to be certain his hard drive hadn't crashed.

"Do you speak it?"

"No."

"Did you ever?"

His aunt and uncle had spoken only English with him, even though on occasion they conversed with each other in Armenian. "No."

"Well, would you recognize it if you heard it?"

"Yeah, I guess." The only place he had heard it spoken was in grocery stores in Watertown, the Little Armenia of the East Coast.

She gave him a strange look, then she pulled out of her briefcase a small tape recorder. "I'd like you to hear this," she said, and she moved it close to his head and flicked it on.

There was electronic hush like the open line of a telephone, some indistinct background noise, the muffle of people talking softly in the background, the distant sound of a jet plane. The sound of breathing. The soft beeps from the monitors. Then a voice that for a split instant registered in the warm core of his soul. *"Ahmahn seerem anoosheeg."* A high, feathery, fluttery voice—a woman's, as if speaking to him through a distant fan.

The next moment Jack felt a jolt of recognition. It was his own voice.

The tape continued as he looked helplessly at Dr. Heller, whose face seemed to dislodge itself from her white smock and dissolve in the soupy sensations in his brain. The margins of his vision became dark as everything began to fracture and sparkle—like viewing the room through a shattered windshield.

Suddenly the beetles hit a trip wire, setting off a wild gyroscope that set Jack into a spin as if his wheelchair had turned into the Tilt-a-Whirl at Canobie Lake Park, whipping him around into a centrifugal blur, sounds muffling and breaking up ... his name ... someone calling his name ... a female voice, the doctor ... Dr. Heller, but he couldn't locate her.

"Room three nineteen ... having a seizure ... Diazepam and Dilantin ... hurry ..."

He felt his body shake as if he were being prodded with an electric rod, cold, wincing ripples shooting across his brainpan.

"Get him flat before he hurts himself."

Lifted. He was being lifted.

And from someplace outside of his body, someplace above the ceiling, he watched them lay him on the slick sheets, the tendons of his legs stretching painfully flat on the bed like a long, bent child. He heard himself making gasping sounds. His eyes snapped open, and for a second he froze, his eyes huge and gaping at Marcy in nameless horror. Then his body spasmed and a scream rose out of his chest.

"Jack. Calm down. Everything's okay. Just relax."

He heard himself whimpering as awareness closed in on itself and warm hands cupped his little fist, rubbing open the tight ball of sad, small fingers.

Ah mahn seerem.

And the moment before the world pulled itself into a pinpoint and blew itself out, Jack felt a small flutter in his throat.

"Maideek."

44

"**H**e had another flashback."

René had arrived at Broadview a little before noon when Nick met her in the lobby. As he led her to the locked unit, he explained how it had happened during a visit Louis had with his wife and daughter. "They were having a nice time when Louis began flipping out about the Red Tent and Fuzzy somebody. I guess it was pretty bad, especially for the wife."

"What did the nurses do?"

"Gave him a shot of Diazepam."

They almost never had to resort to needle sedatives in the homes.

"Except for the bad one," Nick continued, "his daughter says she prefers the hallucinations to his fading away. A few flashback seizures she could live with."

"What about Mrs. Martinetti?"

"I suppose she'll have to adjust. It's better than losing him completely."

"Except he's resisting taking the other meds that have helped reduce the number and intensity of flashbacks."

They arrived at the locked unit, where Nick tapped them in.

"What bothers me," René said, "is what happens if Louis gets stuck in a flashback and can't come out, or doesn't want to."

Nick nodded grimly. "That would be a problem. But that's not why I called you. Have you seen the recent patient census?"

"No."

Nick walked her to a small sitting room down the hall from the Activities Center. "It's another thing the president didn't see the other day." He opened the door.

There were three residents sitting in wheelchairs before a television set playing on low volume. Two of them René knew—women in their eighties who were in advanced stages of dementia. The third woman René did not at first recognize. She moved closer, and for a protracted moment fixed herself on the woman's face. Then recognition hit René like a fist.

Clara Devine.

Over the six months at McLean's Hospital her body had atrophied to the point where she was bound to a wheelchair. She did not look up when René and Nick entered, as did the other women. Instead, she stared blankly at the television, her eyes clotted with fog.

"They brought her back two days ago," Nick explained. "McLean's decided that she was no longer a danger to others or herself."

That was evident, for Clara looked like a pathetic effigy of the once-feisty woman who had eavesdropped on the nursing staff and tapped her way out of the unit. "My God," René whispered.

"Of course, she was taken off Memorine right after the murder. Then about two months later the plaque had begun to return."

The aide held a cup of water with a straw to Clara's lips, talking softly to her. But Clara didn't respond. She was clearly incapable of speech and the ability to feed herself. Her skin hung on her frame like a too-loose seat cover. From her appearance, she didn't appear to have much time to go before she was bedridden. Then it would be a matter of weeks before she'd forget how to eat or before her heart or kidneys failed or her lungs filled with fluid.

"Her sister had asked that the staff not take any extraordinary measures."

Clara's reversal was kept quiet. But there would be no legal repercussions since in the fine print of the consent forms was a clause exonerating the clinical team, researchers, home and pharmaceutical company, et al., from the possible return of the disease. Clara Devine was the only patient to have been withdrawn. And since she had been removed from Memorine, her existence was simply a brief countdown to her death.

They left the room, and Nick walked René to the door. "They did an MRI on her before they sent her back," Nick said. "The plaque's all back. She's a mess."

"Oh, no!"

"That's the bitch of it: Once a subject is on the stuff we can't withdraw them or the dementia returns."

"Which means that if the flashbacks become problematic, taking them off Memorine isn't an option."

"Not without renewed deterioration."

"But nearly everything we use to combat the seizures only dulls them."

"The lesser of two evils. But I do have some good news," Nick said. "Jack Koryan woke up."

Jack Koryan.

When René left, Nick sat alone in his office and from his window watched René cross the parking lot. She looked so lovely as she made her way. A beautiful and bright young woman. He could still hear her gasp of delight at the news, tears of joy filling her eyes.

His eyes fell to a copy of the report of Dr. Heller's interview with Jack Koryan. He fingered open some of the pages that held Jack's answers to standard questions that determined his basic cognitive functionality: Where were you born? Where did you go to school? Name the president of the United States. What state is this? What is your mother's maiden name?

It was that last one that fixed his attention.

What is your mother's maiden name?

And from the opaque, still water well of past time, it rose up like a phosphorescent bubble expanding all the way until it broke the surface with a blink.

What were the chances—maybe one in a million?

Or maybe not.

He watched René pull out of the lot. In a couple of days she would visit Jack Koryan, driven by all the best sentiments—photographic positives of what would drive him.

45

"I remember you," Jack said. "Weren't we once husband and wife?"

Beth nodded. "I'm sorry, Jack," she said with a choke. "I waited and waited, but you didn't wake up and . . ."

"Nothing to be sorry about. You didn't know." He patted her hand. "I'm just glad you didn't have them pull the plug." He could hear the false brightness in his voice.

"They said they didn't think you'd ever recover."

"Forget it. I would have done the same thing." That wasn't true, but what the hell difference did it make? He remembered their marriage was headed for the shoals anyway. The coma had spared him all the anguish.

Beth wiped her eyes with a wad of tissues.

"You're still the best-looking woman I've seen in six months."

"Very funny," she said, half laughing and half crying.

Jack stroked her hair lightly, and his mind flooded with memories. Although he had been told of all the time that had passed, it still seemed like just the other day he had last seen Beth, and overnight she had gotten divorced and remarried.

But Beth looked older: Her face was fuller than he recalled.

She still looked good, dressed handsomely in smart gray slacks and black blazer, a pearl necklace lighting up her neck. He recalled none of the outfit and tried to repress the thought of her posing for her new husband as she would with him in the dressing rooms of Saks or Potpourri or their bedroom. The diamond on her finger was the size of a small olive. But on her other hand she wore an emerald ring he had given her for Valentine's Day, 1998—presented over dinner at Aujourd'hui at the Four Seasons Hotel. In an arrangement with the maître d' it was delivered as her dessert under a silver dome. He remembered speculating on his reaction had the man swapped the ring for a wedge of cheesecake.

Five days ago Nurse Marcy Falco had telephoned Beth in Texas with the good news. She arrived last night. For the reunion Falco and the therapist sat Jack in a wheelchair with a new pair of New Balance running shoes.

"How are the feet?"

"Okay, but they're going back to school."

Jack had been scheduled for intensive physical therapy, which he welcomed, since he couldn't believe how weak he was. According to Marcy, he weighed 127 pounds—a loss of a quarter of his body weight. Yet, just last week he had benchpressed ten reps of 175 pounds at the gym with Vince. Just last week—six months ago.

"So, who's the lucky guy?"

"His name is George King. He's a great guy, and I know you'd like him."

"I'm sure," he said, and tasted acid. It was impossible to get his mind around the fact that what seemed so fresh—his marriage to Beth, who for seven years had been a fundamental condition of his being—had been cleanly snipped away. He felt like some sci-fi character who takes a star-drive trip to the next solar system only to return a few weeks later to an earth that had aged by fifty years. Suddenly it was the future.

"I just wish I hadn't let you go alone," she whimpered. Then in a sudden gush: "Why the hell did you have to take a damn swim in the dark . . . and all those jellyfish around? Huh? What was the point?"

"It wasn't dark, and the water was warm, and I didn't see the jellyfish until I got out to the rock. And my cell phone was in my pants." He smiled, but she did not smile back. A prickly silence fell between them. He had gone alone as a private thing—to connect to a lost artifact of himself—something Beth couldn't understand. "I barely remember what happened." Dark water. Swimming like hell. Stroboscopic flashes of lightning. Aunt Nancy.

Don't rub. Don't rub.

She was standing on the beach frantically waving me in. Then she disappeared. Then she was back. Or someone else. Last-ditch hallucinations before the curtain dropped.

"All I remember was swimming to shore. Next, I'm in this bed." He pulled up his sleeves with his fingers. Faint white scars striped his arm.

"You can barely see them. And they'll fade."

"Not that." He raised his arms. "They look like starched swan necks."

"In six months you'll be Popeye again."

"Until then, Olive Oyl in drag."

She smiled. "At least you haven't lost your sense of humor."

"Speaking of which, who's paying for all this?"

"It's all taken care of," Beth said and explained that when Jack went into the coma she petitioned the court to be his guardian and promptly hired a Medicaid attorney who devised complicated strategies to preserve some assets and convert others to defray the cost of his hospitalization and nursing care. When Beth sold the house, she had put away half in a trust fund, which would co-pay with Medicaid for continued care, the excess of which would be available to him were he to wake up.

"Vince says he's going to help find a place for you. And when you're ready to leave, I'll come back and help you settle in. So don't worry about that. You're going to have plenty of support."

Jack nodded. But she had her own life, and once she left he didn't expect to see her again.

Beth checked her watch. "I've got to go." The nurses had

given them only a few minutes, and his next PT session would begin shortly.

"You can come and visit us. Really. We've got plenty of room. I wish you would when . . . you know . . . you're able to. It's only five hours by plane . . . really." She made a helpless gesture with her hands to apologize for crying. "I'm sorry."

Jack nodded and felt his throat thicken. "Have a nice life," he whispered.

"Don't be so dramatic," she snapped. "This *isn't* good-bye."

"'Course not." In the familiar cast of her eyes, Jack could see that Beth had decided that seeing him again would only make matters worse. And she was right.

She got up and put her arms gently around him. As best he could, he raised his arms around her shoulders, and he closed his eyes for an infinite moment. The aroma of White Linen filled his head as a hundred images flickered in his mind.

"Get well soon," she said, and broke their hold. "Vince will be by tomorrow."

She started to leave, then stopped. "By the way, does the name Mookie mean anything to you?"

"Who?"

"Mookie?"

"They got you doing memory tests on me, too?" He'd had three already, a fourth later today or tomorrow. *Mookie*. The name was like a small node sending up microwaves of recognition, but he couldn't catch them. "I don't know."

"It's not important." She started toward the door again. "Oh, I almost forgot: You're famous." And she pulled out of her bag a newspaper clipping and laid it on his chest. She hesitated again.

"Go! You're going to miss your plane."

She nodded and left.

And Jack watched her pass through the door and listened to her heels against the tile receding down the hall, and for a long moment he stared at the space that she had occupied—a void, a negative space sucking at his soul—thinking from his perch of grief that his old life was over.

The article was from yesterday's *Boston Globe*.

JELLYFISH COMA VICTIM RECOVERS AFTER SIX MONTHS
A 33-year-old Carleton man who had spent nearly two hundred days in a "persistent vegetative state" recently regained consciousness at the Greendale Rehabilitation Center in Cabot, Mass.

The case has been described as "absolutely extraordinary." A former English teacher from Carleton Preparatory Academy, Jack Koryan slipped into a coma after nearly drowning six months ago in Buck's Cove on Homer's Island off the Massachusetts coast, where he was stung by rare and toxic jellyfish. According to experts, the tropical creatures were apparently attracted to the unusually warm coastal waters at that time. . . . Miraculously, Koryan survived the attack and has spent most of the last year in the Greendale nursing home, unresponsive to all contact in spite of the constant stimulation efforts from the nursing staff.

Specialists comment that most patients spend only two to four weeks in a true coma. Contrary to expectations, Koryan is not cognitively impaired. In fact, his mental abilities are "extraordinary," according to his doctors. . . .

Mookie. The word was like a deep itch that stayed with him for the rest of the afternoon.

46

All he gave them was his name, rank, and serial number. That's all he was supposed to give them. Name, rank, and serial number . . . Louis Martinetti. Corporal. US71463961.

And in the snap of a salute, Louis was back in the Red Tent—as the older POWs called it because that was your color when they got through with you. Red. As in bloody-pulp red.

The Red Tent. And Louis was going through it all over again.

He didn't know why or how, because that was not where he wanted to be, but on the mission that Captain Mike Vigna had promised him. The *special*. Operation Buster. Instead he ended up again in the Red Tent. And by now he had lost count—not that it mattered—because it was like a closed loop—a Möbius strip of horror.

Louis was scared—so scared his bowels let loose. So scared that he wished they'd just shoot him in the brain and get it over with. He knew shit, but that wouldn't stop them from what passed for sports with these godless Commie savages.

He remembered from the last time—from all the last times:

no needles, no pliers, no electric prods that had been rumored. And not just him.

It was a large tent, and bound by arms and legs to a wooden armchair in the middle of the dirt floor was Fuzzy Swenson, stripped to his waist. His face was a mess of bruises, and thick strings of blood dripped to his lap from his mouth and nose. His hand kept twitching against the ropes as if trying to wipe himself. When he recognized Louis, Fuzzy moaned and vaguely nodded. He tried to say something, but one of the soldiers shouted him down.

There were five of them—two uniformed NK regulars, an older officer, and Colonel Chop Chop, who stood in the corner shadows and watched as the soldiers placed Louis in a chair facing Fuzzy. With the colonel in civilian clothes, with a shaved head and tinted glasses, was Gregor Lysenko, whom Intelligence had identified as his Russian advisor and had nicknamed Blackhawk. Chop Chop and Blackhawk. Like the comic book. What a fucking joke.

The soldiers bound Louis's arms to a second wooden chair. They also put his helmet between his legs, binding them at the knee so he couldn't release it. He told himself it was to catch his puke when they got down to business.

While they set him up, Blackhawk said something to Chop Chop in what sounded like Russian. The colonel nodded and in a smooth, even voice he spoke a command in Korean to one of his soldiers, not taking his eyes off Louis. An older soldier translated in broken English.

They wanted information about troop deployment. Louis said he didn't know anything about troop deployment.

He and other men of his platoon had been captured four days earlier when they got separated from King Company by a firefight with NKPA units in central Korea. All Louis knew was that they were part of a combat team assigned to defend a sector north of Wonju. But he had no idea where his company had advanced or what the deployment plans were. He also had no idea what other combat, artillery, or tank units were to be attached. That was not the kind of information that Command shared with grunts.

The colonel listened without response to the translation of Louis's words. Then he said something soft and terse, and the baby-faced soldier backhanded Louis hard enough to cause his nose to leak blood and snot into the helmet. Was that what it was for? Couldn't be. This was a torture tent.

The interrogation resumed, questions pelting him like stones: What heavy equipment did they have with them? What other battalion units were they joining up with? How many men? When was the next airdrop of the 187th?

"I swear," Louis mumbled, "I don't know nothing." It was all he could say. It was the truth. He knew nothing. Nor did Fuzzy or the other guys in the platoon. Their mission was to proceed toward a ridge to the east of Wonju. They were not regrouping or reconnoitering with another company. They were just advancing and trying to save their asses.

But the soldier continued, demanding to know master battle plans, refusing Louis's explanation that he knew nothing, that he was just following the leader like Fuzzy and the others.

When the soldier wasn't satisfied, he put on a glove and swatted Louis again, but this time not very hard. And that made Louis suspicious that they were saving him for bigger things. They were.

The same line of questioning went on for several minutes until Colonel Chop Chop appeared to grow weary of Louis's insistence. He mumbled something to the Russian, who responded with a burst of words. Chop Chop immediately conveyed the message to the baby-faced corporal, who gave Louis a look that sent a bolt of electricity through him. The soldier stepped between Louis and Fuzzy and removed a knife from a holster on his hip—a long, wickedly sharp looking blade that flickered in Louis's face and made his heart nearly rupture. The soldier looked at Louis with that flat, inscrutable expression, then in a lightning move that Louis later thought was well rehearsed, he grabbed one of Fuzzy Swenson's ears and sliced it off.

Fuzzy screamed as blood spurted from the side of his head. Still without expression the soldier dropped the severed ear into Louis's helmet. It struck with an obscene *plunk*.

By reflex Louis tried to shake the helmet free. But the soldier whacked Louis in the face to remain still.

Louis looked down at the thing. It was horrible—just the bloodied rim of the ear, a gaping hole for the canal opening still attached to Fuzzy's head. "Please," Louis begged. "I don't know anything. Please. Please."

Fuzzy whimpered and bobbed his head, his hands jerking against the ropes to cup the pain, stop the blood. But he had been tightly bound, and his hands twitched like injured animals.

The interrogator shouted at him to explain the kind of armaments in his company.

Louis looked at the hideous severed ear. *Make something up,* he told himself. *Make something up. Anything, or they're going to cut Fuzzy into pieces and fill the fucking helmet.*

He glanced at Chop Chop, who stood in the corner with the Russian studying Louis through those fucking half-moon black gook eyes—bright with pleasure. The bald Russian beside him looking like a warhead.

Louis began to mumble, trying to compose his mind to come up with something that sounded like military plans. The colonel said something and the translator shouted for Louis to speak up. But all he could do was mumble dissociated words— *southeast corridor light armament northwest Howitzers reconnaissance . . . 17th Infantry Regiment . . .*

But before he could cobble together something that made sense, the knife man pulled Fuzzy's head up by the other ear and sliced it off.

Louis screamed. But Fuzzy only let out a gasp, since he was already half gone from the beating and loss of blood. His head flopped from side to side as if trying to free itself of the pain, his hands jerking fitfully. The soldier dropped the second ear into Louis's helmet.

Louis looked at the officer. "I beg you, please, no more. Leave him alone. He didn't do anything. He doesn't know anything. I don't know anything."

God, help me come up with something, anything, just to stop these fuckers.

Louis mumbled something about a battalion of two hundred

men with armored personal carriers and Howitzers coming from the east toward Wonju. He made stuff up and let it come, scraps of stuff he knew and stuff he just created in the moment. Anything.

The translator passed that on to Chop Chop, who responded. The translator then lowered his face to Louis's and screamed: "No good. You lie. *You lie!*"

"No, it's the truth. I swear."

The Russian grunted something, and the colonel tipped his head at the soldier. He raised Fuzzy's face and jabbed the point of the knife into his left eye, and with a flourish he scooped out the bloody mass and dropped it in the helmet.

Louis felt his gorge rise in his throat. But he held, barely able to register Fuzzy's whimpering and pathetic attempt to free his bound hands to stop the flow of blood and ocular fluid. He closed his eyes and screamed so hard for them to stop that he hoped his brain would short-circuit—that he'd just pass out. Maybe shock himself out of this horrible nightmare place and wake him up on the other side of the globe where he belonged.

But none of that happened.

He was still in the Red Tent, bound to his chair with the bloodied head of Fuzzy across from him, his ears and gory eyeball sitting in the helmet between Louis's legs and the Russian muttering more shit to Chop Chop. Louis tried to mouth pleas of mercy but Chop Chop grunted something, and the knife man jabbed out Fuzzy's other eye and dropped the bloody thing onto the pile.

Louis closed his eyes against the sight, against the groans rattling out of Fuzzy's throat, against the sight of his poor ruined head.

But they wouldn't let him. The soldier sliced off four of Fuzzy's fingers, one by one, and deposited them in the helmet. Then the thumb. Then they began on the other hand.

When Fuzzy appeared to have passed out, Chop gave the final order. The soldier jabbed Louis on the chin with the point of the knife, and in a flash, as his eyes snapped open, the bastard forced back Fuzzy's head and slashed his throat.

That was all Louis remembered of the Red Tent, because

they unbound him and hustled him out to the pen with the other prisoners.

Later that evening, as the sun dropped over the mountains, they brought him and nine other men from first platoon to a low bridge over some river. A detail of soldiers pulled them out of the trucks and lined them up shoulder-to-shoulder against the low rail of the bridge, maybe twenty feet above the water. In the distance Louis could see dark, rolling hills. He focused on a star just above the hills—maybe Venus or Mars, it made no difference—and he thought of Marie Carbone on the other side of the world—his high school sweetheart, the girl he had planned to marry when he got back to the States—and how she had no idea that at this very moment as she was waking up in her parents' home in Woburn, Massachusetts, he was being lined up over some godforsaken river to be shot dead.

Louis heard the metal snap as the machine gunners locked the belt of fifty-caliber shells into the magazine.

He heard the whimpers of the men staggering in terror beside him, knowing that this was their death.

He heard the alien syllables of Colonel Chop Chop's command to fire.

And with his last breath of air bulbed in his throat, Louis heard the moment explode with a ratcheting insistence that propelled him backward over the side and into the water.

By reflex, he held his breath and waited to pass into death.

But he did not pass into death. As he plunged deep into the chilled black water, he was stunned that he had not been hit. Amazingly, he was alive.

He continued holding his breath and let the current take him. Because his feet were loosely bound, he could make dolphin kicks. And when he could no longer hold his breath, he surfaced, took a gulp of air, and resubmerged, his back to the bridge where, if any soldiers saw him, they'd think he was just one of the corpses bobbing on the surface.

Three days later and half starved, Louis flagged an American spotter plane, and in hours a squad of GIs from Baker

Company found him. For nearly two days he slept in the infirmary tent. And for the next fifty years he worked to get those Red Tent images out of his head.

But now they were back with brutal insistence.

47

Jack shook himself awake. Another bad dream.

He could not remember what exactly it was about, and he was grateful—just vague images of misshapen creatures and screams and other nasty sounds he couldn't identify.

Jack blinked around the room, taking in the shapes in the dim night-light as the dream dissipated.

Greendale. His room at Greendale Rehab.

The window with the broken Venetian blinds. The digital clock on the TV. 5:17. Muddy gray light seeped through the slats. Dawn light. He had been asleep since yesterday afternoon when the doctor was in with her test questions—when he had another spell.

Threw yourself a whopper, Jackie boy. Lousy dreams, loony conniptions. Hell, the coma's looking pretty good.

The wall mirror above the bureau. The IV stand. The heart monitors on the rolling console beside the bed. His bed with the baby-blue spread, side bars to prevent him from falling out if he had a seizure. His rebirth crib.

He looked out the window into the predawn gray. How the

world had changed, he thought. How he had changed since a bunch of jellyfish burned a hole in his tape.

In a matter of minutes the outside light grew brighter. The blinds hung at a funny angle, like a gull with a broken wing.

He could smell the ocean. That probably explained why in the dream he sensed being at the sea. Subtle fishy scents from the window had crossed with a dim recall of the jellyfish attack. Crank that through your squeeze box and that explained why he could still dimly make out a dead, bloodied animal near the water—maybe a beached porpoise or harbor seal that had gotten chopped up by some nitwit on jet skis.

(*Blood. So much blood. And battered flesh. So vague.*)

Which sometimes happened in Buck's Cove.

Whatever, it was a bad dream that had left his johnny wet and his brain tender. Yet what stayed with him for the rest of the morning was how *real* it felt. While he couldn't locate any narrative thread to connect the scraps, his mind felt raw with afterimages that made him feel that he'd not been dreaming but had just returned from a scene of brutal horror.

And what gnawed at his mind like an osprey was that he had woken up with his thumb in his mouth.

Later that morning Nurse Marcy brought him back to the PT room where the therapist had him stand for several minutes at the parallel bars. Then they had him lie on the floor pads, moving his legs and arms in different positions. After several minutes of that, they sat him in a wheelchair and worked on exercising his wrists, arms, and neck.

For his upper body they had him do free weights. The last time in the gym he was doing three sets of ten at thirty pounds, and his arms looked like hams. Now he was working out on five pounds, and his biceps looked like walnuts.

This went on twice a day every day. By the end of the first week he was able to move ten feet on the parallel bars, a major victory culminating in his going solo with a walker. To celebrate, Jack asked if someone could run down to the video store and rent him a copy of *The Awakening*.

While his body began to strengthen, Jack read newspapers and magazines to catch up on what he had missed.

But God! How the world had darkened while he slept. America was still at war with insurgents in Iraq, where suicide bombings were a daily event. The Middle East was still a powder keg, with Israelis and Palestinians still locked in bloody retaliations. We still had troops in Afghanistan. Massacres were occurring in Africa. Christ! Maybe nothing had changed. Six months, and the world was no better off than when he had slipped into a coma.

On the bright side, Red Sox fans were talking about their boys pulling it off again this year. And on that happy possibility, Jack dozed off.

48

"Hey, pal, what's with the Rip Van Winkle stunt?"

Jack opened his eyes. "Where the hell you been?"

"Where the hell *you* been?" Vince chuckled and took Jack's hand in his.

Vince Hammond stood at Jack's bedside wearing a black long-sleeve polo and with a big, exuberant boyish face. His hair was shorter than Jack had remembered and spiked with gel, making him look even younger, probably still getting himself carded in bars. But what struck Jack was the difference in their geometry. Against the light flooding through the window Vince looked as if he'd spent the missing months on a Cybex machine. His neck looked like a hydrant, and his shirtsleeves resembled tubes of grapefruits. He had not let the constant exposure to haute cuisine get the best of him. By contrast, Jack felt like a beef jerky.

"How come you're not fat and bald?"

"I'm working on it," Vince said, and squeezed a beer wing. "You're looking a hell of a lot better than you did six months ago."

"Hard to look worse, I hear."

"Yeah, you were something of a mess."

Jack raised the hand mirror the nurses had given him. "And now I'm the Shroud of Turin."

Vince laughed and pulled up a chair. "The important thing is how you're feeling."

"Like a whoopee cushion for all the gas."

"What are they feeding you?"

"White stuff." Jack nodded at the tray of half-eaten mashed potatoes and tapioca pudding.

"When you get your teeth back, some red and green." Vince held up a shiny red bag with the Yesterdays logo. "There's a freezer down the hall."

Jack looked at the bag, which almost looked like patent leather, *Yesterdays* in art deco gold letters. "Nice understated doggie bag."

Vince frowned at the size. "Yeah, maybe our portions are too big."

"I hear you're doing well."

Vince pulled a menu from the bag. "We're doing well."

He handed Jack the menu, a handsomely designed folder of just two pages, instead of the kind of multipage folios that confused your appetite. Desserts on the back side with the list of boutique beers.

"I'll have the calimari with polenta salad and seafood risotto."

"Look, when they let you out, you're gonna be just fine, eating like a king, I'll make sure. Another thing, I know some real estate people who'll find you a nice place. And when you're up for it, you've got a job at the restaurant. So when are they going to let you out?"

"Thanks to you, about six weeks." The nurses had told him how Vince had come in several times a week to help exercise Jack's legs and arms, confident that he would come out of it and wanting to make sure he'd wake up "ready to trot." In two weeks the therapist said he'd graduate to a walker, eventually to a cane. But it was uncertain if he'd have a permanent limp.

"You could be our host, so you don't have to walk much."

Jack smiled. "Sounds fine."

Vince and Jack had been friends since junior year in high school—twenty years of sharing hopes, fears, kid fun, many laughs, some defeats, some painful wisdom, and the kind of closeness that exceeded brotherhood. They both went to Northeastern University, where Jack got his degree in English and Vince in criminal justice because he wanted to be a cop. Four years ago, he got shot by a felon during an arrest and spent two months in a hospital—an experience that made him promise his wife no more police work. So he quit the force, and after some small odd jobs on disability, he saved enough money for him and Jack to begin plans on their restaurant.

"Beth came by."

"I heard."

"She's remarried." He knew Vince knew but he had to give it official pronouncement.

"I'm really sorry about that."

"Yeah." The syllable stuck in this throat.

"But think of it as you turning a new page."

"More like a new book."

"Whatever, it beats the alternative. The nurses say your recall is something."

"So I'm told."

"But you're feeling okay?"

"Except for the weird spells."

"Spells?"

"Like . . . I don't know. Like I'm having memory flashes of stuff from my past. Some crazy stuff, some good stuff—when I was a kid with my aunt and uncle, at the beach, in the backyard, teachers, first girlfriends."

"We all should have such spells."

"Just that they're so real. I don't know how to explain it," he said. "It's more like I'm reliving them."

"I can think of a few nights I'd like to relive."

Jack nodded, but that wasn't what he meant. His brain felt spongy with painkillers and he squished around for the right words. "Sometimes they're so *vivid* I can't tell if it's memory or if I'm in some kind of replay."

"Is that good or bad?"

"I feel like that guy in *The Dead Zone* who has flashes of the future, except I have flashes of the past. Dumb stuff—like taking pony rides at the Mohawk Trail. Playing kickball in the third grade. Christmas Day when I got my first bike. But they don't feel like dreams."

"I don't see what the problem is. You've got a vivid memory."

"I'm telling you, it's not like memory. It's just like . . . just like I'm there—feeling things, hearing stuff, smelling things. My heart races." He looked away, frustrated at the limitations of his words. "Vince, I'm reexperiencing events that I once lived."

Vince nodded as he took it all in.

"Christ, now you think I'm looney tunes."

"No, I get it."

But he didn't. How could he?

"I have dreams all the time, and when I wake up I can swear I was there, someplace else. Everybody does."

"Except I'm not asleep."

"You're not?"

"I could be outside in the sun, but when I look around I'm someplace else—on a beach or in the middle of a thunderstorm, lightning crashing all around me. Yet it's clear blue and I feel the sun on my face, but inside it's storming."

Vince nodded to cover his concern. "Some kind of daydreams. I get those."

No, you don't, Jack thought. Nobody who's right in his head or not on psychedelics gets these. Even with the mushrooms he had tried in college, Jack always knew he was tripping, his anchor self always lurking in the sidelines or flying the thermals just above the Disney pyrotechnics playing across his synapses. But part of him was always in the audience. But this was different, and Vince didn't have a clue. Nor did Jack.

"What do the doctors say? It could be your medication needs adjusting or something."

"They give me some antiseizure stuff that just makes me sleepy, and I've logged enough of that."

"Ask them for something else."

"Yeah."

They chatted more until Jack felt himself turn drowsy. Vince said he'd be back in a few days, and Jack thanked him for coming around. Before he left, Vince gave Jack an MP3 digital player with several of his favorite artists downloaded. "It also records."

Jack thanked him. Maybe the music would help him sleep.

What Jack did not tell Vince was how he dreaded sleeping on his own—without lorazepam or clonazepam or Naprosyn or Tegretol or whatever the hell it was to knock the teeth out of his dreams. No, not the pony rides or schoolyard romps with boyhood chums or lusty moments with Latitia Cole in Erica Hughes's rec room—but the dark, twisted images that were slightly out of focus and just wouldn't stick to his consciousness when he awoke but whose aftereffects left him flayed with anxiety. And as hard as he tried, he could not summon details.

It had crossed his mind that maybe those damn jellics had spot-fried his brain, leaving little lesions that put him just this side of sane—and maybe the lesions were spreading. And wasn't that what all the neuropsycho tests were trying to determine—that maybe all of him didn't come back?

The flash images, the voices in his head, the spells of naked fright. He had said nothing to the docs because he knew that would only prolong his convalescence. And in spite of the fine professional treatment, even after a week he wanted out. He wanted to be someplace other than in this recovery room, this nursing home, away from drip bags and stethoscopes, beeping monitors, and institutional green walls. But more than that, he wanted to be out of his head, because it was like being locked in a room lousy with ghosts.

That's some mouse.

He looked out the window, and from behind the unbroken blue sky he heard thunder.

Shit! It came back to him like a tic. Thunder and lightning on a cloudless day.

He buzzed the nurse for something to sleep on, and Marcy came and gave him a white pill that he gobbled down. And when he was alone again, he turned his head away from the sunshine and the rainstorm raging in his pillow, and he pressed his eyes shut and thought of Beth eight years ago and put her on the moon-washed beach with a sultry breeze and her arms pulling him to her, the heat of her breast lighting his heart.

And he closed his eyes and waited for the Xanax to seep through his brain like sap and douse the lights.

49

Darien, Connecticut

"*Did you ever do it?*"

"*Did I ever do what?*" Rodney Blake felt his insides clench as he darkly sensed what his cousin Nora was asking him.

"*Oh, come on, Rod, you know what I mean, a good-looking boy like you. Did you ever screw a girl?*"

The words passed through him like sparks. Even though it was 1946 he had never heard a girl speak of such matters or use such language. But, then again, most girls were not his cousin Nora, who lived in the sticks of Pennsylvania with farm animals. Besides, she was fourteen, and older than most girls her age, and a year older than him.

"*Not really.*"

"*Well, you musta made out with girls.*"

"*Yeah, sure, of course,*" he lied. He'd never even had a girl-friend. Only kissed a girl in Spin the Bottle, and that was a dry peck in front of other kids.

They were silent for a few minutes. They were lying in his backyard looking at the stars. They had asked their parents if they could sleep in the tents that night—one for her and one for

him, even though either tent could hold two people. But parents
said it wasn't proper to share a tent, a boy and girl at their age,
even cousins. So they lay on the blanket between the tents. The
glow of his family's house through the bushes gave them light
so he could see Nora studying him.

"I don't believe you."

"You don't? How come?"

"I just don't," Nora said. "You must jerk off."

(Did girls really talk this way? Or just Nora?)

Another numbing moment as he tried to conjure up the right
response. If he sounded shocked, he'd look namby-pamby, to
use his mother's term. Yet to admit he had done that was morti-
fying, especially to a girl who was also his first cousin. Father
Cardarelli, who had taught him catechism and who had given
Rodney his missal with the red leather cover and the prayerful
inscription, had warned that "abusing oneself" was a sin in
God's eyes but not as bad as doing "it"—which was "mortal"
and punishable by eternal damnation, which meant something
like those old paintings of demons carving people with long,
evil knives.

In truth, Rodney had played with himself but only experienced pre-orgasmic sensations, which still scared him even
though they felt good. It happened in bed one night while he
was dozing off and his hand started diddling on it own. But it
wasn't a real one because he stopped himself short when he
felt something big was about to happen, something he only
vaguely knew about—a barrier he just wasn't supposed to
cross. Except some fluid rose up, probably what the kids called
"jizz"—a sticky stuff like egg white that dried on his fingers
and sent him to the bathroom to scrub away with soap.

"Sure."

"Then you're not ascared of going blind, which is what
Jerry says will happen, but I think is bulltticky, because every
boy I know's got eyes like a damn hawk."

Rodney didn't know how to respond, but it didn't make any
difference because the next thing he knew, Nora had rolled up
to his side. And before he could say anything, her hand slid
down his front and came to rest on his privates.

"*Wha-wha-what're you doin'?*" In spite of himself, he felt himself harden.

"*Shhh.*"

And she began to rhythmically move her hand up and down across his erection that she had flattened against his belly. Then she slipped her hand into his pants as if she'd done this a dozen times before. Which shocked him. She was only fourteen but so advanced—probably what happened to girls from Pennsylvania where they know about animal husbandry and stuff.

But pecking at his conscience was what Father Cardarelli had said about sex with family members—and what the devil does to those who do that.

Rodney gasped for air as Nora pulled him out of his pants and began stroking him oh so gently. He tried to stop her but he couldn't, and he groaned and moaned with devilish pleasure until he thought he'd explode. But she knew what she was doing and stopped just in time.

Then he felt her take his hand and place it on her crotch. He had never touched a girl. He didn't even know what girls looked like down there. Some of the kids had made crude pencil drawings of huge holes with dark scribbly wreaths of hair, but that did nothing for him. And all the art books in the library showed big fat women with puffy blanks. And medical textbooks only had disgusting diagrams of the insides.

Nora unzipped her bottoms and made him slip his hand inside.

Rodney nearly passed out. My God! All the hair, and she's wet, and slippery and deep, like a gash—just like Buddy Peterson said.

She rubbed up against him, and before he knew it he was pulling her pants down. And she let him. But when he tried to roll on top of her, she pushed him off. "Uh-uh. Just this," she whispered. And she continued stroking him.

Maybe it was some deep animal instinct that powered him or all the things that Buddy and Wade and the older boys had told him, but he pushed Nora's hands back and rolled on top of her, poking her privates with himself, keeping his knees spread so her legs would stay open. Magically he felt himself slip inside *her as if guided by all the forces of evolution—and something broke in his mind.*

This was it. THIS WAS IT. *The epicenter of all adult secrets, all the snickers, the crude pencil drawings, the movies, the jokes, the dirty words. In a stupendous moment of epiphany Rodney connected himself to every other human being on the planet and human being who ever lived, right back to Adam and Eve.*

While his cousin Nora struggled to stop him in time, to get him off her, to muffle her protests before their parents heard, Rodney exploded inside her.

When it was over, she was gathering her clothes and swearing at him under her breath as she tried to wipe away his jizz, saying how oh-my-God *she could get pregnant.*

The next several minutes passed in a blur. Nora disappeared into her tent and he lay there, feeling the chilled air, his sperm crusting on his skin.

Then he was walking across the lawn toward the house, guided by the light and the radio station that played old-time tunes:

Way down by the stream . . . How sweet it will seem . . .
Once more just to dream in the moonlight . . .

But he wasn't naked anymore, or chilled. Instead he was dressed in pants and the striped sweater that Edna had given him for his seventieth birthday a few years ago. Before he passed into the kitchen, he stopped in the living room and removed from the bookshelves the red leather-bound book, its pages now flaky with age. Father Cardarelli's signature still looked fresh.

"Uncle Rod, is that you down there?" Edna asked.

Edna.

He said nothing as he made his way to the cellar door.

"I'm in the bathroom. I'll be right down. Don't forget to take your medicine. The white pills."

Rodney opened the cellar door. He could hear the familiar creaking of the stairs as he made his way down.

He moved to the workbench with the tools neatly lined up on the pegboard, the wrenches ranging from tiny to large plumber items, the same with the screwdrivers and pliers and coping saws. Even the knives—from small carving blades to a steel hunting knife that Nora gave him for Christmas a long time ago. Nora whom they disowned and who took her own life before she turned twenty.

Nora, mother of his daughter, Edna. Secret Edna. Edna who was born far away and whose father nobody knew. Nobody except Rodney.

"Uncle Rod," Edna called from upstairs. "You fell asleep in the backyard. Did the radio wake you? You looked so cute on the blanket beside the tent."

He laid the missal on the bench. Forgive me, dear God. He undid his belt.

"I'll get your pills."

He pulled his pants down.

"But tonight you belong to me. Just to little ol' me . . ."

"The white ones."

He removed himself.

Upstairs water ran from the kitchen faucet into a glass.

Rodney removed his old hunting knife, still shiny and razor-honed the way he left it the other day.

"You were talking to yourself out there." Footsteps crossed the kitchen floor to the cellar door at the head of the stairs.

"I know with the dawn that you will be gone . . ."

Rodney gripped himself tightly.

"But tonight you belong to me . . . Just to little ol' me!"

And with his right hand he slashed.

50

Jack was in his wheelchair in the picnic area listening to Stevie Ray Vaughn on his MP3 when the woman named René Ballard approached him from across the patio.

She was young—in her twenties—very attractive and with a clean, varnished look. She was not in a nurse's smock or an aide's green uniform but a beige pants suit and white shirt. She walked toward him with graceful purpose, promising to be better company than Joe McNamara, who had to be taken inside a few minutes ago because he had some kind of spell.

She also looked vaguely familiar—like a face from beneath layers of film.

Because it was a warm day, Jack had rolled outside to put some color back in his face, which looked like mayonnaise. He had his magazines, still trying to fill the hole. After maybe twenty minutes, Joe came up to him asking if he knew where Father O'Connor was. Assuming that Joe was expecting a visit from the family priest, Jack suggested that he ask one of the nurses. Apparently that didn't register, since Joe cocked his head at Jack like a beagle. Then his eyes saucered and he slipped to his knees, crossed himself, and began to blubber a confession. "Father, forgive me, forgive me, I . . . I . . . Ooooowheeeo oooooh . . . I blinded him in the eye. Lenny Schmidt. I blinded him, and he wasn't doing anything, just standing there in front of Leone's, but I just wanted to scare him, that's all, just scare him, and I didn't think it would hit him in the face really, Father, I didn't, just scare him, hit him on the shoulder or something, but not the eye, I swear to God." One of the aides caught sight of the scene and tried to get Joe to snap out of it. But he was too far gone and started swearing and swinging wildly. Before other aides arrived, Joe asked Jack for forgiveness. As the aides came to haul him off, Jack made the sign of the cross and said he forgave him, reducing Joe to sobs of gratitude. The aides carried him back into his room and shot him up with something to let him sleep off his penance.

Jack didn't know what had clicked in the guy's head—maybe it was Jack's black T-shirt or his saint-gaunt face. But for a brief moment Jack was Father O'Connor. And that wasn't the first weird episode here. Because it was a mixed population, younger rehab patients and elderly dementia victims shared common areas. And the staff encouraged mingling just to help those Alzheimer's residents who weren't that far gone yet. Jack enjoyed talking with them, finding little personality pilot lights still glowing. But some of them would click off to another place all of a sudden, like Mr. Monks at the table over there with the puzzles and the CD headphones. Most of yesterday he spent do-wopping around the ward to Gene Vincent—a seventeen-year-old inside an old guy's skin. Or Marty Lubeck, who for two hours yesterday sang, "Defer, defer, I'm the Lord High Executioner" to the aquarium fish, his face frozen with that same weird intensity, eyes beaded down on some seventh-grade memory. Or Noreen Hoolihan in the rocker over there having a full-fledged conversation about her grandmother with a pot of geraniums.

"Good morning, Mr. Koryan. My name is René Ballard. I'm the consulting pharmacist here, and I'm wondering if I can talk to you a bit."

Her hand was cool and smooth like taffy closing on his fingers. Jack pretended to examine his calendar. "Well, I'm running a tight schedule, but I think I can squeeze you in."

She chuckled. "Thanks," she said, and pulled up a plastic chair.

She had lively blue-gray eyes that pulled you in when she smiled. Her hair was chestnut brown and held back with a clasp fashioned out of some lacy material resembling a rose. She wore gold hoop earrings and a thin gold necklace. Her long fingers curled around a gold pen under a notebook. The woman emanated an intelligent, self-possessed nature, and Jack wondered what she looked like in an evening gown. He wondered what she looked like in a bikini. He also wondered about his interest.

"The nurses say that you're improving remarkably well."

"Rest home food will do that."

"You mean it's that *good?*"

"No, that bad, so you want to heal fast and go home."

She had a laugh like wind chimes that should have settled the low-grade anxiety beginning to nibble at his brain. "I can't say that I blame you. And from all reports, that won't be too long, given how well you're doing. I remember when they brought you in."

"Sorry that slipped my mind."

She smiled. "Your wife and friends told me a lot about you."

"Former wife."

She nodded. "Yes, I heard. I'm very sorry about that."

As they chatted, Jack could not repress the mounting unease that had nothing to do with nursing home food or being stuck in a wheelchair surrounded by demented geriatrics. It was this woman—this lovely, shiny young woman with her sincere big eyes and perfect teeth and kiss-me lips—who made him painfully aware of the white-stick legs showing from his pants and birdcage chest and the long empty lane ahead of him. Just the other day he was a creature of satisfaction and desire, and he had a life.

"Dr. Heller showed me your memory tests. She's not seen anything like it before. Your recall is at the far end of the curve."

"The universe loves a balance."

Her manner was guarded as she let a couple of seconds elapse before responding. "The PT people here are the best around. I'm sure in a few months you'll be a hundred percent better and back to living your life."

He smiled. "If there's a God." She opened her notebook and he could see a list of questions she had written. "I have a funny feeling you're not here to check my meds."

"Actually, I'd like to ask you about your memory, if that's all right."

"You're the fourth person this week." Her pupils dilated as she waited for his response. He could have lost himself in those eyes.

"You mean you're tested out."

"Mazes, picture tests, digit recall, word recall, blocks, card tests, and every time I turn around somebody asks me to repeat what they said. I'm beginning to feel like an echo chamber."

She laughed. "None of that, I promise. But you're right: I'm not here about your medication although if you have any questions or problems, I hope you let me know."

"Since you mentioned it. I know it sounds like a bad punch line, but I'm having problems sleeping."

"You're not getting enough?"

"Not deep enough. I want to sleep without dreaming. Just a blank."

"You're having bad dreams?"

"Yes." He didn't want to elaborate.

She wrote something down for the nurses. And he nodded a thank-you to this lovely, inaccessible woman who would give him something not to dream. She slipped her notepad into the clip and looked at him to say it was business time.

"Let me explain. In addition to my consulting role, I'm part of a research project for a local pharmaceutical company that's conducting clinical trials of a drug for Alzheimer's disease. You might have seen it on the news or read about it."

He had. "Some kind of breakthrough cure."

"Yes, it's called Memorine. In fact, several of the residents here are enrolled in the trials."

"You mean I've got Alzheimer's, too?"

"Hardly," she laughed. "But, coincidentally, the jellyfish that attacked you contains a toxin that affects memory."

"I've got more than I can use."

"So I've heard, but that's not what I mean."

Me, either.

"So, I'm wondering if I could ask you a few questions about your memory."

"Why?"

"Because we've discovered a similarity between your neurological activity and that of patients on the drug. While you were in a coma, the doctors ran some MRI scans on your brain to check for problems—tumors, lesions, or any other abnormalities. Thankfully, there were none. But the images showed that areas associated with memory have experienced enhanced activity, and I'd like to ask you about the kinds of things that are coming back to you."

"What's the connection to me?"

"Just that several test patients are experiencing some unusually deep recall. I'm just wondering if you've had anything like this—you know, memories of early experiences." She hesitated a moment as he stared at her without expression. "Flashbacks."

Flashbacks. She'd given it a name. And Jack felt his pulse rate spasm. *Yes,* he thought. "No," he said.

Her eyebrow shot up like a polygraph needle. "Really?"

"No flashbacks."

He could not determine if she looked disappointed or incredulous. Maybe something in his face gave him away, because she settled back in her chair and studied him. Then after a moment she said, "May I ask, then, why you want something to let you sleep without dreams?"

"That's not the same thing, is it?"

"Neurologically the activity is coincident."

If you tell her yes, she'll poke you with questions until you're a damn dartboard—which means they'll never let you out; in fact, they'll make you some kind of adjunct study for that drug they're pushing. "What can I tell you? No flashbacks."

Nice mouse. Big mouse.

Die, goddamn it.

Her eyes hardened. She didn't believe him. "I see, then it's just a coincidence—the images and the fact that on several oc-

casions you called for your mother, actually sounded as if you
were having a conversation with her."

"My mother?"

"One of the nurses caught it on tape."

The initial hospitality lost its warmth. Nice ploy: Send in a
clever female with sunny good looks and knockdown charm to
coo him into submission, and you got yourself that grant and a
fat bonus.

But right behind that thought another muscled it's way up:
*Sour. You're a damn self-pitying sour old man before your
time. Which is why you belong in this geriatric terrarium.*

"You mean you've never talked in your sleep before? Talked
to a dead relative or friend?" he asked.

"Yes, of course."

He could hear the caution in her voice. "Given all the medication they were pumping into me, I'm surprised I wasn't
chatting with Cleopatra."

"That may be true, but what made these episodes different
was your voice. You sounded like a child, which suggests that
you were reliving some deep-past experience. So I'm wondering if you're aware of these flashbacks—if you've had them
while awake, if you can tell us what you're experiencing when
they occur."

She held him with those big eyes—beseeched him to tell her
what they both knew was the truth: That he had flashbacks, that
he talked to dead people, that he had been to places he hadn't
thought of in years, relived moment-to-moment interludes that
he didn't want to return from—splendid little kid-fun vignettes. Also the dark other stuff that came back to him in
quick-fire snaps that left him quaking in horror.

"What we'd like is to determine the kinds of activity your
brain undergoes during certain conditions of recall. In other
words, conduct some functional MRI tests." She went on to
explain.

"I'm afraid I can't help you, Ms. Ballard."

Her body slumped as she made a polite nod of resignation.
"Well, I'm sorry to have bothered you." She stood up, holding
her leather-bound clipboard and all her questions to her chest.

"I'll talk with Dr. Heller about adjusting your medications to help you sleep better."

And while you're at it, he thought, *maybe you and your neuro pals could climb into my head and tell me what the hell is squatting in the closet—what that friggin' ooga-booga thing is staked out in the shadows and watching through the slit. The thing with the big sharp head. That's what I'd really appreciate. Something from that script pad of yours that would nail shut that damn door.*

"Thank you."

She opened her shoulder bag and pulled out a business card and laid it on the table. "Should there be any changes," she said, and thanked him.

He watched her leave, cutting a rippling wake across the ether of the patio—admiring and hating her pert little gabardined bottom and long legs and bobbing chestnut hair as she made her way into the building and through the lot for her cute little BMW to drive to her cute little condo where later in the day she'd crack open a cute little pinot noir with her cute little geek stud . . .

To hell with you, René Ballard.

To hell with you, Beth King.

Suddenly he felt like crying.

To hell with you, Jack Koryan.

Shit! He closed his eyes and wished they'd fuse shut.

51

"**M**r. Reynolds, you put your clothes back on or I'm going to tell my daddy!"

The little elderly woman shook her finger at the large naked man with his arms spread.

A few feet away, two college women who were admiring the bronze sculpture near the entrance of the Museum of Fine Arts turned around. The black woman in the Northeastern University baseball cap looked at her white companion and started to snicker.

But the elderly woman with the flowered dress and large shopping bag was not joking. She snapped her head at the young black woman and squinted. Then her expression opened up. "There you are, Lucy Goosey! Where's my Jello?"

"Beg pardon?"

"You were supposed to be watching him and not running off to Patty's house." Her mouth began to tremble. "Now he's missing."

"Lady, I don't know what you're talking about."

Mary gave the black woman a sharp look and stamped her foot. She then turned to the young white woman. "My mother's going to wring her neck when she finds out. She wasn't supposed to let him out without the leash. Now he's lost, and it's going to be dark soon."

The black woman studied the little elderly woman in the blue flowered housedress and floppy canvas hat. Her legs looked swollen, like bologna rounds pressed into dirty white walking shoes. "I'm sorry, lady, but I think you're confused."

"I know what you said to Barbara Chin. Miss DuPont told me. I don't care if I *don't* go to your party." And she stuck out her tongue.

"What party?" the white woman asked. "What's she talking about?"

The old lady snapped her face toward her then dropped her eyes to the small granite pedestal with the bronze plaque: "*Appeal to the Great Spirit,* Cyrus Edwin Dallin, 1909."

"What are you talking about? That's not Jello. That's the Murphy's dog, Boris. Jello's yellow and nice—not like him." And she kicked at the stone.

"Oh, boy!" the white woman said. Then to her friend she whispered, "She's got a medical bracelet."

Mary looked up at the black woman again. "You're always doing ten things at once." Then she snapped her head up at the statue. "What's Mr. Reynolds doing here? It's not his backyard. And I wish he'd put his clothes on."

The black woman made a move to read the bracelet, but the elderly woman snapped her hand away and squinted at the band as if it were a watch. "It's almost five o'clock. My daddy's going to be home soon, and when he does he's going to call your parents for this." Then her voice broke. "He's still a little puppy," she said, looking nowhere. "Mommy and Daddy gave him to me for my birthday."

The black woman made big eyes at her classmate to say the woman was totally delusional. "I'm sure you'll find Jello. But can you tell us your name?"

A passing trolley train squealed against the tracks, and the elderly woman squinted toward the street. "Lady, can you tell us your name?" the white girl asked, a little louder.

But the old woman paid no attention. Her eyes were transfixed on the MBTA train on the far track moving down Huntington toward the Northeastern stop.

"Ma'am, can you tell me where you live?"

"Seventh."

"Seventh what?"

"I got him for my seventh birthday, dummy." She shook her head. "Lucy, you were there, and Patty, too. Okay for you if I'm not invited. I wouldn't go even if I was. So there!" Then her expression sharpened. "And since when have you been black?"

The black woman's eyebrows shot up. "Pretty long," she said and pulled a cell phone out of her bag. The elderly woman looked at the thing and gasped.

"It's only a cell phone, for God's sake."

Blinking, the old woman stared at the device. And while the black woman punched numbers, her white companion leaned down toward the elderly woman. "Can you tell me your name?"

"Jello, you know that."

"No, *your* name, not your puppy's."

The old woman looked around at the traffic grinding down Huntington. They were at a crosswalk to the MBTA Green Line stop at the nearby corner. The traffic was thick and people were waiting for the oncoming train. While she glared across the avenue, distracted by whatever she was taking in, the white student stooped down and read the bracelet. "Mary Curley."

The black woman nodded. "I'd like to report a missing person," she said into the phone. "I mean we found her. We're in front of the Museum of Fine Arts on Huntington. Yeah. She's an elderly woman who's definitely confused. She's got some kind of medical alert bracelet on. Her name's Mary Curley; it says 'I am an Alzheimer's Patient.'"

Before the young woman could read the address on the back, Mary yanked her arm free. "Jello?" She reached into the giant Gap bag and pulled out a red mangled slipper. "Here's Mister Slippy. Come on, good boy."

Both women looked behind them, but there was no dog in sight.

"I mean, like she's spaced out," the black woman told the dispatcher. "She's talking to statues and trees like she's Mr. Magoo."

"Mary, where do you live?"

But Mary just glared at the street.

"Jello," the white woman said, to break her attention.

Mary snapped her head at her. "Where?"

The girl took Mary's shoulders and stuck her face into hers. *"Where do you live?"* she asked, punching out each syllable.

Mary glanced at the museum with its four Doric columns and massive granite portico above huge bronze doors. "Four fifty-two Franklin Avenue." She sang that out in perfect little-girl rhyme.

The black woman nodded, and into the phone said, "I don't know. Maybe she escaped from a nursing home. No, I don't know how she got here, and I don't think she does, either. She thinks she's lost her dog. Yeah. And you better come fast. . . . Yeah, she's wearing a dress and sneakers and holding a shopping bag. The Gap."

Mary glanced back at the spot she had been glaring at— someplace beyond the line of cars, busses, and trucks that inched down Huntington.

"How did you get here, Mary?" the white woman asked.

Suddenly Mary jerked out of her trance. "There's my baby," she said in that little-girl voice. "Jellooooo? He's in his house. Where he was all the time."

The white girl took Mary's arm as she started toward the street, when suddenly Mary turned on her and bit her wrist.

"Shit, lady!" the girl shouted. "Jesus! It's bleeding," she said to her friend, who was still on the cell phone.

Mary shot into the street. Some inner-lane cars screeched to a standstill, and she just made it to the outer lane. But because the cars had stopped bumper to bumper, the college women could not catch Mary, who seemed not to notice the traffic or even the close call as a delivery van screeched to a halt just inches from broadsiding her. It was as if she were following a beam of awareness within a landscape that had nothing to do with the outer world.

"I see you," she squealed with delight, and scurried through the traffic. "I see you, my baby."

"Jenny, stop her!" the black woman shouted.

Jenny ran into the street, but neither she nor her friend nor any of the people on the sidewalk could stop Mary Curley because the traffic had made a tight chain of cars for half a block. Without distraction, she moved to the stopped train as if powered by some invisible force. From across the street, Jenny, still holding her bleeding wrist, shouted to her, "Mary, stop."

But Mary did not stop, nor did she hear Jenny or her friend with the cell phone or the people in their vehicles or the last *ca-ching* of the money falling into the collection machine or the train's doors closing behind the last passengers. Mary had dropped to her knees so she could look into the doghouse.

"No, Mary! Noooo!"

Jenny and her friend were scrambling over the hoods of the stopped cars screaming at Mary to stop.

But Mary was down now and crawling under the massive coupling that connected the two Green Line cars. "There's my good boy."

52

An elderly woman from Brookline killed herself yesterday by crawling under the wheels of an MBTA train in Boston . . .

But authorities are still baffled how the seventy-eight-year-old woman suffering dementia had managed to find her way to Boston's Museum of Fine Arts three miles from her home.

According to her daughter, Mary Curley had been furloughed from Broadview Nursing Home in Cobbsville. Somehow she had managed to slip out of her Brookline home and found her way to the museum.

According to witnesses at the scene, Mrs. Curley appeared to be delusional and did not realize she had crawled under the Green Line train. . . .

*I*t was the fourth flashback-related death. This had to stop, Nick thought and clicked off the radio.

He pulled into the parking lot of Broadview Nursing Home, thinking that maybe Peter Habib was right—that this was a flawed drug that should be tabled.

He parked and made his way inside, where he stood in the lobby waiting for his party to arrive. Also burning like an ember in the forepart of his brain was the report about Jack Koryan. It was as if he had been raised from the dead, and with impossible recall—with an incandescent hippocampus that might harbor stuff that could turn things topsy-turvy.

My God!

Nick shook the dark possibilities from his mind as he watched the GEM group march up the front walk from the parking lot for the two P.M. meeting. *This was not going to be good.*

Gavin Moy was in the lead, his bulldog face preceding him like the grille of a Mack truck. He was dressed in an olive green sport coat, and with the dark glasses he looked like a military commander striding his way toward the front. Flanking him was Jordan Carr, moving in steady cadence like Moy's shadow in the afternoon sun, and behind them marched Mark Thompson, the GEM Tech medical director, and Mort Coleman, chief legal officer for the company.

Nick met them at the door, then led them across the lobby, a spacious and well lit area newly furnished with padded chairs and sofas upholstered in bright floral patterns and clustered around coffee tables and large floor plants discretely arranged for attraction and privacy, giving the room the feel of an upscale country inn. And, like the rest of the wing, all provided by the generous grant money of GEM Tech, according to a plaque hanging in the entranceway.

They took the elevator to the second floor and passed through the security doors leading into the Alzheimer's unit. Although Jordan Carr had worked on the ward in the early days of the trials, he had been back only a few times since Nick had taken over the site. And he was here because Gavin, with his penchant for corporate hierarchy, had named Carr assistant principal investigator of the trials.

This was Gavin's second visit to the home since the GEM-sponsored renovations. But it was not why he and his entourage were here. For the benefit of the others, Nick walked them through the ward for a quick overview before they got down to business.

The new dayroom, nearly twice the size of the original, was a skylighted cheerful area set up with clusters of chairs and tables, a wide-screen television set, and bookcases with a surround-sound system that was currently playing some soothing, innocuous instrumental CD music meant to keep patients calm. A whole collection of easy-listening and memory-lane CDs filled the shelves—from *The Fabulous Fifties* and *Favorite Irish Ballads* to collections of Perry Como, Johnny Mathis, Nat King Cole, and the big bands. Safe, soft nostalgia.

The unit was now fully air-conditioned and equipped with an elaborating lighting as well as a fail-safe security system, ceiling-mounted cameras at the elevators and all exits. No more repeats of Clara Devine.

Nick could feel Moy's restlessness as they made their way through the ward. But Nick kept up the pace and the tour-guide chatter not out of perversity but to humanize the issue for Moy and his suits—and to show where GEM's grant money had gone.

Nick flicked a wall switch twice, turning on a primary then a secondary bank of fluorescence. "Double lighting because afternoons are stressful," he explained. "The sun goes down, and they get agitated. It doesn't always work, but it helps."

A few elderly women were in chairs, some talking to each other, some talking to themselves. One woman in green sweatpants and white sneakers sat in a wheelchair holding a doll. One man paced by the rear windows, looking outside and muttering to himself. A few others shuffled on wheeled walkers.

Of the forty-eight patients on the ward, more than half were on Memorine. Because the trial was designed to be a single blind study, patients did not know if they were receiving the active drug or a placebo. And great care had been taken that the placebo tablet looked like the active medication. The reason, of course, was to prevent patients from acting differently because they knew they were taking an experimental drug. Although some medical staff knew who was in the control group, the participants were randomly assigned; and all effects observed—beneficial and troublesome—were documented then analyzed with cold, hard statistics. Even for those staffers who did not know which subjects were on Memorine and which were not, the distinction became progressively apparent over the months, especially since some of the more recovered patients, particularly those with no other morbidities or physical infirmities, were beginning to wonder why they were still in a nursing home.

Nick showed them a few sample rooms. The interiors were neat and cozily appointed in soothing pastels. Most had three beds, some two; a few were singles. Stuffed animals were bunched on the pillows in some of the women's rooms. The walls and bureau tops held personal belongings—toiletries, religious statues, bowling trophies, war medals, and photos of the patients and family members from earlier times. One man had Red Sox banners and an autographed photo of Ted Williams. Most photographs had labels naming those in the pictures, including the patients themselves. Many residents not receiving Memorine forgot who they were.

Around the beds in one room were crayon drawings, some saying, "I love you, Gramma." There was also a sheet with a poem, "To Aunt Wanda." On the wall beside one bed was a cracked black-and-white photo of the patient as a little girl in pants and floppy hat posing with a pony. The name on the label was "Margaret, age 9." She was the woman outside in the day-room with the rubber doll in her arms.

"She's a real gabber, this one," Nick said. "Born in Ireland and can tell you lots of good tales from her childhood."

"Is she one of ours?" asked Moy.

"Yes," Nick said. "Three years ago she couldn't recall the last four decades of her life, including the death of her husband and daughter. But you'll be happy to know that she's coming back."

Moy nodded with pleasure, the smile relaxing his scowl.

"What's interesting," Nick added, "is that she recalls her early days like they were yesterday."

They left the room. As in most homes, the nursing staff had

made every effort to individualize the patients. So outside of each room was a computer-printed biography of the residents.

Margaret O'Bannion was born in Ireland on January 30, 1921, and retired as a history teacher at Arlington High School. She enjoys her family and activities. She has 3 children and 7 grandchildren. She has a great sense of humor and enjoys rock-and-roll music and playing cards.

The next room's bio read:

Herbert Quinn was born in Lawrence, Mass., and worked in the mills as a young man. He is a very proud grandfather and likes to sing and socialize.

The door of the next room, a single, was closed, apparently because the patient was taking a nap. Outside of it was this bio:

Louis Martinetti was born in Portland, Maine, but lived much of his life in Woburn, Mass. He's a decorated soldier from the Korean War. He has a wife, Marie, a daughter, Christine, and a grandson, Steven. He likes oldies music, history, and baseball, and he enjoys playing cards and watching movies.

Nick led them into one of the large activities rooms where eight patients sat at a table as a recreational therapist instructed them in cutting and pasting pictures onto construction paper. "Hi, ladies," Nick said, as they entered. "Hope we're not disturbing you. I'm just showing my friends what a lovely place you have here."

"How are you girls doing today?" Moy asked. He walked up to the table smiling and inspected their artwork.

"Fine," two women said in unison.

Some others just nodded. One woman squinted at Moy and muttered something. Nick flicked the switch to double the lighting. "Oh, he's adorable," she said, nodding at Gavin Moy. "He looks just like my Jimmy without his hair."

"Jimmy's my cat's name," another woman piped up.

"That's not a cat's name, Jimmy." She made a face and turned toward Gavin Moy. "What's your name?"

Before Moy could answer, the other declared, "Yul Brenner. He's Yul Brenner."

"Yul Brenner?" another said, her eyes squinting at Moy. "Nahhh, go on. That's not Yul Brenner." Then she scowled at him, when suddenly her eyes widened. "Oh, oh. Omigod, it's Yul Brenner!" and she burst into snickers.

"No, it isn't."

"Yes, it is—"

"Thank you very much, ladies," Moy began. "I'm flattered, but—"

Sudden shouting behind them cut off Moy. Nick shot outside.

Margaret, the woman in a wheelchair, was sobbing uncontrollably as a nurse and two aides at her side tried to comfort her. "He's not breathing," she blubbered. *"He's not breathing."*

"Who's not breathing?" Moy asked. "Who she talking about?"

"He's dead!" Margaret cried. "He's dead." And she began to wail.

"The doll," Nick said.

Lucille, one of the nurses, moved over to Margaret. "He's not dead, Margaret," she said, and put her hands out to take the doll. "I just think he's just sound asleep." Then, as everybody watched, she gently pried the doll out of the woman's clutch and laid it on the floor where she began to stroke the doll's chest as if performing CPR.

"Look, he's beginning to breathe," one of the aides said. And the others, like a Greek chorus, agreed. "Oh, yeah. He's breathing again."

Lucille continued rubbing the doll for a few more seconds, then handed it back to Margaret. "There you go, little guy. He was just in a deep sleep, but he's fine now."

The others cheered quietly, as through huge eyes Margaret reexamined the doll for a second. Then she kissed it on the head and pressed it to her chest as if nothing had happened.

"Very good," Moy said. And he gave a thumbs-up sign to the nurse.

"Something about fighting fire with fire," Nick whispered.

"We've had several dress rehearsals," Lucille said.

Nick was about to tell Moy that Margaret had lost an infant child decades ago, when somebody shouted, *"It's a goddamn doll."*

Louis Martinetti.

He had stepped out of his room in a bathrobe and pajamas. "Just a stupid doll, anyone can see that. She's nuts. She does this five times a day. You can't even get any sleep around here." Then he shouted, *"I want out of here!"*

One of the aides went over to Louis in an effort to console him. "Oh, Louis, poor Louis, were you asleep?" Yolanda asked. "We're sorry."

"Goddamn loony bin in here," Louis continued. "Take that thing away from her. She's only going to do it again."

Margaret scowled at Louis, clutching the doll to her chest, trying to block its eyes against the bad man.

"It makes her feel good," Lucille explained.

"Thing's made of rubber," Louis said. Then to Margaret he yelled, "Rubber. It can't be dead, right?"

Margaret began to whimper and sway with the doll clutched to her breast.

"Oh, forget it," Louis said. "Just don't get so damn noisy next time." Then he rubbed his face in exasperation. "I want out of here," and he glared at Nick. "I don't belong here and you know that. I'm all better."

He started back to his room when his eyes fell on the men with Nick. Instantly Louis froze. His eyes filled his glasses as he glowered at them. "Uh, uh, uh!" he muttered.

"Louis, what's the problem?"

Suddenly he became very agitated, muttering to himself and cowering. "Louis, calm down. What's wrong?" The nurse tried to take his arm but he yanked free, then began to chop at his forehead with his right hand.

"What the hell's he doing?" Moy asked.

Louis looked possessed, standing there in a slight crouch with his eyes bulging while muttering nonsense syllables—

"koppy choppy tu san ingee jop jop"—all the while chopping the side of his forehead.

"Louis, calm down," Nick said. He tried to take his hand, but Louis jumped away. "Come on, Louis. Everything's okay. Nothing to be afraid of."

Louis glowered at them, and for a moment he looked as if he were about to attack. Then he seemed to realize something. "Buster," he muttered.

"What's that?" Nick replied. But Louis shook his head, then let out a howl and bolted back into his room, slamming the door.

"Louis! Louis!" Lucille called through the door. "What's the matter? Everything's okay." She opened the door, but Louis shouted for her to leave the room.

"What's his problem?" Moy asked.

Nick shook his head. "Something spooked him."

"He was looking at us," Jordan said.

"But who knows what he saw." Nick moved to Louis's door and tapped. "Louis, it's Dr. Nick. May I come in?"

No answer.

"Louis, I think Margaret's okay now, and you can take your nap. But you seem pretty upset. Maybe you can tell me what the problem is." None of the patient rooms had locks, but instead of pushing his way in, Nick decided on giving Louis an option to open up and explain what had spooked him. Nick tapped again. "Louis, may I come in?"

Nothing.

Nick whispered to Lucille to get some meds, and he tapped once more. "Louis, I'm going to come in if that's okay. Then we can talk about it." He opened the door.

Louis's single was empty. The windows were closed and still intact. The bed was flat. Nick opened the door to the toilet and pulled back the shower curtain. No Louis.

On the small bureau sat familiar photos of a younger Louis posed with other GIs in Korea. On the floor, probably tossed off when Louis got out of bed, were two CD cases, *The Real Johnnie Ray—Greatest Hits,* and Peggy Lee's *Is That All There Is?* But nothing looked out of place.

"Louis, I know you're here," Nick said to the closed closet door. "There's nothing to be upset about. Those gentlemen with me are my friends." He tapped the door. "Louis, it's Dr. Nick. I think it's a good idea if you came out so we can talk about what's bothering you."

Nothing.

"Then I'm going to open the door."

Nick opened the door. Louis was there all right, but he was crouched down among his slippers and shoes and a suitcase.

"Hi, Louis. It might be more comfortable if you came out into the room."

Louis looked terrified. He mumbled something incoherent, but after a few moments Nick coaxed him into standing up.

But then Louis spotted Jordan, Moy, and the others behind Nick. His pupils dilated and he began to jabber nonsense syllables again, his voice rising in a ululating pitch. "I swear I don't know nothing. Please."

"I think it's best if you waited outside," Nick said to the others. Then to Louis, "It's okay, Louis. Everything's all right. No one's going to hurt you. You can come out now."

Jordan, Moy, and the rest began backing into the dayroom. But before they disappeared, Jordan looked back.

Louis Martinetti was standing in the closet dressed in army fatigues, combat boots, and fatigue cap. Although it was too small for him, his shirt was adorned with ribbons, a Bronze Star, and a Purple Heart. A set of metal dog tags hung around his neck. In his left hand he held a furled umbrella.

Louis muttered something to Nick.

"What did he say?" Moy asked.

"His name, rank, and serial number."

53

"He had a flashback."

"A what?" asked Coleman.

Nick had filed several reports to GEM Tech scientists with cc's to Gavin Moy about the seizures. But apparently Coleman had not been informed. "A flashback seizure," Nick said after they had settled in the conference room. "It's what I called you about. We have a problem."

The nurses had given Louis Martinetti an injection of Haldol and put him back to bed. Nick put his hands on a stack of notebooks of cumulative data on the trials. "As we all know, the majority of test patients have experienced reversals of their pathology and are enjoying increased functionality and lucidity—a success level as defined by the company's endpoint objectives. But for some patients the turnaround works too well."

Moy looked at him nonplussed. "What do you mean 'too well'?"

"By stimulating the growth of new neuron formations in the hippocampus, memory functions are regained."

"We know how it works," Moy snapped.

"Of course, but over the last several weeks, we've noticed some disturbing side effects that we need to address. For a number of patients the compound dislodges them from the objective present and sends them into flashback modes. In short, they relive long-forgotten experiences."

"That's impossible," Moy growled. "Our brains aren't like some Blockbuster video collection, for God's sake."

"True, but Louis out there has been experiencing some kind of throwback to his Korean War days. In his mind he's twenty years old and with his buddies in Korea."

"That's ridiculous," Moy said. And his medical director nodded agreement.

"But that's what we just witnessed," Nick continued. "And it's what I think happened with Mary Curley. From police reports, the woman was clearly delusional, thinking she was a child again looking for her puppy. And she crawled under the trolley. In her mind she was back seven decades. Like Louis Martinetti, she was locked into continuous dissociative experiences."

Nick glanced at Jordan, whose face looked like red camouflage. The episode with Louis Martinetti had clearly upset him. Or maybe it was the way Moy was glaring at him. Jordan knew about these problems, of course. He had experienced similar episodes at his own trial site. So had the other investigators. "Luckily, nobody raised the question of a connection between Memorine and Mary's suicide."

"And there isn't one," Moy said.

The party line. Nick opened a file folder. "And they're not just anomalies here. Maurico Rucci, who's PI at the Providence trial site, reports similar problems. So does Peter Habib in Plymouth. He's got a resident who refuses to change out of a party dress she's worn around the clock for several days, and she becomes violent when aides try to make her. Apparently the dress was like one she had worn to her high school prom. And every time she has it on, she would hold full conversations with old classmates. It's bizarre."

"I don't believe it," Moy declared. And the others nodded.

"Another patient in the study from Schenectady was caught

at the last minute trying to drown his three-year-old grandson in a sink."

"What?"

"The mother stopped him in time. Later he said he thought the little boy was a fox. Then we learned he was raised on a chicken farm. He was trying to appease his dead abusive father, he said. This was not a violent person. Nor was Mary Curley suicidal."

"Dr. Mavros, how do you know these anomalies weren't the results of neuropsychiatric problems?"

"Because none of the placebo patients have flashback seizures. Look, I'm telling you that what we are seeing are intrinsically significant side effects that must be addressed."

Thompson asked, "Any idea what these flashbacks are rooted in, Doctor?"

"No, but my guess is abnormal brain plasticity. Some people might be genetically susceptible to psychomotor seizures. Or it could be demographic. Whatever, we need to make a thorough dose response profile of the population, since the numbers are high."

"How high?"

"Thirty percent, maybe more."

Throughout the exchange, Jordan remained quiet. But now he seemed to rise in his chair. "I beg to differ," he said. "I've seen several reports, and these flashbacks are simply isolated cases that are clearly the result of the prior dementia and not Memorine."

Nick nodded. "That was my suspicion, too, but when I withdrew patients from the drugs, the episodes disappeared. Unfortunately, that presents an even worse problem, as you know. Withdraw them too long, and the plaque returns."

"So what are you recommending?" Moy asked.

"That we try to create a demographic profile while determining proper dosages and treatments. But we'll need more time—maybe a year or two."

Gavin's face looked as if it had turned to brick. "We don't have a year or two. The first weekend in June you, I, and every

GEM Tech trial clinician are scheduled to meet at Bryce Canyon, Utah, to work out the final details of the application to the FDA. It has to be submitted by midmonth for a year-end market release. And you know that."

Jordan cut in. "Nick, we're talking about people who've suffered years of brain deterioration. And we all know that connections of the different areas lose control and get repatterned, resulting in different behavioral aberrations. With all due respect, dementia patients have adverse episodes—flashbacks, if you wish—but they're caused by the rerepatterning from the original damage. In short, it's the pathology, not the pill."

"Then that's something we better determine before we rush to the FDA."

"Any idea what sets off these flashbacks?" Thompson asked.

"From what I've observed, external stimuli—odors, loud sounds, something somebody says, flashing lights. Almost anything can bring them on, in fact. Depending on the flashbacks, the experiences can be traumatic or delightful. Mr. Martinetti had clearly experienced trauma. So did Clara Devine and others, including one of Peter Habib's patients, a Rodney Blake, who bled to death after he castrated himself for God knows what reason. Mary Curley's was just the opposite, and it killed her horribly."

"And what do you do to stop them?"

"Dilantin, some of the other antiseizure medications. Heavy doses of anti- anxiety and antipsychotic drugs have been necessary also."

"And how would you characterize the majority of these flashbacks?"

"For the most part pleasurable."

"Is that a problem?"

"It is if they're addicted."

Thompson's face screwed up. "Pardon me?"

"Many *want* to go back to their past," Nick continued. "For them the present is a dull reality—like Dorothy returning from Oz to black-and-white Kansas. And they know that it's Memorinc that will get them to return."

"You're talking dependency."

"Big time. And if they can't get their flashback fix, some of them will try to bring themselves back by whatever means."

"Such as what?"

"For Mary Curley, it was returning to a place where her parents had taken her—the Museum of Fine Arts. When her daughter brought her home, she somehow managed to make her way. But this was not your typical aimless dementia wandering. This was marked by purpose and destination. Others employ queer little rituals to trigger the flashbacks—like what you saw out there with Louis's hand movements."

"You mean hitting himself in the head?"

"He wasn't hitting himself. He was saluting."

"Saluting?"

"Yes, but on some weird fast-forward. It's how he induces a flashback."

"You've got to be kidding," Moy said.

"I'm not kidding. Some subjects set off events by stimulating different sensory zones—rubbing parts of their bodies, pacing, bouncing on one foot. Or they play nursery rhymes and Christmas carols on their CD players. Whatever sends them back."

"But Gavin's right," Thompson said. "Past experiences aren't stored intact in the brain."

"Yes. True memory is a matter of flashbulb recollections. With these patients, there are just more flashbulbs and a strong autosuggestive component, allowing them to create the illusion of being back when."

"That guy was acting normal one minute, then he snapped."

"Yes, and something set him off."

"I am not happy about this," Moy growled. "We've spent hundreds of millions of dollars in years of studies examining the efficacy and tolerability of Memorine with two dozen test groups and hundreds of patients, and consistently across all the damn scales the drug improved cognition—in some cases a hundred percent compared to placebos—and with no deterioration in global functioning and behavior. And now we have these goddamn flashbacks or whatever the Christ they are."

Nick was aware that GEM's marketing plan was to send scores of sales reps to physicians and health care people across the country to encourage use of Memorine once it hit the markets. According to Gavin Moy, that program alone was costing the company forty million dollars. Adding to the rush was the fact that FDA director George Orman-Witt was retiring at the end of the year, and his replacement might not be as sympathetic with flashback reports and could ask for a complete review. So they were playing Beat the Clock.

Mort Coleman, GEM's legal counsel, turned to Nick. "So, what do you suggest?"

"I suggest that we do an internal review of all clinical data and try to determine the correlation between these flashbacks and patient profiles—demographics, ethnicity, environment, genetic markers, medical profiles, and any other possible parameters. If something comes out of it, perhaps we can determine if certain patients should be excluded from use of the drug."

"That could take months, maybe years."

Nick heard the edge of panic in Coleman's voice. "It may also save lives and beat lawsuits. We rush this to market before it's ready and we could end up with the greatest medical flop since thalidomide."

"And if we don't, it might be the greatest medical crime against humanity," Thompson declared.

"Then maybe you should speak to some family members," Nick said.

"What does *that* mean?" Moy asked.

"At Webster Smith Rehab in Maine," Nick explained, "an eighty-two-year-old male lies in his bed all night talking to kids at the YMCA camp he went to as boy—I mean full, coherent conversations about canoeing, rope swinging, et cetera to people who aren't there. He had his wife bring in mosquito netting, and he's got it draped over his bed like he's back camping. Most of the time he doesn't acknowledge her presence and it's driving her crazy because Memorine has brought back a son instead of a husband."

"He's suffering other problems."

"You saw what happened to Louis Martinetti out there."

"I saw a demented patient banging himself in the head."

"Even if there are these flashbacks," Thompson said, "what's the problem with patients reliving parts of their childhood every so often? It's better than sitting in front of a television like a turnip."

"Then maybe you should come with me." Nick opened the door and led them down the hall to another room. "We're still waiting for the family to claim her belongings, so the place hasn't been changed over yet. But this is the single that Mary Curley occupied for the last year." Nick swung open the door.

The interior was a mausoleum to little girlhood. The walls were draped with posters of kittens and puppies and cartoon decals. The bed was covered with appliqué floral bedspread patches in pinks and yellows, and the pillow was stacked with stuffed animals and Raggedy Ann and Andy dolls. Pasted on the headboard were large floral letters in pink spelling out "Mary." Beside the bed was a nightstand with a pink lamp whose shade had cartoon figures of bees and bluebirds and a framed black-and-white photograph of a puppy with a label "Jello." On the bureau were ceramic figurines of ballerinas and puppies as well as a grouping of the Cowardly Lion, Tin Man, and Scarecrow. Beside the bed was a pink rocking chair whose back was a carved heart with the hand-painted inscription: "Time out to think about the things you do!" In the corner was a large plastic pumpkin structured as an armoire with shelves lined with small dolls.

"Jesus!" Moy muttered.

"She wanted to be a little girl again," Nick said, "And in her mind she was."

"Where did all this stuff come from?" Coleman asked.

"Family members. As she became more functional, she began to demand mementos from her childhood. But since most of them were long gone, relatives brought all this stuff, which made her want more. The problem was that she'd sit in here for hours playing."

From a bureau drawer Nick removed a small black-and-white photo of a little girl beside a man in a suit. They were standing in front of a statue of an Indian seated bareback on a horse with arms extended. "According to relatives, the MFA was a favorite place her parents took her to as a child. She liked the mummies."

Then Nick picked up a throw rug in the shape of a yellow puppy. On the floor were crisscross lines where tape had been applied. "Her nephew did that."

"What is it?" Jordan asked.

"A hopscotch grid," Moy said.

"It was," Nick said. "And she was pretty spry for her age. You would hear her singing and trying to hop about. We peeled the tape off when she took a fall."

Jordan looked rattled. "But if she was happy, what's the problem?"

"If Mary was your mother and you didn't mind her playing with dolls and doing hopscotch, that wouldn't be a problem. But if she's doing it all day long, you may yearn for Alzheimer's.

"The other thing is that she'd turn violent when it was time to take her antiseizure pills because she knew what they did. But it was the little blue pill that brought back her childhood."

Nick held up a folder with a small stack of letters from family members. "These are requests from family members to withdraw their relatives from Memorine. Mary's daughter had threatened legal action if we refused. We complied, but not soon enough."

"So you recommend we ask for an extension to work out these problems."

"Yes."

"We have a strategy meeting in June. We'll work it out," Moy said, and left the room. The others followed through the door. In the corridor Moy stayed back until he and Nick were alone. "You really believe they're remembering that far back?"

"Yes. We're rewiring areas in their hippocampus that's sending them back."

"How far?"

"Mary Curley's daughter says she recalled events in the

Ohio house where she was born—where they lived before the family moved east."

"And how long ago was that?"

"Seventy-five years."

Moy's face appeared to shift slightly.

"She was less than three years old."

Moy held Nick's gaze for a moment until Nick felt something pass between them. Then Moy turned and left.

54

Five, six, seven more days passed, and Jack added another nine, twelve, and fourteen minutes to the time he could walk unassisted. Every day he made mincing little steps of progress.

According to the doctors, he had sustained no impairment to his thinking and reasoning skills, nor would he need speech therapy. So the rehab team focused on making him physically stronger and getting him to walk again. Thus his day was blocked out in sessions with the whirlpool, foot hydrotherapy, the rehab gym, and the physical therapist who had him keep active four or more hours a day.

His progress was considered remarkable by the staff, the result of his own determination to get back on his feet and out on his own. And they would hoot and high-five him and praise his strength of will. His recovery had pushed the envelope.

But it was more than strength of will and muscular reconditioning. Jack wanted out of Greendale. Call it bad karma or superstition or sour psychic residue. But the place was buggy with nightmares and bad flashes—so much so that he began to dread sleep for fear of being assaulted by grade-B horror flick snips. The nurses gave him different drugs that sometimes helped.

But the good news was that Vince had located a place to lease—a small Cape cottage he could have for the next nine months. And it was in Carleton, Jack's hometown.

That was also the bad news, for it was near the old neighborhood where he and Beth had shared their home.

"**Hi, Jack. This is** Dr. Nicholas Mavros."

A squarish middle-aged man with thick gray hair stood next to Marcy. In a black sport shirt and chinos, he didn't look like a doctor—maybe because it was Saturday or because the docs here didn't dress in white. The man had a wide, toothy smile and dark eyes that were hidden behind thick Coke-bottle glasses.

"Dr. Mavros assisted Dr. Heller when you were first brought to MGH."

Mavros's hand was meaty and cool. "Good to finally meet you awake. How you doing?"

"Better."

"Good, good. You're quite the Comeback Kid." Mavros smiled broadly. "The PT reports say you're progressing marvelously. And there's no evidence of any neurological damage. In fact, quite the contrary. The memory centers of your brain are very active. Which is the most important thing, right?"

Jack nodded. Dr. Mavros's large opaque eyes bore down on him. And though it was barely perceptible, Jack felt his innards tighten.

"You're a medical wonder. And if you don't mind, I'd like to run a functional MRI on you someday."

Jack was not interested in more tests, and made a noncommittal nod.

"Do you recall anything about the actual accident—swimming, the jellyfish attack?"

"Not really. Just jumping into the water, some vague image of jellyfish, then I'm here."

Mavros nodded woefully. "They got you pretty good."

"I don't recommend it."

"I'll say." Mavros smiled brightly. Almost too brightly, as if trying to slide into the next question without notice. "And just out of curiosity, what were you doing out there on Homer's Island? Seems like a rather remote place to be."

"We used to rent a place out there."

"We?"

"My family."

"Your family . . . ," Mavros repeated, leaving an inviting gap for Jack to fill in.

"A vacation rental."

"I see. Were you staying there at the time of the jellyfish attack?"

Outside thunder cracked. Jack had already tired of the line of questioning. "Just wanted to see the old place."

"I see."

But it was clear that the good doctor didn't see.

"Do you remember how old you were when you first started going out there?"

Jack shook his head. "I was a baby."

"Do you remember the name of your first-grade teacher?"

"My first-grade teacher? I already had memory tests."

"Just checking." And Mavros flashed a thousand-watt smile.

"Miss Van Zandt."

The doctor jotted that down on his pad, and Jack wondered how he'd check for accuracy.

"What were your adoptive parents' names?"

Jack told him.

"Do your remember your biological parents?"

"No. My father died when I was six months old, my mother when I was two."

"So you don't remember them."

Jack felt himself slump. "No."

The doctor looked at his notepad. "The nurses say that you've complained of bad dreams, which is consistent with the reports while you were in the coma. Do you remember anything about those dreams—any specifics?"

"Nothing very clear."

"Can you characterize them in any way?"

"Disturbing."

"Disturbing?"

"Violent. Images of someone getting hurt." Jack felt his heart rate notch upward.

"Can you see who it is? Who's involved, or how they're—"

Jack cut him off. "No, and I'd rather end the questions, if you don't mind. I'm very tired."

"Of course. I understand, and I'm sorry about this." Then his face brightened again. "But thank you. And you should know that we're delighted with your progress."

Jack nodded. He was drowsy all of a sudden, as if he'd been drugged.

Before the doctor left he said, "I hope I didn't upset you with my queries. It's just a routine thing, you understand."

"No problem." Jack closed his eyes.

"Just one more, if you don't mind. One of those standard memory test things."

Jack opened his eyes.

"Your biological mother. What was her maiden name?"

"Sarkisian."

Mavros looked at him for a protracted moment. Then he nodded.

But he did not ask to spell it, nor did he write it down on his pad. He just stared at Jack without expression, then thanked him and left the room, leaving Jack thinking that this was the third person in a week who wanted to know his mother's maiden name.

55

"**W**e have a problem," Mark Thompson announced.

Of the thirteen chairs around the huge shiny cherry-wood conference table in the boardroom of GEM Tech, six were occupied. Five men and one woman: Gavin Moy; legal counsel Mortimer Coleman; marketing director Marilyn Pierce; medical director Mark Thompson; principal investigator for the clinical sites in Connecticut Zachary Mello; and Jordan Carr. Conspicuously absent was Dr. Nicholas Mavros.

"Peter Habib has gotten Nick thinking there's a causality between these so-called flashback seizures and Memorine. Since the suicide-ruled death of one of his patients, he is asking for an immediate review of clinical protocol."

"Even before Utah?" Moy asked.

"Even before Utah."

"What about Nick?"

"He's more open-minded but he's susceptible. Apparently Peter has forwarded him data."

"Wasn't it Peter who first raised a flag?"

"Yes. And now he wants to alert the agency."

"What about Nick?"

"I think he's willing to wait until Utah. But the point is that he's losing his proper vision on this project," Thompson continued. "And frankly that makes him something of a liability for this trial and this organization."

"If you're suggesting we replace him as chief PI, that's not going to happen," Gavin Moy declared. "That'll only invite the press to ask why, raising the kind of speculations we don't need."

Mort Coleman agreed. "Axing Nick because we don't like his position on the drug's efficacy is not the way to go. He's an iconic figure in the medical community and is identified with these trials and GEM Tech. That would be counterproductive."

Marilyn Pierce cut in. "Not to mention how the FDA would react once Nick began talking to the press about his termination. That's not a viable option."

"But there is a viable option," Moy said. "Hiring an independent clinical research organization. Not only is that the most legitimate way to go, but I'm betting it'll get Nick to come around."

"Come around to what?"

"To stop suggesting that we ask the FDA for a friggin' two-year extension."

"Christ, is that what he's doing?"

"Yes." Moy poured himself some coffee from the decanter. "So what we do is consult an expert clinical research organization. We submit them all the clinical data, have them go through each case report, put them on spreadsheets, blah blah blah, and determine any problems and if so whether they fall within the projected end points of the target population blah blah blah."

"But that could still take months," Jordan said.

"Not if we make it worth their while," Moy said. "But Nick's right. It's better safe than sorry."

Coleman agreed. "We don't want to explode onto the market only to discover that we've got a billion dollars' worth of lawsuits dogging us like with Fen-Phen or Vioxx or those rotavirus vaccines that got yanked."

"And what if this CRO determines there's a . . . correlation?" Jordan could hardly word that possibility.

"If that's the case, then we have to determine that segment of the population for whom these side effects can't be eliminated. But, at least, usage of the drug can be screened and made available only to people not susceptible, who meet specific eligibility criteria—or under conditions where the benefits may outweigh the risks. That's what warning labels are for."

"Even in the worst-case scenario, say thirty percent are risk cases, seventy percent of the market is still blockbuster proportions."

"I think the CRO option makes sense," Jordan said. And the others agreed.

Moy named the Klander Group, a New York organization GEM had used in the past. Moy also was good friends with Allen Klander. All agreed. "Good, that settles it," Moy said.

Before they headed for lunch, Jordan pulled something out of his briefcase. "I assume you're aware of this news item." He handed Moy a photocopy of the *Boston Globe* article as well as copies to the others. The headline read: "Jellyfish Coma Victim Recovers After Nearly Seven Months."

A 33-year-old Carleton man who had spent six months in a "persistent vegetative state" recently regained consciousness at the Greendale Rehabilitation Center in Cabot, Mass. . . .

"Is this a problem?" asked Marilyn Pierce.

"Is what a problem?"

"The article goes on to say that the guy returned from the coma with memory powers that baffle his doctors. Some sharp-eyed neuro-pharm person from another lab might find a connection to the Solakankji jellyfish and scramble to come up with a competing compound for treating dementia, you know, tweak the molecule a little and get their own patent."

"Hardly," Coleman said. "We've got the patent for the parent compound, plus patents on sixteen molecular 'for use' variations. Nobody else is even close, unless they've got a variant synthesis we haven't thought of."

Coleman was right. Those patents represented proprietary as well as legal rights to scientific property. For another company to develop a competing compound, it would have to be an ingenious and unforeseen molecular variation that also demonstrated pharmacological uses in combating Alzheimer's or other forms of dementia—a process of biochemical identification, extensive three-phase testing of animals and humans, and the implementation and organization of the R&D required to launch a decade-long process. Even if some little-known lab could secretly put together a competing drug, there'd be a leak—if nothing else, word filtering down from the FDA, one of the many Alzheimer's associations, or employees in the very tight and incestuous pharmaceutical industry.

"Someone would have to make a connection between the jellyfish and the guy's enhanced memory," said Thompson. "And there's no way anybody would. You just have a miraculous recovery. And sometimes that happens."

"Not a problem." And Moy slipped the article into his folder.

But Jordan thought that he detected a lingering concern in Gavin's face.

Whatever, they would take the CRO route. And if all went well, they'd go to market before anybody else. Thanks to marketing, Memorine was not just a household term already; it had become to the needy an incantation.

Gavin Moy sat alone at the head of the table after the others had left. From outside he could hear the sounds of jets on their approach to Logan Airport over Boston Harbor.

His eye fell on the newspaper article again.

Jack Koryan.

It sounded French or maybe even Irish (like one of his neighbors at Bayside, a guy whose face was the map of County Cork—named Kevin Lorian). Maybe even Israeli—à la Moshe Dayan. Possibly Arabic, a variation of *Koran*. Whatever, the guy had been sent into a coma for nearly seven months.

Moy had wondered at the odds of a casual tourist on Homer's Island getting stung by Solakandji. Those things don't come around but once in a blue moon—could be decades between occurrences. An absolute rarity.

But who was this Jack Koryan? And what the hell was he do-ing out there taking a swim with a storm brewing?

A simple statistical coincidence. Nothing more, nothing less.

Maybe Mark Thompson was right. Maybe the real problem was Nick Mavros.

56

It was dumb, but Jack still went.

Another three weeks would pass before he was released from Greendale; and he had circled the day in red on his calendar. But on occasion an aide would take him for a field trip to a local park or mall where he could exercise his legs. Of course, the aide was always at his side with a medical kit—the football, as Jack called it.

But that Friday morning, Jack convinced the aide, Andre LeVal, to swing by his old place in Carleton where he and Beth used to live. He also convinced Andre to let him stroll up Hutchinson Road by himself while Andre kept an eye on him from his parked car. Andre saw no problem and let Jack out.

It had been a long time.

Jack made his way with the cane, moving along as if he were crossing a minefield, taking little mincing steps not because of his legs but because if he didn't sneak up on the place it might come at him too hard. So he stopped across the street, under the maple in front of the Helms's place. Tom and Marilyn both worked, so they wouldn't catch him, come out, and ask him in for coffee and a good cry.

He looked at the house and waited for a reaction. But there was none, probably because the anticipation had all but anesthetized him.

The place looked the same—white colonial, green shutters, sloping lawn, low stone wall, azaleas and boxwood bushes that he had planted. The paint looked brighter than he remembered. The flower garden was still there, blazing with daffodils. Beth had sent away for hundreds of bulbs one year, and for several hours they planted them all, getting goofy on the dirt and sweat.

Jack thought about crossing the street, but there was no sidewalk, which did not make for casual strolling, especially with a cane. So he stood under the tree, hoping no cars would come by and wonder if he was some kind of stalker.

You don't live here anymore, Jackie Boy. That was pre-coma you.

He moved down the street.

Why are you doing this, asshole? The last thing you need is a good-old-days fix. Only going to make you more miserable.

Niggling thoughts, and he shook them away. *Just this once.*
Bullshit.

Jack's mind was a fugue. He had not been here in months, and this was coming to terms with that. Reality test, turning point, sayonara—your basic parting shot.

The lawn was a brilliant green, looking better than he remembered it. But it always did look greener in April before summer turned it New England brown. The house looked the same, but the setting looked reshuffled. At the top of the lawn sat the pink dogwood he had planted the spring they moved in. It had been pruned, and the shrubs looked taller—or maybe it was his imagination. At the side of the house was a child's riding toy fashioned after a train engine. A kid or kids lived there now. He and Beth had wanted to fill the place with babies— three or four of them. Whatever, somebody else's tree, somebody else's shrubs. Somebody else's kids.

Jack felt disoriented from the double vision. To a major portion of his brain, this was his house. He and Beth had lived there just a few weeks ago. Now people with unknown names filled the rooms with their voices, there furniture, their kids, their own *I-wish-I-may-I-wish-I-might*s. Different voices hummed the walls, warmed the bed. Same stage, different cast.

Suddenly a fierce sadness sliced through him like a sickle. This was what grief was like—grief for the loss of it all: for his Beth, his world, the old Jack. Sure, he was alive, but was that really better than the alternative?

Shit! Just what he didn't want was to get locked into yearning for what no longer was. He needed to rise above the swirling muck of anger and self-pity. This wasn't a matter of getting on with his life since there was no life to get on with. It was a matter of your basic makeover. Renewal. Renascence: Jack Koryan II.

About the past and that place across the street, he just wanted to forget. But, man, it was hard, and there were times like this when he envied the Greendale old guys their forgetting. He'd kill to go blank, erase the palimpsest of his old soul and get an all-new impression.

He started up the street and glanced at the house again . . .

One big fucking mistake, pal! Go back to Andre and get out of here.

And he was hit with a recollection so vivid that for a moment he nearly lost his balance.

It was November: He was standing high on a ladder cleaning the gutters. Beth appeared in the bedroom window right next to where he was scooping out the leaf mash. She had just gotten out of the shower and was toweling off when she spotted him and tapped the window. He peered within to see her flash him a full Monty, a sly cartoon grin on her face. "Hey, Ladderman, want to climb this?" He made a huge stupid face. "Uh, climb what, ma'am?" She closed the towel across herself and opened it again in an exaggerated stripper flash and jiggled her breasts at him. "This, nitwit." "Ah just do gutters." She rolled her eyes. "Well, have I got a gutter for you!" she said, and snapped her pelvis at him. "Oh, okay, if you say so," and he gave her a look of moronic complicity. Beth cracked up, and Jack was down the ladder in a wink and up the stairs and into the bedroom before she could settle in their bed. "Shower first," she said. And he did. And they did. And it was wonderful.

He headed back down the street toward Andre's Toyota, repeating just what a bad idea this was. He should have just gone to the North Shore Mall instead. Andre was reading a newspaper.

Jack got in the car. "Okay, let's go."

"Nobody home?"

"Nobody home."

As Andre pulled away, Jack felt the tug of the house at number 12 for one last little peek—for auld lang syne. He glanced through the window, gazing at the house through a mist, too distracted by the receding visions to notice the black SUV following them.

57

Peter Habib turned his bright red Harley onto Ocean Drive and cranked the throttle. At one in the morning there were no other vehicles on the road.

Peter did this whenever he couldn't sleep. Instead of tossing around in his sheets, he'd take his candy-apple-and-chrome stallion for a spin.

And this was one of those glorious early spring nights when the sea air was laced with sultry hints of summer yet still cool and moist and requiring a leather jacket.

He loved this drive because there were several strips where the houses and trees gave way to open vistas of beach. His favorite was a straightaway about a mile long with no obstacles between him and the ocean save for a concrete breakwater barrier erected a few nor'easters back.

Rising among scraps of clouds was a three-quarter tangerine moon that blazed across the black expanse of water and set the sky in motion. It was one of those nights when Peter felt privileged to be alive.

He whipped along the winding course of Ocean Drive, feeling that he could do this all night long, except that the Massachusetts coastline would not allow endless oceanside cruising. Maybe after the trials were over, he'd head for California— growl up the Pacific Coast Highway from Los Angeles up through the Big Sur. And why not? He could afford an early retirement. And his wife wouldn't mind if he and one of his biker friends did a guy thing. Might even take the hogs across country. The other option was flying out and renting bikes in L.A. Or buy them and have them shipped back. Whatever. He was making great money.

Ahead the road opened up to the straightaway, and his heart throttled up.

Amazing. Not another car on the road, and there was the endless Atlantic and that splendid moon you could almost pick out of the sky with your fingers.

Peter pushed the bike to about forty. He liked the way the roar of his engine echoed off the barrier as he whipped through the scene, the moon to his right over the water. He throttled up.

But it wasn't the only light. Out of his left eye he saw something in his mirror. The moon. But reflecting off something else.

He checked his right mirror, but it happened all so fast that he did not process that a large black vehicle had closed in behind him. Or that its headlights were off. Or that it had come up on him at full speed, the only indication being the moon glancing off its windshield in his mirrors.

Peter also did not have time to process how the driver of the vehicle could have missed the bright taillights of his Harley. All he knew was that the large dark mass suddenly closed on his left flank pressing him into the strip of barriers.

By reflex, Peter braked. And the moment exploded into a void.

58

"**H**e died instantly," Nick said.

"That's terrible." René had met the man only a few times, but she felt as if she had lost an old ally. And Nick was devastated.

"The police say that he lost control of the bike and hit a concrete breakwater."

"He was such a nice man."

"And a first-rate clinician. It's a real loss." He was also the one vocal ally Nick had in his effort to postpone the FDA application of Memorine.

According to Nick, Peter had been cremated and a memorial service would be held in a few weeks.

They were walking on a trail through conservation land about two miles off the South Border Road exit of Route 93. It was where Nick would hike to get in shape for the Utah trip in June. Most of the trails were through tall oaks, although the land climbed to huge glacial outcroppings of granite from the top of which one could see the skyline of Boston.

They continued in silence for several minutes. The cool breeze felt good, a relief from the confines of nursing homes and an opportunity to deal with their sadness. In a couple of hours they had to be back at Broadview to consult with the Martinetti women. Louis was protesting that he wanted to go home.

"The other news is that GEM's decided to hire an independent clinical research organization to go through all the data and come up with recommendations."

"To what end?"

"GEM's mandated to explain any problems with the trials to the FDA, so they'll try to determine if the flashbacks are the result of the drug or the disease. It's what Peter was pressing for."

"But we can tell them that."

"Except they don't want to hear our argument."

"I thought once the Zuchowsky affair was resolved, they'd stop putting their heads in the sand."

"The Zuchowsky affair cost them a million dollars. This could cost them five hundred times that."

Nick had been working out here and on a home treadmill, so he cut up the trail like a mountain goat, René right behind him. "Any idea which CRO?"

"No. Some gerontology specialists."

"And what about flashback cases?"

"We continue fine-tuning dosages and noting behavior changes. Any problems we continue to treat with antiseizure drugs, antipsychotics, sedatives."

Two other clinical PIs had bowed out of the trials in disagreement with GEM Tech's pressure tactics and had been replaced by GEM-approved physicians. And now Peter Habib was dead. "Are we the only ones who think they're rushing a faulty drug to market?"

"I think Brian Rich and Paul Nadeau agree, and possibly Jordan Carr. He may be coming around. Unfortunately, that's up against a powerful flood of appeals by AD groups to get it to market by Christmas, no matter what."

"But a CRO review could take months."

"If pushed, they could review the data in a week. They've also got to have it done for Utah. That's seven weeks from now."

"So there's a deadline."

"Absolutely. Meanwhile, we box up all case report forms,

records, whatever, including all files on CDs, and continue the trials."

They came to a clearing and climbed the granite boulders to the top, where they had a three-hundred-and-sixty-degree view. Nick sat down on a rock and took a deep breath.

"You okay?"

He smiled and let out his breath. "Just a little dizzy."

René handed him a water bottle from her day pack. "How long have you been having these spells?"

"Since I've been thirty pounds overweight." He guzzled some water and stood up. "I'm fine."

Toward the east the skyline of Boston shimmered in the milky blue mist. Nick took his camera out of his backpack and snapped off a few shots—of the local rocks, the Boston skyline, and René.

"The Utah conference is just an hour's drive from Bryce Canyon. Imagine the views."

"I take it the FDA knows nothing about these flashback problems."

"Not officially, even though that was what Peter was pushing for," Nick said. He snapped another two shots. "Nor will they unless that's in the report by the CRO."

"And if the CRO concludes that the problem is drug-related?"

Nick shrugged. "Then we go back to the drawing boards— determine where the problem is—dosages, interactions with other medications or other diseases, population demographics— whatever it takes. We've done nothing about determining a correlation. Maybe Italian Americans or Eastern European Jews are susceptible to such seizures. Or people with a particular genetic signature. Or those patients with high blood pressure. We just don't know why some have flashbacks and others don't, but we'd better determine that before the stuff hits the market."

"And if this CRO concludes that the flashbacks are not drug related?"

"It goes to market."

What bothered René was how GEM Tech reps were categorically dismissing the flashbacks as anomalies unrelated to the drug. Even Mary Curley's death was ruled an unintentional suicide as the result of advanced dementia. The same with a man from Connecticut named Rodney Blake who had cut off his own genitals.

"Meanwhile, we continue feeding hope to victims and caregivers."

"And isn't that a shame."

59

"I don't want him home like this. He's not right yet, I'm telling you. He's not right."

René and Nick were back at Broadview with Marie Martinetti and her daughter, Christine. Louis was insisting on being released from the home and had called a lawyer.

"The tests say he's improved nearly fifty percent," Christine said.

"Yeah, but he's worse."

Mrs. Martinetti was in her seventies and ailing with arthritis, and Louis was still strong and more active than ever. And given his cognitive improvements, Louis had outgrown the nursing home. That fact made this a circumstance that nursing homes had never before had to confront—not since Memorine. And René could feel Nick struggle with the dilemma.

"Well, you're free to sign a release for him if you choose to bring him home," he explained.

"That's what I'm saying. I can't handle him the way he is." Marie looked pleadingly at René. "It's that Memorine. You gotta take him off it. It's making him crazy."

Christine's face was drawn in dismay. "Mom," she began.

"Mom, nothing. You don't know the half of it. You got to take him off it."

"Mrs. Martinetti, we really can't do that," Nick said woefully.

"What do you mean you can't do that? Of course you can do that."

"If we withdraw Louis from the drug the disease will come back."

Mrs. Martinetti glared at Nick as if he had just spit something up. "What?"

"That's the problem with this medication, I'm afraid."

"What's the problem? What are you saying?" She shot René a frantic look for an explanation she could accept.

But Christine cut in. "Mom, they're saying that the plaque will grow back. That he'll get Alzheimer's again if he's taken off it."

"What?" Mrs. Martinetti looked back at Nick. "You didn't know about this?"

"It never occurred in the early phases of the trials with lab animals. No reversal of any kind. Even in the second phase using humans we didn't see any evidence of a reversal."

Nick was correct. René had scanned some of the reports from GEM and outside protocol test labs, and nothing in the data had indicated that withdrawal from Memorine in any dosage caused animals or healthy nondemented humans to develop the amyloid plaque. Not until Clara Devine was returned from McLean's.

"It was completely unforeseen," Nick said. "I explained to Christine the other day. I'm very sorry."

"Sorry? But they said this was a miracle cure." Then the realization set in and her face crumbled. "Oh, my God."

"But, Mom, he can still take it," Christine began. "He's still recovering."

But Mrs. Martinetti disregarded her. "So, what does that mean? Louis will have these flashbacks the rest of his life—go back someplace in the junior high gym or in the army? Sweet Mother of God, what are you telling me?"

"Mom, please. It's better than him just wasting away."

Her head snapped at her daughter. "No, it *not* better! It

scares me, he goes off like that, talking to dead people, getting all scared he's got to watch them cut out Fuzzy Swenson's eyes, that Colonel Chop Chop bastard."

"Colonel Chop Chop?" Nick asked.

"Some North Korean commander," Christine said. "Chop Yong Jin, or something like that. I think he was in charge when my dad was taken prisoner. That was his nickname, Colonel Chop Chop." She explained that he was a high-ranking Korean officer who brought a Russian advisor on military campaigns— a guy they nicknamed Blackhawk, from an old military comic book character. In the book Chop Chop was his loyal sidekick. "Dad escaped, but he saw some bad stuff he never talked about."

"No, he didn't escape," Marie Martinetti cried. "They still got him. He keeps reliving them. And he talks about it and he's back again and again, but you're not there. I am. I *am*."

"I don't care if he has a couple of flashback things," Christine continued. "Those were the best times of his life, when he was young and full of himself. And he's fine in between, and he's not hurting himself or anybody else. And maybe you can come up with something that keeps them under control."

"But you don't know what he's reliving," Marie protested. "I've seen him. I'm here almost every day and you're not. It's horrible what I seen him go through. *HORRIBLE,* pressing his hands to his eyes so he can't see what they did to his friend. We'd be having a nice visit, and suddenly he's back in the Red Tent, he calls it—the torture place in the Commie camp. You don't know what he saw. He screams and cries . . ." And she broke down. "It's horrible . . ."

Christine put her hand on his mother's knee. "But I don't want him taken off it, Mom. I don't want to see him slip away again. I don't."

"But I can't handle it. I can't. I know what it does to him, how he gets so upset. Because in his head it's real what he sees. I prefer him . . . forgetful."

"*Forgetful?* You prefer him turning into a vegetable, just sitting there with dead eyes and a bag on his side? Not me! And I'm not going to let that happen to him again."

"But you haven't seen him suffer. That stuff's a curse. A damn curse. I wish to God we'd never signed him up on it." Then her voice broke into a whimper. "Oh, Sweet Mother, give me strength."

As René listened, she uttered a silent thanksgiving that her own father had never been afflicted with such war delusions. He rarely talked about the war, so God only knows what he might have relived on Memorine.

"Mrs. Martinetti," Nick said, "the lab is working on fine-tuning the dosages and coming up with some combination with other drugs to control these episodes. Believe me, there are a lot of very talented people working on this."

"Well, hurry up, because I want him back the way he was."

"In the meantime," René said, "we're giving him antiseizure medication that will help keep him stable."

"But that stuff makes him dopey," Christine said.

"I don't care *dopey*," said Mrs. Martinetti. "I'll take him dopey. It's better than being back in the Red Tent."

"Well, he certainly can go home on a furlough," Nick said to Christine. "It's unusual for patients with Alzheimer's, as you can imagine. But maybe some weekend soon."

"That would be great," Christine said, her eyes brightening.

"Then we'll put something on the calendar."

"But only if he had his antiseizure pills," Mrs. Martinetti insisted. "Otherwise, he can stay here. I can't take his torture. He was better off with Alzheimer's."

60

"**S**orry to bother you, Jack." It was Marcy.

Jack opened his eyes. He was still lying on his bed in his jeans and sneakers. After his morning walk—the forty-yard dash up and down the hall in just seven minutes—he had stretched out on his bed with the television on mute and closed caption and a copy of *U.S. News and World Report* across his chest. He had dozed off.

"This is Theo Rogers." With Marcy was a man in a T-shirt that said "We Fix It." "Mr. Rogers is going to repair your Venetian blinds."

"Call me Theo." The man held out a large rough hand that felt as if it could crush Jack's like twigs.

"How you doing?"

My legs ache, I'm built like a tuning fork, I wake up in the middle of the night with visions of gory mayhem, there's a six-point-two Richter scale quake rumbling between my ears. "Just dandy."

Theo nodded. He looked to be in his early thirties. He was maybe five-eight and built like a gymnast. His hair was dark and held back with elastic bands in a short ponytail, and his face was smooth and open. Either he had non-Caucasian blood or spent time in the tropics or a tanning salon, because his skin was a coffee color. Around his waist hung a tool holster with a hammer, pliers, and other tools. He opened a small stepladder.

"This won't take long."

Outside the window deep-bellied rumbles rolled across the sky and lightning flickered, making Jack squint.

"A bit bright for you, huh?" Theo said. "We'll take care of that," and he began to work on the blinds, which hung at a crazy angle in the window frame.

"I'll leave you two guys on your own," Marcy said. Before she left, she checked Jack's heart and pulse and took a temperature reading. While the workman inspected the blinds, Jack closed his eyes. Through the open window he could smell the ocean.

"I read about you in the papers."

Jack opened his eyes to see the man looking down at him from the ladder.

"Waking up after almost seven months. That's something."

"I guess." Jack closed his eyes again. He was tired and didn't want to chat.

"I never heard of jellyfish attacking people before. Musta been one hell of an experience."

"I don't recommend it."

"I bet. Remember it any?"

"Not much." Jack thought about asking Theo to let him sleep but decided that the guy meant well. Besides, the sound of the tools and the shades rattling sabotaged any nap taking. Jack closed his eyes again.

"The papers said something about your memory coming back strong. That's great. Sometimes coma patients come back with lots of blank spots, I hear."

Jack cracked open an eye. On the monitor some doctors were talking about that Alzheimer's drug René Ballard had mentioned. "Experimental drug for Alzheimer's disease," read the caption.

Theo removed the hammer from his holster and banged the

end of the screwdriver to pry loose a fixture. And Jack felt a small sensation jog through him.

"So you remember stuff before the accident pretty good, huh?"

"A little."

"Well, that's all that matters, if you ask me. As somebody said, 'You are what you remember.' Right? Same thing if your house caught fire."

"Pardon me?"

"If your house caught fire. They took this poll, asked if your house was burning down and there's only one thing you could save, besides your family members or pet, of course—what would it be?"

On the screen some doctors in white were being interviewed. Mass General Hospital, read the caption.

A slumping feeling. Maybe because that's where Jack was taken after the accident.

"The family photo album." Theo gesticulated with his hammer hand. "What nine out of ten people said. And me, too. It's the same with memory, know what I mean?"

Jack closed his eyes. "Guess I'm pretty lucky."

A few moments passed, then Theo started up again. "Just out of curiosity, what were you doing out there on Homer's Island? Kind of an out-of-the-way place, you ask me."

Jack was growing tired of the interrogation. "Bird watching."

"Bird watching," the man repeated. There was a long silence. Then he said, "The papers said something about you swimming. And a storm."

Why is this guy pressing me? And why the feeling that this was going beyond idle chitchat. "It came up fast, and I hadn't checked the weather report."

"Got your own boat?"

"Took the water taxi."

"So you remember stuff before the accident pretty well, huh?"

What is it with this guy? Why won't he shut up? Why's he playing Twenty Questions with me? "A little."

"That's my point: You still got what's most important." And

he tapped the side of his head. Another long pause. "How far back do you go?"

"Pardon me?"

"How far back can you remember—like when you were a kid?"

"Not really."

"Uh-huh. Some people say they remember when they were babies. Sign of intelligence, they say."

Jack did not respond.

"I can't remember before I was ten," Theo snorted. "Guess I must be pretty dumb. How about you?"

Jack eyed the man. "No. No. Nothing."

Suddenly things turned strange. In a protracted moment, the man became a still life, freezing in place on the ladder with the hammer raised, his mouth moving in slow motion, pulsing out queer utterances, the syllables stretched to alien phonics. As the man's eyes bore down on Jack for a response, Jack felt something like an eel slither through his gut.

Bad feeling.

"Don't remember stuff from when you were small? Me, neither, but I wish I did."

Jack couldn't speak—as if what had slithered through him shot into his brain and bored a hole in the language centers, leaving him gasping for words and quaking with an irrational sense of dread.

"Hey, you all right?"

"Mmmm." Which was all Jack could squeeze out.

"You looked a little . . ."

God, what the hell is this? What's passing through me?

His lungs caught some air and he sucked it up to his voice box. "I'm okay," he rasped. "Little dizzy."

"Uh-huh." And the guy turned back to the shade.

Jack's head was soupy and he closed his eyes as the man tapped away. Outside, the thunder was growling out to sea, the lightning flickering through Jack's eyelids. The man hammered away, and with each smack a small seismic crack shot through Jack.

Jack opened his eyes. Something about the image of that guy on the ladder clawed at Jack's consciousness. Something not right. But he couldn't grasp it. Whatever, it flitted across his mind like a bird coming in to roost, then just at the last second shot away.

Jack was positive he had never seen this Theo before because the man's face didn't fit any memory template. Then again, Jack had not laid eyes on a lot of faces of late. Maybe all the toxins had turned sections of his brain into Swiss cheese. A reasonable explanation, except the guy would surely have said something.

So why the dark sensation? Maybe someone from a dream. And he'd had a boatload of those of late.

"You want some water or something?"

"I'm okay." Jack could hear fear in the breathy scrape of his voice.

The man eyed him suspiciously, then nodded and went back to banging something in place, his mouth still moving.

Jesus, what's happening to me? Jack asked himself. *What the hell is going on in my head?*

Without expression, the man locked hard eyes on his. "I asked you a question."

Jack didn't remember the question. Maybe he'd nodded off for a moment and just dreamed he had. He looked up at Theo to reply, but the sensation was back, and worse—leaving him thinking that he had lived these moments before. Some wicked déjà vu.

In an instant an inexplicable anxiety set Jack's diaphragm in spasms. His throat constricted as if a snake were coiling around it. His forehead was a cold aspic of sweat, and his chest and neck were a flash of prickers.

Heart attack. I'm having a heart attack.

"Hey, you want me to call the nurse?"

Jack could not answer.

Shit. Worked yourself into cardiac arrest. A killer surge of self-inflicted anxiety, and you won yourself a permanent flat line.

But another thought cut across that one: *No. Not a heart attack.* His heart was strong, they had said, and at the moment was pounding so hard that his shirt was pulsing. No, something else. What had passed through him was a bolt of black horror.

Something about this repairman.

He wants to hurt you.

The guy glared down at him. And in Jack's mind, he jumped off the ladder and smashed his head with that shiny ball-peen hammer.

"You having a seizure?"

A skim of panic formed over Jack like ice. *Seizure. How did this repairman know about seizures?*

But the other voice was back: *You're being an asshole. The guy's perfectly friendly in his Mr. Fixit overalls and body shirt, up there on his ladder being chatty and doing his business with the blinds. And just because he's a repairman doesn't mean a limited vocabulary. You've got the problem, pal, not him.*

The repairman continued to stare at Jack, the individual slats making razor-edged slashes of light and shade across his features. He look demonic, his mouth a black gash in his brown face, his features jagged. And hot black auger eyes boring through him.

Suddenly the guy climbed down, the hammer in his fist.

Oh, Jesus! God, no. No! his brain screamed. A faint squeal pressed out of a clenched larynx.

The man took no notice and came up to the bed, the hammer still in his hand. Jack let out a gasp and in a flash he saw the hammer come down on the crown of his head with a sickening crack, blood and brain matter splattering all over the bed.

Under his pillow Jack's hand scrabbled for the nurse-call button.

"This will take care of you," the guy said.

Jack pressed the button and closed his eyes against the blow. Nothing.

"Here you go," and Theo handed Jack a glass of water.

"Everything okay?" Marcy said.

Jack opened his eyes. Theo was standing over him with a glass of water, Marcy by his side. "You okay, Jack?"

Jack grunted. "Can't sleep." Theo went back to the blinds.

"No problem." And she produced a pack of pills. "Theo looks about done, right?"

"Just about." And he slipped the hammer into his holster and popped the blinds in place and pulled the strings. They were fixed. He dropped them closed to darken the room.

"Great." Marcy gave the lorazepam to Jack.

Theo gathered his things. "You hang in there, buddy." And he walked out of the room.

In a matter of moments, the horror had flushed from Jack's mind.

There, asshole. There's your crazed psychopath in farmer johns.

Jack sipped more water and closed his eyes, concentrating on the liquid flowing down his parched throat. *Damn lucky the proverbial cat had your tongue, or you'd have some fancy explaining to do.*

So just what was *that?* Jack asked himself as he lay there. *Just your hot imagination—like those dreams of misshapen creatures killing people.*

But that didn't satisfy. There was something he couldn't put his finger on. Maybe the guy looked like somebody else. Maybe someone in a movie. Maybe someone in a dream.

A dream. His mind kept on coming back to that.

Like the dream about someone sneaking in here one night and trying to squirt some bad juice into your tubes.

But the other voice was back: *The guy's just some friendly innocent you're hanging your loonies on. Period. The meds. It's all the crap they're giving you, playing crazy dreams when you sleep, giving you the ooga-boogas when awake. That, or you're losing your mind. Spent six months in the Twilight Zone and came out with half your luggage. Could be worse. Could be sleeping with the jellies.*

Nothing made sense, but the incident had left him weary and yearning for oblivion. Marcy dimmed the lights, and Jack closed his eyes. He wanted to sleep for a week and wake up whole and ready to get out of here.

"You sleep tight," she said.

Besides, Bunky, who the hell would want to kill someone who's been in a coma for half a year?

PART
4

61

On April 24, Vince drove Jack to a rented house about two miles from the colonial he had shared with Beth.

In spite of the memories, Jack wanted to return to Carleton because he liked the town and because it was close to the Lahcy Clinic where he had his physical therapy. He also wanted to be near Yesterdays, where Vince talked him into being host now that he was back on his feet. Two weeks ago he had renewed his driver's license and would get around in rentals until he could afford a car of his own. "Maybe I'll check the Yellow Pages for Rent-a-Wife," he told Vince.

The place was a neat six-room Cape painted dark green, making it look like a giant Monopoly piece. Low trimmed bushes formed a border around the front, which sat on Old Mystic Road, near the Mystic Lakes and the town line of Medford, where he could buy beer since Carleton was steadfast in the virtues of its Puritan ancestors—holding dry and proud of it. The house came furnished, which was fine, since Jack harbored no sentimental attachment to what he and Beth had shared. Nor did he want to be reminded.

He and Vince spent a few hours putting things away from

boxes stacked in the different rooms. And when most of it was done, Jack walked Vince to his car. " 'Thanks' doesn't come close."

"It'll do." Vince gave him a hug. "You need anything, you call." He got into his car, a 1992 green Mitsubishi 3000 VR4 twin turbo. Jack tapped the rear spoiler. "Does this do anything?"

"Keeps me out of the trees." Vince started the car. "You take it easy and work on your Charlie Charm."

Jack started hosting at the restaurant in three nights. "No reservations, fuck off! Next."

"Perfect," Vince said and pulled away.

As he turned on his cane, Jack noticed a black SUV with tinted windows roll down the street. He wouldn't have noticed it except that it rolled by slowly, then sped away as Jack looked up.

A moment later, Jack forgot about that car, thinking how one of his own would be a good way to jump-start the rest of his life.

Before she moved to Texas, Beth had placed all of Jack's belongings in a warehouse to be stored for five years, after which they would be donated to Goodwill were Jack still in a coma. For the next two days Jack put stuff away in bureaus, closets, and bookshelves. But several cartons of old stuff still sat in the cellar—stuff he'd long forgotten about.

A stairway through a kitchen door led to the cellar. For more than an hour he went through the boxes, which Vince had arranged in neat stacks along wall shelves. In black marker they were labeled: "Jack's Stuff. College Notes. Books. Photos." Beth's printing. He ran his finger over the neat block letters, thinking that when the ink was wet Beth was his wife, he was still Jack.

Yeah, and your marriage was on the rocks.

He slit open a box. Inside was a pile of photo albums. Beth had spent days arranging the snaps chronologically in the plastic sheets. He thumbed through them—shots of him and Beth, of Vince and other college friends. One album contained pictures of trips they had taken to Jamaica on their honeymoon, to

Yosemite a couple years later, visits to friends in Chattanooga and California. Also in the box was their wedding album—a padded white faux leather folder with calligraphic gold script on the cover: "Our Wedding." He did not open it.

Another album contained some foggy and cracked pictures of his aunt Nancy and uncle Kirk before they were married. And at the very end were black-and-whites of his biological mother and father, including a wedding portrait of them from 1966. His mother, Rose, was a slender, attractive woman with a simpatico face. His father, Leo, looked like a foreign dignitary with black eyes, a long sharp nose, and a baronial mustache. He stood just a few inches taller than Rose. According to Jack's aunt, Leo was born in the Armenian sector of Beirut, Lebanon, where he studied languages and was fluent in several. In the old-world custom of marriage arrangements, he married Rose, thereby securing American citizenship. Jack knew nothing about their marriage—whether it was a good one or not—and little else about Leo, except that his plane went down just short of the runway on his way to visiting relatives in Chicago.

Because Jack was only six months old when his father died and about two years old when his mother disappeared, he did not remember his parents, just these few photos of them. But imagination had a way of conspiring with memory, creating a reality of its own—a kind of kinescopic synthesis of stories his aunt told with these old photos.

Another shot of Rose showed her beaming at the camera with an infant swaddled in her arms. Himself. She was in the kitchen of their five-room flat in Worcester's Armenian neighborhood just off Chandler Street. She was wearing a pullover with some lettering that he could not make out. Leo probably took the photo. As strange as it was, Jack had convinced himself that he remembered that apartment and his mother as she appeared. Which wasn't possible. Human memory couldn't reach back that far, he was sure, no matter what that repairman said.

Jack studied the photographs. *Who were these people whose twisty genetic stuff was filed away in his cells? What had they looked like? sounded like? smelled like? Had they spoken with accents? What stories had they told? What dreams did they dream?*

For some reason, he felt a stronger affinity to his mother, whose dark almond eyes seemed to talk to him. Relatives had said that he had inherited her strong will and her bunions. She was clever and spunky, a little scooter of a woman on whom nothing in the natural world was lost. According to his aunt, she had an almost religious appreciation for the sea and would spend hours walking beaches looking for crabs, worms, and mollusks. She had a collection of shells from all over the world, some she had picked up herself, others from friends. So it was not surprising that she had studied marine biology, having won a scholarship to Tufts University, then moving into the doctoral program at Harvard. And here she was, this remarkable woman whose blood gurgled through his veins, who gave him life and dandled him on her knees—and he never knew her.

The only other photo showed her posing with other people in front of an auto parts store. They looked like colleagues since she and two others were wearing what resembled lab coats.

The album still in hand, Jack moved toward the basement window for better light. But a spike of pain shot up his left leg, throwing him off balance so that he stumbled into a shelf of laundry detergents and sent a bottle of Clorox onto the floor, the bleach draining into a puddle. Fortunately, the bottle was only partly full, so he was able to soak it up with a sponge mop, squeezing the stuff down the drain of a small sink. Yet the fumes filled his head, and he had to steady himself against the table to get the noxious odors out of his lungs.

An odd sensation rippled across his brain. It was not unpleasant, nor did it seem to affect him in any way but for a moment's dizziness. Maybe the fast turn on his feet, he told himself. But as he started to move, he felt himself shut down for a second—a miniblackout. He braced himself against a support pole and looked around, gauging his awareness.

He knew where he was—in the basement of the Mystic Street rental, between a utility table and the washer and dryer.

He was also aware of the cool cellar air, the heft of the album in his hand, the slight throbbing of his left leg, the discomfort in his shoulder and other joints—all the orthopedic white noise. He laid the photo album on a table and took a few steps.

Again that odd fugue—as if he had passed through a blank in the time-space continuum. He rested against the table and closed his eyes. He could hear himself breathing. He could hear the distant sounds of traffic. He could also hear something else: A woman's voice. Faint, feathery faint, high, but clear enough to make out singing.

"You are my sunshine, my only sunshine . . ."

A shard of ice passed through Jack's heart. He snapped around, half-expecting to lay eyes on some strange female gawking at him from the shadows.

Nothing.

Boxes, storage trunks, lamps, old armoire, furnace, oil tank, small workbench, Christmas decorations, washing machine, and dryer. No demon woman. The room was empty of any other presence.

Christ, now it's phantom voices in the daytime.

All the shit you're on, man—all conspiring to scramble your squeeze box.

He got the photo album and shuffled over to a pile of boxes and sat down. His head felt slow, as if operating on a sluggish strobe. He closed his eyes and took a deep breath to steady himself. *Just a little misfiring that'll pass,* he told himself. He opened his eyes and began thumbing through the photo album again.

Then from behind him he heard the voice again: *"You are my sunshine, my only sunshine."*

Jack bolted straight up, the album tumbling to the floor. For a moment he stood perfectly still, his body throbbing to the fright in his blood. He took a deep breath and slowly turned to get a fix on the voice, certain that it came from the shadows by the furnace. He crossed the floor by the workbench. Who the hell would be down here, and why hide in the shadows and sing?

I'm going crazy. I can't tell if it's external sound or it's inside my head.

He removed a ball-peen hammer from the pegboard. His heart took a huge surge of blood as he crossed the stairs and looked up to the light of the kitchen.

"You are my sunshine, my only sunshine."

Jack let out a shuddering gasp. "Who-who's there?"

This time he was dead certain. A woman's voice, and not just in his head but in his ears. Real sound that still registered vibratory stimulation. Real sound: A clear, thin female voice singing. But not from the kitchen.

Someone's down here with me.

He moved into the cellar, his fingers in a tight, cold grip on the hammer. Jack didn't know the people who owned the house, nor did he know anything about them. The arrangements had been made by Vince, who said that personal problems had forced the couple to move out of state with their daughter. But it crossed Jack's mind that those personal problems could mean that said woman of the house was psycho and had sneaked back home and was hanging somewhere in the shadows.

Jack moved toward some tall furniture against the far wall. "Okay, game's up."

"You are my sunshine, my only sunshine . . ."

An involuntary cry fluttered up Jack's windpipe. The woman's voice was right on top of him. He snapped around, his hand fused to the hammer, but he could not get a direction. He dipped his head into the black gaps between the furnace and the armoire. He wished he had a flashlight. "I know you're there. I can hear you breathing."

Nothing.

He tapped the doors of the armoire with the hammer. "Come out, goddamn it."

Nothing.

He raised the hammer and snapped open the door. The armoire was lined with shoe boxes, but nothing else. He walked toward the rear of the cellar. "All right, I'm calling the police."

Nothing.

He circled back toward the laundry table.

"You are my sunshine, my only sunshine . . ."

Jack froze. Movement. He saw movement. He was standing before the opening to a small recess that decades ago had served as a storage room for coal.

"You are my sunshine, my only sunshine . . ."

"I see you, goddamn it," he said to the shadows, the hammer in his fist ready to swing if some lunatic woman rushed him. "Get out here!" His heart pounded so hard he had trouble putting breath in his words.

In the coal room hung an old wooden framed mirror, resting at a tipsy angle, the glass cracked and smoky. But he could see himself clearly, his pale face, his eyes like holes in his skull, the solid-bodied silver hammer in his hand.

As he stood there contemplating his image, he heard the thin falsetto. But this time she wasn't singing. *"Ahmahn seerem anoosheeg . . ."*

Jack let out a shudder. *The voice was coming from him.*

In the reflection he saw his mouth form the syllables, their sounds piercing his ears like slivers of glass. His voice. His voice. He could still feel the muscle sensations in this throat. He could hear the vibrations in his ears.

God Almighty!

A black rush of horror passed through him. He had spoken—or someone or something had spoken through him, as if from another brain. Or worse: He really *was* losing his mind.

What made him all the more horrified was the realization that the words he had uttered were not words he comprehended. They were a foreign language. But he was certain that the words were those of his long dead relatives and ancestors. That he had spoken Armenian.

Disbelief flooded his mind because Armenian was a language he did not know, had never learned, had never spoken. Yes, he recognized phonemes and sound patterns picked up from friends of his aunt and uncle when he was a kid. But he was no more conversant in Armenian than he was in Danish or Inuit. But he would bet his life that the words he had uttered were Armenian.

Jack turned off the light and went upstairs one step at a time, thinking that this had nothing to do with medication or blood pressure or tricks of the light and that, given the option, he preferred to think there had been a crazy woman down there and not that he was going insane.

62

Jack sat by the phone staring at Dr. Heller's number and running through his head what he would tell her: That yesterday he had had a bout of auditory hallucinations—that he was in his cellar, and suddenly he began hearing a woman singing in a voice that appeared to emanate from inside his own head.

Some kind of seizures like what that pharmacist woman, René Ballard, had said the dementia patients were experiencing on that new Alzheimer's drug. Maybe just a coincidence, maybe there was a connection. She had called them flashbacks.

Maybe that's what was happening, except it gets worse, Doc. Oh yeah, much worse, because then I began speaking in a language I've never spoken before and in a voice that wasn't my own. What do I think, Doc? That I've got a haunted head. And what I did was pop three Xanax tabs and fall into an eight-hour hole.

For maybe a full fifteen minutes he sat by the phone. If he told her straight out what had happened, she'd call him in immediately, set him up with neuropsychologists, psychiatrists, dementia specialists, flashback experts, whatever, then submit him to another battery of tests, put his head in the MRI hole again, wire it for bugs. But, frankly, he just didn't want to go through all that. Besides, he had a scheduled appointment next week. He'd leave it at that.

In the meantime, he'd keep out of the cellar. *Oh, yeah.* In fact, he'd minimize his time in the kitchen to avoid the pull of the damn door. He'd also double his dosage of Dilantin to keep the ghosts in their coffins. Sure, he should have consulted Dr. Heller. Sure, only a fool was his own pharmacist. Sure, he could probably trigger some nasty side effects—although he had none. On the contrary, the extra hit had the effect of a pop-up stopper. For eighteen hours he was dream-free, flashback-free—not even a slice-and-dice still out of the blue.

The bad news was that because he refused to take any more sleeping pills, Jack had traded bad visions for insomnia. For the next five nights he logged no more than twenty hours of sleep, some nights getting maybe two, spending the remaining hours twisting in his sheets until dawn. He even went online and found a Web site for insomniacs that offered a list of a dozen sleep-inducing strategies: take a warm bath; listen to soft music; drink warm milk at bedtime; visualize something boring . . . He tried them all, but nothing worked. He just became more alert in his desperation.

He also dreaded dusk. In fact, it got so bad that when the evening news came on his heart rate increased and his mouth went dry. At about nine-thirty on the fifth night he actually felt sleep weigh heavily on his eyelids. So he slipped into the bedroom, trying not to think about how he was pretending to yield to drowsiness like most normal people. He took his medicine, resisting the temptation to down a few tabs of Xanax, turned off the lights, and got into bed.

He closed his eyes, trying to settle into his drowsiness as if he were just your average Joe—stable, relaxed, retiring after a long and exhausting day at the office. At 10:18 he was still awake and even more alert than ever. He stared at the dark ceiling, trying to pretend that he was fighting sleep, forcing his eyes to remain open until the last possible moment when he'd close them and slip into the warm well of oblivion.

But it didn't work.

And his mind filled with the illuminated dial of the radio clock, the cable box, light strips framing the window shades from the street, sounds of the house settling, the fridge compressor kicking in, Logan jets . . . goddamn butterfly wings in Peru.

He got up and draped towels over the radio, then found some duct tape and sealed the shades against the window frame. The black was now total, but his brain was hot with frustration. He closed his eyes and tried not to think of the sounds of his heart clicking in his ears, hoping the white noise would lull him to sleep as with any other normal person. Except that he wasn't like any other normal person but a man cursed to lie awake holding his breath for the subtlest decibel to pin his affliction on.

At 1:46 he was still awake.

By 2:11 his mind was a flywheel. *If there was a God,* he thought, *he or she didn't have a sleep problem.* The cable box clock. As a light source it wasn't intrusive, but he knew that every time he opened his eyes there was the countdown in glowing red—and as long as the digits were visible, he'd be tempted to gauge the passage of time.

Shit!

He got up and covered the cable box.

An hour later, he headed down to the kitchen for another warm glass of milk. He thought about reading a dull book or maybe catching some mindless movie on TV. But that would only stimulate his brain all the more. So he sat at the kitchen table and sipped warm milk out of a blue glass under the garish fluorescence of the circular tube on the ceiling. He closed his eyes and rested his head on his elbow, thinking about warm milk coating his stomach and magically transmitting rock-a-bye-baby signals to his brain. But that didn't work.

Jack opened one eye. It fell on the cellar door.

The cellar.

Don't think about it, he told himself. Then another voice cut in: *Yeah, sure. Like don't think "elephant" and suddenly there's Dumbo flapping his ears at you.*

His eye dropped to the hexagonal glass knob.

Turn me.

Click.
Pull.
He closed his eye and sipped more milk.
Come on, guy. Peek-a-boo.
His eye slitted open.
Thata boy, I see you . . .
The door, and just behind it a black shaft and twelve little steps down, light switch at the top. He closed his eyes again.

He got up, scraping the chair noisily against the floor, and downed the rest of the milk and rinsed out the glass. Then he turned and leaned against the sink, staring at the door. *So, what's it going to be, Jacko? Stay out of the cellar for good until your laundry rots in the machine—been five days now, still sitting in a damp twist at the bottom, never did make the dryer. Going to have to send them through again for the mildew.*

He crossed the kitchen and opened the door.
So what's the big deal?
Well, you see, the last time I did this, there was this poltergeist thing that took me over.
What are you afraid to find? Just a lot of boxes of old stuff. Maybe glug up the throat on nostalgia, but that's an old friend by now.

He flicked on the light.

Empty stairs, no goggle-eyed zombies gaping up at him, and no ooga-booga vibes registering. Plus, a few low-sleep cobwebs aside, your head feels clear for once.

He took the steps one by one, holding on to the rail. Someplace in the front hall he had left his cane, which would have been comforting to grip at the moment. But he decided not to bother going back up.

At the bottom he turned slowly until he faced the rear wall and the armoire. Nothing.

He moved across the floor to the washing machine and put his hand on the lid, thinking that this is where the thing with the KKK hood jumps out and crushes your skull. Nothing but his clothes in a fused ring around the base of the agitator. They were still damp but they didn't smell mildewy, so he put them into the dryer.

He limped across the old carpet and stopped in his tracks. Along the metal shelves were boxes. He didn't know why he stopped, but as if following some radar beam his eyes fell on a single carton. He had been through all the boxes—all but this one, which still had tape across the flaps. On the side in small black letters it said "Jack's Stuff."

As if by remote control he went over to the shelves, his mind funneling all attention onto that parcel, that plain brown cardboard box with no commercial lettering. It was maybe eighteen inches on a side, but surprisingly light. He placed it on a table and opened the top.

Old newspapers were balled up as packing. He unfolded one double page that was discolored from long repose in the box— October 1979. He felt around under the upper layers until he hit the source of the weight. Smooth shape—soft, cloth, pliable. His fingers began to hum as they sent up crude premonitional images to his brain like a sonogram. He pulled it out.

A large tan stuffed mouse with round sausagey limbs, floppy round pink ears, a red knobbed nose, big startled cartoon eyes in white and black, a thick brown tail. Instantly every inner sensor focused on that stuffed mouse.

"Mookie."

63

"It's a damn joke. Klander and company gave them just what they wanted to hear: *It's the dementia, stupid.*"

René had not seen Nick so upset. His face was red, as if too full of blood. The Klander Clinical Research Group report sat in a black folder on Nick's desk.

"They hired a bunch of fancy-sounding neuro people and threw a ton of money at them and got the validation they were looking for."

"But we gave them reams of data and documentation of the problems."

"Yeah, and they concluded that the events were not Memorine-related but the results of the brain's deterioration from Alzheimer's. And they bolstered the claim that since the flashbacks are treatable with standard antipsychotic meds, the phenomenon equals demented delusions. QED." He pushed a copy toward her. "You can read it yourself."

René took the report and thumbed through it. There were pages of data from outside literature documenting hallucinatory behavior of AD patients. "But the evidence is overwhelming."

"Not when the conclusion is predetermined. So instead of

burying the evidence, they hire so-called neutral specialists to say the problems aren't drug-related. Pretty clever, huh?"

"But can't the FDA see through that?"

"No, because the FDA wants this to go to market. So does the president. He sees it as a sixty-billion-dollar savings of taxpayers' money. So, it's fait accompli."

"What about the investigators at some of the other sites? I thought we had some support on this."

"We do. Paul Nadeau wants an extension. So does Brian Rich. In fact, Nadeau reports he's got a patient who keeps having flashbacks of finding his father hanging in the closet when he was eight years old. And Dr. Rich says one of his keeps reliving her days as a child at Dachau. And the only treatment is to dope them into a stupor."

"God, the cure is worse than the disease."

"Exactly, but GEM's going to deny that."

"So we treat the flashbacks with the usual stuff."

Nick nodded. "And if people recede into the past, let them stay there. If they get out of hand, sedate them, and to hell with the burdens on the families."

"I don't believe this." And in René's mind she saw Louis Martinetti blanching with horror as he was suddenly transported to the Red Tent where he was forced to watch his captors do unspeakable things to his buddy, pleading for them to stop in some kind of pidgin Korean speak.

"Believe it. What we have is a fifty-billion-dollar piggy that's going to market, no matter what—ethics and good business practice be damned. It's the same sealed mind-set you saw with Enron and Tyco. Nobody wants to hear bad news. And if you have any or you raise ethical questions, you're not part of the team—and don't get the rewards."

"But this didn't happen on its own. Somewhere along the line somebody made a decision to compromise the truth."

Nick nodded. "There's an old Greek expression: 'The fish rots from the head first.'"

In all the years she had known Nick, René had never seen him so worked up. His face was flushed and his eyes filled his glasses. He looked like another person pressed to the surface under internal heat. In the classroom he had held forth on the need for strong ethical safeguards, especially in the cloudy interface between drug companies and physicians. But the lectures were always cool and reasoned. And never had she heard him criticize colleagues or staff behind their backs. If he had a problem, he was always diplomatic and respectful, stating his differences in objective and conciliatory terms. And if someone was wrong, he always gave second chances. "We're all allowed one mistake to learn from," he once said. "It makes us better and stronger people."

"So what do you think will happen in Utah?"

"I'll lodge my protest, but I don't expect to turn a lot of minds. As somebody said, it's like trying to stop a train in its tracks."

Then from the floor he lifted a large cardboard box full of Memorine marketing products—gym bags, umbrellas, hats, decals, letterhead stationery, rain ponchos, a jewelry box with a pearl necklace. He slapped down a CD. "They even have their own soundtrack—*Back to Life*." As on the other items, the diamond GEM logo was prominent. Also in the box were brochures on Bermuda, Gstaad, and Italy—junkets for the principal investigators. "Hard to fight all this," she said.

"A flawed medical miracle whose benefits exceed any risks, they claim."

64

Jack had not been in Mass General since the days of his coma, so he remembered nothing. He made his way across the lobby to the elevators in the Lane Building and up to the eighth floor, where he found Dr. Heller's office. He was let in to see her almost immediately.

"Every time I go down into the cellar, I get hit with bad visions. Maybe I'm cracking up."

"You're not cracking up, Mr. Koryan. You're having some kind of seizures."

"What about my muttering Armenian phrases in a woman's voice? I don't even know the language."

"Did you recognize the words?"

"Not the exact translation, but they're words of endearment you'd say to children."

"Maybe your relatives spoke to you in Armenian and you just forgot."

"From thirty years ago?"

"It's possible. Your deep recall is remarkable. Perhaps you were just pronouncing them from rote memory—maybe from your aunt or other relatives."

"Then how do you explain the image of some misshapen creature with a witch hat and a large animal with the bashed-in head? Those were as real to me as you are now."

"I'm not a psychologist, but I think you're making some kind of association. Tell me about the visions."

Relaxing a bit into the gentleness of her manner, Jack described them. Their occurrences weren't predictable or even restricted to bedtime: Daymares that would strike while he'd be taking a shower or out for a walk or sitting on the porch having a beer. But the bad flashes were always violent and thematically consistent—a darkened figure with a pointed head coming for him, then suddenly attacking another figure with some sort of bludgeon to the brutal sound of skull bone cracking. And always the flashes were perceived from the same point of view—by a window, about chest high, and through some obstruction, as if from the inside of a cage of some sort. And the banging sounds and flickering lights. What baffled Jack was that the location was deeply familiar. And although it lacked none of the non-Euclidean geometry characteristic of ordinary dreams, recognition eluded him.

"Simple nightmares."

She had a cleanly rational explanation for things that didn't feel clean and rational but alien and clammy. "But it felt like real time, like I was reliving it."

She nodded and jotted something on her pad. "But this isn't the first time you've had vivid recollections."

"No, but these are different."

"How are they different?"

He explained that these were not pleasant periodic flashes from his youth—warm vignettes of childhood play in the schoolyard or in the neighborhood park with friends, or interludes with girls he liked. What had distinguished them from daydreams or ordinary recollections was that they were violent and exquisitely vivid.

"Dreams often feel very vivid."

"What about the possibility that it was the toxin?"

"It's possible." She flipped open a folder of his medical

charts. "According to your most recent blood test, there are negligible traces of the toxin in your system from the original attack." She looked back at him. "But a more likely possibility is that the massive amount that entered your system has permanently enchanced the physiology of the memory centers of your brain and, as a result, you may be experiencing memory-related nightmares. But that will require running tests on you, which you've refused."

He was still not interested, but her words sent an uneasy ripple through him. "What I don't understand is why the same violent scene."

Dr. Heller studied Jack for a moment as she absorbed his words. "Do you recognize the figure?"

"No. But I can see its form."

"Do you recognize the victim?"

"No."

"And how long have you been having these spells?"

"The bad ones, since I've been out of Greendale—since I moved into the house."

"Do you recognize where the violence takes place?"

"I have a sense of being near the ocean, but I also recall a swimming pool smell."

"A swimming pool smell?"

"Yeah, chemicals—chlorine, I guess."

Dr. Heller folded her hands. "Mr. Koryan, I'm a neurologist, not a psychologist, but I know some very good people I'd like to refer you to." She pulled out her pad and scribbled down a name and held it out to him. "He's very good."

Jack took the paper and laid it on her desk. "I'm sure. But I really don't like the idea of some specialist shrinking me back to my toilet training then giving me a prescription to the same stuff you could write."

Dr. Heller stared at him for a long moment parsing his comments and her own possible responses. "It might be wiser to try to get to the source."

Maybe I don't want to. The thought just popped up. He said nothing.

"Have you ever been physically attacked or assaulted?"

He'd had a few tussles in high school and college but nothing to produce recollections like this. "Not that I remember."

"Have you ever been in a severe accident?"

"No."

"Were you in the military or in any disaster—fire, earthquake, anything like that?"

"No."

"What about traumatic childhood experiences? Any frightening events?"

Jack heard a slight hum in the back of his mind but shook it away. His uncle Kirk had died of cancer when Jack was twelve, his aunt Nancy when he was a sophomore in college. Their deaths were sad, of course, but not traumatizing. "No."

"Well, it sounds to me as if you're having intrusive recollections or some kind of dissociative episodes that leave you with a sense of having relived some disturbing experience, yet you say you can't recall any such event."

Jack wanted to leave.

"Let me just ask if any of these episodes are associated with your drinking alcohol."

"No."

"Are you drinking much?"

"A beer once in a while." He checked his watch. The hum had begun to buzz through his limbs. He wanted to be out of there.

"Do you find yourself avoiding particular thoughts or feelings, people, or places?"

"Uh-uh." God, he wished she'd end the session.

"What about feelings of detachment or estrangement from other people?"

"Sometimes."

"I mean in the extreme?"

"No."

"Any sense of foreboding?"

He shook his head. His leg was bouncing.

"Well, can you think of anything that might specifically set off these flashbacks or illusions—internal or external cues that might symbolize or resemble some aspects of the events?"

Yes. "No."

"Do you have suicidal thoughts?"

"Suicidal thoughts? Yeah, sometimes. But it's more that I just want to escape, not kill myself, if that makes sense."

"Tell me the difference."

Jack thought for a moment. "I don't feel masochistic, like I want to punish myself. It's just that I feel like Humpty Dumpty with too many pieces to put back—and a few missing."

"I see."

"But it's not all the time, just when I'm feeling sorry for myself. But I'm not braiding a noose."

Dr. Heller smiled, then blanked her face as she studied him, looking as she were trying to read a ticker tape across his skull.

"So what can you give me?"

She handed him the slip with the name of the neuropsychologist. "Call him. You're clearly blocking something, and if you still choose not to"—and on her prescription pad she wrote something down—"take this to your pharmacy." She handed him the second slip. "It's called Zyprexa—it has sedative effects and has been shown to reduce nightmares associated with PTSD."

"PTSD?"

"Post-traumatic stress disorder. But I think you really should see an expert if you want to do something about these episodes. Because what concerns me is that you appear to be blocking something."

65

Dr. Heller was right: He was blocking something, all right. And he was avoiding places—the cellar, for instance. *Oh yeah, Nightmare Central,* and that had sent him and his laundry to the Scrub-a-Dub coin place in town, convinced the basement was cursed.

She was also right that maybe in addition to his new PTSD pills he needed a good shrink to get behind all the memory flashes, bad dream scraps, and little pockets of horror his mind would pass through, because they had gotten worse since he'd been out of Greendale. Maybe he should call that name on the script sheet and talk all the vomit from his soul until he got to the bottom.

Aye, and there's the rub, sweet prince, because you know as well as I do that you don't need a shrink, because when you look down those stairs, you know what you see.

That large stuffed mouse with its head bashed in.

Maideek Mookie. He'd looked it up. Armenian for *mama mouse.*

———

Because the archives of local newspapers from thirty years ago could not be accessed online, Jack rented a car and drove to the Boston Public Library the next day. There, in the basement, he located microfilm for the *Boston Globe,* New Bedford's *Standard-Times,* and the *Cape Cod Times* for August 22, 1975. One headline blared "Nor 'easter Pounds Mass. Coastline. Millions in Damage."

The New Bedford paper gave more details of the search-and-rescue attempts for the next several days. There were several different articles covering various aspects of the storm, including one that reported on the damage to coastal homes and boats.

One mentioned the disappearance of Rose Najarian.

COAST GUARD SEARCHES FOR MISSING MASS. BOATER
A Massachusetts boater has been missing since Friday, when her sailboat was apparently capsized by high winds and choppy seas in the waters off Homer's Island in the Elizabeth Island chain off the coast of Massachusetts.

Coast Guard vessels went into action at daybreak, when a call went out from Falmouth police after island residents discovered the washed-up and damaged remains of an Oday 17 belonging to Rose Najarian of Watertown.

Seeing his mother's name listed was like putting his finger in a wall socket. For as long as he could remember, she was simply the biological circumstance of his existence and a label to someone in old photographs. But seeing her name in print had the effect of connecting that existence to a life he knew almost nothing about. What he did know—and it came back to him like a heat-seeking missile—was that she had handmade that stuffed mouse.

He continued reading:

According to officials, Mrs. Najarian was apparently attempting to batten down her vessel in anticipation of yesterday's nor'easter, characterized by northeast winds of 30 to 40 mph. Police reported that her two-year-old child was found inside a beachfront cottage over a mile from where her boat washed up.

It is not known if life a jacket was worn since four were found in or near the boat, adding to official's theory of why Mrs. Najarian was in the boat. According to a Coast Guard spokesman, even if she had worn a life jacket, exposure for a few hours even in warm water would lead to hypothermia. No sign of Mrs. Najarian has yet been found.

Rose Najarian, a widow, was a research biochemist affiliated with MIT. Her two-year-old son, Jack, was found the next morning in the beach cottage in fair condition . . .

The fast-moving storm caused coastal flooding and damage to homes on the islands and to southern Massachusetts . . .

Jack made a photocopy of the article, then scanned the next days' papers. Two days later a second article appeared in the *Boston Globe*.

COAST GUARD GIVES UP SEARCH FOR MASS. BOATER
The Coast Guard officially ended its search for a Massachusetts woman, which began Saturday morning after her sailboat capsized off Homer's Island . . .

Rose Najarian was apparently drowned when trying to secure her boat in anticipation of last week's storm. The search included a Jayhawk rescue helicopter from Coast Guard Air Station Cape Cod and two rescue boats from Station Pt. Judith, R.I. "The decision to suspend a search is never an easy one," said Petty Officer James Fagan of the First Coast Guard District Office.

"However, we've saturated more than 125 square miles with rescue and air assets for 28 hours and, based on that information, we feel that if the victim was on the surface, we would have detected her. . . ."

Jack wrote down the officer's name, although he didn't need to. The details of the articles stuck to his mind like frost.

When he reached home later that day, Jack called the Massachusetts Coast Guard Station at Woods Hole and explained that he was investigating the disappearance of his mother some years ago. After two holds, he was connected to a public information officer who asked if he were a policeman on a cold case. Jack was tempted to say he was, only to avoid the obvious questions: Why do you want to know? And why now?

"I'm sorry, we don't keep records from that far back."

Jack then called Vince and explained that he needed a contact at the Coast Guard. In vague terms Jack explained that he was interested in how, exactly, his mother had died, and that he had time on his hands. Vince didn't know what to make of Jack's explanation, but half an hour later he called back with a name: Fred Barboza.

Two hours later, Jack reached Lieutenant Fred Barboza, who said that it could not be done over the phone, that Jack would have to come to the CG Falmouth office in person. And tomorrow was not a good day.

On Friday he drove his rental to Falmouth for an eleven A.M. appointment.

The Coast Guard station was located on the southwest shore of Little Harbor in Woods Hole. The administration building was a long, narrow, two-story cinder-block-and-brick structure that sat in the middle of a long dock along which several CG vessels were docked. Jack checked in at the security desk, and after a brief wait a man in a uniform appeared and introduced himself as Fred Barboza. He led Jack to a small office.

"It's an unusual request—something police or other investigative agencies pursue when they've got a cold case involving foul play."

Foul play.

"May I ask why you're doing this?"

He wanted to say, *Remember the story of the princess and the pea? Something poking me under all the layers.* "Just that she was never found, and I'm wondering if I can learn anything about the circumstances of her disappearance." He showed Barboza the photocopies of the news clippings.

"It says that a storm was forecast and small craft warnings had been issued."

"Yes."

Barboza looked at him with a flat, uncomprehending stare. "Mr. Koryan, it's been thirty years. We don't keep records going back that far. Besides, this seems to tell it all. She got lost in a storm trying to tie down her boat."

He was right, of course. But he also could have told him that over the phone and spared him the three-hour round-trip. "Maybe you can tell me about the kind of efforts that went into finding her."

"I'm sure they gave it their all. The article says two search-and-rescue boats and a chopper." Then he added, "Maybe it's better to leave the dead in peace."

It's not the dead who need the peace. "Do you know where I might find James Fagan? He was a petty officer at the time."

"No."

"But you didn't even look."

"He retired ten years ago."

"And you have no records where he may have retired to? Nobody here who keeps up contact—old friends, guys who still keep in touch, retired officers' clubs, reunion parties?"

Barboza had irritation scored across his brow. But he glanced at the wall clock, then pushed himself up and crossed the floor to a file drawer and ferreted through a thick batch of folders until he found one. He slouched back to his desk and ripped off the top sheet of his pad, then jotted something down and handed it to Jack.

A telephone number with a Massachusetts area code.

Jack had no idea if he was chasing white rabbits, but he called Fagan and explained his request for a meeting. Fagan was either a generous man or desperate for something to do. Whatever the motivation, he agreed to meet the next day in the parking lot of Grasso's, an Italian restaurant just off the Rockland exit of Route 3 South.

Jack said he'd be dressed in jeans and a black shirt and

carrying a cane. Fagan met him at the door. He was a compact man about sixty with a ruddy broad face, and he was wearing a Red Sox cap.

The hostess led them to a table with a view of the parking lot. After some small talk about baseball, Jack showed him the photocopy of the newspaper article about the failed search operation. When Fagan finished reading it he asked, "If you don't mind me asking, why after all these years are you looking into this?"

Again Jack anticipated how weak his reason sounded. "Because she was never found, and I'm wondering what efforts went into finding her."

Fagan nodded and sipped his beer.

"The article doesn't say anything about divers being sent out."

"You're talking thirty years ago. I don't think the Coast Guard even had a scuba-ready search-and-rescue unit like today. Even if they did, where would you send them? It's a big ocean, and there were ten or twelve hours before you had sunlight, and given the turbulence from the storm the visibility would be nil for days."

"Sure. Do you remember searching for her?"

"Yeah, vaguely, but only because it was a new cutter, and one of my first search-and-rescue operations. We patrolled the coastline for a couple days—maybe two other boats out and a spotter plane. The thing is that the storm was a nor'caster, which didn't make sense."

"I don't follow."

"Well, the storm came from the northeast, which means the winds were onshore and, like the article said, with strong gusts. Under those conditions, drowning victims almost always wash up. And when they don't, it's because of offshore winds or the currents—which weren't the conditions that night. I don't mean to be graphic, but drowning victims are floaters—they eventually come to the surface."

"Which means that a body would most likely have washed up."

Fagan nodded. "Of course, there's the problem with that channel out there. Even during a nor'easter you've got crosscurrents moving as much as seven knots."

"Meaning what?"

"Meaning the storm passes, and she's carried out to sea; and being August when it happened, the water's pretty warm."

Fagan seemed to realize what he was saying and pulled back his explanation and guzzled some of his juice.

"What about the water being warm?" Jack asked.

Fagan sucked in his breath, looking like he wished Jack hadn't picked him up. "Well, I don't know if you're familiar with the waters out there, but the island's at the outer edge of the Elizabeth chain and there's a channel that occasionally draws in some pretty unusual sea life from the Gulf Stream, including some deepwater pelagic fish, well, you know, like sharks and all. I mean . . . sorry," and he took a bite of his scrod.

"Sure."

They ate without saying much for several minutes. When they finished, Jack paid the bill and walked outside with Fagan.

"Wish I could've been more help."

"No, you were very helpful," Jack said, feeling a hollowness in his midsection. What he had learned was that his mother might have been eaten by sharks. He prayed that she had drowned first. "I appreciate your time, Mr. Fagan."

"No problem." Then he said, "You know, there's another thing I remember that bothered me back then, just came to me."

"What's that?"

"Funny I didn't think of it before, getting caught up in all the meteorology," Fagan said. "The boat was an Oday 17, the article says, which means that she was probably out there prepping it for the storm. You were too young to remember, of course, but do you know if there was anyone else in the cottage with her? Your father or other people?"

"No, just my mother."

Fagan took that in, then made a *humpf* and shrugged.

"What are you trying to tell me, Mr. Fagan?"

"Well, two would have been faster, but one could have done it. I assume it was moored in the cove, so depending on the wind it could take some time, you know, rowing out there from the shore in a tender. She'd be fighting the wind, of course, which would slow her down, having to remove the mainsail, bagging it, then putting it away in the cutty cabin—maybe put another safety line on the mooring, whatever. But with all the back and forth, that would take some time. Plus it's dangerous trying to keep your balance, all that pitching. Like trying to stand up on a seesaw. One false move and you're overboard."

Fagan shook his head. "Forgive me, she being your mother and all, but what I still don't understand is how she took the chance, leaving a two-year-old baby unattended in his crib."

Jack felt a cold flash up his back, but all he could do was nod in reflex.

Fagan shook his head. "That's something that just never sat right with me, a storm kicking up the water just a hundred feet away. I've got a grandchild about that age, and he can climb out of his crib like a monkey. Not something me or my wife would've chanced. Hell with the boat's my attitude."

"Thank you, Mr. Fagan."

"No problem. Good luck."

Jack watched Fagan walk into the parking lot toward his car, his words sizzling in Jack's brain.

66

René heard the familiar high-compression growl out her window, and she looked out to see Jordan Carr pull up in front of her house in a new Ferrari—this one a black lacquered thing with huge chrome wheels.

Over the months, she had seen Jordan Carr at meetings with other clinicians working on the Memorine trials, but her social relationship was restricted to a few quick lunches in nursing home cafeterias. But it was evident that he was attracted to her. On a few occasions he asked her out to dinner, a movie, or a concert, yet she politely refused, saying that she was busy with work or other engagements. He seemed to take it well, coloring and nodding, bowing out with an exit line—"Maybe another time." Eventually he stopped asking.

René knew she probably came across as aloof or old-fashioned, maybe even prudish or anti-men. But she was none of those. In fact, she had decided that she wanted to meet new men and go out, and that when her work on the trials subsided, she would start exploring the dating scene. But at the moment she was swamped. About Jordan Carr she was just not interested. What made tonight different was that Jordan insisted that she meet old acquaintances of his to talk about investments and financial planning. With her school loans, the grant money she was making on the trials, plus the growing value of her GEM stock options, her economic situation was becoming more complicated, so she agreed to a dinner date.

"What do you think?" Jordan asked when she stepped outside.

She looked at the low, sleek machine with the midnight-sculpted luster. "Did you and Batman do a swap?"

"Very funny," he said with a blank face, and opened the passenger-side door.

René got in thinking that that was one problem with Jordan Carr: that he found few things funny, that he had almost no sense of levity, that she could not imagine him having a good belly laugh. Perhaps he was above the display of humor as with real anger. If he got angry or upset, he tended to internalize his reaction, perhaps in accordance with some mannered protocol of behavior—as if the control of his emotions underscored a superior virtue. Ironically, the blotching of his face would betray him. And that's what bothered René the most about him: She was never completely certain of his true feelings. And in that uncertainty Jordan Carr made others aware that he was superior.

Jordan started the car and they pulled away.

It was Friday afternoon, and they were driving to the cliffs of Manomet, a few miles north of the Cape Cod Canal, where Grady and Luanne Vickers had a summer place. Grady worked for a Boston mutual funds company and was Jordan's portfolio manager. Luanne was a Boston bank manager.

"But she really doesn't need to work," Jordan said "She's from old Yankee money."

Old Yankee money.

And that was another thing. For Jordan, money seemed to be a prime mover. Perhaps it had to do with making up for the divorce lawyers, but when once she complained how in the trials there seemed to be more emphasis on the financial than medical, especially regarding the clinicians, Jordan reminded her, "Look, it takes eight to ten years to get trained—school, internship, residency, not to mention high professional expenses and staggering malpractice insurance. Maybe not you, but some people would argue that docs are entitled to financial rewards." She saw no point in counterarguing and said nothing.

As he ate up the highway in his stallion hat and leather driving gloves, she decided that Dr. Jordan Carr really *was* that Michael Douglas character—and proud of it.

A little after five, they turned off Exit 2 and onto ⌒A, and from there they found a tree-lined side street that led to the cliff-top house—a gray-shingled two-level place with a deck offering a spectacular view of Cape Cod Bay.

As soon as they arrived, Grady came out of the house. He was a heavyset man with floppy brown hair and an eager, pleasant face. He shook René's hand when he was introduced. "You're going to have to forgive me, but I have to leave." Then, with a woeful expression, he explained that their four-year-old daughter, Leah, who was staying with Luanne's parents in Wayland, had developed a high fever and had been taken to the local emergency department. Luanne had left earlier and called to ask Grady to join her. The girl had had a seizure.

"How high was her temperature?" René asked.

"One-oh-four point seven. They put her in a cool bath but decided to take her in."

"That was smart."

Grady checked his watch. "Luanne called twenty minutes ago and it was down to one-oh-three point six. I'm sure she's going to be fine, but Leah is asking for me. But you're welcome to stay, of course. We'll be back later, depending on how things go. And I'll be happy to talk financial planning."

"I understand," René said.

Grady led them inside and showed them what would be their room if they wanted to stay over. René noted a queen-size bed. She also noted that across the hall were the master bedroom and a smaller room for Leah. But downstairs in the living room there was a couch. She didn't know how Jordan had characterized their relationship, but she had no desire to share a bed with him. Jordan dropped his bag in the guest room. He had brought a change of clothes. She hadn't. An overnighter was not part of the evening.

René followed Grady and Jordan down the stairs, where Grady grabbed his keys and headed outside again. He walked over to the Ferrari and shook his head. "Guy's got it rough," he said to René. "House in the country, vintage Ferraris, getaway perks to Park City and Aruba." He winked at her. "All those drug company kickbacks."

Jordan's cheeks instantly blotched. He didn't like that, but he covered well. "And how's the insider trading going?"

"Touché." Grady smiled. "But apparently not as well, 'cause I'm still driving a Toyota and you're running around in Stealth fighter jets." Grady jiggled his keys. "There's a shrimp and scallop casserole in the oven, rice on the stove, and a terrific salad Luanne made in the fridge. Plus plenty of beer in the cooler and a rack of wine in the kitchen. Enjoy. Again, I'm sorry about this. But maybe later."

René thanked him and added, "I'm sure Leah will be just fine."

He nodded and his smile faded. "Luanne's kind of worried about the seizure . . . you know, possible consequences . . ."

"That's highly unlikely," Jordan said. "Febrile seizures are over in moments, with no lasting damage. Besides, her temp was too low. It's when the fever is over one-oh-seven for an extended period of time that there could be some problems."

"I'm feeling better already."

Jordan pretended to write something out on his palm. "That'll be two hundred and fifty dollars."

"Which will just cover room and board for the night," Grady laughed and got in the car. "And don't wait up for us. Nice meeting you," he said to René. "See you later."

Room and board? It began to feel like a setup.

René followed Jordan inside. The place was designed for the view—cathedral ceiling, open living-room-dining-room-kitchen area, a corner fireplace, and a huge floor-to-ceiling glass wall with sliding doors that led onto a deck. The sun had set behind them so that in the fading light the blue-gray sea made a seamless fusion with the sky. From the canal, a few miles to the right, to Provincetown, the full sweep of the Cape's arm could be seen. On a clear evening, Jordan said, you could make out the lighthouse in Provincetown straight out.

"Well, we might as well make the best of it," Jordan said, and began to spoon the casserole onto two plates. René opened a bottle of red wine, chiding herself for her earlier suspicions. They would make the best of it, have dinner, and head home, no problem.

They ate the dinner and drank some of the wine they had brought. Then they moved onto a wicker couch on the deck to take in the view. It was a perfect spring night, warm, with a gentle breeze and an opaque sky fretted with stars. To the right, a crystalline moon rose over the water, making a marbleized path all the way out to the horizon. In the distance pulsed the P-town lighthouse.

Jordan poured himself his fourth glass of wine and made a toast. "To us and continued success. And I hope we all make a ton of money." He was beginning to slur his words.

"Yes, continued success," René said, and clicked his glass.

"Which reminds me," Jordan said. "Did you see the Klander Report?"

"Yes, I saw it."

"So, what do you think?"

She really didn't want to get into it over wine. "Well, I think it's something of a whitewash."

"Whitewash?"

"It dismisses flashback seizures as incidental events."

Maybe it was the wine, but Jordan's face darkened. "Because that was the conclusion of the CRO—that they're simple anomalies unrelated to the drug."

More likely, that was the conclusion of GEM Tech execs who had vigorously denied any rumors of side effects—rumors that had kept deep-pocket investors awake at night. *Unrelated delusional behavior.* And helping to counter such anxieties was the frenzy created by the FDA's decision to fast-track Memorine's development—the deluge of calls and e-mails to clinicians and trial site administrators from AD victims, their families, health care people, and government reps wanting to know when the drug would be available. (The unofficial response was, this coming Christmas.)

However, that was not the unanimous agreement among clinicians, a few of whom had made their concerns known. Even though it was still impossible to prove conclusively that Memorine caused flashbacks, the observational correlation was overwhelming. "It's still rudimentary," René said, "but Dr. Habib's MRI studies were beginning to confirm a connection between flashbacks and neurological repair. I'm sure they were sent to you following his death."

Furthermore, the MRI configurations of Jack Koryan's flashback seizures were identical to those of AD patients during flashback seizures. The EEG readings were also similar. And Peter Habib's independent study had confirmed the similarities. The only problem was that Jack Koryan refused to submit to any more MRI exams or tests to determine the effects of the jellyfish toxins. Understandably, he had had it with being probed. Besides, he was a "civilian" again and getting on with his life.

Jordan studied her for a moment as he selected his words. "Well, some have argued that those are exaggerated claims." He got up and went inside to get another bottle of wine.

When he returned, he poured more wine into his glass. René still had half a glass. He took a sip. "I'm not sure what to make of Peter Habib's findings, but let's say there is some connection, just for the sake of argument. We're addressing the problem with standard meds and good results, right?"

He put his hand on hers. "And, look, ask yourself this—if your father were still alive, which would you prefer: him drying up layer by layer until he's nothing more than just the shell of himself, or him alert and reliving some good old times with old friends?"

She hated the question and deflected it. "If these people were all experiencing delightful nostalgic moments, it wouldn't be so bad," she said. "But many of them are being thrust into past traumas over and over again, like Louis Martinetti. He keeps reliving the torture of himself and a soldier friend back in Korea. And others get lost in equally horrible experiences from childhood. For whatever reason, these traumas overwhelm any other recollections and keep pulling them back."

Jordan made a dismissive gesture with his wineglass.

"Jordan, these flashbacks are turning out to be worse than the disease. Worse than fading away to nothing. The stuff is making some of them prisoners of their worst experiences. And the meds we use to treat the flashbacks not only wear off but they dull them so that they're barely functional."

Jordan took a sip of his wine and made a smooth grin. "Whatever, once we get to Utah all the laundry will be sorted and all issues will be resolved with one mind. And if there are those who disagree—me, Nick, or anybody else—they can file separate reports with the FDA."

Just then the telephone rang and Jordan went inside to catch the call. But that wasn't necessary since a portable was sitting on the side table. She could hear muffled talking from inside and what sounded like Jordan chuckling. Maybe it was the wine, but Jordan never chuckled. He just made polite, smooth grins when he thought something was supposed to be funny.

A couple minutes later, he returned from the kitchen. "That was Grady. Leah is fine and sleeping comfortably. They'll be back tomorrow for brunch."

René felt herself tense up.

"So," Jordan said. He lowered himself to the couch again and put his arm around her shoulder. "I've got a question for you, if you don't mind," he began. "I asked you out four times, and four times you turned me down. I'm just wondering what there is about me you don't like. Is it my appearance? Was it something I said? Do I have bad breath? Every time I ask you say you're busy."

"Well, I have been. That's the truth."

"Well, you're not busy now." He lowered his face to hers, at the same time sliding his hand over her shoulder toward her breast.

"Please don't," she said.

"Please don't what?"

"Don't this." And she removed his hand.

Jordan snapped his head back. "What's your problem?"

"I don't feel like being pawed."

His face was nearly the color of the wine. "Pawed? Is everything fucking protocol with you . . . or should I say *no* fucking?"

She got up to move to the chair, but he grabbed her arm. "Where are you going?" He glowered hotly at her.

"Jordan, stop this."

"Stop what? I haven't done anything but try to give you a damn kiss, for God's sake."

"You're hurting my arm."

"You're hurting my arm," he mimicked, his face making an ugly distortion as he spit out the words. His other hand jerked as she spoke, spilling wine onto his white pullover and making a large red stain. But he held his grip.

His face was maroon and eyes were glassy and wild-looking. Suddenly René felt afraid of him. She was seeing another being in Jordan that had resided below the surface. His face was the color of rage. "Jordan, please let go of me."

He glared at her for a long moment, still holding her, scrutinizing her face, his own hot and on this side of erupting. He did not let go.

"Please let go of me," she insisted.

But he continued to study her without expression. So with her other hand she dug her nails into his wrist and snapped her arm free. Then she shot inside.

"Fucking little bitch," muttered Jordan, and stumbled after her. "Where you going?" he shouted, as he entered the living room.

In an instant, René decided not to go upstairs for fear of being trapped in a bedroom. So she bolted to the fireplace, grabbed a fire iron out of the rack, and raised it like a bat.

Fucking little bitch.

She had not heard him utter such language nor imagined this heat in him. Maybe he was just a bad drunk, but what crossed that thought was that her reaction was confirming the menace she saw in him. And that maybe it was all he needed to assume the role.

Jordan stopped in his tracks as she raised the poker, and for a moment he just stared at her without expression. But in her mind she rehearsed her moves if he came at her. He was drunk, unsteady in his step, sloppy in his movements, seeing double—and she wasn't. Maybe it was the adrenaline thundering in her veins, but she felt twice her size. One flinch of aggression from him and she'd split his skull.

He must have picked up her radiation, because his face slackened and his mouth creased into a stupid grin. "What the hell you doing? I'm not going to hurt you."

"You bet your ass you're not."

"Put that thing down." He was wavering and had to steady himself against the couch. "What the hell's your problem? I was just trying to be romantic, for God's sake." And he flopped onto the couch, spilling more wine on himself. "Shit," he said taking in the big red stain.

"Who was that on the phone?"

"What?"

"Who was that on the phone?"

"Grady. Who do you think it was?"

"And what did he say?"

For a moment Jordan had to regroup himself against the wine. "What do you mean? You know, that Leah wanted them to stay with . . . the grandparents . . . Why?"

His face was in flames. He was lying. He could have answered on the portable, but he took the call inside. It *had* been a setup—to get the Vickers out of the way. And now things were out of hand, and Jordan was too drunk to drive her home.

With the poker in hand, René ran up the stairs knowing that he was in no shape to follow her but certain that if he did, she'd nail him. She felt that close to the edge. (Once Todd had hit her in a moment of craziness, and she nearly scratched his eyes out.)

But Jordan didn't come after her, and from the bedroom she called a cab and said it was urgent. "Five minutes, lady. Got a guy in the neighborhood." She waited several minutes before going back down.

When she did, Jordan was sprawled on the couch, holding

his head and groaning. "Where're you goin'?" His shirt and pants were stained with wine.

"Home."

Suddenly he was alert, his eyes huge glass balls. "You're not taking my car!"

"I called a cab."

"A cab? Aren't you overreacting?"

Maybe, she thought. Then she remembered how he looked at her when she asked him to let her hand go. And the hot eyes.

Fucking little bitch.

He tried to get up, making it only halfway. He groaned. "God, my head." Then he looked at her. "You're being a . . . You're being hysterical, you know that? I'm a doctor, for chrissake. I'm not going to hurt you."

Outside a horn honked, and she headed for the door.

"You're being ridiculous," he said.

She stepped outside.

"Goddamn bitch!"

With her bag, she hustled to the cab. As she got in, she looked back to see Jordan stumble after her. She could hear him still muttering curses.

The cab pulled away and made a U-turn at the bottom of the street. As they passed the house, she noticed Jordan leaning against his Ferrari and vomiting wine and casserole onto the driveway.

67

You're nuts! Fucking whacko Looney Tunes nuts!

That's what Jack told himself as he pulled his rental into the Harbor Line parking lot in New Bedford to purchase his round-trip ticket.

Homer's Island.

It was located at the southwesterly end of the Elizabeth chain, about eighteen miles south of the old whaling port of New Bedford and four miles southwest of Cuttyhunk. Privately owned and devoid of strip malls, clam shacks, minimart Mobil stations, or any other commercial blight, the island consisted of seven hundred unspoiled acres and maybe a couple of dozen august mansions that sneered down from their cliffs over million-dollar yachts as reminders that you were not a member of the Lucky Sperm Club. In spite of the exclusive domain, the summer months drew a few boaters to the tranquil anchorage and the wildlife. The ferry left three times a week at ten A.M.

Jack arrived a few minutes early with a growing sense of unease. He really didn't know why he was doing this. It was not a casual trip down Memory Lane. Yes, something happened out there when he very young. Maybe on the night his mother had disappeared. Perhaps something would come back to him if the projection guys messing around in his hippocampus would play him a recap. Or perhaps not. But at least he'd get the bug out of his belly.

From the upper deck he could make out the water taxi he had taken last August. The captain's name was Jeff Doughty. A few days after Jack emerged from the coma, he called Jeff to thank him for alerting the Coast Guard and to tell Jeff that he was back from the dead. Jeff was delighted to hear that.

It was a cool, overcast Saturday, so only a handful of people was on the boat. The trip took a little more than an hour, making only one other stop, at Cuttyhunk. Most of the Elizabeth Islands lay low against the sky, and as the boat pulled out of port Homer's rose like a gentle ruffle on the horizon.

Approaching from the east, Jack could make out a few mansions along the southern ridge, at the end of which sat Vita Nova, the Sherman estate. Only a few cars and a couple of taxis were on the island. Jack hired one to take him along Crest Drive to about a quarter mile short of the property, preferring the exercise of walking and the gradual approach. Along the way, he passed open sweeps of full-ocean views, some woodland stretches, and a few homes perched along the brow.

Vita Nova was a twelve-room structure of weathered clapboards—one of four homes that looked down on Buck's Cove, a horseshoe anchorage rimmed with white sand, dune grass, and granite outcroppings. From the road one could not see the complex of flower gardens or the flagstone walkways or the brown caretaker's cottage. Jack had been inside the estate only once or twice when he was a boy, as tagalong when his aunt dropped in to say hello or report a leaky window. Rental issues were handled by mail or phone, and the Shermans did not socialize with the Koryans or come down to the beach. Jack never understood how people who owned one of the most stunning spots on the New England coast never took a swim at their own beach or put a boat in the water. In fact, he almost never saw activity at Vita Nova.

He also never learned how his family was so privileged to rent the cottage. The Shermans surely did not need the money,

and Jack couldn't imagine why they'd welcome strangers with
a couple of screaming kids in for two weeks out of the year.
According to his aunt, Jack's mother had befriended Thaddeus
Sherman, the patriarch of the estate, who had offered her the
use of the place before Jack was born—an agreement that apparently continued on and off for ten years following her
death. Since then, Jack had not returned until college, coming
out a few times on a friend's outboard. They'd drop anchor in
the cove, watch the sun go down, and under outrageously
starry skies get beer-philosophical.

Vita Nova looked lifeless—dark windows, closed garage
doors, no gardeners pulling weeds. Adding to the eerie calm
was the fact that at this westerly end of the island you almost
never saw cars, people walking dogs, or joggers. Except for the
wind ruffling a flag, it felt as if he had entered a still-life canvas. And walking by the place he felt as conspicuous as a kan-
garoo. About fifty yards west of the estate was the beach
access, an unmarked set of wooden steps hidden by scrub and
dune grass.

From the time he woke up that morning, Jack kept thinking
about descending these steps and how the cottage would
emerge on the left and in the cove Skull Rock. He did not
know how he'd react—if he'd be assaulted with flashback images and freak out. But he doubted that, since for the last week
he had been on the new PTSD Whack-a-Mole pills, and they
worked. No seizures, no flashbacks. Nothing. But in anticipation, his heart thudded as he made his way down, fixing his
eyes on the water that under the bright gray sky looked
chrome-plated. A few steps down, he watched the cottage
emerge over the boulders, and he half-expected a blast of psychic shrapnel that would send him scrambling up the steps. Instead, all he felt was emotional blankness. Nothing.

But Skull Rock stopped him cold.

At eleven-thirty, the sea was just coming off high tide, so
only the black crown cut the surface like some cryptozoic sea
demon arising from slumber. Jack looked away and continued
to the bottom, feeling the rock tug at him as he crossed the
sand to the shelf of grass that aproned the cottage. The place

looked the same as it had for decades—a four-room Cape Cod cottage in weathered shingles, echoing the manse above. The roofing had been patched in places, and the window boxes had been recently painted, but the same wicker rocking chair sat on the patio as on Jellyfish Night.

The interior was dark. As he took in the house, he could feel suction at his back—the kind of sensation you get when you know you're being watched. Skull Rock. He turned, and keeping his eyes low, he walked to the edge of the water, where a dead skate had washed up, its white underbelly torn open by seabirds. Jack took a breath and raised his eyes.

The rock was black against the horizon, maybe a ten-foot arc crowning the surface. As if in tunnel vision, everything else in the cove fuzzed to a blur, but that rock cap—and it came back to him with stereoscopic clarity: the heavy black clouds, the leaden water, the squawking gulls, the deep-bellied rumble of thunder, the flicker of lightning across the horizon. He could feel the cold grip of the barnacles under his feet, wavelets lapping at his ankles, and the apprehension as he estimated the stretch between him and the beach in his standoff before the mad fifty-yard dash into a coma.

He remembered from mythology class that the ancient Greeks had believed that two rivers led to Hades. One was called Lethe; and on the way to the Elysian fields, departed souls would take a drink of it and wash away all memories and sorrows as a condition of reincarnation and return to the upper world. The ancients also believed in recycling, since the other was the River Mnemosyne—one drink and you remember everything. As Jack stood at the edge of the water, he wondered which was the worse curse.

He headed back toward the cottage, wondering if anything had been changed, if the same honey-colored pine walls, stone fireplace, and red furniture still warmed the room. What it would be like to be at that window looking out—if things would click into place and if some little bone of recollection would float up from the gloom.

Of course, the proper thing would be to go back up to the house, introduce himself as someone whose family used to rent the cottage—might even remember him—then ask if he could please take a peek for old time's sake. It had been a while. But that would mean reclimbing the fifty steps, and if anyone was home try to explain that he came all the way out here with cane in hand—a two-hour car ride from Carleton followed by another hour by ferryboat—on a cold, bleak Tuesday morning for a casual nostalgic hit. Sure, pal, and pigs have wings.

The other option was the truth—*You see, I think when I was not even two years old, my mother . . . and I just want to run a test, see if anything comes back—so don't mind me while I cuddle up under the window. Got an old crib lying around?*

No problem, Mr. Koryan. First, just one little call.

And a police chopper would be out here like that to drop him into the nearest foam room.

He climbed the stairs, feeling his legs throb, stopping every so often to catch his breath and let his heart catch up. By the time he reached the top, his whole body pulsed. And to think that last year at this time he could have gone up and down these stairs ten times. *"In time, in time."* Marcy Falco's words chimed in his head.

Jack pressed the bell and could hear a muffled ring from inside. He waited a minute and tried again, but still nobody came to the door or peeked out. Nor could he hear footsteps. The momentary flash of relief was quickly crossed with anxiety—there was no excuse not to break in.

He headed back down to the cottage again. His head ached from the blood booming through his veins. He tried the door, but it was locked, and cool relief flushed through him.

Good, head home. Nothing here for you. Dumb idea from the start.

But just as those thoughts passed through his brain, his head snapped to the right—to the window box with the bright ragged geraniums, because under it a plastic key box used to be nailed to the shingles out of view—house rules to lock up when leaving the place, since the cove drew boaters who sometimes came ashore to explore.

Jack walked over to it and stuck his hand below, and like a

small electric shock his fingers felt the plastic box. He snapped open the lid and a tarnished brass key tumbled out—the same slightly bent number from twenty years ago, maybe even more. It sat in the palm of his hand, humming like a talisman. With ease it slipped into the tumbler and, with a sticky crack, the door pushed open.

But he did not enter immediately. The blood swelling his head had produced a ten-megaton ache that threatened to split the lobes of his brain.

Don't do this, man. You're gonna step in there and get nothing, or it's gonna set off another Wes Craven gore-fest you may not escape from.

Fuck it! Came this far.

He stepped inside . . . and nothing.

But instantly the old cottagey seabreath filled his head like a dream. From a cursory glance, the Sherman fortune had not been squandered on makeover. The interior was just as he remembered it from twenty-five years ago—golden knotty-pine paneling, red plaid upholstery on matching sofa and chairs, rectangular coffee table with a glass top under which sat an arrangement of seashells, sand dollars, and starfish, fireplace with the dried wreath, logs in a wrought-iron pot. Familiar pine furniture in the bedrooms, and the same kitchen—an old four-jet gas stove, double white stainless steel sinks, but what looked like a new refrigerator. It was like stepping into an old movie set.

As he walked through the place his mind ticked off the kinds of things he'd do to restore it, were it his, wondering why the Shermans with all their money hadn't upgraded the place. Maybe it had something to do with not separating old Boston Brahmins from their millions.

He also half-expected goblins to jump out at him. But nothing like that. The dark kinescope of his brain had blown a fuse. Not even a flicker of recollection. Nothing came back. He looked at the room, and the room looked at him, and that was it. So maybe it was a blessing in disguise, he thought. Maybe this was the point in the story where the beleaguered hero finally shakes the gargoyle off his back—in this case to be replaced by his new best friend, Zyprexa, ten milligrams daily. So say adios, take the next boat home, and get on with the rest of your gray-mush life.

"Who are you?"

Jack froze. A woman's voice. From behind him. For an instant, he thought he was having another spell—that shortly he'd lapse into Armenian lullabies.

But behind him stood a real woman in real-woman flesh and a lavender sweater. "This is private property."

Before he could respond, a volley of angry barks cut the air like gunshots. And from behind the woman emerged a large German shepherd with about fifty flashing incisors.

"Brandy, stop!" And the woman yanked the dog back on its leash. The dog instantly heeled and ceased barking. "What are you doing here?"

"I tried your house, but nobody was home."

"That still does not excuse your breaking in."

He held up the key. "I didn't. I remembered where the key was kept. My family used to stay here during the summer. I don't know if it rings a bell, but my name is Jack Koryan." He pushed down the impulse to extend his hand because he did not expect the woman wanted to take it nor did he want to give Brandy a target.

"I don't recognize the name," the woman said. "And that doesn't explain why you're here."

Wish I knew myself.

"You may recall someone nearly drowning out here last August. The Coast Guard found him and he ended up in a coma. It was in the papers."

"Yes."

"Well, that was me."

"Oh. Well, I'm glad you survived."

But he could see that she was still wondering what he was doing in her cottage. "I'm just trying to put some pieces together," he began. "I don't know if you remember the story, but thirty years ago the woman who was staying here disappeared one August night and was never found. That was my mother. She had stayed here a lot."

And Jack explained: How he was found the next day by a groundskeeper who had shown up to assess the damage from the storm, only to discover Jack sitting in dirty diapers on the floor clutching his stuffed mouse. How he was rushed to a hospital in New Bedford, where he was treated for dehydration and shock and released two days later to his aunt and uncle. How he was unable to relate any of the events of the evening even in the most rudimentary baby talk, so it was assumed that he remembered nothing that had happened that night in the cottage—if anyone else had been there or the circumstances of his mother's disappearance.

"That's an unfortunate story, but I still don't understand why you're here."

"It's crazy, but I was hoping that something would come back. I've been having dreams of her."

The woman looked at him in bewilderment for a moment. "My father sometimes took in odd sorts and occasionally let them stay here."

"Odd sorts?"

"Oh, I didn't mean it that way." She had stepped into the room and was now standing with her foot on the stone lip of the fireplace. Brandy settled beside her, panting and looking bored. "Special people interested him. Artists, writers, naturalists . . . Did your mother paint?"

"No. She was a biochemist."

The woman's face suddenly opened up. "Oh, good heavens. The sea-creature lady."

Sea-creature lady?

"From Harvard."

"Yes."

"Well, I'll be. She had something to do with a joint lab at MIT."

"Yes."

The woman's eyes expanded, and as if a valve had been turned open, turned effusive. "Yes, yes, yes. You see, Thaddeus was a trustee of the institute, which explains how he met your mother. She must have written a paper or given a talk or something which caught his attention. I think I was maybe ten or twelve at the time, but I remember her—a quick little lady with lots of energy. Yes. She used to come out and gather specimens, wade in the water with a face mask and net."

Jack could barely breathe as he took in her recollection.

"I don't know if you're aware," she continued, "but the waters out here are very special, because every twenty years or so the Gulf Stream brings in some odd creatures from the tropics—beluga whales and sunfish, Portuguese men-of-war, and smaller things. Sharks, too, even had a hammerhead caught just beyond the cove. But I remember her."

"Rose."

"Rose. Oh, yes: Rosie." And she pronounced the name with warm recollection. "A lovely woman. Wore her hair in a bun. She had a whole collection of things in jars she put on the shelves over there. Even set up a little lab in here of sorts with a microscope and things. She used to show me her collection—little starfish and crabs . . . and jellyfish. Such a lively, lovely woman."

"Jellyfish?"

"Yes. She must have been a marine ecologist—you know, someone who fought to save the whales or whatever, because Thaddeus was a great proponent of the save-the-sea movement, of course, and a charter member of the Cousteau Society, but that's before your time . . . ," and she went on.

Then she looked around the room and nodded at the corner. "She even had some mice, a cage with half a dozen or so. And a little maze she had built. She let me play with them."

"Mice?"

"I don't know what the connection was . . ."

Just then her cell phone chimed, and Brandy let out a reflexive bark. The woman produced a phone from her pocket and explained that she was down at the cottage talking to a visitor. She clicked off and stuck her hand out. "And, by the way, I'm Olivia Sherman Flanders." She checked her watch. It was time to leave.

Jack handed her the key as they walked outside. She locked the door and dropped it in her pocket, probably thinking about calling a locksmith. They headed up the steps, Brandy ranging ahead on the leash. As they reached the top, Olivia said, "You said something about having dreams of her."

"Yes, just dissociated images, nothing that makes sense."

"But you must have been a very young child when she drowned."

He nodded. "I can't explain. But I apologize for letting myself in like that. I was just hoping that something would jar my memory."

"Humpf," she said with a shrug, and offered him a ride to the ferry.

But he refused. He could use the exercise to build up his leg muscles, in spite of the ache.

"I understand," she said.

He dry-swallowed a Motrin and limped away.

The sun had broken through, warming his shoulders and turning the cove into an open bowl of green mercury. His eyes fell on the Skull Rock, drying to a dusty gray.

Jesus, jellyfish.

68

To save her money, the cabby had driven René directly to Logan Airport, where she caught a shuttle bus to Dover Falls, New Hampshire, where, on a call from the shuttle driver, another taxi met her to take her home. It was well after two A.M. when she had finally climbed into bed, drained and wondering if she had overreacted. Wondering how far it would have gone if she hadn't reacted. No, every instinct told her she hadn't overreacted.

On Sunday morning, René was at her dining room table working on the trial data for Nick in preparation for the Utah conference. A little after eleven, her doorbell rang, startling Silky from his sleep on the chair beside her. Outside was the black Ferrari. And the sight of it set off a small burst of adrenaline in her chest. Jordan was at the front door with a huge bouquet of flowers.

She couldn't pretend she wasn't home because her car sat in the driveway, and Jordan had spotted her looking out the window.

She opened the inside door, but not the screened storm door.

"I just wanted to stop by and apologize for the other night." He was dressed in chinos and a sleeveless polo shirt and looked as if he were heading to a golf course. Except on his feet were boat shoes.

"I don't remember half of what happened, but I think I acted badly. Really. I'm terribly sorry."

She could still feel the heat from his eyes as he gripped her arm and swore at her with hot conviction. Maybe he was just a bad drunk. "Accepted." Maybe she had overreacted, for she could still see herself in the middle of the living room with the fireplace iron raised like Uma Thurman in *Kill Bill*. Bullshit! Jordan was tall and athletic, and he was gassed. Who knew what he was capable of? Besides, she felt in peril.

Jordan looked at her through the screen with a supplicating expression. It was clear that he wanted to come inside. She opened the door and took the flowers. "Thank you," and she closed the door again.

"Well, I just want you to know that that wasn't the real me."

"That's a relief."

His face blotched as he didn't quite know how to take her comment. Then he made a flat smile of resignation. "I guess I had too much to drink."

"I guess."

"In any case, I'd like to make it up to you—you know, start afresh. I've got tickets to the auto show at the Exhibition Center."

"I don't think that's a good idea right now. Besides, I'm swamped with work."

Jordan's facial muscles tightened, and his left eye twitched slightly. And for a moment she expected him to push his way inside. But instead he nodded. "Okay, fine. I said what I was going to say."

René watched him walk down the driveway to his car. As Jordan opened the door to get in, René noticed somebody in the passenger seat. A man. She didn't recognize him at first, but she did register a large fleshy head and sunglasses.

Jordan lowered himself into the driver's seat and started the car. But before he pulled away, he cast a final glance at René as he rolled by her mailbox. In the next moment the car roared away.

And like the afterimage of an old television set, it came to her that in the passenger seat was Gavin Moy.

69

Mother's Day fell on the first Sunday in May. And because it was a glorious day, Yesterdays was bustling with celebrants.

It was Jack's second week of working the reception desk as host, and he was enjoying it. He felt engaged and useful. Several of the patrons were his old neighbors, a few former students, and town acquaintances who knew Jack's story and who were delighted to see him back and on the mend. Between customers, he grabbed a few moments' rest on a barstool behind the desk. During a lull that evening, Vince came over to Jack with a soft drink to see how he was doing.

Jack nodded that he was fine. "By the way, anyone you know own a Ford Explorer?"

"What color?"

"Black."

"Yeah, about thirty guys. Why?"

Maybe it was a grand coincidence, but it was now the fourth or fifth time he had noticed the car—the last on his return from the port at New Bedford. "Not important."

The evening passed well for Jack until, relieved by one of the waiters, he took a break and stepped into the kitchen for a snack. He stopped by the stove—an eight-burner industrial monster with all gas jets blazing—to watch the chef and three assistants moving from one burner to another, stirring and shaking with choreographic precision. On a butcher-block island, sous-chef Rico was carving a flank of beef, making cuts around the bones, trimming off the fat, and exposing the bright red muscle. Jack watched in amazement at the flourish of Rico's hands, the blade slicing with surgical deftness, leaving neat red slabs, the white bone glistening in the light. Beside him his assistant Oliver lay the cuts flat and began to hammer them with a heavy cast-metal tenderizing mallet.

From the other side of the kitchen Vince came over with a dish of homemade mango sorbet. "Hey, Jacko, I need a sampler."

Suddenly something happened.

"Jack?"

Jack did not answer. He was stunned in place—his eyes huge and fixed on Oliver hammering the red meat.

"Hey, man?"

But Jack was mesmerized by Oliver. Then Jack's mouth started twitching as a low groan pumped up from his lungs.

Vince swooped over to him. "Jack, it's okay."

Jack's body hunched over, his knees collapsing, his face a rictus of horror.

"What the hell's happening to him?" Rico asked.

"Some kind of seizure," Vince said. The others in the kitchen clustered around them, and somebody handed Vince a cold cloth. "Jack, snap out of it. Everything's okay." He dabbed his face.

Rico found a chair and they lowered Jack onto it. He was still making those small weird grunts.

"What's that, Jack? What are you saying?"

Jack had folded into the chair with Vince holding him in place, but all the while Jack's eyes were fixed on the butcher block and the red wet meat and the bright metal hammer.

"*Jack!* Snap out of it." And Vince slapped him on the face. That worked, because Jack let out a sigh, his mouth went slack, and his eyes closed. "Jack, come on, man. It's okay."

Jack opened his eyes and looked at Vince, then at the circle of people gaping at him. "What?"

"It's okay. You had a little spell is all." He handed him a glass of water. Jack's face was tight and drained of color, his lips gray, his eyes all pupils. His face was slick and cold. "Somebody call an ambulance," Vince said.

"No, no," Jack said. "I'm . . . okay. Outside. Just need some air."

They helped him to his feet and moved away as Vince took him through the back door. Rico followed with a chair and bottle of water.

The night was warm and clear, the stars hard white points against the black sky. Cicadas chittered in the trees. "Scared the hell out of us, pal."

"Sorry."

"Sorry, shit! I want you to call that doctor of yours tomorrow and tell her your damn meds are screwing you up is all. She must have better stuff you can take."

"I just saw her."

"Well, see her again, because whatever they gave you isn't working."

Jack didn't say anything but stared off into the sky.

"Are you hearing me?"

"I hear you."

"Well, I'm telling you, it was freaky, man. First I thought you'd had a stroke, then it was like . . . I don't know . . . like you'd turned into a frightened child or something."

Jack didn't say anything.

"Whatever, promise me you'll call and tell her what happened."

Jack nodded.

"Promise me. I want to hear the words."

"I'll call her."

What Jack did not tell Vince was that he was off the meds—

off the Zyprexa because it was numbing his brain, killing the
flashbacks.

And he wanted them back.

Jack still felt scooped out by the time he got home.

He changed and got into bed, thinking about taking a triple
hit of lorazepam to slam-dunk his head into oblivion. Thinking
about packing up again and moving to a different town, a different state, maybe even Canada—just to get away from Carleton,
the restaurant, Massachusetts, all the places with past-life
hooks into his psyche. Someplace where he could reincarnate.

*Fat chance, because even if you could afford to move, you'd
still be stuck in the padded cell behind your eyes. And there's
only one way out, me boy.*

In the dark his hand fell on the little amber vial. He shook it.
He could tell in the dark which pills they were from the sound
of the rattles—at one end the tiny one-milligram lorazepams,
little more than grains of sand to the Zyprexa bombs, and in
between enough maracas to rhythm out a salsa band. He undid
the cap and fingered out two tabs.

*Ten would do it. Okay, maybe twenty, given the tolerance
you've built up. Thirty tops. A couple of gulps of water and no
more Freddy Kruegers.*

He stared up at the ceiling. Just enough light leaked from the
windows to cut the total black. If he popped the pills, he'd drain
away in under five minutes, wake up four hours later. Then, if
his legs began to fuss, pop another tab and a pain pill, send himself back to black until dawn—the pattern of the night.

"Thought you'd had a stroke or something."

A stroke would have been a gift. The *something*'s the thing.

"A frightened child or something."

*Other possibility is you're losing your mind. Makes sense—
lost everything else. Why not a clean sweep?*

"You're blocking something." Dr. Heller's words floated up
like big yellow balloons.

He dropped the tabs back into the vial and got out of bed
and went downstairs. The kitchen was a small space with very

little counter area, filled mostly with ceramic cannisters for sugar, coffee, flour, and a wire spice rack with jars of different powders and herbs, a microwave, a small Mr. Coffee, and teapots. All the utensils were in two drawers.

He cleared a space on the counter and pulled open one of the drawers and dumped the contents onto the counter. Knives of all sizes and shapes, forks, spatulas, pie cutters, and other things tumbled out like pickup sticks.

He picked up one black-handled carving knife with a ten-inch blade of shiny, honed blue steel that came to a stunning point. He slowly turned the knife, and the overhead light arced across the curved honed edge like neon.

Nothing.

He picked up another, a heavier cutter with a thicker steel stock, probably for heavy carving or chopping. He held it in his right palm, felt the heft.

He put it back. Nothing.

He stirred his fingers through the pile looking for some connection, some zap of awareness.

Nothing.

He swept the knives and other utensils into the drawer and closed it. He then tore open the second drawer—handles of rolling pins, serving spoons, barbecue forks, whisks, eggbeater blades, spatulas, and small steak knives, all under a pair of pot holders and oven gloves. He removed the pot holders and gloves to expose the full contents of the drawer.

For a numbed moment his eyes rested on a single object: the heavy-duty wooden-handled stainless-steel mallet, one side tooled flat for pounding thin cutlets, the other a cross-hatch of tiny pointed pyramids for breaking fibers of flesh or cracking bone.

Jack picked it up and felt a hitch in his breathing.

He did not gasp in recognition. He did not become assaulted with shakes or break out in a sweat or feel a rush of blood to his head. Just the solitary hitch in his breathing, as if on some level just below the surface the *something* beamed up an impression like a sonar image almost too blurry to make out.

A meat mallet.

A meat mallet.

At two-thirty he lay in bed staring into the black as he had for the last two hours. His mind was very alert, as if a bungee cord had been affixed to it and every few minutes that drawer down there would give a yank.

A goddam meat mallet.

The sickening whacks against bone cap.

Sweet Jesus!

He kicked off the covers, pulled on his jeans and shoes, and went back down to the kitchen, tore open the drawer and removed the meat hammer. Still on a weird autopilot, he made his way through the dark to the garage, where he found a shovel, and cut across the lawn to the rear edge of the property by an anchor fence, and under some yews he dug a hole and buried the mallet. He returned the shovel to the garage and went back inside, where he cleaned up and got back into bed.

For another forty minutes he lay in the dark feeling his heart pony around the inside of his chest and trying to shut off his mind. He rolled around on the sheets, concentrating on regulating his breathing, calming his heart rate, and composing his mind to sleep. Several times he grabbed the vial of lorazepams, but he knew they would do little to block the pull of that mallet. It lay under two feet of dirt out back, but it might just as well have been strapped to his head for the way it kept slapping against his mind.

Die, goddamn it, die.

It was a sick, crazy, obsessive compulsion of the purest ray serene, but he could not shake it, and doping himself into slumber would only put off the next assault. And daylight would only make it worse, because the freshly overturned dirt would be glowering at him until he couldn't stand it anymore.

"Shit!"

He kicked off the covers once again, got dressed, and went out back with the shovel and dug up the mallet. He put it in a paper bag so he wouldn't have to touch it. Then he headed down the driveway in the dark and onto the Mystic Valley Parkway that led to a small bridge over the Mystic River where it drained into the lower Mystic Lake. Because of the hour, no cars were on the road. He removed the hammer, and with all his might he flung it into the water.

For a long moment he watched the water smooth over itself as the moon rode the ripples.

He was sweating yet chilled by the time he returned to the house. Because his mind was still on high alert, he got himself a beer and went to the porch and sat in the dark, his insides trembling as if he were sitting in wet clothes. He took a sip—always the best part—but it was not satisfying. He tried to distract himself with the bright electric sounds of the cicadas, a hoot owl, the moon whitewashing the yard grass. None of that worked.

As he gazed into the dark corner of the yard where he had dug the hole, the pieces came together with such clarified horror that a squeal rose up from three decades of merciful sleep.

A man.

He could not see his face or morph together the body from the shadowy flashcard form, but it was a man. And something had happened and he had pushed her or she had fallen, and she was on the floor by the fireplace . . . then he was bending down over her muttering . . . *Oh, shit, no!*

Then a towel across her head to the muffle the sound—
Goddamn it, die.

And blood . . .

Dark clothes, bending over, legs straddling her as she lay groaning, twitching horribly on the floor by the stone fireplace.

Her feet moving, as if trying to catch traction on the air. Groaning. The arm raised, hammer arching upward, coming down and down and cracking the bone.

Die . . . Die . . . Die . . .

The bright red spot spreading across a towel and puddling onto the floor.

Looks this way, thinks twice: Do him, too—the kid in the crib?

Stop that screaming.

Charges over . . . the big shadow face.

And all goes black.

70

"Tell me about the jellyfish drug."

"What about it?"

"You said it had something to do with enhancing memory."

It was the following afternoon, and Jack and René Ballard were sitting in a booth at the Grafton Street Pub and Grille in Harvard Square. The luncheon crowd had left, and it was three hours before the dinner menu kicked in. Jack had surprised her with his call, reminding her of her offer to help if he had any problems.

René looked very stylish in jeans and a black silk top and red paisley scarf, her shiny chocolate hair framing her face like a feathered wreath. Her face was smooth and well designed. Her nose was thin and sharp, her cheekbones high, her mouth full and expressive. Her eyes were perfect orbs of reef-blue water. It was a beautiful and intelligent face, and Jack took pleasure in it. "It reverses the damaging effects of the plaque that builds up in the brain of Alzheimer's victims."

"And it restores memory."

"In patients with the disease, yes."

"Short-term and long-term?"

"Yes. May I ask why you're asking all this?"

"In a moment. But just tell me approximately how far back, the recall." He could feel something pass through her mind as she considered the question.

"In some cases very far."

"Even early childhood?"

René's eyes were calm but guarded. "Yes. But why do you want to know?"

But he disregarded the question. "And if they go off it, what happens?"

"The process is reversed. The plaque returns. But . . ."

"What about in non-Alzheimer's patients? Any signs of plaque or dementia from taking the stuff?"

"No. Now, why are you asking me all this?"

"Because I think I witnessed the murder of my mother."

"What?"

"I was very young at the time, but I'm almost certain somebody killed her in my presence. And I'm just remembering it by way of memory-related nightmares and flashbacks."

"Flashbacks?"

"Yeah. Sometimes when I'm awake I have these spells. Just scraps, like a filmstrip with lots of frames missing." And he described some of the episodes. But as disturbing as they were, he felt relief in getting them out, in telling her—and it was not just like lancing a psychic boil. For some reason he wanted her to know. He wanted René Ballard to know about him.

At the moment, she seemed transfixed. "Go ahead."

"I think it was at the cottage on Homer's Island the night she disappeared," he continued. "And I think she knew whoever it was, because I don't sense immediate hostility as with a stranger. I think there was a fight, because I remember shouting and commotion. The next thing, I'm looking outside and the man is smashing her skull with a hammer—actually, a meat mallet, I think.

Die, goddamn it. Die.

"My sense is that the killer was desperate to finish her off, because I keep seeing him hanging over her and hammering away."

René studied him suspiciously. "Do you have any idea who he was?"

"I couldn't see his face—just a vague dark shape with a pointed hat or something covering his head. Maybe a rain slicker. I couldn't make it out. But I have a strong feeling it was somebody she knew. Besides, a storm was brewing so there wouldn't have been strangers boating up, and the only other male in the area was a frail old guy in the mansion who couldn't have made it down the stairs."

"And you're certain you're recalling something you'd experienced, not just a recurring dream."

"I know the difference between a dream and these spells. It's like I'm reliving a very bad thing in flashes, but I can't get the whole footage."

Silence fell between them as the sounds of the restaurant filled the gap. René took a sip of her drink. "What's the connection with Homer's Island?"

"I'm not sure of the exact details, but Thaddeus Sherman let her stay in the caretaker's cottage." And he explained what Olivia Sherman Flanders had told him. "The official story is that she got swept off her boat while trying to secure it."

"And you don't believe that."

"No."

"But someone she knew entered the cottage that night, had a fight with her, then killed her with . . . a meat mallet, you're saying."

"It's my grassy knoll."

He knew how absurd it all sounded—trying to piece together evidence of a thirty-year-old murder when there was no physical evidence and no body, where the only witness was a two-year-old baby and suspicion was rooted in bad flashes following emergence from a coma. Not exactly a hard-and-fast case.

Even on the off chance that his mother was murdered, Jack had no idea how to mount an investigation. Most island residents from back then were probably dead or in parts unknown. Even if he had money to hire the best private investigator in town, there was virtually nothing to go on. And he had neither the energy nor the resources to play Sam Spade.

"What I'm having problems with is how old you were at the time. Memory consolidation doesn't start until a child is three or four years old."

"You don't remember things from very early in life?"

"Not that early. And what little I do remember is mostly fictionalized."

"Fictionalized?"

"Yes. I know my father took me to the Statue of Liberty when I was five, and in my head I have a recollection of being there. But in reality I only remember the memory—what my father told me. I just put together the details and re-created the scenario, but not the experience itself."

"But isn't that what's happening with your dementia patients, the ones you've been testing at Greendale?"

"Those are more interactive, autocreative."

"So you're saying that I'm experiencing meaningless vignettes put together from some old horror flicks."

"I don't know where they're coming from."

He thought for a moment. "Maybe I *am* crazy."

"Doubtful, but I can suggest something to help counter the experiences."

"I've got enough meds. And that's the problem. They're working too well."

"Too well? What does that mean?"

"It means that I don't want to bury them. I want to catch them. I want to go back."

A sucking silence filled the space between them.

Her eyes narrowed. "What are you saying?"

"Memorine. I've seen how it works on people with dementia—sending people back in their heads. I've seen what the stuff can do."

René's eyes flared at him. "Jack, what you're suggesting is ridiculous. It's also impossible."

"Maybe, but to me it's worth a try."

"Not to me. One, it's a trial drug not for public consumption. Two, it's not something you can fine-tune, just dial a date and pop a pill to relive it. Three, if I gave you samples it would also cost me my job. And that's not going to happen."

He leaned forward and lowered his voice. "But nobody would have to know if a few pills are missing."

"Jack, every pill, every capsule, every cc of patient medication is accounted for, rigorously documented on forms and signed off by doctors, nurses, and pharmacists."

"You mean to say that you can't cop a few tabs and write down that Mrs. Smith took them?"

René looked at him in disbelief. "No, I can't."

"Or you won't."

"And I won't. Besides, we don't know what the effects would be on you."

"But you said there were no effects on non-Alzheimer's patients. Besides, they couldn't be any worse than what I'd already experienced. Unfortunately, that's gone the way of Zyprexa."

"Pardon me?"

He tapped his head with a finger. "My VCR's dead. Not even a lousy LED light. That stuff killed the flashbacks. I haven't had one for days."

"Then maybe you should count yourself lucky."

So much for that idea, Jack told himself, and he dropped the subject.

When it was time to go, Jack said, "By the way, doesn't it seem odd that the same jellyfish that knocked me into a coma happens to be your Alzheimer's drug?"

She thought of that for a moment, "Just a coincidence. No more so than if you'd gotten stung by a bee. Ever hear of apitherapy?"

"No."

"Bee stings can be fatal to some people, by causing such a severe allergic inflammatory reaction that the person can go into shock and die. But in small doses, the toxin is sometimes used to treat other inflammatory conditions such as rheumatoid arthritis or neuralgia. Just a matter of the right dose." And she stood up to go.

"While we're playing Scrabble, maybe you can tell me just what species of jelly it was. They said it was rare, but nobody ever gave it a name."

"Solakandji."

71

The woman with the child froze when she saw him.

Louis had just buried his parachute in a flowerbed and was crawling on his belly toward the water, his weapon in his right hand, two ammo clips and a grenade belt over his left shoulder. An enemy gunship was rounding the bend in the river. He could make out men in the machine-gun nests. One scream from her, and Commie soldiers would be all over him like ants. And if they didn't kill him on the spot, they'd haul him off to another prison camp and finish him off for good. Or, worse, take him back to the Red Tent to beg Chop Chop and Blackhawk for death.

Louis fanned the woman and kid with his carbine, looking down the barrel capped by the black military-issue silencer.

Thwump. Thwump.

And she and her kid would be gone—and he'd be out of harm's way and back on his mission.

God damn you, woman!

Less than twenty-four hours ago, Louis and other select combat paratroopers were summoned to a group briefing at battalion HQ where recon officers displayed large photos of a small village with a cluster of buildings around a pavilion that was HQ of high-ranking North Korean officers who had fled Pyongyang. Because American POWs were believed housed in the same locale, they couldn't carpet-bomb the site. So, their mission was to make a surgical combat parachute assault—their drop zone being a mountain clearing northwest of Jinan. Their assigned target was that pavilion.

At Kimbo Airfield, Louis and the others boarded the *Dixie Dame,* a C-119 transport piloted by Captain Mike Vigna. They would take the plunge from six hundred feet up, knowing that if anything went wrong, they were seconds away from an abrupt death. Each man had been issued ammunition, rifle, grenades, pistol, extra ammo, three days' assault rations, and a T-7 parachute. Louis must have weighed over 250 pounds with all that was strapped to him. But he didn't mind, since among the attendees ID'd by recon was NK 23rd Brigade commander Lieutenant Colonel Chop Yong Jin and Russian military advisor Gregor Lysenko. Who made Operation Buster special. What Louis had been waiting for all these months.

Colonel Chop Chop was the most hated man in the NK command—the same guy who had ordered his soldiers to pillage South Korean villages and massacre unarmed civilians. Same guy who had disregarded all international conventions on the treatment of POWs. Same bastard who had captured five GIs from King Company and left their bodies in a railway tunnel. And the same guy who had ordered the mutilation and death of Fuzzy Swenson and the summary execution of Louis's buddies from the first platoon.

That was four months ago, and since then Louis had declared his own private war against Colonel Chop Yong Jin and General Gregor Lysenko. Although Command had given him a copy of those men's photos, their faces had permanently scored themselves into Louis's memory banks that night in the Red Tent.

He checked his watch. Right now, Marie was in bed in Woburn, Massachusetts, and here he was in the middle of a gook village on the Yesong River. It had been a bad drop.

Unexpectedly, Jinan was being defended by automatic

weapons, including forty-millimeter ack-acks. At 20:15, just fifteen hours ago, under a clear, moonlit spring night, the *Dixie Dame* took off. The plan was to fly due north along the usual C-119 route, then break off over the sea and drop to seven thousand feet, where they'd make a left correction, drop again toward the water until they were at eight hundred feet, then bank right until they made landfall.

All went according to plan as Vigna pulled up off the sea and rode the contours of the land. At about five minutes before target, the jumpmaster gave his command to hook up to the cable running down the aisle of the plane and face the door. But as they were doing equipment check on the next man's chute, antiaircraft batteries opened up at them. Within seconds, Louis felt the plane get punched. In moments, they began bucking wildly.

The jump door flew open, and Louis felt the 120-mile-an-hour rush of air. He could barely register the fire ripping at the right wing or the groan of the plane or the other bodies pressing him against the opening. All he remembered was the green light and the shout: "Go!"

Hours later he woke up to morning light feeling stiff but unhurt. He had passed out under a thick willow, its branches stretching to the ground like a curtain—a perfect blind. He had just buried his chute among some tulips, when a village woman happened by with her son, a kid about eight or ten. Hard to tell with Asians.

Slowly the woman backed away, shielding her son with her body.

The kid said something to his mother. Louis had no idea what, but he lowered his gun because the kid looked terrified. He couldn't shoot them. But he raised his fingers to his lips to warn them not to blow his cover. The woman nodded and took off with her kid.

A quick surveillance of the area told Louis that he had landed in the People's Garden. He could see lots of manicured green grass, some sort of garden park with flowers, fountains, walkways, even a footbridge—right on the banks of the Yesong River. Although he couldn't see enemy troops, he could hear the din of their armored vehicles on the move toward Highway 1 to Kaesong. His heart sank because it meant Chop Chop and company were miles away by now. They had given him the slip.

Louis crawled out from under the tree. He had no idea where the other crew members were or where the plane went down. He hoped they'd made it to the sea where allied patrol boats could pick them up.

He made his way on his belly toward the river's edge. Villagers were walking about, but Louis's attention was fixed on a small fleet of boats. They were clearly Chinese because they were painted green with red trim, and the pilot's cockpit was camouflaged as a large white waterbird. He also noticed that the pilot was actually peddling.

Shit! The bastards were sporting a U.S. flag at the stern, and the troops were all disguised as U.S. civilians—which meant they were heading downriver to sneak up on allied warships for a midnight raid.

God in heaven! He had to stop them.

Louis positioned himself at the base of a large bronze lantern. Over his shoulder was a statue of a rider on a horse facing the other way. Maybe Chop Chop. This was his region, his town, his people. Louis steadied his weapon at the patrol boat emerging from the low bridge. It passed noiselessly in front of him, the troops playacting normal, like it was a typical day in the park. He had studied the movement of the previous boat, so he knew it was going to round the island, then head downriver. And as soon as it did, he'd open up with everything he had.

In a matter of seconds, the patrol boat rounded the island. Louis tracked the pilot in his crosshairs. Plug him then blow enough holes in the port side to beach the bastards. Do the same with the next one just nosing its way under the bridge. He knew he'd go down, but he'd take a lot of Reds with him. Slowly he began to squeeze his finger.

"Hey, what the hell you doing?"

Louis froze.

Over his shoulder were two North Korean cavalry regulars on horseback. He rolled on his back with his gun raised.

"It's a hockey stick."

One Commie got off his mount and grabbed Louis's gun barrel.

Thwump, thwump.

Louis squeezed off two shots, but the soldier didn't flinch. Probably wearing a bulletproof vest.

"What the hell you think you're doing?"

"I think he's been in the sun too long," the other soldier said, taking Louis's gun out of his hands.

After two years of duty Louis knew some Korean. *"Kop she-da mama-san!"* he said, telling the gook to go screw his mother.

"What he say?"

The mounted soldier shrugged and took hold of the reins of the other's horse. "It's all right, folks," he said to the small crowd of villagers that was gathering. "You can leave."

"Poor guy," one of the peasants said. And he took a picture of him with his camera.

Louis held his arms high in the air. "Go ahead, shoot me, you Red bastards. Get it over with."

Louis thought about making a run for the water, but either they'd nail him in the back or the gunners in the duck boats would get him. The gook on the horse radioed for support while the other kept interrogating him.

"Can you tell me your name, sir?" The soldier took Louis's arm and inspected his wrist.

They were trying to steal his watch. "Louis Martinetti. Corporal. US71463961." They'd have to shoot him before he named his company and location.

"Some uniform," the first soldier said. "Pretty old."

"Go to hell," Louis said.

"Mr. Martinetti, where do you live?"

Louis looked defiantly at the small crowd. Some took photos of him to show their relatives a real American POW. In the distance he heard sirens, and his heart leapt up. An air raid.

U.S. planes were approaching, and they'd blast these animals to smithereens. But nobody seemed concerned. They just mumbled and shot pictures.

"It's a medical tag. Alzheimer's," said the first Commie, still trying to steal his watch.

Louis did not resist. He had nothing else to lose. But he'd hold tight when they brought him to the Red Tent. He'd die before he'd reveal anything about the mission. And if he ever got out alive, he'd finish it. *Oh, yeah!* And he glanced at the high statue of the horseman. *Someday, you son of a bitch.*

The soldiers began to lead Louis away, when from the mob of peasants a woman burst forth.

"Dad!" She ran to the soldiers and took Louis's hand. "I'm sorry, officers. We were in line for the swan boats, and he just wandered off. I'll take him, he's fine." Then to Louis, "Dad, you've got grass stains all over you. What've you been doing?"

Louis looked at the woman, and for a long moment he had no idea who she was.

72

To celebrate the end of the trials, the GEM Tech clinical team and executive administrators met at the Red Canyon Resort Hotel, a rustic but grand hundred-year-old lodge located near Bryce Canyon and Capital Reef on Route 12. It had been selected for its privacy and because it was located within driving distance of the splendid canyon and Rocky Mountain scenery crisscrossed with endless hiking trails and whitewater rapids. It was also near Gavin Moy's ski condo.

Although people had arrived on Friday, the official opening of the conference was Saturday at noon with a formal kickoff luncheon and talk, followed by the clinical investigators' meeting behind closed doors for the FDA strategy session.

Nick's overriding impression of the conference was the expense. Little had been spared. GEM had flown in sixty people from various parts of the country—execs, medical officers, marketing VPs, legal staffers, clinicians from outside the company, as well as the twenty-three clinical physicians who, for nearly two years, had headed up various trial sites. They had rented out half the lodge and the adjoining Mountain Lion Room, where later in the day the principal investigators would determine the final application report to the FDA. In the balance lay the hopes and fate of millions of Alzheimer patients, their families, and caregivers. Also billions of dollars.

The afternoon began with a five-course meal served in the elegantly appointed Ponderosa Room, where a SWAT team of waiters had assembled. Dinner consisted of leek and potato soup, carpaccio of tuna, salad greens, a choice of filet mignon, salmon, or lobster tail served in elegant presentations, assorted spring vegetables, and fancy Italian desserts. There were the finest wines from Napa Valley as well as endless bottles of Taittinger champagne. Table conversation sparkled with talk of skiing in Utah versus Gstaad and Chamonix, diving on the Great Barrier Reef, trekking in New Zealand's Milford Sound, the comparative virtues of Mercedes and BMWs.

It was an afternoon of well-decorated egos assembled in celebration of scientific success, of historic possibilities, and, of course, high personal rewards. While the setting and glittering promise were very alluring, Nick could almost hear folks calculating how many millions they were about to make in the next few years. If the projection of GEM's bean counters was accurate, the value of Nick's own shares would top ten million dollars in two years, maybe twice that when the European markets opened up. Then there was Asia, the Middle East, and the rest of the world.

What ate at him was how all the others would react once, with the backing of Brian Rich, Paul Nadeau, and Jordan Carr, he dropped a bomb.

After lunch, Mark Thompson, GEM Tech medical director, introduced Gavin Moy, reminding the audience of his humble beginnings as a medical resident who decided to start his own lab in a cramped basement behind MIT.

"What separates Gavin Moy from the rest of us mere mortals is the genius to recognize possibilities. What to a lesser man would have been merely a happy accident was to Gavin a discovery humming with neuropharmacological benefits. And he was clever enough to get patents on a whole family of base compounds from the jellyfish toxin.

"Not only did he believe in himself, but he also had the courage and tenacity to pursue a dream that led to this very room. Yes, it took years of isolation and synthesis, research and development. But over those years Gavin raised enough capital to expand his labs and to create a certain esprit de corps, a palpable feeling of shared enthusiasm that may not be found in every such scientific enterprise. That energy and sheer pride is a reflection of the man who resides at the top."

More applause and cheers filled the air.

"It has been nearly four decades since young Gavin Moy and a couple of local grad students first fired up their Bunsen burners in that small room below Junior Dee's Auto Parts Store. Today we are at the culmination of that determination, vision, and genius as we are about to give to the world the fruits of such great labor and science—the world's first cure for Alzheimer's disease, a scourge of aging humanity for generations and generations. Ladies and gentleman, I am proud to introduce Gavin Moy."

To a thunderous standing ovation Gavin Moy rose to the podium, looking elegant in his black pinstripe suit and tanned shiny head. Nick looked around the room. Brian Rich and Paul Nadeau shared a table with Jordan Carr, who had told Nick that he had reconsidered the data and was behind him in his recommendations for an extension.

Jordan caught Nick's eyes and nodded. And Nick felt a warm rush of gratitude.

"For the first time in history," Moy began, "we have demonstrated a plaque eradicator in the treatment of mild to severe Alzheimer's disease, thus representing the world's first treatment . . ."

And he cited impressive statistics on patient improvement while faces glowed with wine and expectation. "In one study alone, one hundred and sixty patients with moderate to severe dementia had experienced an average of seventy percent improvement in cognitive behavior as measured by various mini-mental and higher cognitive tests . . ."

Bolstering Moy's claims was a video of AD patients moving about the wards of different nursing homes looking purposeful and alert. Other patients answered the questions of interviewers. Responses were sometimes halting but focused and generally lucid. In one sequence, subjects—including Louis Martinetti—happily explained how wonderful it was to regain their memory. But what the video did not show was that Louis, home on furlough, was having continuous and traumatic flashbacks to his POW days, and yet for some mysterious reason he resisted taking medications prescribed to control those flashbacks.

The video segued into testimonials by members of the Alzheimer's Association who had witnessed miraculous improvements. Also tearful and touching reports of nurses, home staffers, and family members who expressed profound gratitude that their loved ones were improving. Heartfelt applause followed the testimonials.

The video presentation ended with a slick promotional on the healing power of the drug—elderly patients having fun moments with younger family members, concluding with a voiceover pronouncement: "The Memorine Solution."

Gavin Moy concluded with the reminder that they were at a turning point in medical and social history. "The world is waiting, and it is morally imperative that we respond accordingly and in a timely manner."

A standing ovation exploded. The pep rally had come to a conclusion.

73

There was a half hour break as people stretched and mingled, some execs and invited guests retiring to one of the bars. Then the twenty-three PIs moved to the Mountain Lion Room for the closed-door strategy meeting.

At the center of the room sat a large oval table with twenty-three chairs, each with place cards—nineteen men and four women. Although Nick thought it rather excessive, each clinician had been sworn to secrecy, their signatures appearing on a confidentiality document drawn up by GEM's legal department.

Nick took his seat. He looked over at Paul Nadeau and Brian Rich. They nodded. From the other side of the table Jordan flashed Nick a thumbs-up. His backers—renegades in dissent, as René called them. (He would telephone her and, of course, Thalia when it was over.)

Nick called the meeting to order and offered sincere appreciation for the arduous work by the researchers and their various staff members. "I share with my colleagues the high enthusiasm over the successes of Memorine and the hopes that it can eventually live up to expectations. I need not remind anyone of the global impact of this meeting and the decisions we make. But I'd like to say that our purpose here is to evaluate the accuracy and legitimacy of our application report to the FDA and not to agree on strategies that would ensure smooth sailing through that process."

An uneasy rustling circled the table.

Nick then asked for each doctor's comments on the collective findings of the trials. And one after another the comments were expectedly praiseful. Some spoke of how exciting it had been to work on such a miraculous compound, others saying how personally gratifying it was to witness such positive results. Murmurs of "Hear, hear," arose from others.

When it was Jordan Carr's turn, he shot Nick a nervous glance and said he had nothing else to add but high expectations. Nick felt confused. It was agreed that Jordan would initiate the concern about the flashbacks and begin to quote troublesome data. But he just looked away.

When it came to Paul Nadeau and Brian Rich, they also concurred with the others' praise and expectations, although Nadeau did mention a few cases of regressive delusional behaviors that were correctable by standard antipsychotic medications.

Nick was beginning to read the portents. "Thank you for your comments," he said. "And while I appreciate your enthusiasm, I heard only passing reference to what I believe are serious adverse reactions as manifested in over thirty percent of the trial subjects—namely, the flashback seizures. And if we are to offer a balanced report of our findings, it is incumbent upon us to highlight those problems which have resulted in a number of deaths, including one murder and three suicides, several injuries, and some arrests, not to mention the effect on family members and caregivers."

"I beg to differ," said Harvey Schultz, a PI from Trenton. "I'm not sure where you're getting your figures, Nick, but I have not experienced such adversities. And frankly I thought we had clarified this problem—namely, that these alleged flashbacks are delusions stemming from structural changes from AD and not the application of Memorine."

Nick was ready for that. "We have not clarified the problem but buried it."

A grumble arose. Jordan looked at Nick, his face reddening.

"A significant number of patients are receding into hallucinatory delusions of past-time—even early childhood—experiences. And many are very traumatic, locking patients into flashbacks. We've documented several cases of residents becoming highly agitated, including Louis Martinetti, from the video earlier, who out of the blue is back in a Korean POW camp. Another keeps getting stuck in a house fire that she was in when she was ten years old. Another relives the discovery of his father's suicide by hanging. These are terribly traumatic flashbacks that they just can't seem to escape.

"Furthermore, these episodes have not only created great difficulties for nursing home staffers, but, as you can imagine, they have had devastating effects on family members."

Then he read a few sample letters from caregivers. " 'You have made my husband into a guinea pig and into someone I don't know. His behavior is erratic. One minute he's himself, the next he's talking crazy things to people who died years ago. At least when he was demented, we knew what to expect. Now he's like a lost child who cannot come out of his trances.'

"Another writes: 'I don't like what this has done to my father. It's frightening and painful for our family to see him reliving painful experiences once forgotten. Our only option is to fill him up with tranquilizers and other drugs that send him into a stupor. You've created for us a horrible emotional seesaw. At least with the Alzheimer's we knew what to expect and learned to deal with it. But this is awful.'

"Another says of his eighty-two-year-old wife who plays with toy animals all day: 'I spent fifty-four years growing old with Helen, but I'm not sure I can grow young with her.' "

Silence filled the room.

Then Brian Rich spoke up. "As you know, Nick, I've scrutinized the data and given this a lot of thought over the last few weeks. But with all due respect, I've decided that our job is to cure diseases, not the social consequences of our successes. What we should be discussing is how best to make our deadline with this report. The world is waiting."

And from around the table voices made a spontaneous chorus: "Hear, hear!"

"Can you demonstrate that once a patient is off the drug the flashbacks subside?" asked another physician.

They all knew the answer. "No, since we can't take anyone off the drugs without bringing back the plaque. And that constitutes a double punishment by limiting our treatment of the flashbacks."

"Then where's the evidence that Memorine causes flashbacks if you cannot demonstrate the inverse?" Josh Rubell from Pittsburgh asked.

"Because in most cases the subjects experienced no sustained delusional activities prior to the trials."

Rubell jabbed a long yellow pencil at Nick. "Those complaints wouldn't have arisen had you not alleged that these flashbacks were the result of Memorine. You and you alone have poisoned the well, Nick, and I resent that."

The place hushed. And Nick felt his face burn.

Another added, "Frankly, I'm getting tired of all this talk of flashbacks and adverse drug reactions. We hired an independent outside CRO to review all the data and make a determination. We have the Klander Report, and I'm going with that."

Agreement passed around the table. Nick looked to Paul Nadeau and Brian Rich, who had shared Nick's decision to seek an extension on the application. They were both nodding and muttering, "Hear, hear." Across the table from them sat Jordan Carr, who was also nodding, his eyes steadfastly avoiding contact with Nick's.

Et tu, you son of a bitch, Nick thought.

In three weeks, the Klander Group had pored over all the clinical data that René Ballard and others had helped amass—med schedules, behavior reports, charts, clinical observations, progress reports, test scores, and any alerts raised by Nick and others. But it was a foregone conclusion that the Klander Report would dismiss the flashbacks as a consequence of the disease.

It was also understood that Nick's rejection of the Klander Report could mean the end of Nick's participation in the trials, his funding, the support for the MRI lab—a financial and image loss to the hospital. But institutional politics and fiduciary health was not what this was all about. "With all due respect, I think the Klander Report is bullshit."

"Then you're all alone, Nick," Dr. Rubell said.

For the first time that night Jordan Carr raised his hand. "Look, Nick, we've worked together on this for a long time. And for the most part we shared the analysis and interpretation of the data. But I've studied the Klander Report, and I must say that I am comfortable with its conclusions. We've treated hundreds of people with dementing conditions, and most have been brought back from inevitable oblivion. That's confirmation enough for me."

"Hear, hear."

"More than that, behavioral anomalies are to be expected in such a wide-ranging population." Then Jordan thumbed through the report to its core argument. "It's a proven fact that during the deterioration of the brain, connections are repatterned, while good ones become dominant. Which is why AD patients sometimes have sudden recall and forgotten talents—like sitting at the piano and playing the *Moonlight Sonata* when we thought there was little left inside. This is precisely what occurs with these flashback victims."

And he continued in his smooth high-reasoned tone as he quoted statistics. When Carr finished, the others applauded. And Jordan flashed Nick a smile that could barely disguise the "gotcha" glow. René was right about him: He was a self-serving chameleon who said all the right things if it advanced his cause.

"If I may quote Mark Twain," Nick said when the place quieted down, " 'There are three kinds of lies: lies, damned lies, and statistics.' What we did was hire the Klander Group to give us what we wanted to hear: That Memorine is a miracle cure with no side effects. Period. Frankly it's disingenuous of us to claim that this report offers a fair and neutral evaluation of our data. And I won't be part of it."

"I don't like what you're suggesting."

"What, that money talks? Well, that's what's happened. And I cannot live with myself were I to vote to accept this report and, thus, make what I assume will be a unanimous endorsement of our application."

"Nick, we've got spectacular results, and you're harping on some minor problems. Just what do you propose?"

"That we request an extension of up to two years before approaching the FDA."

"But we have a deadline," someone shouted over the protests.

"Yes," Nick said, "a deadline of GEM Tech's marketing department, but *not* the health needs of people suffering from Alzheimer's disease.

"Let's say we accept the report and Memorine hits the market. What happens if we get another suicide or murder? Remember the multimillion-dollar settlement against GlaxoSmithKline after a man shot his wife, daughter, and granddaughter? The jury decided there was enough scientific evidence that it was the Paxil he was on. Do we want GEM taken over by the courts?

"What happens when caregiver complaints over flashbacks force the FDA to put a hold on distribution? And while we scramble to figure out what to do, millions of victims begin to slip away again. Meanwhile lawsuits fall from the sky like hail, and GEM Tech stocks won't be worth the paper they're printed on.

"And what happens when outside medical studies conclude that GEM Tech clinicians cut corners and pulled strings to get FDA approval? GEM Tech and every one of us in this room would be litigational toast. And the only ones celebrating would be the lawyers and the competition."

Jordan spoke up again. "Nick, for the sake of argument, let's say that some of these flashbacks are the direct result of the drug. So what? The alternative is dementia and death. But if the flashbacks don't intrude, don't threaten anyone, why not live with them? Look at Louis Martinetti—his Mini-Mentals are over seventy percent. That to me is a miracle."

More chants of "Hear, hear."

"I say we vote to accept this report while initiating an aggressive demographic profiling of patients who may have such seizures. This way we determine susceptible target groups."

"You mean we conduct a demographic screening after approval?" Nick asked.

"Yes," Jordan said. "And that population with a propensity for flashback problems would be warned to avoid the drug, and at the same time GEM could offer a free test to screen for it."

"But that's putting the cart before the horse," Nick said. "I think it makes better sense to make those determinations *before* we submit our application. Even if it takes a year or so, it's to everybody's advantage to determine which patients might be susceptible to these flashbacks. The alternative is a dangerous rush to market that is unacceptable to me."

"The other option is a black box," Paul Nadeau threw out.

Nick chuckled. A black box was the warning that the Food and Drug Administration required in a drug's labeling— nothing a pharmaceutical company welcomed. "Sure: 'If you don't want your elderly patients to play Ding Dong School all day or attack the postman because he took your marbles, then this drug may not be for your dementia patient.' "

Nobody else found that amusing.

"What you are asking, Nick," said Rubell, "is that we tell millions of people out there that they'll have to let the fog close over them while we work out these little details. In my book there's no crueler punishment—show them the light, then blow it out. We are simply not going to stop this train."

"I agree," said Jordan.

"Well, then," Nick concluded, "I have to say that I cannot in clear conscience vote to allow this report to go to the FDA without a disclaimer statement. It's a whitewash job that feeds false hope to sufferers and caregivers. And I refuse to contribute to the perception that we researchers are so embedded with GEM investors that we have collectively voted to look the other way."

Hard eyes beamed at him, as heads bowed together in judgment. And for a second, Nick felt like the centerpiece of Leonardo's *The Last Supper*.

"That being said, I will write my own letter of recommendation that the FDA postpone review until further tests are conducted."

A gaping silence filled the room as the blank ballots were passed around. Two minutes later the count was made: twenty-two in favor, one opposed.

Nobody said anything to Nick as he left the room and took the elevator upstairs to his room.

74

Two thousand miles away Jack Koryan lay in his bed thinking about his biological father's remains lying in a grave somewhere in a Cranston, Rhode Island, cemetery.

75

A little after nine that same evening, Gavin Moy called Nick to join him at the bar downstairs. "I didn't see you at dinner." Moy was sitting alone in a private booth at the dimly lit rear of the room.

"I had room service." Nick was tired and wanted to go back up to bed.

They shared a bowl of mixed nuts. "You ate all the almonds," Moy said. "All you left me are friggin' peanuts."

Nick swirled the bowl with his fingers and pulled out an almond. "Here's a *friggin'* almond."

Moy took it and popped it in his mouth and crunched it down. They sat quietly sipping their drinks for a few moments. Then Moy said, "I heard what happened this afternoon."

"I said what I've said all along. No surprises."

"Except that your dissenting report will be a major setback for us."

"Just one voice in the wind. I doubt it."

"But a big voice."

"Then you might consider reevaluating the rush to market, because the drug is badly flawed."

"Bullshit, it's not flawed."

"Gavin, the only thing worse than Alzheimer's is experiencing the same horrible trauma over and over again. And that's what this compound has done to many victims: It keeps sending them back to relive terrible events. And that's worse than Alzheimer's. That's worse than death."

Moy made a hissing sound and batted the air with his hand. "I heard your arguments. I just wish I could talk you around to our view. A letter from you could derail the train."

"Sorry, Gavin, but I can't."

They sat in silence for a long moment sipping their drinks. Moy flagged the waiter for a refill and another bowl of nuts. Then out of his jacket pocket he removed a sheet of paper and handed it to Nick. It was a photocopy of the story of Jack Koryan emerging from his coma.

"What about it?"

"It's our jellyfish," Moy said. "You know who he is?"

Nick felt himself tighten. Jordan Carr had requisitioned a blood assay on the guy. He had also asked for a frozen sample of his blood to check how much toxin was still in his system. "Yes."

"I understand he's been complaining about bad dreams."

The son of a bitch is baiting me. "Yes. He's been having flashbacks."

"Flashbacks," Moy repeated. "Something about nightmares of violent confrontations of some sort."

"That's my understanding." Nick kept his voice neutral.

Moy nodded, not taking his flat eyes off Nick's face, and picked out a couple almonds and crunched them in his molars. "I'm just wondering if you think there's anything to it."

He's playing tricks with me, Nick thought. *Some kind of twisted blackmail thing.* "It could be recollection; it could just be bad dreams. I'm not really certain. There's no way to know."

"It doesn't bother you? You don't see a problem here?"

"We're talking about stuff in the subconscious mind—nothing one can substantiate."

"Well, it seems we've both been wondering about this guy and what he remembers, and if that's a problem."

"I don't believe it is. Besides, our interest in him was strictly scientific."

"Of course," Moy said, and he clinked Nick's glass where it sat on the table. "And, frankly, I'm getting tired of this fucking ghost dance."

Nick took a deep breath. "Me, too." He checked his watch. "I've got to get up early tomorrow."

"Oh, yeah, your sunrise safari."

Nick had mentioned that he would be heading off to Bryce Canyon.

"You know that the forecast is for freezing rain in the mountains."

"Cuts down on the crowd."

Moy chuckled. "A crowd of one."

Nick's plan was to get up around four-thirty A.M. and make it to the canyon before sunrise. "You're welcome to join me."

Moy made a *humpf*. "The option of getting up in the cold and dark to drive twenty miles to watch the sun rise, or stay in bed. What we call your basic no-brainer."

"How often does one get the chance to catch a sunrise on Bryce Canyon?"

"Almost as often as sleeping in. You can show me your pictures."

Nick left thinking that maybe he was wrong. Maybe they *were* dancing with ghosts.

76

"My God," Nick whispered to himself as he looked down. He was standing a few feet from the four-hundred-foot drop-off ledge that made up Inspiration Point at the southern rim of the canyon. The only sound was the rustling of chilled winds through the ponderosa pines and jagged sandstone promontories—a sound unchanged for a hundred million years.

Bryce Canyon gaped at Nick's feet—a deep series of amphitheaters filled with thousands of limestone and sandstone spires, fins, and towers carved by wind and rain into whimsical shapes, creating a maze of ancient hoodoos. Overhead, the indigo vault was rapidly fading to an orange fire as the rising sun spread from the eastern horizon, bleaching out the last few stars. A crystalline quarter moon rocked in the northwest sky.

Nick inched closer to the drop-off for another shot.

He had gotten up as planned, and made it out here in his rental in about half an hour, stopping for coffee and donuts at a gas station mini-mart. Of course, the roads were wide open with no one else on them. He had checked out of the hotel at four-thirty A.M., his rental packed to take him back to Salt Lake

City for his afternoon flight back home—after this glorious pit
stop, of course. The last couple days had been stormy, but today the clouds were breaking. And because of the nearly nine-
thousand-foot elevation, the air was still chilled and the trails
dusted with snow.

The most amazing thing was that nothing moved. He could
see for over a hundred miles, and there was no motion but for
the junipers and pines. Not even a falling stone. Given the hour
and the frigid, windy conditions, not another hiker or tourist
appeared to be within miles of the place. Nick's rental was the
only car in the parking lot. From his perch, not a road or car or
building or urban light violated the primitive panorama. Not a
single sign that this was the twenty-first century and not a sunrise during the Mesozoic age. In fact, this could very well be
another planetscape—a vista on Mars, given the reddish
stones. Yet the stunning lack of sound was a gratifying relief
from the noisy, crowded conference rooms and dining halls.

Nick mounted the Nikon with the three-hundred-millimeter
gun-barrel lens onto the tripod, attached a shutter release cable, and began taking shots of the predawn light glazing the
towering fins rising from the canyon floor.

He would take maybe four or five shots, then move along the
rim as the light changed. When the sunlight began slanting into
the canyon, he switched to the two-and-a-quarter Mamiya 7
with the wide angle and headed for the very edge to shoot vistas. One must sustain a near-religious trust in the integrity of
limestone, for he was at the very edge of a sheer drop-off, the
sight of which sent electrical eddies up his legs.

He aimed at the sunrays gilding a row of rock blades.

Click click click.

Then back to the eighteen-millimeter wide angle.

Click click click.

The light was changing by the second. He shot off the rest of
the roll and put in another, then moved up the rim. There he
crouched down at the edge and shot down at the sunlight
glancing off a clutch of sun-enameled fans of limestone. It was
amazing how they resembled a colony of fire coral, but in

monstrous proportions. Of course, despite the calcium carbon-
ate structures and the fragile flamelike shapes, so-called fire
corals are not true corals but rather a hydrozoa whose stinging
cells are equipped with needlelike projections containing
burning neurotoxins closely related to those of jellyfish.

Jellyfish.

Amazing how lines converge. Of all the people on the planet
to meet up with Solakandji jellyfish, Jack Koryan. And what
had brought them together was a confluence of seemingly random geophysical events—cool Pacific seas, warm Atlantic
highs, errant Gulf Stream waters, a man on a swim in the right
place at the right time.

The jellyfish effect.

Statisticians would put the odds at one in a million—except
that this was not a statistically random convergence of the
twain. Far from it. Nick didn't know to what extent things connected, but when he got back to Boston he'd check. But it was
amazing how the closer you looked at life, the fewer accidents
there were. In fact, maybe there were no real accidents.

Oh, Jack Koryan, he thought. *Poor Jack Koryan.* You've got
demons clawing at your brain, and you don't know what to do.
The sad thing is that nothing can be proven after all these
years. And even if it came to that, how do you explain? It's all
so garbled by time. Even if you could explain, what can you do
about it?

But maybe you should, Nick told himself. *Maybe do the one
decent thing that would free the guy. And isn't that your play-
bill role out here: Dr. Ethics?*

*Deep down, Jack, we're really not bad people, just humans
in conflict—like the rest of the race. Except the stakes are
higher.*

Nick looked at the sun rising between a fissure in a hoodoo
blade rising out of the chasm. A shaft of gold sent spikes in all
directions like a crown of glory.

*Sorry, Jack Koryan, for the long bad nights. But, I swear,
when I get back I'll open the door for you.*

Nick moved to another outcropping of rock where he hung

over the edge with the Nikon. He clicked off three shots. The light was rapidly shifting, shafts of gold shooting from the horizon through the cloud holes. He traced one to his right when he thought he spotted some movement on the higher ledge. He swung his camera around to zoom in on what appeared to be a clotted shadow among some pines just below where the rays lit the treetops.

In the split instant he depressed the shutter release halfway for autofocus, uncertain whether the shadow was an animal or a person, sudden movement from behind him sent a reflexive shudder through his body.

Before he knew it, a figure rushed out at him. In the instant before impact, it all became clear to Nick. But in a hideously telescoped moment he felt the wind punch out of his lungs, and his body was propelled off the rockface lip and into the abyss.

From a perch fifty yards to the upper right, the only sound was a solitary note of recognition—a short "ahhh" escaping from Nick Mavros's lungs as if he had found a misplaced key—then maybe ten seconds in real time the soft smack of his body against the rock rubble below . . . then some muffled afterechoes as he and his camera tumbled to their final resting place in the cretaceous layers of ancient seas.

It was done, and Dr. Jordan Carr signaled below to his accomplice to return to their car before day hikers began to show.

Jordan's guess was that Nick would eventually be found by backpackers or park rangers—a battered thing in a red North Face parka and jeans. And, depending on how long it took to recover the body, the newspapers back home would run the sad obituary of Dr. Nicholas Mavros of Wellesley, Massachusetts, senior neurologist of MGH and chief principal investigator of clinical trials of the new experimental wonder cure for Alzheimer's, who had apparently lost his footing during high winds on a slick and crumbly rim in Bryce Canyon National Park while alone on a photo hike. He had been in Utah attending a meeting of clinical physicians for blah blah blah, as Gavin Moy would so eloquently put it.

Jordan took a final glance into the abyss.

The only barrier between him and the Promised Land now lay below. *And God's in his heaven, and all's right with the world.*

77

Solakandji.

Jack had written the word on the back of René Ballard's business card.

It was a warm afternoon, a fine day to be outside. And Jack's rehab people were of the Kamikaze School of physical therapy, encouraging him to get out and walk twice a day.

The Robbins Memorial Library was no more than two miles from his house—maybe an hour's walk at his rate with the cane. Located in the center of town on Massachusetts Avenue, the library was a beautiful Italian Renaissance building whose interior might have been one of the most stunning in the Northeast—high vaulted arches, Doric columns, carved marble niches, paintings, and multicolored marble floors. Beyond the rotunda was the reference room, where a bank of online computers stood against a wall. At this hour most students were in class, so there was no wait for a machine.

On Google, he came up with hundreds of hits for "Solakandji jellyfish." He scrolled down the list, uncertain what he was looking for, but positive that this was preferable to laundry and housecleaning. Besides, he was curious about the little critters that had taken a half-year bite out of his life.

Some of the sites contained general info about jellyfish with sidebars about Solakandji; other sites were for naturalists, students of marine biology, and underwater photographers. Several explained treatments of jellyfish stings. Aunt Nancy had been right—vinegar, and don't rub.

He clicked on a few sites that included color photographs of the animal. And there it was: *Solakandji medusa*—a smoky yellowish translucent mushroom with spaghetti tendrils. It looked so innocently pretty.

This highly venomous jellyfish is extremely hard to detect in the water . . .

. . . its tentacles can grow up to 2m long and are near invisible under water.

The Solakandji sting causes a rapid rise in blood pressure and a cerebral hemorrhage . . .

There is currently no anti-venom available for the sting because scientists have struggled to capture enough of the jellyfish to develop an antidote . . .

Coelenterates have stinging cells called nematocysts, which are made of a spirally coiled thread with a barbed end. On contact, the thread is uncoiled and the barb delivers the toxic substance . . .

(St. Thomas, V.I.) By the time the emergency helicopter arrived, he was screaming in agony; a few hours later he was in a coma . . . died four days later . . .

There were similar news items about rare encounters in the Caribbean with swimmers and snorkelers, but none in North America. The news account of his own attack had apparently expired.

As he continued down the hit list, he found more technical sites cued by scientific terminology—"Coelenterate," "envenomations"—and linked to lengthy abstruse articles for marine biologists and not the beachcomber or sport diver.

Jack clicked on a few terms and found himself getting lost in the details. After nearly an hour, he came to a cluster of links to more medically slanted sites concerned with the toxin and possible neurological problems. A few enumerated the venom of various species that were clearly dangerous to humans but which were being researched for potential medical application—all very scientific. Out of curiosity he explored some of the archival abstracts of papers published in obscure journals.

Scrolling down a long list Jack came to a dead stop. For a long moment he stared at the screen in numbed disbelief:

Sarkisian N., Nakao M., Sodaquist T. A novel protein toxin from the deadly *Solakandji* jellyfish. *Biotechnology Today* **66:** 97–102, 1969.

What nailed his attention was the name buried in the authors list: *Sarkisian, N.* Nevard, Armenian for "Rose." Her professional name.

His mother.

The realization came to him in a stunning moment of awareness: She had coauthored an article about the toxins of the same jellyfish that had rendered him comatose. As if in autoreflex he read the beginning of the abstract, trying in a side pocket of his mind to put it all together:

The deadly Solakandji jellyfish *Chiropsalmus quadrigatus Mason* is rare and distributed in the tropical Caribbean and equatorial Atlantic. Four fatal cases due to stings from this species have been officially reported. C. quadrigatus toxin-A (CqTX-A, 43kDa), a major proteinaceous toxin, was isolated for the first time from the nematocysts of *C. quadrigatus* . . . CqTX-A showed lethal toxicity to crayfish when administered via intraperitoneal injection (LD50 = 80 g/kg) and hemolytic activity toward 0.8% mice. . . .

The arcane scientific language meant nothing to him. But it was his mother's words, her fierce intelligence expressed in her adoptive language. The coincidence was almost too much to grapple with. And yet, he sensed a logic and some greater import, like watching a Polaroid photo slowly develop.

He moved the cursor back to the search box, typed in "Solakandji N. Sarkisian," and hit the Search button. Four articles came up listed under "Hydra Library":

Sarkisian, N.A., 1969. Isolation and determination of structure of a novel polypeptide extracted from marine organism *Chiropsalmus quadrigatus Mason. Pure Appl Chem* **14**: 49.

Sarkisian, N.A., 1970. The potent excitatory effect of a novel polypeptide, protopleurin-B, isolated from a rare jellyfish (*Chiropsalmus quadrigatus Mason*). *J Pharmacol Exp Ther* **14**: 443–8.

Sarkisian, N.A., 1972. Pharmacologically active toxin from a rare tropical jellyfish. Various neurological activities demonstrated in maze-patterned behavior in laboratory animals. *J Pharmacol Exp Ther* **17**: 226–233.

And there were others with her name and coauthors. From what he could determine, his mother had been involved with the identification of some properties in the jellyfish toxin that over time had been found to have some effect on lab animals with potential pharmacological implications.

He then went back to the less technical sites, those of general information on the species, and looked up pages that gave its habitat. After scanning several articles about the creatures' encounters with swimmers off various Caribbean islands, he got the hit he was looking for—an article written by a reporter for the *Cape Cod Times:* "Fish Out of (Home) Waters," with the subheading: "Writer finds tropical fish in an unlikely place—Homer's Island"

For years scuba divers have reported seeing exotic strangers such as butterfly fish, triggerfish, and angelfish around the point of Buck's Cove of Homer's Island in late summer and early fall. They are not so much visitors as prisoners of the sea—swept north by the Gulf Stream when they're the size of a button.

For most of them, the journey is a one-way trip, and their time is limited. They're doomed to die when the water temperature falls as winter approaches. . . .

Among the visitors spotted by aquarists are cobia, black drum, and stingrays. Even a juvenile lionfish was captured two years ago. . . .

But the most unusual finds in recent years were the meter-long Solakandji jellyfish, which are usually found in the Caribbean and Pacific . . .

Jack was not certain what he had found, but what stood out in his mind was the fact that his mother had decided to publish under her maiden name and not her married name, Najarian. Had she gotten caught up in the woman's liberation movement? Did she decide to distinguish her professional self from her married self? Or were she and his father so estranged?

That last possibility sat festering in his brain as he left the library and headed home.

Jack knew almost nothing about his biological father or his parents' marriage. He had also never visited his father's grave.

So why all of a sudden was he calling ahead for the exact location? And why spend the better part of two hours driving to Cedar Lawn Cemetery in Cranston, Rhode Island?

A little late to be showing respect for the man who had sired him, he told himself.

Or do we smell the proverbial rat?

The cemetery officially closed at sunset.

In his rental, Jack arrived an hour before that. The directions given to him by the administration office were perfect.

LEO K. NAJARIAN

There was no inscription. Just the incision of the Armenian cross and the dates.

What Jack knew about his father was that he had come to this country from Beirut, Lebanon, and settled in Rhode Island, where he had relatives, all dead now. That was the Armenian immigrant pattern. But apparently the two sides of his family were not close; after his mother's death Jack had almost no contact with the few people on his father's side.

Perhaps it was strictly a professional decision to use her maiden name. Perhaps their marriage was in trouble and she was receding from it. His aunt and uncle told him nothing about their relationship. And even if they had marital problems, what was the point of his knowing?

He looked at the headstone, his eyes filling up as he took in the name of the father he had never known. The man who was just a name and a couple of faded photographs.

For most of his life, Jack felt the absence of a real father the way amputees suffer phantom limbs. His uncle Kirk was a nice man, but too infirm and too distant to fill the void that left Jack wondering just what it would have been like to have had a real father to have done things with. *"Hey, Dad, let's play catch."*

Who were you?

Who am I?

"Sorry, Dad," he whispered, feeling a deep, searing guilt that he had ever entertained the hideous suspicions that the man buried here was the creature in the dream—the thing in the hood with the mallet.

He put down the pot of flowers he'd bought and through the mist took in the headstone. It looked so stark. Only the years were listed: 1931–1972. No month and date—which seemed odd, since the surrounding headstones gave complete birth and death dates.

Whatever, he had come and paid his respects, and now it was time to get back to the here and now. And he limped back to his car and drove home, thinking about calling René Ballard. She had some explaining to do.

78

Nick's funeral took place that Saturday morning at St. Athanasius Greek Orthodox Church in Arlington, Massachusetts. René was numb with grief.

Hundreds of people had turned out, drawn from the greater medical and health-care community. She recognized several faces and joined Alice Gordon and staffers from Broadview, Morningside, and other nursing homes. In the front pews sat Nick's wife of thirty years, Thalia, their two sons, and their grandchildren. He was always showing René his photos of them. Now they looked lost in disbelief that he was gone.

From her aisle seat at the rear of the church she watched the mourners file in, recognizing several of the trial PIs and MGH people. She also spotted GEM Tech executives and scientists. Gavin Moy, in dark glasses, and some associates seated themselves in a pew ahead of her. Jordan Carr was with them. As he passed by, he stopped and gave her a squeeze of condolence on her shoulder. "I'm so sorry," he whispered, then filed in beside Moy. René nodded and wept quietly.

In a short time, the vast interior of the church filled up,

dozens of people standing ten-deep in the rear and pressing down the outer aisles under the stained-glass windows.

The official story was that Nick had lost his balance—a combination of precarious footing, strong winds, and possibly vertigo. Rumor had it that Nick had been given to dizzy spells—and at the high elevation in early morning light he might have had a destabilizing experience for one fatal second. Park authorities had reported snow flurries during the night and early morning winds with gusts up to fifty miles an hour.

All throughout the service, René was distracted by a small filament of uneasiness glowing in her gut. Every so often it would flare up, but she would close her eyes and will it away.

Later, at the grave, where the priest in his robe and head-piece pronounced the final benediction, her eyes floated over the large crowd of mourners and came to rest on the entourage of GEM Tech people standing in close file around Gavin Moy—various executives, marketing people, physicians, lawyers, officials from the FDA, and other power brokers.

Jordan Carr acknowledged her with a nod and a flat smile. Their collective somberness was appropriate, but it still could not dispel that little hot-wire sensation spoken earlier by one of the nurses in a whisper: *How convenient was Nick's death.*

79

Jack had left several messages on René Ballard's cell phone and had nearly given up on her when she returned the call on Tuesday. She had taken some personal days following the death of a friend, she said.

Because it was a bright, warm day, Jack suggested they meet at Fins, a seaside bistro in Portsmouth. René was waiting for him at a table on the deck under an umbrella. Behind her, the Atlantic spread out gloriously, the sun dancing off the surface as if covered with diamond dust. Jack ordered a sparkling water and under the table he slipped his briefcase with printouts of some of the material he had found online. When René removed her sunglasses, her eyes were red and tired-looking, her face drawn.

"I'm sorry about your friend."

She nodded. "It just shouldn't have happened. He was such a good person." Her mouth began to quiver and she shook her head. "Sorry."

"Nothing to be sorry about."

The waiter arrived with Jack's drink.

René took a sip of her wine. "So, what did you want to show me?"

She looked up at him, and for a brief moment he felt himself taken in by her eyes. The hard blue crystals were softened by her tears. He felt a warm rush in his chest and wanted to put his arms around her. But he pushed away those thoughts. "They're gobbledygook to me," he said, and laid before her what he had printed from the journal archives.

René looked at them. "I found some of these myself when I first heard about you."

Jack lay his finger on the authors' line. "That's my biological mother. Her maiden name was Sarkisian. Koryan is from my adoptive uncle."

She looked at him in disbelief. "What?"

"But it's not so grand a coincidence when you put it together. Homer's Island is one of the only places on the Northeast where these creatures ever show up, and she had rented the place specifically for that reason. She was a biochemist, and from what I gather . . . Well, you tell me."

While Jack sipped his water, René silently scanned the pages of the articles, occasionally nodding and humming recognition to herself. After a few minutes, she looked up. "This is incredible," she began. "But I think your mother helped identify the biochemical structure of the toxin. Her name is listed first, which is protocol for principal investigators. And this one a year later links it to its neurological effects on cognition and memory."

"Which is why the last one she coauthored talks about lab mice and maze problems."

"Yes, which means . . . I don't believe this . . . not only did she help identify the biochemical structure of the compound, but I think your mother discovered the neurological benefits of the toxin."

"You mean the Alzheimer's drug?"

"Yes." She looked up at Jack in dismay. "You're sure this is your mother?"

"How many biologists from MIT named N. A. Sarkisian do you think there were?"

René nodded. "Then she must have known Nick Mavros."

"Nick Mavros?"

"My friend who just died." She reached into her handbag

and pulled out the obituary from the *Boston Globe*. The headline read "MGH Neurologist Falls to His Death in Utah." "He
was chief PI of the Memorine trials," she said in dismay. "He
also did the imaging work on you when they brought you into
MGH. This is unbelievable."

Jack stared at the photo of Dr. Nicholas Mavros. "He came
to visit me at Greendale."

"He did?"

Jack felt a hole open up in his gut.

"Just one more question, if you don't mind."

"One of those standard memory test questions."

"He came to ask about my mother." Jack stared at the obit
photograph, then pulled up his briefcase and rifled through the
papers until he found the photograph he had discovered in the
old albums boxed in the cellar of his rented house. "Son of a
bitch." He turned the photograph so René could see it.

"That's Nick," she said.

Shot in front of an auto parts store, the photo was of a younger,
leaner Nick Mavros with long, black, shoulder-length hair, smiling at the camera, his arm around the shoulder of Jack's mother,
who grinned happily, her head tilted toward Nick Mavros. They
both wore white lab smocks. And they looked so together.

"They must have been in the same research group as grad
students."

Jack's eyes were stuck on the image of Mavros. "He asked
me twice if I remembered her."

"One of those standard memory test questions."

"What was your mother's maiden name?"

But they already knew that from Dr. Heller's tests days earlier. Then Jack thought of something and fingered through the
packet of articles until he found what he was looking for:

"He even wrote about it with her," he said and showed her
the abstract.

Sarkisian N. A., Mavros N. T., et, al. 1971. Neurotoxic activity on the sensory nerves from toxin of the deadly Solakandji
tropical jellyfish *Chiropsalmus quadrigatus Mason*. *Chem
Pharm Bull* **17**: 1086–8, 1971.

"My God, I found the abstract for this same article, except I didn't know she was your mother." Then she picked up another article and scanned the pages. "Listen. 'Proteinaceous toxin from the nematocysts of *C. quadrigatus* found effective in facilitating attentional abilities and acquisition, storage and retrieval of information, and to attenuate the impairment of cognitive functions associated with age and age-related pathologies in mice.' "

"Translating as what?"

"That they were moving down the pipeline toward Memorine." She looked at the other articles and abstracts he had printed up. "Nick's name appears only on this one, but she's on all these. The last with her name on it is from March 1975."

"Because she died in August that same year." Jack was quiet for a moment. Then he said, "He was testing me."

"Testing you?"

Jack could still see the shift in the man's face. "I think he wanted to know how far back I could remember. Like early childhood. Like the night she disappeared."

René's eyes seemed to veil over. "Jack, what are you trying to tell me?"

"That he may have known something about her disappearance. That he may have been the visitor to the cottage that night. That maybe he's the figure in those flashbacks. That maybe he killed her."

René's head recoiled as if Jack had punched her. "That's outrageous." Her voice was scathing. "Nick was a wonderful and compassionate man." Suddenly her face began to crumble. "How dare you say such things? He just died, for God's sake."

"He knew her and never said anything. He never said, 'I remember your mother.' "

"Maybe he didn't know she was your mother. You have a different name."

"Then why did he ask her maiden name? Heller had already established that. He wasn't there to check for brain damage. He wanted to hear it from me. Son of a bitch! I had a weird feeling about him the moment he showed up. He probably wanted to know if I remembered him from that night."

"Why would he want to kill her?"

"I don't know. I know nothing about him and practically nothing about her, except that they knew each other. And he wanted to know if I remembered her. You put it together."

"That's absolutely insane."

"Then tell me why he was pussyfooting around, why he didn't say he had been friends with her." And he held up the photo.

"I don't know why. But he's dead, and I don't want to hear his name slandered, okay?" Her eyes blazed at him through her tears. She looked down at the photograph. "Besides, it's been thirty years, for God's sake. There's no way to know what happened that night."

"Yes, there is."

For a moment she stared blankly at him.

"It could take me back to that night."

"Christ! We've already been through this. I'm not stealing any Memorine. Period."

He expected that, of course. And she was probably right. The stuff can't be fine-tuned. It's unpredictable in its effects. It may not even work. But as he sat there under her angry glare, it crossed his mind that deep down where the sun didn't shine maybe René didn't want him to remember what he saw that night—and who was under that rain slicker.

"This is the last I'm going to say about it, but I think you're stuck on a foolish and sick idea just to satisfy some neurotic obsession."

Jack said nothing, just nodded as the syllables seeped in one by one. "Maybe so." Then he looked out at the sea, and into the reflective light of the sun, feeling possibilities dance before his eyes.

"By the way," he said as they got up to leave. "What kind of a car did Nick Mavros drive?"

"Why?"

"Just wondering."

"Some kind of SUV . . . I think a Ford."

"What color?"

"Black."

80

Jack had not been back to Greendale for nearly two months. So when he showed up that Wednesday morning, he was welcomed like a famous alumnus returning to campus. Aides and administrative staff flocked around him and in tears Marcy Falco threw her arms around him. Jack had been one of her "witchcraft" successes.

"I just wanted to stop in to say hello and thank you for all you did for me." He had brought a large bouquet of flowers for the ward and a five-pound box of chocolate for Marcy. He said that he wanted to see how some of the residents were doing. He had heard that a few were progressing well in the trials.

Marcy took him upstairs to the ward, where it was morning rounds, and patients were getting their meds.

"How's Joe McNamara?"

"Up to his own tricks," Marcy said. "He won't take his meds. Connie's coming along now." She led him into Joe's room, where Joe was sitting up in his bed. He had apparently slipped and injured his hip.

"Hey, old-timer, remember me?"

Joe looked at him, his face straining in confusion to place Jack.

"Joe, you remember Jack," Marcy said.

Still Joe scowled as he rummaged in his brain for recognition.

"In any event, Connie will be by in a moment," Marcy said. "I'll leave you two to catch up."

When she left, Jack whispered into Joe's ear. "Father O'Connor."

Joe's mouth dropped opened as recognition swept across his brain. "Oh, Father, Father, forgive me."

"How've you been, my son?" Jack asked.

Joe was beaming. "Pretty good, Father, pretty good, but I hurt my hip, you know." And he pulled up the blanket to show a huge black-and-blue bruise along his flank. "It looks worse than it feels, though."

Jack could hear a wad of phlegm in Joe's throat. "Well, that's a blessing."

Just then Connie came in with a small tray with juice and a cup of meds. "Look who's here," she chortled, as she placed the tray on the table. Joe said nothing but studied the contents of the pill cups.

Jack pulled Connie aside. "I hear Joe's not being very cooperative."

She lowered her voice as Joe stared at the orange juice. "He likes the blue pills, but the white one he spits out."

"How come?"

"He claims they make him dull." And she made a what-are-you-going-to-do face.

"What's the blue?"

"His Alzheimer's drug."

"And the white?"

"Zyprexa."

"Of course." Then Jack lowered his voice. "Maybe if just the two of us are alone, I can get him to cooperate."

Connie thought that over. "Whatever." Then she moved to the bed. And in a loud, clear voice she reserved for the elderly patients, she said, "Joe, you're gonna do Jack a favor and take your meds like a good guy, okay?"

Joe looked at her but didn't answer. Then he picked up the cup with the square blue pill and gulped it down with orange juice. Connie watched from the doorway. Nurses were supposed to witness patients' taking their meds so they could mark the charts.

"Joe, it's me, Father O'Connor."

Joe looked up and his eyes saucered.

Jack held up the cup of Zyprexa. "You're going to make me proud, okay? You're going to be a good lad and take your pills for me." Jack did all he could not to lapse into a Barry Fitzgerald brogue. He laid his hand on Joe's shoulder, glaring at him with a sanctimonious smile. "Come on now, lad." And Jack raised the cup with the single pill to Joe's lips.

Joe opened up, Jack poured it in, then raised the orange juice to his lips. And Joe swallowed.

At the doorway, Connie grinned and flashed a thumbs-up. When she left, Jack sat at the corner of the bed. His eye fell on the suction bottle with the hose connecting to the wall.

"I don't like her. She makes me take that crud. They just put me to sleep. I like the blue ones better. They're kinda fun."

"How's that?"

Joe's thin dry lips cracked into a wry grin. "They bring me back to some good times." And he gave Jack a naughty wink.

Jack checked his watch. Marcy would be back in moments. "Joe, did I tell you the story about the new nun at her first confession?"

"Uh-uh," Joe said, looking up at him with an eager face.

"Well, there was this new nun, and she tells the priest that she has a terrible secret. The priest then tells her that her secret is safe in the sanctity of the confessional. So, she says, 'Forgive me, Father, but I never wear panties under my habit.' The priest chuckles and says, 'That's not so serious, Sister Katherine. Say five Hail Marys, five Our Fathers, and do five cartwheels on your way to the altar.' "

Jack waited a moment until he was sure Joe got the joke. Not getting a reaction, Jack began to explain, when it all clicked in Joe's brain, and he started to laugh. Jack took Joe's hand and laughed along with Joe, which made him laugh even more, until Joe started coughing. In a moment, Joe got locked into a coughing jag and Jack shot out of the room. Connie was just rolling by with her cart. "I think Joe needs to be suctioned," he said. And hearing Joe trying to catch his breath, Connie rushed inside the room.

The moment was Jack's, and his awareness was crackling. He had less than two seconds as everybody else in the room was distracted—Marcy at the other side of the dayroom with another resident, the aides with their backs to him. And the cart sat right there, drawer open, folders of patients' meds all in a row—Joe McNamara's gaping at him. And inside of it the card of blue pills in shrink-wrap windows.

Connie never locked the cart when she ducked into the rooms. Officially, she was supposed to, since it was a fundamental regulation in the nursing home that medication carts be locked when the nurses were out of view of them. But in all the weeks that Jack had spent on the ward he almost never saw the nurses lock the carts, unless they had to leave the area for a length of time—but never for a fast dip into a patient's room. And why bother, since everybody on this ward was mentally out of it?

In a flash, Jack's hand shot into the folder, and a moment later a card of thirty Memorine tabs was inside his shirt. He ducked his head into Joe's room and said good-bye. Joe had caught his breath and waved. "Good-bye, Father. And thanks for stopping by."

"Any time, m'lad, and God bless."

Half an hour later, Jack was home.

It would take them another day to realize that a card of thirty was missing. And nobody would connect the absence to Jack. Even if they did, it would be too late to stop him. He looked at the card of pills.

And the son of a bitch also had a black SUV. He'd been tailing him for weeks. He knew Jack was on to him. He knew, and now he was dead and had taken it with him.

81

MEMORINE CLEARED BY THE FDA FOR
THE TREATMENT OF ALZHEIMER'S DISEASE

BOSTON—GEM Neurobiological Technologies of Walden, Mass., today announced that it has received marketing clearance from the U.S. Food and Drug Administration for Memorine, a new drug for the symptomatic treatment of mild to severe Alzheimer's disease. Memorine has proven highly effective in reversing the damage done to patients with mild to advanced Alzheimer's disease while enhancing cognition and patient functionality.

"GEM Tech's dedication to the needs of patients and their families and our commitment to human health care and Alzheimer's disease research have fostered this new breakthrough therapy," said Gavin E. Moy, president and chief executive officer of GEM. "For generations, Alzheimer's disease has been a family tragedy affecting millions of people. Memorine represents the first cure of this dreadful affliction, thereby all but eliminating the anguish of families and terrible deterioration of patients."

Controlled clinical trials in over 900 patients demon-

strated that more than 70 percent taking Memorine dramati-
cally improved in tests of cognition over the course of the
studies and assessment of patient function and behavior and
activities of daily living, in comparison to patients taking
placebos, after 24 weeks of treatment.

The efficacy of Memorine was established by placebo-
controlled Phase III clinical trials. In the trials, patients diagnosed with mild to severe Alzheimer's disease received
single daily doses of either a placebo or 10mg of Memorine
for 24 weeks. . . .

Cognitive improvement and memory were measured by
the Alzheimer's Disease Assessment Scale-Cognitive Sub-
scale (ADAS-cog). Patients on Memorine achieved results
nearly 80 percent higher compared to placebo groups. Likewise, patient function was markedly improved, based on clinicians' observations and interviews with patients and
caregivers. . . .

Memorine will be available by prescription by the beginning of next year. . . .

The telephone pulled Jack away from the morning paper. It was
the administrator from Cedar Lawn Cemetery returning his
call from the voice mail messages he had left yesterday.

It was an unusual request, and Jack had to answer a few
questions to prove his identity. But they had the information he
had sought.

Leo K. Najarian was born on July 19, 1931, and died on
March 30, 1972.

Jack asked the man at the other end to repeat those dates,
and the man did so. They had come from the coroner's certifi-
cate of death.

Jack thanked the man for his time and effort and hung up the
phone.

And for a long moment Jack stared at what he had written
down. Leo Najarian had died eleven months before Jack was
born.

82

It was cloudy, and the forecast was for an evening thunderstorm. Jack was packed and just leaving the house when he heard the doorbell ring.

It was René. Her face was stiff and white. "What the hell do you think you're doing?"

"And a good morning to you." He closed the door behind her.

She glared at him. "The nursing staff at Greendale reports that a thirty-tab card of Memorine is missing from the med cart. They also report that you had dropped in for a visit on the same day."

"And they sent you over here to see if I know anything about that."

"No, they didn't, because they can't possibly imagine why you'd be interested in the stuff. They're still searching for it."

"Well, that's a relief." A week had passed since he was out there.

"Jack, what the hell do you think you're doing?"

He picked up his travel bag. "I'm going to find out who killed my mother."

"This is absolutely crazy."

"No crazier than the stuff I'm carrying in my head."

"First, you don't even know if it's going to work for you. Second, you can't just pop a pill and wait for flashbacks. It has to build up in your system. Third, I resent your suspicions of Nick Mavros."

He reached into the travel bag and pulled out the card of tabs. Nearly a third of them were gone. "It works, but all I'm getting is snippets—nothing connecting. I need the proper stimulus. The right setting. The right conditions, like the weather."

"What if something goes wrong? What if you trigger some awful psychotic reactions?"

"It's a chance I'm willing to take."

She tugged at his arm. "And what the hell do you hope to accomplish?"

"The truth."

"What truth? That you've got some sick obsession about your mother's death and you're trying to pin it on an innocent man?"

"I'm stuck in a little horror loop and it's going to continue until I do something about it."

"Like what?"

"Like opening a door."

"This is insane. You don't know what you're doing. I'm telling you, you're not going to do anything but set off more seizures."

"That's what I'm hoping for."

She stomped her foot. "Jesus Christ! You could damage your brain."

"Been there, done that. And just in case . . . ," and he reached into his pocket and pulled out four vials of pills. Dilantin, Depakote, Tegretol, Zyprexa—antiseizures, antipsychotics, anticonvulsants, you name it.

She looked at the labels. "I don't believe this," she muttered in exasperation.

"If I begin to trip out, I pop some of these. Isn't that what you do on the wards?"

She looked at him nonplussed. "Did it ever occur to you that you may not be in any mental condition to take any of this?"

He nodded. "Then want to come along and hold watch?"

"Where?"

Jack checked his watch. "The boat leaves in three hours."

They arrived at New Bedford just in time to catch the one o'clock ferry. Jack had brought with him a travel bag with enough food for the weekend. The sky was a bundle of dark clouds, and rain was beginning to fall.

René had continued to protest as they drove along until she realized it was a lost cause. Jack was adamant, but he was also touched by the fact that maybe René Ballard cared enough to come along to keep watch. Or maybe it was to defend the reputation of her friend and former professor. Whatever, he was glad she was with him.

Earlier Jack had called Olivia Sherman to ask if he could rent the cottage for the weekend. She said that the weather would not be good, but he said that he didn't mind. In fact, he preferred the beach under dramatic conditions. She didn't seem to understand but welcomed him to come.

For most of the boat trip to the island René remained in a quiet funk. But at one point she asked, "What if you take your little trip and convince yourself you saw Nick in the cottage that night? What do you have?"

"I already told you—the truth."

"Bullshit. You'll have a self-fulfilling delusion," she said. "You've lined things up in your head so you can arrive at a predetermined conclusion—that Nick had something to do with your mother's disappearance."

"I'm counting on recognizing the difference between delusion and memory."

"Yeah, and thirty percent of the patients on Memorine are conversing with people from their childhood."

"But in their heads they're back there."

She shook her head in frustration.

They arrived at the island at about one-thirty and hired a taxi to take them to the Vita Nova. They had begun to descend the steps to the cottage when Jack felt a small shudder. Overhead the sky was a dark, roiling canopy of clouds. And in the distance they could hear the rumble of thunder accompanied by explosions of light in the clouds as if from an unseen battle at sea. The conditions were nearly the same.

They made their way down to the cottage without saying a word. The key was back in its plastic container under the flower box, and with it Jack let them inside.

In spite of his adamancy, he really had no idea whether this would work or how long it would take even if it did—or how long René would tolerate the experiment. But for the last several days, all the drug had done was turn his head into a kaleidoscopic run of dissociative past-time vignettes that had no connection to that night three decades ago. But the storm resonated in some deep place.

And Jack knew that the flashbacks needed just the right stimuli—like some of the old people on the Greendale ward hearing an old tune and suddenly they would be back in grade school. And although René might turn out to be right—that it was insane, dangerous, and probably a dead end—it was also a last-ditch effort to satisfy a festering unknown that he knew would not otherwise go away until his death.

Around three P.M. Jack took his first tab. By then René had resigned herself to the absurdity of the experiment and saw herself as simply on standby alert should Jack flip out. Over the next few hours Jack tried to make small talk with her. She gave halfhearted answers about where she was born, where she went to college, about her parents.

By six, Jack still felt nothing, so they made a dinner of pasta with a jar of store-bought sauce. At one point, while they were working in the close confines of the small kitchen, Jack turned to her. "René."

She turned toward him from the stove where she was stirring the sauce.

"Why did you decide to come out here with me?"

The question caught her off guard. "To make sure you don't hurt yourself."

Jack could not help it, but as he took in those clear blue eyes and full and faintly disapproving lips, he felt a warm longing flood him. Here was a beautiful, desirable, and intelligent woman—the kind who dated famous brain surgeons, business execs, or movie stars—a woman who was so far above his league yet who had come all the way out here in the middle of a storm because she cared. Yes, maybe it was academic or out of some professional sense of obligation—but he didn't want to believe that. And now he was sharing a very small space with her and enjoying it in spite of the bizarre circumstances. "That's very nice of you." And for a second he thought he was going to slip and lower his face to kiss her.

But a sudden sizzle cut the air.

"The pasta water's overflowing."

Gratefully, Jack snapped off the gas jet as foam poured over the sides of the pot. With a fork he snagged a strand of spaghetti and handed it to her. She blew on it, then tasted it. She nodded. "Perfect."

As he poured the pasta into a colander in the sink, he said, "By the way, do you like Armenian food?"

"You mean like shish kebab?"

"Yeah, and pilaf, stuffed grape leaves, and lamejun, which is Armenian pizza."

René was setting out the dinnerware and dishes. "I've never really tried it. Why?"

"I'm just thinking that once this is over, what do you say we give it a shot? I know a nice place in Watertown. They also have takeout."

He could see that she clearly was not in the mood to talk about some future date. "We'll see."

Jack nodded and stored that away, glad that he had not yielded to his foolish impulse and spoiled the moment. Besides, he reminded himself, another reason she was out here was to vindicate her old friend and mentor, Nick Mavros, from the nuttiness of Jack's experiment. But her "we'll see" gave him hope.

With dinner, Jack took another half tablet. Still nothing happened, and the storm was getting closer.

After they ate, René settled on a couch with a book. She did not want to talk any more, sending the message that she was not a participant in Jack's nutty experiment.

At eleven Jack took another tab—swallowing a whole pill to René's protest. By one o'clock he still felt nothing but drowsiness. He put more logs on the fire.

Meanwhile, René sat with her book and sipped wine. Vials and syringes of antiseizure agents were lined up on the coffee table. Every so often she'd mutter how she couldn't believe she was doing this. And on the other side of the coffee table Jack sat in another sofa, where the crib had been, and stared at the door.

After a while he felt a fluidy warmth spread throughout his brain. The lull of the rain against the roof and the fire conspired against him, and he closed his eyes as a delicious drowsiness settled over him.

He could hear the rain pelt the roof like BBs. And in the distance, a deep-bellied rumble of thunder.

On the coffee table sat a shiny metal meat mallet he had brought. Also, the photograph of him on a pony beside a statue of an Indian; his mother was holding him in the saddle. According to the faded ink on the back, it was taken on the Mohawk Trail when Jack was fourteen months old.

It was the last image in his mind as the warmth of the fire pulled him under.

He knew he must have fallen asleep, because sometime later he vaguely felt himself being lifted and carried to another room, which was dark and where he was laid onto a bed and covered.

"And here's Mookie."

And he felt something nuzzle up against his side.

"Ahmahn seerem."

(How did René know Armenian?)

"His eyes are moving."

"That's good, he's dreaming."

"Jack, I'm right here."

(Beth? I thought you were in Texas.)

"They're just going to take some pictures."

He could hear her through the door, on the far side of the living room. He tried to open his eyes, but they wouldn't work.

"You won't feel a thing."

Thunder rumbled.

"Almost there."

(I'm coming. I'm coming. I'm coming. . . .)

He was in a deep sleep when he heard a knock at the door. His eyes cracked open, and through the space of the open door he saw René let in the visitor. "I thought you'd never make it," she said in a low voice.

(How did René know somebody was coming out here?)

Jack saw the figure pass the opening of his door. Because of the storm, he was wearing a dark, hooded slicker that blocked his face. René closed the door and asked how he managed to make it in this weather, and he said something about the sea not being bad yet.

Jack did not identify the voice. And René's voice sounded strange, accented. And she looked smaller, darker than he recalled. And her hair was in a bun.

Jack knew he wanted to stay awake—he knew how important it was that he take watch . . .

The big replay, pal. What you've been waiting for, stole all the blue beauties for . . .

But for the life of him, he could not keep his eyes open.

A sharp voice woke him again. "I'm not going to do that. Simple as that."

"I'm a part of this, too."

"I don't give a damn."

"You never give a damn."

"I do, but I'm not going to give it all up for him. It's as simple as that."

"Stop shouting, you're going to wake him. Stop it."

Jack climbed out of the crib and onto the floor. He walked to the opening and looked into the living room.

The next moment exploded in a flurry of movements. The man's back was to him but he could see the woman slap her hand at him. "You son of a bitch," she cried.

The man's own hands rose to block her attack, but she continued to swear and swing at him, and he slapped her back, connecting with sounds of smacking flesh, her screaming.

Her screaming . . .

"Call the friggin' cops. Go ahead."

And with a fist he backhanded her in the face. The blow sent her stumbling backward, and her head cracked against the stone edge of the fireplace—the contact passing into Jack's brain like a hot needle.

Jack heard himself cry out—a sharp, bright cry that sliced the air.

"Shut up, goddamn it."

But Jack could not shut up. The man turned toward him, his face still out of view, and a terrified Jack scurried back into the bedroom. A moment later the man slammed the door shut.

Jack crawled under his crib, his stuffed mouse pressed against him, the hard wood floor cold against his legs. He could see movement in the light strip. And he could hear movement and the man's voice. "Oh, shit, Rose! Rose!"

Then a long silence. Jack crawled out from under the crib and padded to the door, his mouse still held against him. There was no lock on the door, and he knew how to open it—just push the metal handle down.

He did, and through the crack he saw the man with the slicker on his head dragging her out the front door, a thin dark trail smearing the floor.

Jack could feel the cold breeze rush into the room. A moment later, the man closed the front door. Thunder cracked overhead and the window flickered blue light.

Jack went to the front door.

"Goddamn you, die."

Jack opened the big door to see the man hanging over the woman on the ground. In the man's hand was the meat mallet. In the dark wet the woman was whimpering and her feet were twitching horribly, as if she were trying to walk on air. And the mallet came down and down.

Jack let out a cry. And the man looked up, his hood casting a sharp shadow over his face. Jack ran back to his room and closed the door and climbed back into his crib.

But the door flew open and the man filled the light, his head a large black bullet, the mallet still gripped in his hand.

Jack heard himself crying so loudly that it felt as if pieces of his throat were breaking loose.

And the man just stood there taking in the screams, watching Jack squirming, cowering in the corner of his crib, clutching Mookie to him, the blanket over his head but with just enough of a hole in the folds to see the man who continued to stand there in the doorway staring at him, his terrible head and slanting shoulders—thinking about what he should do about the baby in the crib eyeing him through his blanket.

Jack could hear himself whimper, wishing he could stop, wishing he could just disappear, blink out of existence.

"Won't remember a thing."

And then the room lit up in an electric blue light as a crack of thunder shattered the air.

The man closed the door.

He must have cleaned up the mess in the other room, because Jack could smell something—bleach—as he lay there in the dark waiting for the door to burst open again. But it didn't.

And some time later he heard the outside door bang shut.

Jack heard a warbling cry and snapped his eyes open.

He had slipped to the floor. His throat felt thick and his chest hollow as if he had been sobbing deeply. His mind was raw. He looked around the room.

All was still, and outside a gentle rain pattered against the roof. The fireplace was a bed of glowing coals and burnt log ends. A soft yellow night-light burned in a lamp on the table. The clock on the wall said 3:35.

René was curled up on her couch under an afghan.

Jack must have made sounds as he awoke, because René rolled onto her back and sat up. "You okay?"

He nodded. "I saw his face."

PART
5

83

"**D**ad, we have to be there at six. Might be time to get dressed."

Louis had just stepped out of the shower. Through the door he could hear her voice calling up the stairs. "Okay," he said. He could hear the excitement in his daughter's voice. She had been that way since the invitation came. In fact, since he'd been home on furlough.

Then she added, "Remember, you're going to be one of the star guests tonight. You excited?"

"Yup."

Then another voice yelled up the stairs. His wife's. "And don't forget to take your pills. The white ones. They're on your bureau with the water."

"Okay." He found the pills. The white ones. The ones that dulled his brain. He dropped them into the toilet.

Then he toweled himself off and looked in the mirror. He raised his arms and flexed his muscles, which bulged up thick and tan from going shirtless under the hot Asian sun. He inspected his teeth—white and straight. Then he smiled at the smooth young face staring out at him. With a comb he slicked back the thick black hair so that it looked like an ebony plate across his head. He had his father's hair. Unfortunately, Dom had gone bald by the time he was fifty. Louis still had thirty years to worry about that.

On the bed lay the black tuxedo his wife and daughter had gotten him. That would be his cover.

Before he got dressed, he checked the map again and the recon photos, trying to fix in his head the layout of the village center and the entrances to the pavilion. When he had them burned into his brain, he slipped them back into the plain envelope.

He put on his watch: 18:22 hours. All was going according to schedule.

He slipped on his fatigues, then the monkey suit. In the mirror he fixed his bow tie and sent the comb through his hair for the last time. He wished they had some kind of hat to complete the look.

Under his jacket he fixed his weapon, certain that the layers would hide the bulge. He took one last look in the mirror and gave the soldier a stiff salute.

Then he headed out. At last. This time it was the real thing: Operation Buster.

84

Following the announcement of the FDA'S approval of Memorine, Alzheimer's organizations, support groups, caregivers, and allied health-care people everywhere celebrated the good news. And so did the White House.

And on this balmy Saturday evening, a huge victory gala was held at the seaside estate of Gavin E. Moy. In the setting sun, the place glowed like a huge and magnificent jewelry box on the Manchester cliffs overlooking Moon Harbor, where Gavin Moy's boat the *Pillman Express* lay moored in a black-glass sea. Inside, a small regiment of tuxedoed waiters moved throughout the crowd with trays of canapés and champagne.

There must have been two hundred people spread throughout the thirty rooms and out on the patios, but mostly filling the first-floor ballroom, the library, and various parlors. There were executives and scientists from GEM, of course, and medical and health-care folks from all over New England, as well as representatives from different Alzheimer's organizations, the FDA, the state legislature, Capitol Hill, and, of course, the White House. The president himself could not be there, but he sent a telegram that was read by Gavin Moy over the PA system.

Partway through the evening, Jordan Carr silenced the crowd. The house lights dimmed as monitors positioned around the rooms flickered to life. The videos contained old and new footage of AD success stories, including some of Louis Martinetti, who addressed the camera in a clear and lucid delivery. Louis was then introduced. He was wearing a tuxedo and was flanked by his daughter and wife. He did not give a speech. In fact, he looked overwhelmed, even anxious, mumbling to himself. But through tears of joy, his daughter thanked everybody for making Louis a living miracle.

A thunderous applause arose from the group, many of whom were wiping tears from their own eyes, René included.

More video presentations and testimonials followed. Also, a television commercial for Memorine that would begin airing on all major networks and cable on Monday. The spot was mostly visuals, with swelling background music, as happy and focused elderly folks played in grassy green yards with grandchildren, pushed them on swings, sat around dinner tables. And the only words were those of the unseen narrator: "Alzheimer's: At last a cure. Ask your doctor about the Memorine solution." And at the bottom of the screen the name GEM Tech and its sparkling diamond logo.

Following the video, Gavin Moy gave a brief speech in which he thanked all those scientists, researchers, physicians, nurses, and others for their dedication and determination to bring to an end the scourge of Alzheimer's disease.

After the cheering, people formed a line to congratulate Gavin.

With a briefcase in hand Jack waited patiently behind people he didn't know, in front of people he didn't know. Somewhere in the crowd René was talking to the Martinettis. She had told him about Louis and how he had become a very special patient of hers and how his successful comeback from dementia had been like a redemption for her—a final exorcizing of her own guilt and of those tormenting memories of her father as he faded away. Louis's recovery was a kind of recovery for her too.

When his turn came, Jack took Gavin Moy's hand.

"Hi," Moy said, his large, smiling, tanned face taking focus on Jack.

"*Meds Gama.*" Jack's voice was barely audible over the din of the crowd.

"Beg pardon?" Moy said, cocking his head toward Jack.

Jack repeated the words. "*Meds Gama.*"

Moy's expression ruffled. "Nice to meet you," he muttered, and tried to pull his hand away.

But Jack did not release Moy's hand. Nor did he release the grip of his stare. "*Meds Gama*, also known as *Meds Garmir*, also known as Big Red."

Moy looked at him, startled. "Sorry, but I don't believe I know you." The others in Moy's entourage were beginning to take notice.

"I think you might have an idea."

"No, I don't."

"Jack Koryan. Son of Rose Najarian, also known as Rose Sarkisian."

Something passed over Moy's face as he held Jack's glare, then he turned to the others. "I'll be right back," he said, and tortured his face into a smile.

When a bystander offered to accompany him, Moy said he'd be fine. He looked back to see René suddenly tailing Jack. He raised a cautionary finger at her. "I think you can stay here." And she fell back. Jack did not like the threatening gesture, but he said nothing and nodded for her to fall behind.

Moy continued to smile as he cut his way through the crowd, making terse comments to people, a big strained Happy Face preceding him as Jack followed him out of the ballroom and into the hallway.

Jack expected Moy to turn on him when they were alone, but he said nothing and led him down a corridor, then up some back stairs and through two rooms and doors and into a corner room overlooking the harbor. Moy's home office was furnished with bookshelves, a robust marble table, and a large desk in the windowed corner. Moy moved behind the desk and sat in the big black leather mitt of a chair. He folded his hands and leaned across the desk glowering at Jack. "Okay, what's this all about?"

On the walls behind him were photos of Moy and other people on his boat posing with fish. Others showed him in hunting outfits with dead deer. Also on a table were trophies for pistol marksmanship. "It's about the death of Rose Sarkisian."

Moy stared at him impassively and said nothing—a withering ploy he probably used to bring his employees to their knees. "I don't know what the hell you're talking about."

"You don't recognize the name?"

"No."

"Think hard. Rose Sarkisian." And Jack enunciated the syllables with deliberate clarity.

"Look, I've met thousands of people in my travels over the years."

"She was my mother."

"So, good for you."

"You killed her."

Moy's face froze for a moment. Then he leaned forward menacingly. "I don't know who the fuck you think you are coming in here making such claims, but I've heard enough." His hand moved toward the telephone.

Jack pulled out a photograph of Rose and Nick and slid it across the table.

"That's Rose Sarkisian and Nick Mavros taken about thirty years ago. I did some research. They're standing in front of Junior Dee's Auto Parts store, which used to be where Kendall Square is now, behind MIT. It's where you had your lab down below."

Jack watched Moy intently, but there was nothing in his face that betrayed him—not a flicker of his eye or a microtwitch of his facial muscles.

"So I knew her."

"And you were at the cottage the night she died."

"What cottage? What night?"

"Homer's Island, August 20, 1975, Vita Nova."

"I don't know what you're friggin' talking about."

Jack pulled out of his tuxedo jacket a photocopy of the story of Rose Sarkisian's disappearance.

Moy glanced at it. "You know nothing," he said. He picked up the phone. "You've got ten seconds to get out of here or I'm calling the police."

"You murdered her. I was there. You came in. You had a fight and pushed her. She fell backward and hit her head and went unconscious. But that didn't satisfy you, so you smashed her on the skull, then dragged her outside to finish her off with a kitchen meat mallet that she used to make dinner for you. Then you came back in and cleaned up the mess with bleach. Then you left to dump her body in the water."

Moy looked at Jack as if he were an alien. His eyes were intense and his mouth in a twisted rictus. He looked positively stunned. "How?" That was all he could say.

"How do I know?" Jack pulled out a single blue tablet and slid it in front of him. "The Memorine solution."

Moy stared at the pill for a telescoped moment.

And in Jack's head he heard that voice: "*Die, goddamn you, die.*"

Moy raised his face again. He settled into his chair and stared at Jack for several seconds. "So, I knew your mother," he said, as if in a trance. His body seemed almost to deflate into the confession.

And the sound of the words sent a cold flush through Jack. His hand reflexively slid up the front of his jacket to the lump under his arm.

"But no pill will conjure up the truth."

"And what's that?"

"She tried to blackmail me." Moy stopped and waved his hand in the air. "I've said enough." He straightened up in his chair. "I want you out of here. You've got nothing on me."

"Except my memory."

"Get out of here before I call security." And he picked up the desk phone.

"She discovered the toxin, and you ran off with her patent."

"Bullshit."

Jack reached into his briefcase and pulled out the down-loaded stack of articles and abstracts. "Her name is all over these, until you killed her and appropriated her discovery."

Moy looked at the pile as Jack fanned out the collection.

"She was on the ground floor of your wonder drug."

"And what do you think you can prove by these, huh? You going to take me to court after thirty years?"

"It's evidence of a motive for murder. I saw it all, but you didn't think I'd remember. I was too young—just a toddler. But it all came back because of your magic jellyfish. Pretty funny, huh? What goes around comes around."

Moy's face was bright red. "She fell and hit her head . . . We had a fight, and she fell and hit her head."

"And you finished her off with a hammer because you feared she'd report you—report that she was the one who discovered the toxin and saw the potential benefits and demanded equal billing with you." Jack pulled one of the articles from the pile. "She was the one who determined how the stuff stimulated the adrenal medulla to activate the brain's beta-receptors on neurons that receive noradrenaline, resulting in an enhanced emotional memory. It's all in here—her experiments with mice. She's the one who should be celebrated down there, not you, you son of a bitch. You killed her. *You killed her.*"

Moy's face looked as if it would explode. "Yeah, I killed her and she deserved it. You happy now? I killed her. She tried to extort money from me. And it wasn't because of the goddamn science. It was because of you. *You!*"

Jack's breath caught in his throat.

"I was married, and just starting all this, up to my ass in debts, and she was threatening to destroy everything. She wanted me to leave my wife and marry her. And when I said that wasn't going to happen, she started threatening to sue for child support."

"Child support?"

"Yeah, child support. You."

"I don't believe you."

"Don't." Moy started around the desk toward him.

"This is pure bullshit."

Moy pointed to his face and pressed toward Jack. "Yeah, then look at these eyes and look in a mirror."

Jack stared at Moy's eyes, and a sensation slithered through his body that left him thinking how the universe had just shifted on its axes.

"The fuck's going on?"

A voice behind them.

Jack turned, and a thick, short man in a tuxedo entered. Behind him was another, taller man.

The Mr. Fixit guy from Greendale—the guy who came to repair the blinds. Theo.

Behind him was some physician Jack had met outside. A Dr. Jordan Carr. And Mr. Fixit was holding a shiny silver pistol on Jack.

Jack had been gone for over twenty minutes, and René was beginning to worry.

As she looked around the crowd, she spotted Louis Martinetti. He had slipped away from her and his daughter and wife, who were now talking to some FDA officials. They were laughing over something. Meanwhile, René tracked Louis moving through the crowd toward the rear of the hall and corridor leading to the staircase to the executive offices.

She excused herself from the people she was with, saying she was going to find a rest room. She scanned the crowd, but Louis had disappeared.

Corporal Louis Martinetti slid behind a tall bush growing out of a pot. The entire headquarters staff was assembled. It was like a Who's Who of the North Korean General Command. Operation Buster. The big payoff.

He surveyed the crowd—most of them officers of the 23rd Brigade, a few regulars standing guard, ready for some grunt command. He didn't know how much time had passed as he remained staked out—ten minutes, twenty, an hour. But suddenly his body clenched.

Corporal Martinetti raised his field glasses and adjusted the sights. And his heart leapt up. Colonel Chop Chop had stepped out from the masses. And he was heading for private consultation with Blackhawk.

"The real question is: what do I do with you now?" Moy said. "You *are* my son."

"A mere technicality."

"Ah, yes, a slip of biology. But I still can't let you go, you know."

"What's this?" Carr looked confused. "I thought Teddy was—"

"He is also, and it's a long story," Moy said. "I'll tell you later."

"He hasn't got anything on you," Teddy said to his father.

Jack looked at his half-brother or whatever the hell he was. His overly developed body was pressed into a tuxedo, making him look like a small orca. And it all came clear to Jack as he stared into the stolid eye of the gun barrel: this Teddy had visited him at Greendale in his Mr. Fixit role under the cover name Theo Rogers so the staffers wouldn't connect him to Gavin Moy. (He probably even used a false ID.) And his purpose was to determine if Jack remembered anything because Moy must have told him that Jack was his blood son out of wedlock; and Theo/Teddy here was checking up on Jack's recall, maybe in protection of his father, maybe sweating potential conflicts over who was rightful heir to the Moy fortune. Whatever, the guy had come out to spy on him.

"No, but he's the type who won't let go. Unfortunate, but it's in the blood."

"If I suddenly disappear," Jack said, "people are going to wonder, and there are a hundred of them downstairs who saw me."

"I'll get the boat," Teddy said.

"Oh, look at that," Jack said. "A chip off the old block, bro."

"Fuck you, asshole."

"And silver-tongued at that."

"Yes," Moy said. "The boat."

"Another replay, right? First your lover, now her son."

Moy looked point-blank at Jack. "I don't care who you are. I don't like you. And I'm not going to let you fuck things up for me. I've worked more friggin' decades to get here than you've been alive. And you mean nothing to me. Nothing."

"Wait a minute," protested Carr. "I don't think this is a good idea." And he looked from Moy to Teddy. "Really. He suddenly disappears, and people are going to get suspicious."

Teddy snapped at Carr. "No time to turn chickenshit."

Carr flashed a look at Jack. "But he's right—a lot of people saw him tonight."

Teddy nodded toward a rear door. "He went for a stroll on the rocks and slipped. It worked in Bryce."

"Get him out of here," Moy said.

Teddy jabbed the pistol at Jack. "Move it."

"Freeze!"

Jack turned. Behind them in the shadows was an older man aiming something barrel-like at them. "Hold it right there. Hands behind your heads, legs spread, and don't move." He stepped into the light.

Louis Martinetti.

He must have been wearing his tux over his fatigues, because he was dressed for combat, with a chest full of medals, including a Purple Heart. When they turned, Louis dropped down to a squat behind a table with flowers shooting out of a huge Chinese porcelain vase. The problem was that he was holding a furled umbrella on the gunman. Suddenly Louis began shouting over his shoulder for his men to advance on the eastern flank of the compound. They had the colonel and Blackhawk cornered.

"What the fuck?" Teddy said. He began to swing his gun arm toward Louis, who ducked behind the table making shooting noises.

Someplace in the shadows of the outer office Jack heard a scream. "Louis, no!"

René.

A shot rang out, and instantly Jack heard a grunt as Louis fell backward. He had dropped his umbrella and was clutching his arm.

Before Teddy could get off a shot at René, Jack flew at him, knowing instantly that in his condition he was no match for Teddy. So he sunk his teeth into Teddy's wrist. The guy screamed and released the gun, but not before catapulting Jack off of him. But Jack grabbed the pistol and rolled away, his muscles paining him with the effort. It passed through his mind that he had not held a gun for a couple years, since target practice with Vince at the police range. But now a gun felt good in his grip.

The next moment exploded with a scream from René as Teddy made a move to stomp Jack. Without thought, Jack took aim and squeezed the trigger. And Teddy hit the floor with a huge grunt, grabbing his leg. The bullet had hit him in the calf.

Out of the corner of his eye, Jack saw Moy pick up a crystal sculpture of his company's logo to hurl at him. But Jack flashed the gun at him. "Drop it or you're dead," Jack said.

Moy dropped it and Jack pulled himself to his feet, holding the pistol in both hands.

"I should have taken care of you, too," Moy said.

"Yeah, you should have."

From the shadows behind them Louis sprang up. His injured arm didn't stop him from flying at Jordan Carr and pulling him to the floor and flailing at him with his elbow and good hand. Louis was muttering odd syllables and swearing at Carr and saying something about Fuzzy. Jack didn't understand, but Louis had Carr pinned to the floor.

René shot over to him to pull him up to tend his wound. But Louis kept pummeling Carr, who yelled for help. René shouted for Louis to stop and managed to pull Louis off him. She removed Louis's shirt and fashioned a tourniquet for his arm with the bow tie. His shirt was soaked in blood, but Louis insisted she put it back on him.

"I'm fine. I'm fine. Just had a little—" Louis cut himself short, seeing Jack tying Moy's hands behind him. Louis's face lit up. "We got 'em both, Fuzz. Hear that? We got 'em."

Jack didn't know what Louis was saying, but he seemed pleased. He pushed Moy on his front while René bound his hands and Jack fanned the gun from Moy to Theo to Jordan Carr, who had pulled himself to his feet again.

Jack aimed the gun at him. "Playing both ends against the middle, right?"

René looked at Jack. "What are you doing?"

"He's with them." With his free hand Jack knocked a small lamp off Moy's desk, pressed his foot on it, and tore the electrical cord off it. He tossed it to Carr. Then he pulled telephone wires out of the phone and wall. "Tie him," he said, nodding to Teddy Moy, who was writhing on the floor. "Good and tight."

"Jack!" René said, glaring at him for an explanation.

"I think they had something to do with Nick's death."

"The fuck you doing?" Teddy protested as Carr began to tie him up. "Get the gun."

Carr looked back at the gun in Jack's hands and began binding Teddy Moy's arms behind him, then his legs to the thousand-pound marble table.

"What are you saying?" René asked as she came over to Jack. She glared at Jordan Carr on his knees tying a tourniquet on Teddy's left leg. Then she looked back at Jack for confirmation. Jack nodded, and René flew to Jordan. She grabbed Jordan by his shirt. "You killed Nick? *You killed Nick?*"

"I didn't. He did."

Teddy swore at Carr from his facedown position. "And you were right there calling the shots."

"But why?" René cried, and she whacked Jordan in the face.

Jordan put his hand to his cheek, which looked branded. "Because he was in the way, that's why. Because he wanted to stop something that was good. And maybe before you go sanctimonious on me again, you can ask yourself this: If you could have saved your father, wouldn't you have done anything? Wouldn't you?"

René said nothing.

"Sure you would, even if it meant eliminating anyone who stood in the way of his cure, right? You would have done the same—anything to keep him from dying layer by layer, even if it meant a few flashbacks. Right? Right?"

For a stunning moment René could not respond, as if she did not know how to answer the questions. But she backhanded Jordan in the face.

The moment was broken when Moy's cell phone cut the air. Jack reached into Moy's jacket pocket and pulled it out. It was someone identifying himself as GEM's executive vice president.

"Yeah, everything's just dandy," Jack said. "We're on our way down."

When Jordan Carr was finished binding Theo, he looked at Jack and René. "So now what?" he asked, trying an ingratiating smile on Jack.

Louis was sitting in a chair muttering to himself. But he looked okay. Just a flesh wound.

Moy was in his chair, his hands bound behind him. Theo was tied to the marble table and going nowhere. Jack aimed the gun at Jordan Carr's chest. "You've got thirty seconds to tell us about Bryce or I'm going to start shooting holes in you."

All the way down the stairs and through the corridor they could hear the chant of the crowd initiated by his management team: *"Gavin! Gavin! Gavin!"*

They paraded into the hall, Gavin leading the way, his hands bound behind him, Jordan Carr in tow, also bound. And behind him came Jack with the gun and flanked by Louis and René. Teddy was back in Moy's office enjoying a view of the underside of his father's pink marble table.

For a moment, cheering flared up as people at the rear of the hall spotted Moy. But instantly it began to mute as people saw the spectacle of him being led at gunpoint to the podium. In the distance the sound of police sirens from Jack's 911 call. But he had plenty of time before they arrived.

At the microphone, he introduced himself, then said he would like to make an announcement. He felt for the lump in the breast pocket of his sportcoat and he removed the small silver MP3 recorder that Vince had given him. He held it up to the microphone and pressed Play.

"You killed her. Admit it."

"Yeah, I killed her and she deserved it. You happy now? I killed her."

Epilogue

Homer's Island • Seven Weeks Later

A small sign on The beach read BEWARE OF JELLYFISH!

"Nice timing," Jack said, and handed René a plate.

They sat on beach chairs by the water's edge picnicking on shish kebab, stuffed grape leaves, pilaf, and stewed vegetables.

"In the late sixties, she was on a marine science panel in Cambridge with Jacques Cousteau—something about the threat of industrial pollution and global warming on the oceans of the world. Thaddeus Sherman was impressed, and they started talking. One thing led to the next, and he invited her to stay here because it was the only place in the northeast where Caribbean sea life shows up. One visit, and she fell in love with the place and started collecting specimens."

Jack poured two glasses of chardonnay.

"Sounds like she was a very special woman."

"I think she was." They clicked glasses.

Today was the thirty-first anniversary of Rose Sarkisian's death.

"She apparently had an affair with Gavin Moy, who was more her type—academically speaking—than the man she married. Who knows? Records say they were in divorce proceedings before he was killed in a plane crash. They hid that fact on the gravestone to save face."

Jack also learned that Rose had specialized in the therapeutic properties of marine toxins. After having bagged some Solakandjis, she had chemical assays done on the toxin and found that the compound demonstrated beneficial properties on the neurological system. When Moy decided to start researching these neurological properties, Rose went to work with him as a partner. They apparently became lovers. And when she became pregnant with Jack, she insisted that he either marry her or provide financially for Jack's upbringing. Moy refused. They fought, and she was killed. Moy and his people went on to develop an FDA application of the compound for the treatment of dementia. But Rose Sarkisian was the prime mover. She had identified the agent and its therapeutic properties with lab mice.

Mookie. Where's Mookie?

And that stuffed animal was what she had made for her little boy.

Jack looked out over the water to Skull Rock and the glittering azure expanse beyond. And for a moment he thought he heard thunder.

"I didn't know that Nick knew your mother. He never said anything."

"Except he must have suspected when he saw me on his MRI patient list. Then he did some name and date checks."

"He must have suspected foul play all along, since she had identified the toxin's benefits, then mysteriously disappeared."

"My guess. And then Moy appropriated the discovery and slapped his name on the patents."

"Which is why Nick kept pressing to discover whether you remembered anything."

"He even sent you after me. Kind of glad he did."

She smiled. "Me, too." He felt a flush of warmth as she took his hand.

Because there was no statute of limitations in Massachusetts, Gavin Moy had been indicted for murder, the evidence being his own confession on tape. Likewise, Jordan Carr and

Teddy Moy were also indicted for the murder of Nick Mavros. After the discovery of Nick's body, the film in his camera had been developed. At first it had meant nothing in the investigation of the accident. But when the police heard the tape of the exchange recorded in Moy's office, they went back to the film to discover on the last frame a face staring out from a clutch of dark bushes. When blown up, the face in the dark looking directly at the camera was Jordan Carr's.

But that was not the only evidence for the prosecution undercutting Carr's insistence that he had not been at Bryce Canyon. Teddy Moy had decided not to go down alone. He confessed that Jordan had been complicit with him and Gavin Moy, although Teddy had done the actual dirty work of pushing Nick off the cliff. There was suspicion that Teddy was also responsible for Peter Habib's death, now being investigated as a possible homicide.

"How's Louis doing?"

"Fine. I was out to their place the other day. He sends his regards."

"He was a real hero."

"Yes. He really was. No, *is*."

As René had explained it, that night at Moy's estate Louis had apparently experienced a memory-induced hallucination, believing he was engaged in a long-anticipated assault on North Korean military high command including individuals who had participated in the torture and execution of members of his platoon. And although he had experienced no more such hallucinations since, he could not be taken off the drug, of course. But he was being more closely monitored and treated with different doses of medications that would block his flashbacks and possible hallucinations without sending him into a stupor. His short-term memory continued to improve, and he was living almost a normal life again.

But understanding why some patients like Louis Martinetti were susceptible to flashbacks clearly required more research. The problem was that after four to six months of regular dosing, sixty percent of the patients showed cognitive and functional improvement; yet, for some reason, nearly half of those experienced disturbing flashbacks. As a result, Memorine's FDA application was withdrawn. Those trial patients already on the compound would be continued and closely monitored and properly treated for flashback seizures. Meanwhile, the FDA had mandated that GEM Tech scientists in conjunction with outside research groups make aggressive efforts to determine what genetic, chemical, or demographic factors might account for the phenomena before reapplication of Memorine or any refashioned compound for approval.

Understandably, thousands of AD patients, caregivers, and health-care workers were disappointed at the news. But Orman-Witt, the director of the FDA, said that this was medical progress. "This initiative is going to push drug companies to be more thoughtful when testing their products and not rush them to market or cover up damaging evidence." The hope was for a safe and efficacious treatment within two years.

Alas, the world would have to wait. And when some safe variation of Memorine eventually reached the market, Rose Sarkisian would share credit for its discovery.

Jack's own flashbacks and related nightmares had also faded, as if on some deep level a ghost had been laid to rest. He was back at the gym with Vince and pumping chrome once again. And next month he'd be back in the classroom at Carleton Prep and helping Vince out hosting Yesterdays on weekends.

Jack got up and took René's hand as they walked to the water's edge.

Fifty yards out, Skull Rock sat glistening in the golden sun. And hanging over the sea like a pale ghost was a crescent moon that smiled down on them.

"You know, for all the jelly I took in, I still don't remember what it's like to kiss a woman."

"I bet it'll come back to you."

"Well, you can't tell."

She pulled his face to hers and kissed him.

"I never told you, but I was always a slow learner."

"You goof," she laughed, and kissed him again.

He closed his eyes real hard. "Getting warm."

She kissed him again.
"Warmer still."
"This could go on all day."
"I hope so, and into the night."